CROSS-CHECKED

Boston Rebels Series
Book 3

JULIA CONNORS

Cover Design by Qamber Designs
Developmental Editing by Melissa McGovern of Memos In The Margins
Copy Editing by Nice Girl, Naughty Edits
Proofreading by Amy Pritt and Elizabeth Solomon

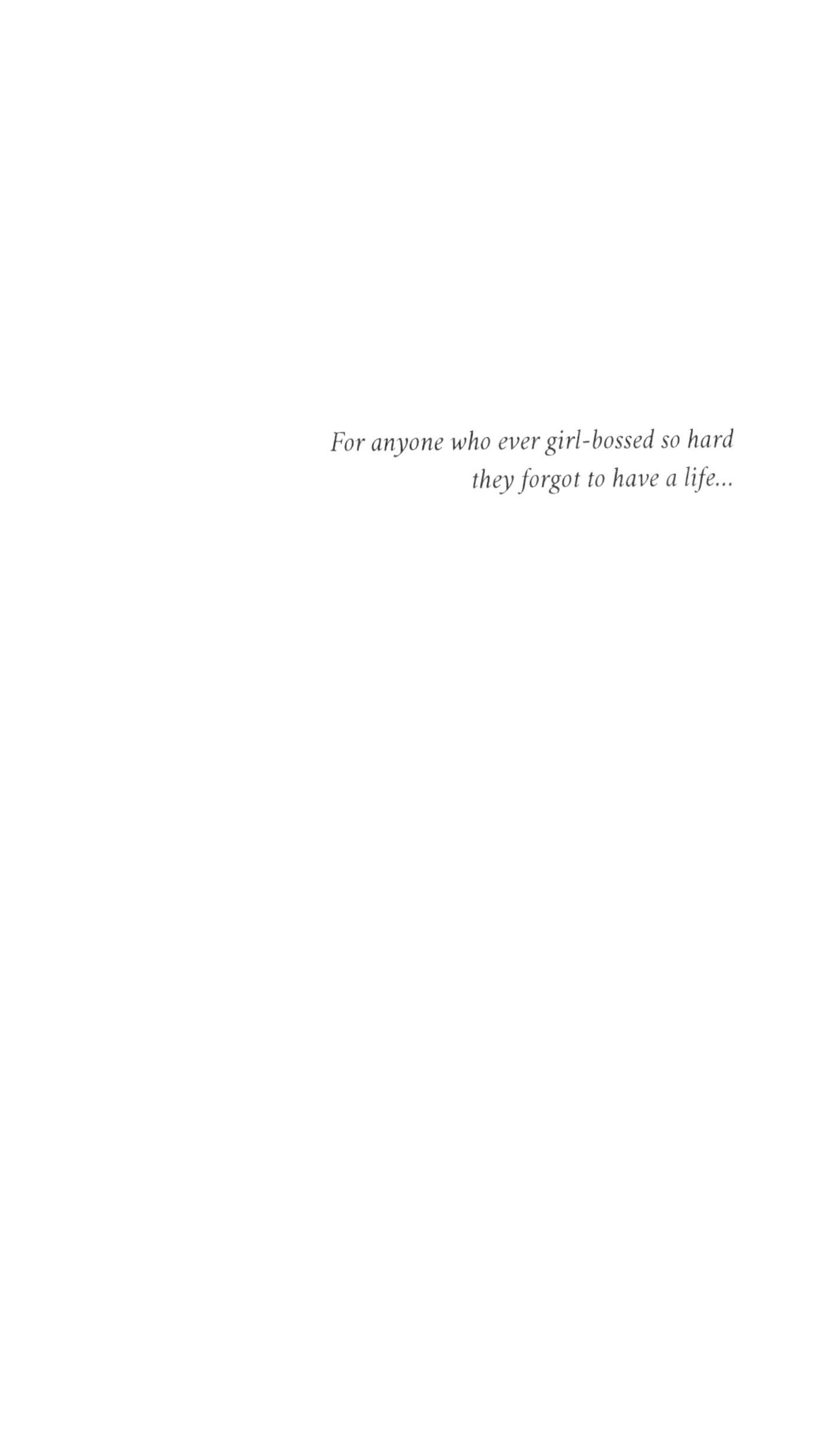

*For anyone who ever girl-bossed so hard
they forgot to have a life...*

Author's Note

Cross-Checked deals with topics that may be sensitive for some readers, including infertility, past emotional abuse, and cheating. For a full list of content warnings, please visit my website: juliaconnors.com/cross-checked

Please note that, for the sake of the story, some liberties were taken with the teams and timing in the playoff rounds, as well as the timing for voting on the GM of the Year award. And, due to various trademarks, the actual names of the annual pro hockey awards were not used.

Chapter One

AJ

"And what do we think about the rumors that Alessandra Jones, general manager for the Boston Rebels, may be a finalist for the GM of the Year award?" The voice of Ted Deveney, one of the country's most beloved sportscasters, has my head snapping up from the contract I'm reviewing. Now, with my heart pounding, my attention is entirely focused on the TV on the opposite side of my office.

"I'd say it's long overdue," Stefanie Flowers, Ted's co-host, responds, and I let out a small sigh of relief. "She's taken that organization from consistently breaking the hearts of their fans, to consistently being one of the top teams in the entire league."

"That's true," Ted says, his trademark white mustache flattening into a straight line as his lips curve up and he chuckles.

"Division champions four out of the six years she's been

GM, conference champions twice, and Stanley Cup champions once. I'd say she's earned *at least* this nomination, if not the actual award."

As one of the few female sportscasters covering the NHL on the national level, I'm thrilled that Stefanie is showing the same passion I have about seeing a female GM do well.

"And," Ted adds, "with one win already under their belt in this second round of playoffs, and Boston basically outperforming Carolina in every way, I'd say they're off to a good start securing a fifth division championship."

"We'll see what happens in Game 2 tomorrow night, and then as Boston heads down to Carolina later this week," Stefanie says. "With most of their lineup already in place for next year, and minimal changes in the roster, the team really seems to be jelling."

"The latest news from the Rebels is that Aidan Renaud will be coming off the IR in time for next season."

"I'm sure they're excited about getting Renaud back. But the question remains," she says, and I groan internally, because I already know where this is going, "whether Ronan McCabe will be staying next year."

"Sounds like a classic case of a star player and his team not being able to agree on what he's worth," Ted says, an air of nonchalance in his voice.

"Well, we're all eager to see how that works out. It's hard to imagine the Rebels without McCabe leading them, but we're also hearing rumors that he may be interested in potentially moving to another team."

I can feel my nostrils flare. Given that we haven't reached an agreement, I know his agent must be starting to look at other teams. But the fact that we're still in season and he's not being more discreet about it pisses me off. And we haven't reached the free agency interview period yet, so no actual conversations should be happening.

Sometimes, it feels like McCabe wants to leave. The number of times he's tried to step down from being captain, and his obvious distaste for me, make it seem like he has one foot out the door and is just waiting for me to beg him to stay. And I'm not the type to do that, no matter how good he is.

"They still have a few weeks to come to an agreement, but it'll be interesting to see if that happens, or if McCabe becomes an unrestricted free agent," Ted adds.

"Yeah, interesting is one word for it. If he continues to perform in the playoffs as well as he has all season, it would be crazy for the Rebels to let one of their star players go. But I personally can't wait for this round of playoffs to conclude, so we'll finally know who those GM of the Year finalists are."

"You holding out for the first female nomination in the history of professional hockey?"

Stefanie's smile is broad as the camera zooms in on her. "You know it, Ted. I think we're watching history unfold."

The knots in my stomach tighten, and I close my eyes, taking a deep breath and releasing it slowly. I want to relish this moment, when the nation's most well-known hockey sportscasters are talking about my success, but all I feel is the overwhelming pit of dread at the thought of letting people down.

Straightening my spine, I remind myself that Frank Hartmann, owner of the Rebels, took a huge risk bringing me to Boston six seasons ago—and all he's ever asked of me is that I rebuild this organization with players who care about our fans and bring home the Cup. He didn't ask for me to win awards, he asked me to focus on the team. Doing that may have made me a stand-out GM, but this has never been about me. It's *always* been about the team.

I relax my shoulders and open my eyes, almost jumping out of my seat at the sight of my Director of Marketing and Communications, Lauren, standing on the other side of my desk.

"Where the hell did you come from?" I ask as I exhale the breath that just caught in my throat.

One of her arms is folded as it holds her laptop against her chest, and the other reaches to pull out a chair. "I assume that's a rhetorical question," she says with a laugh as she sinks into the seat across from me, "since you put this meeting on my calendar."

"But I didn't even hear you sneak in," I tell her as I pick up the remote on my desk and mute the TV.

"Yeah. You were so focused on that amazing news coverage that you didn't notice me knock at your open door or walk in here."

I let out a tight laugh, and Lauren raises her eyebrow in response.

"You okay?" she asks.

Pressing my lips together, I nod. "Never been better."

Lauren looks at me like she sees right through this *the pressure doesn't bother me* charade. And she probably does. Over the last year and a half that she's worked for me, she's gradually become my best friend as well. "It's a lot of pressure."

I appreciate how she understands that every single decision I make is viewed through the lens of "the first female

GM in the history of the league . . ." It's a privilege to serve in this role. And yet, sometimes the pressure is stifling.

Over the last six seasons, we've set pretty much every individual record in Rebels history—most shutouts, highest number of goals scored in a single season, most goals scored by a defenseman, most assists by a single player, highest save percentage, and the list goes on. If we can win the conference championship this year, we'll be the winningest team in Boston hockey history.

That pressure isn't on my shoulders—I've done everything I can leading up to and during this season to put the team in a position to bring home the Cup again. Now, it's up to them. But if it doesn't happen, I already know I'll hyperfixate on what I could have done differently to set them up better.

And one of the questions I'm sure I'll be asking myself is whether it was a mistake to bring Frank Hartmann's son, Luke, to Boston as our newest goalie. I did it against his wishes because while he was concerned it would look like nepotism, my primary concern is finding a replacement for our top goalie, Colt, who will likely retire at the end of next season.

Luke is fresh and young, a player who I knew would work well with and learn from Colt. He came here with no ego. He's the kind of selfless team player we need, and I wish some of our veteran players—particularly our team captain Ronan McCabe—were more like Luke Hartmann.

And while Hartmann did well in the regular season, now that we're in the playoffs, he isn't playing at the level I need him to be. I remind myself that he's still growing, that this is only his third season in the pros and his first time making the playoffs, but the self-doubt creeps in, making me question myself and my past decisions.

"What the hell is going on, AJ?" Lauren asks. It's only then that I realize I'm so lost in my own head, I never responded to her.

"Nothing. It's a lot of pressure is all, just like you said."

"Are you doing okay with everything?" Her sweet voice carries notes of empathy.

"Yeah, I'm fine. It's just that this damn award is adding a whole other level of stress to an already overwhelming time."

"It's like Stefanie said, though. It's long overdue. You've earned this."

The finalists for the award are voted on by every general manager in the league, plus a few league executives and a few members of the media. The stats for our team—the way we've grown and improved over the six seasons I've been here—would have had any other GM nominated years ago.

And yet, I've never been a finalist.

I could speculate on all the reasons why, but I've been down that road before, and it doesn't end well for my mental health.

"You turned this team around, AJ," Lauren reminds me. "And whether you're a finalist for this award or not doesn't change that. Not when you've already come this far."

I lean back in my chair, relaxing for the first time in too long. "I know you're right. And I know that carving out a space for women in such a male-dominated sport is an uphill battle—"

"One you've already *won*, by the way," Lauren chimes in.

"—and I'm not doing it for the recognition, you know? I'd never tell anyone else this," I say, glancing at the open door to make sure no one's outside my office, before I drop my voice lower. "But for once, it would be nice for the men who hold the same position I do to look at the work I've done here and to finally say 'good job.' Frank took such a huge risk bringing me here, and I'm honored to have been the first female GM in the league. I just want to make sure I'm not the last, you know?"

I want my legacy to live on. It sounds so selfish and cliché when I say it in my head. But I don't want this for my own ego. I want this so that other women know they can do this, too.

But I keep the thought where it belongs—in my head— because I don't know how to say that without it sounding like it's about me.

"You won't be the last, AJ. But it's a huge honor to have been the first. And even if you had sucked at it," Lauren says with a laugh, "which obviously you *haven't*, you still wouldn't be the last female GM. Because now that you've done it, even more women are going to set their sights on upper management."

I raise an eyebrow at her. "Like you?"

She laughs again and holds both her hands out in front of her like she's pushing the thought away. "No, I have my hands absolutely full at the moment. I couldn't take on any more responsibility, even if I wanted to. Which I don't, so stop trying to put ideas in my head."

Lauren's got three-year-old twin girls, and this summer she's getting married to one of the best men I know. Jameson Flynn is not only one of the most well-respected agents in hockey, he's also incredibly loyal, trustworthy, and fair. He's brought me talent I didn't know I needed, and helped me rebuild his former team behind the scenes. The fact that he also introduced me to Lauren when she was looking to get back into sports marketing has only made me like him more.

"You sure?" I tease. "Because I'd love to have a female VP on staff."

"Listen, I'm not saying *never*. I'm just saying no time soon."

"So now you're handing out promotions without even running them by me?" Frank Hartmann's voice bellows as he strides through the door to my office.

A broad grin splits my face at his teasing tone. One of the things I love most about Frank, besides the fact that he's like the dad I wish I had, is that he isn't a micromanager. I run things by him out of professional courtesy, but aside from my decision to bring his son onto our team—which he was concerned would look like nepotism—he never questions me. He trusts me to do the job he hired me to do, and that's been one of the best parts of coming to Boston.

"No, no," Lauren says with a shake of her head. "AJ just promoted me to my current position. She's not promoting me again."

"Have I told you recently that you're doing a fine job?" Frank asks her.

"Fine like mediocre? Or fine like high quality?" Lauren's auburn eyebrows, a couple shades darker than her hair, scrunch together as she looks over to Frank, who's taken the seat next to her.

"Which do you think?" His pale eyes practically dance with amusement above his rounded cheeks. The man is an absolute teddy bear.

"Definitely high quality," Lauren says with a decisive nod.

"You would be correct. Now, we have a bit of an issue that I need y'all to deal with in the quickest and most professional way possible." He glances between us. "We've had three fights break out in the stands during the playoffs. In every instance, security footage shows that it was our fans, wearing our players' jerseys, that started each altercation. I know people get excited and tensions are high, but we don't want Boston fans to be known as aggressive shit-starters any more than we want our players to have that kind of reputation."

"So you want us to . . ." Lauren drags the word out. ". . . change the fans' behavior?"

"I want you to figure out how this organization can show the fans that this behavior isn't acceptable, without coming off as preachy or heavy-handed," Frank says.

Lauren sinks her teeth into her lower lip, and I can tell she's trying not to laugh. Fighting is part of the game, and I know immediately that she's thinking it would be pretty hypocritical for a hockey team to tell its fans that fighting is wrong.

"Okay," I say decisively, because Frank wants solutions. "We'll take care of it."

"How?" he asks, as Lauren turns to me with the same question in her eyes.

"We'll figure it out," I tell him. "But off the top of my head, it seems like it would be easy to get a friendly reporter to lob a softball question about this to one of our players during post-game press, and then have the player remind fans that the only fighting that belongs at our games is on the ice."

"Make sure it's McCabe," Frank says.

"Why *him*?" The question bursts out of me, followed by a

laugh. Of all the players on the team, no one is less likely to engage in friendly banter with reporters, or ask fans to leave the fighting to the professionals on the ice, than McCabe.

"He's the team captain," Frank says as he stands and shoves his hands in his pockets, clearly done with this conversation. "It needs to come from him."

It takes everything I have not to push back on this, not to tell Frank that there are other players who are just as respected by the fans and far more likely to help us out with this.

"Understood," I say as he turns to head out the door. Because when your billionaire boss writes your very hefty paychecks and mostly leaves you alone to do your job however you want, you don't question him when he asks for something minor. Even when you know it's just going to make your life more difficult.

Lauren leans back in her chair, looking relaxed for the first time since Frank walked into the office. "Want me to talk to McCabe?"

I look at the ceiling as I bite the inside of my cheek. Everyone knows that McCabe and I have a contentious relationship on the best of days, but it's grown even more tense this season because his contract is up and he's making ridiculous demands for us to keep him. Still, I'm his boss, so I can put on my big girl pants and tell him what he needs to do.

"No, it's fine." I shake my head, glancing over toward the wall of glass overlooking the practice rink. "It should come from me. Just let me know who the reporter will be, and I'll tell him what the plan is before our next home game."

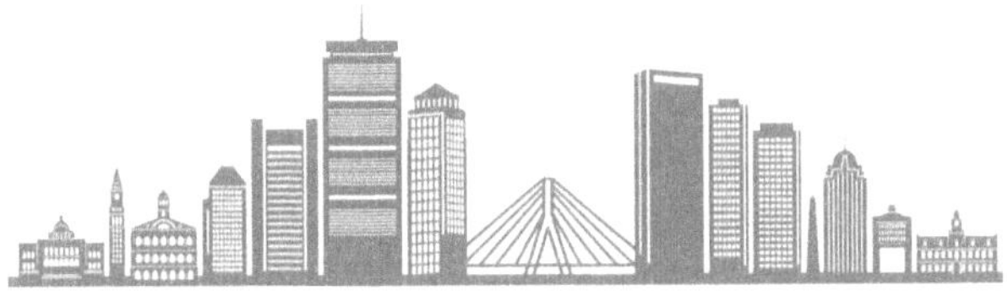

Chapter Two

McCabe

COLT

Where the hell did you go? AJ was looking
for you, and I didn't know what to tell her.

hit. When my nanny called me to say that my
daughter was running a fever and I needed to come
home right away, I didn't even think twice about
leaving the children's hospital our hockey team partners
with, where a few of us were visiting with sick kids this
afternoon.

Since finding out I was a dad nine months ago, Abby has
been my first priority.

I never would have imagined that my ex-girlfriend would
just show up and dump a baby I didn't know about into my
arms, claiming that motherhood would get in the way of her
acting career. It didn't matter that she couldn't act for shit,
and had never landed a role outside of a commercial here or

there—Jenna was naive enough to believe that she was destined to be a star, and selfish enough to not let anything stand in her way.

But from the moment I held Abby in my arms, there was no question that, for her, I'd be the best dad I could be. The second she wrapped those impossibly tiny fingers around my thumb, her big eyes staring up at me, she carved herself right into my soul. I knew at that moment, with Jenna still standing in my entryway before she turned and fled, that I'd love and protect Abby, even if it was us against the world.

Balancing hockey season and single-fatherhood was hard enough, but lately, with the pressures of the playoffs, I feel like I'm failing more often than I'm succeeding.

MCCABE

Abby's sick, I had to head home.

I type out the message as I wait for the elevator in the lobby of my building, willing it to hurry the hell up so I can get upstairs and see what's wrong with my daughter.

COLT

You might want to explain that to AJ
because she definitely muttered something
under her breath about you not leading by
example.

I never wanted to be the team captain. I prefer to lead quietly and not be the center of attention. Being captain has forced me into the spotlight in ways I'm not comfortable with. The only thing I want my teammates, the fans, and the media to focus on is how I play. Leading the team in a public way, that's the dream for guys like Colt, who have a way of putting everyone at ease but can still light a fire under your ass when you need it. However, Colt's a goalie, so he can't wear the C on the ice.

When our previous captain retired a few years ago, I was already an alternate captain and the logical back-up choice. And while no one's ever tried to make me feel like it should have been Colt in the first place, I know the only reason I have this distinction is because league rules prevent him from having it.

Every year I suggest maybe it's time to give the honor to one of our alternate captains instead, but my team and management both seem to want me in the role. Honestly, I think they don't want it to look like they've taken it away from me, even though I keep trying to step down.

MCCABE

Will do. Thanks for letting me know.

I appreciate Colt warning me, because my contract is up at the end of the season, and I'm still in the negotiation phase with the Boston Rebels. This shit should have been settled long ago, but my agent, Trevor, and my general manager, AJ, couldn't come to an agreement over my next contract.

According to Trevor, AJ insists that my salary demands are selfish and will prevent her from acquiring new players who will round out the team. But I'm one of the top-scoring players in the league, and I'm not taking *less* for my next contract than I got for my last one. When negotiations broke down, AJ left it at *we'll revisit this at the end of the season.*

So, right now, I can't afford to look like I'm not invested, even though my mind is already made up to leave. Partly because management not settling my next contract during this season feels like a huge fuck you to the years I've spent here—years that pre-date AJ coming to Boston.

Unfortunately, I've worked for her almost my whole career—she was the assistant GM when I played for St. Louis, then she came to Boston a few years after I was traded here. Other players love her, but I just keep my head down and try to make sure she doesn't screw me over again like she did years ago in St. Louis.

If we can't come to an agreement after the playoffs, I'll be an unrestricted free agent. Trevor is already talking to Nashville, and they're interested. Signing with them could be perfect, because my sister lives there with my nieces. We're the only family each other has, and now that we're both single parents, we've been talking a lot about living in the same city.

I'd miss my teammates, many of whom are like brothers to me, but getting to see my daughter grow up with her cousins and having family around is worth more than what I've built here with the Rebels. I never thought I'd say that, but I guess fatherhood changes you.

My phone pings again as I step into the elevator, and I glance down at a text from Colt, followed immediately by another text from my nanny.

COLT

Hope Abby's feeling better soon. Let us know if you need anything.

LUCY

Are you almost home?

I often get the sense that my nanny, Lucy, can't wait to

leave, and today is the perfect example. Abby is prone to fevers, so we've been to the pediatrician multiple times. The doctor always tells us that if there are no other symptoms and the fever doesn't go above 102 degrees, Abby's just fighting something off and we can relax and treat the fever with infant acetaminophen. But instead of following those orders, Lucy called me and insisted I come home.

She came with amazing references—the kind that are apparently too good to be true, since she's proven to be flighty and unreliable.

At least this is just a summer gig. As soon as I know where I'm playing next season, my first order of business will be to find a new, more reliable nanny.

I glance back up as the elevator closes, and in the quickly diminishing space between the doors, I swear I see AJ walking into the lobby of my building. Her head is bent as she glances at her phone, but even across the wide marble space, and without seeing her face, I'm confident it's her.

What the hell is my boss doing in my building?

I have a sinking feeling in the pit of my stomach as I wonder if she's here to check up on me after I left the chil-dren's hospital early. *No*, I assure myself, *she's not the kind to make house calls.* And even if she were, we're barely on speaking terms, so she'd know better than to show up at my door.

What the hell is she doing here, then?

My phone buzzes again as Lucy puts a question mark on the message she sent five seconds ago because, clearly, it's taking me too long to respond.

MCCABE

Yes, I'm almost home.

I resist the urge to add a snarky comment, which is exactly the kind of sarcasm I typically employ when I think someone is overreacting. But I need her to keep showing up until the end of our postseason, so I can't afford to piss her off.

When the elevator doors open, I stride down the hall. My condo is at the end, the last door on the left. It's a nice corner unit with walls of glass on one side, and floor-to-ceiling glass sliders leading out to a full-length balcony along the other.

The condo across the hall from me—the last door on the right—was for sale last month, and I halfway considered buying it since it's a mirror image of mine, taking up the corner opposite me. Our condos share a wall from the end of the hallway all the way to the balconies along the exterior of the building.

If I'd bought it, I could have opened the wall between the two units and made an incredibly sweet six-bedroom, four-bath place for Abby and me. But it didn't make sense to purchase it since I don't even know if I'm staying in Boston.

So the condo sold, and the people who lived there moved out without so much as a goodbye. I've never even met my new neighbors. The anonymity of living in an insanely expensive building in a big city used to be something I loved. I could come and go without anyone bothering me. I could bring home women whenever I felt like it, and there was no one to judge me. I could retreat in solitude when that's what I needed, but the lights and parties of the city were right outside my doorstep if that's what I was looking for.

Now that I'm a dad, it all grates on me—the bustle and the noise outside, and how quiet and lonely it is inside once Abby goes to sleep. I want to live in a place where I have family close by, where I can sit on my front porch and know the people living in my neighborhood, and where my daughter can learn to ride her bike on the street in front of our house.

And that condo across the hall with the nameless, faceless neighbors—who, if the sound of the door opening and shutting is any indication, come home late and leave early in the morning—has gradually become the perfect example of why I want to move.

With a quick glance at the 1706 on their door, I turn toward my condo, number 1705, and push my key into the lock. When I make it to the living room, I find Lucy is sitting on the couch with Abby curled up against her chest. Lucy's eyes are closed and they're both breathing steadily, and for a moment, I'm taken back to the first time Lucy met Abby, when she came to interview for the summer nanny job.

She seemed like she loved babies when I first met her— the perfect person to fill in for the summer, between my last nanny leaving to move to a new state, and the new nanny I'll hire once I know where I'm playing next season. Now, I know what she loves is that I pay well enough that she can hang with her rich boyfriend and his trust-fund friends as if she actually comes from money herself.

I clear my throat, and Lucy's head whips to the side. "Oh good," she says quietly, hugging Abby to her chest as she stands. At least she's trying not to wake her. "You're here. She needs her dad."

I eye Abby, whose cheeks do look a little pink, but it could be thanks to the heavy blanket Lucy has her wrapped up in like it's the middle of winter.

"She looks okay to me," I say, not because I don't want to

be here with my daughter, but because I'm annoyed that Lucy had me rush home.

Management already knows I hate doing PR shit off the ice—the visits to hospitals and schools, the media appearances, the charity work—and the last thing I want in the midst of contract negotiation is to act in a way that reinforces the narrative that I'm not a team player. And *this* doesn't seem like the emergency she claimed it was.

"Well, she's not. I'm going to let you take over from here because I need to go pick up my boyfriend."

Lucy's boyfriend lives in a penthouse condo that makes mine look like a hovel and drives a sports car that costs more than my first year's salary as a hockey player in the AHL.

"He couldn't just drive himself?"

"My car's in the shop, so I have his car," Lucy says, and it occurs to me that, because I left my car with the valet so I could get up here as quickly as possible, I didn't see his car parked in the spot beside mine that I let Lucy use.

If that prick doesn't have more than one car, I'd be shocked. And I *know* he has access to a driver, or could just grab a ride through a rideshare app, the same way any of us do.

He doesn't *need* her to come get him; she *wants* to go.

"I see." I fold my arms across my chest. "And would needing to go get him have anything to do with why I had to come home?"

"What?" She sounds shocked, her eyebrows pinching. "No, I just told him that since you're coming home, I could pick him up before we go out to dinner. Oh, and"—she reaches her arms out to hand me my sleeping daughter—"not this weekend, but next, I'm going to need a couple days off to go to Nantucket with Tim's family. It's his grandmother's birthday, so not something we can miss."

I take Abby and bring her up to my chest, where she opens her eyes and fusses for a moment. Snuggling her into me, I sway back and forth from one foot to the other, humming her favorite song as I breathe in her baby scent. She settles right down, closing her eyes. Her lips are turned up at the corners, like she's realized Daddy's home and she can relax.

God, I hate being away from her.

"Uhh, that's not how this whole nannying thing works, Lucy. That weekend will be the start of Round 3 of the play-offs, and I'll need you here with Abby," I tell her. Even though we are just starting this series, we're already dominating.

Our goalie, Colt, just broke Carolina's best player's nose so he'll be out for at least a couple of games. If we don't wrap this series up while we're in Carolina this weekend, I'll be shocked. But even if we have to play into next week to clinch the division title, I can't fathom a situation in which we're not moving on to the next round.

"Okay," she says breezily. "I'm sure we can work something out."

"The only way it'll work out is if you're here when I need you to be here." I don't want the words to come out in the low, almost menacing way they do, but I can't help it. I don't have anyone else to watch Abby, not even during the day while I'm at practice, much less overnight, and she knows it.

"Okay, I'll find out the details and let you know," she says, giving me a broad smile, like she just knows she's going to get her way. I don't think she understands that work is supposed to come first, especially when your job is caring for a baby.

"Alright. I'll see you back here tomorrow, right?" It makes me nervous that I even need to ask this. She's staying here with Abby for the next five days. After tomorrow afternoon's game, we're flying south to play our next two games against Carolina at their home arena.

"Yeah, of course. But what if she's sick?"

"Then you'll need to take care of her, and maybe take her to the doctor. You can handle it. You've taken her to the pediatrician before."

She inhales a shaky breath, and not for the first time, I wonder if I made a huge mistake hiring a college kid to take care of my baby on her summer vacation. A month ago, she seemed like she was going to be perfect. Now I've got serious reservations, but no alternative.

I absolutely hate feeling like I might not be doing what's best for Abby, but I have a contract, and I have to be there to play. I'm the leader of that team, and showing up for work seems like the bare minimum, especially when so many of my teammates also have kids. None of them are single dads, though.

"Okay," she says, heading for the door. "See you tomorrow."

I really hope she shows up.

Chapter Three

AJ

"Can someone please tell me why the hell we haven't taken off yet?" I grumble, wondering why we're still sitting on the tarmac. I need this plane in the air so I can get my laptop on WiFi. I don't have time to waste sitting here doing nothing.

"We're waiting on McCabe," Charlie Wilcott, our head coach, says from across the aisle. He must see something on my face, because he adds, "He'll be here in five minutes. It's fine."

"Why wasn't he on the bus from the arena after the game, like everyone else?" In the cabin behind us, Walsh is blasting the song the team always plays after a win, and the guys are singing along at the top of their lungs.

"Apparently, his nanny's car is in the shop and she borrowed someone's car, so she didn't have Abby's car seat. Since he's gone for the next five days, the nanny needed him to bring her the car seat he had in his car."

I sigh.

McCabe had texted me last night to let me know that he'd needed to leave the hospital early yesterday because his daughter was sick, and now he's delaying our flight. I'm a "family first" kind of general manager, and I know he's a single dad and all, but I can't shake the feeling that he doesn't think it's a big deal that he left early yesterday and is making the whole plane wait for him today. Or maybe it really is his nanny's fault in both cases. With him and his entitled attitude, it's hard to tell.

Ronan McCabe is the kind of player who seems to think I pay him millions of dollars a year to play hockey but shouldn't expect anything from him off the ice, even though he knows that's not the kind of organization I'm running.

As captain, he has no problem holding other players accountable for stepping up like I've asked, but he doesn't seem to hold himself to the same standard. And when he does step up, it's with equal parts attitude and resentment.

I glance over at Wilcott. "And they couldn't have figured this out *before* the game?"

Charlie just shrugs, like *What can we do?*

I focus my eyes back on my phone, where I'm reading today's headlines. And when I hear McCabe come through the door to the jet, several rows behind me, loudly apologizing to his teammates as the music comes to a stop, before rushing up front to apologize to Coach Wilcott, I close my eyes and pretend to sleep.

Next to me, he explains that he would have just ordered a new car seat with overnight delivery, but he didn't trust Lucy to install it correctly, so he had to return and switch his into her loaner car to make sure it was safe. I assume Lucy must be the nanny? He's making her sound awfully incompetent, which, in turn, makes me wonder why he'd leave his baby with her.

When he's done explaining the situation to Charlie, he turns toward me—I can feel him staring down at me. But I take slow, steady breaths, even as I hear Charlie chuckle like he knows exactly which avoidance strategy I'm using.

It might not be the most mature choice, but we're in a tough negotiation period right now, and the last thing I need is any sort of confrontation with him, especially in front of everyone else.

We'll save that for behind closed doors, like we always have.

———

I'm sitting at the upscale hotel bar the next night, enjoying the overly heavy pour of a delicious Cabernet Sauvignon the bartender gave me, when Charlie walks up.

"The guys are all going to dinner together, with strict instructions to be back in their rooms by 10 p.m.," he tells me. "Larry and I are going to grab something at a restaurant down the street. You want to join us?"

"Nah," I say. "I'm good. But thanks for the invite."

"Please tell me you're not having wine for dinner." His voice has that overly concerned tone I'd expect from a father figure—someone like Frank Hartmann—not one of my employees. It's probably my own fault for insisting the entire Rebels organization is one big family.

"I just ordered a steak. Does that meet your approval?"

"Yes, but it wouldn't kill you to go out and eat socially, with other people, you know."

I tend to stick to myself on road trips, except for the very rare occasion when I can convince Lauren to come, too. There's no real reason she *needs* to be on these trips, and she hates leaving her girls, but every once in a while, there's a good reason for her to tag along—like a potential sponsor we can meet with while we're on the road.

"Tonight is the only time while we're here that I have any downtime," I say, and watch as the bartender's head turns toward us. I don't know if he's eavesdropping or just looking over to make sure I don't need anything, but I drop my voice a little lower either way. "I plan to enjoy having a couple hours to myself. Besides, we're having lunch together tomorrow, remember?"

He lets out a low grunt of acknowledgement. He's as pleased as I am to have to share a meal with the coaching staff, GM, and owner of Carolina's team. But Frank is old friends with their owner, and he insisted.

"Yeah, Frank said he wants the captains there tomorrow too," Charlie says, "so I told them they'd need to come with us after our practice skate in the morning."

"Absolutely not." My tone invites no disagreement, but I suspect Charlie doesn't want his players forced into this lunch, either. Every hockey player has his own pre-game rituals, and almost all of them include an afternoon nap, followed by a series of superstitious behaviors they have to run through. Even though, obviously, they'll all need lunch anyway, they shouldn't be forced to sit through this ridiculous charade—especially because our goalie Colt just broke one of their player's noses, so tempers between the players are bound to be high. "I'll talk to Frank about it."

Charlie just laughs and shakes his head. "Good luck with that."

"I don't need luck. Frank may own this team, but he pays me very well to manage it. And he's always trusted me to know what's best for our players." Am I really this confident that he'll see it my way? No. But am I certain that I can convince him? Yes.

"Alright. Well, enjoy your dinner and I'll see you tomorrow. Should I tell our captains that they don't need to be at that lunch?"

"I'll let you know once I have confirmation from Frank."

"Alright then." He gives me a nod before turning to leave.

I scroll on my phone for a few minutes, ignoring what I sense are the curious eyes of two men farther down the bar. And when the bartender finally brings over my plate, which has a filet artfully arranged over some asparagus and mashed potatoes, my stomach grumbles so loudly I'm pretty sure the whole restaurant heard it. I can't help it; this smells fucking fantastic, and I was on a series of calls all day, meaning I only had time for a protein bar for lunch. If we were back at the office, my assistant, Colleen, would have ordered me something so I didn't skip a meal—because, let's be honest, I get hangry and no one should have to deal with me when I haven't eaten.

The bartender smiles as he sets the plate in front of me, and a row of perfectly straight teeth sink into the right side of his lip like he's holding in a laugh. "It does smell good, doesn't it?"

"Honestly, I'm so hungry I was about to eat my own arm.

You could have brought me a bag from the closest fast-food joint and I think my stomach would have reacted the same way."

"Luckily for you, you'll probably enjoy this more." He gives me a wink as he licks his lower lip, and it occurs to me that this man who looks like he was a child yesterday is flirting with me.

"Maybe I *prefer* fast food."

He looks me up and down, taking in the dark hair that's kept the perfect shade of brown with my monthly hair appointments, the smooth face that's kept wrinkle free from regular visits to my aesthetician, the large pearls that adorn my earlobes, and the silk blouse beneath the burgundy blazer. "That would surprise me."

"Oh yeah?"

"You seem like a woman who . . . knows what she likes."

"I do know what I like," I tell him, letting my lips curve up at one side. "But that doesn't mean I don't prefer a greasy hamburger over a filet."

He crosses his arms and leans forward, resting his elbow on his side of the bar. "So why are you here having a seventy-dollar steak, then?"

"Seems like a waste of a perfectly good food allowance from my work if I go to McDonalds, you know?" I say as I unwrap my cutlery from the napkin and lay the cloth across my lap.

"So what do you do for work?"

I don't know why I still haven't found a good way to answer this question. I'm not the kind of person who throws around my job title to impress people, nor do I want to invite the questions it inevitably generates from perfect strangers. "I work in sports."

Leaning in a bit closer, his eyes focus on my lips as I lick them —a nervous habit I've never quite gotten over. "Tell me more."

I pick up my fork and knife, sinking them into my steak as I flick my eyes back up toward him. "No thanks."

His eyebrows lift in surprise. "Are you always hesitant to talk about work?"

Yes.

"No. But you just watched me turn down dinner with my colleagues, so obviously I'm not looking for work talk."

I watch as his pupils dilate, his eyes lingering on my mouth. I know that my lips, and the wide smile they afford me, are the physical feature I'm most known for. So his intense interest in them shouldn't surprise me, but it still does. He's a damn baby compared to me.

Then he stands, spreading his hands along the edge of the bar. His forearms are dusted with blonde hair over his tanned skin. The color matches the natural highlights in his slightly overgrown waves, giving him a touch of southern surfer boy charm.

"So what *are* you looking for?"

Such an open, honest invitation. And in the past, right after my divorce, I'd have probably taken him up on it, even though he's easily fifteen years younger than me. But I grew tired of that long ago. Now, I just want peace. My job is stressful—hell, my whole life is stressful—and honestly, a good night's sleep sounds way better than sex.

"Just to eat my meal alone." I give him a sympathetic smile to soften the blow.

His lips turn up into a half smile as he nods, before turning and heading down the bar to flirt with the much younger lady at the other end. As I take the first bite of my steak, then wash it down with my wine, I know I made the right choice. Because the only thing worse than the loneliness of being divorced and forty, is the empty feeling I'm left with after meaningless, and often mediocre, sex with a stranger.

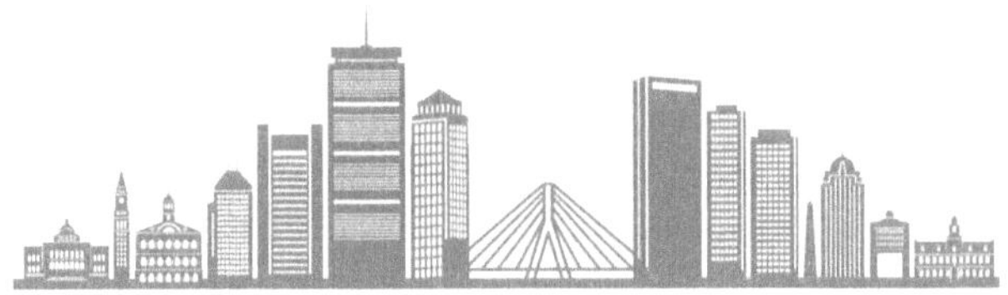

Chapter Four

McCabe

I walk into the rink exhausted because I couldn't sleep last night.

Lucy called me after Abby was down for the night to tell me that even with the acetaminophen, she was *still* running a fever. She didn't have any other obvious symptoms of being sick, but since she's still an infant, it's not like we can ask her how she's feeling. It could be a sore throat or stomach pains or anything, really. Lucy said she'd call the pediatrician when they open in the morning and try to get an appointment.

I tossed and turned all night after that, worried about Abby, hating that I'm not the one there with her, and praying that Lucy will take good care of her.

Though I love Abby unconditionally and am trying so hard to be the dad she needs, I can't help but think that maybe I'm not enough. Maybe what she really needs is a parent who can be there with her all the time, not a different nanny. Maybe what I need is a partner.

Unfortunately, most of the women I meet are interested in me primarily because I'm a professional hockey player—none of them seem like they're ready to settle down with a kid who isn't theirs.

"What the hell's wrong with you?" Drew Jenkins asks after I push open the door to the locker room and stalk inside. He's new to our team this year and having himself one hell of a season. He only had one year left on his contract when we acquired him in a trade from Colorado last summer, and AJ has already re-signed him in a six-year deal. Unlike with me, she had no problem increasing his salary, even though my stat line is more impressive.

I like Drew, and I'm glad we've locked him down. But it's yet another reason this whole contract negotiation has left a sour taste in my mouth regarding AJ—this isn't about the money. She doesn't want to keep me on the team and is hiding behind the salary cap as an excuse.

She's gone and made this personal.

Which she might not have done if I hadn't fucked up eight years ago. Beating the shit out of her then husband wasn't my smartest move, but I have zero patience for men who verbally abuse and physically intimidate women.

It doesn't matter that she, as assistant GM, was technically his boss, or that he, as my assistant coach, was technically my boss. That shit's not cool, and when I called him on it, he told me to mind my fucking business and that he'd speak to his wife however he damn well pleased.

I probably shouldn't have hit him the first time . . . or thrown any of the ten punches I delivered after that. But he was an asshole, and I was standing up for her. And she fucking traded me because of it.

Once I was playing for Boston, my contract was renewed with a no-trade option before she signed on as GM. So this is the first time we've had to negotiate since the incident.

"Slept bad."

"Is that code for 'I stayed up too late fucking some random chick?'" Colt asks.

"Unlike you before Jules, I don't sleep with someone new in every city we're in." It's a bit of a shit thing to say to someone who's a long-time friend, but I'm tired and my give-a-fucks for people's feelings aren't showing up today.

Besides, there's nothing inaccurate in that statement. Colt *was* the most notorious fuckboy in professional hockey until he started secretly dating his best friend and agent's younger sister, Jules. Now they're happily engaged, and Drew is engaged to Jules's sister, Audrey, so they're going to eventually be brothers-in-law.

Colt snorts. "Yeah, because you're a fucking saint, McCabe." His voice drips with sarcasm. I never had a reputation like his, so I know his statement is just because he gets testy when he's away from Jules for too long. Which is funny because, until a few weeks ago, none of us even had any idea they were dating, much less secretly engaged.

"Alright," Walshy says, clapping his hands together. Our alternate captain, Patrick Walsh, has a big mouth on the ice, but off it, he's a total peacemaker. It's probably part of why he's so happily married. "Let's get ourselves ready for our practice skate, and save this energy for our opponents tonight."

"McCabe, a word?" AJ says after I've navigated the long hallway where we walk into the arena. I tried to put on a happy face because I know everyone wants to see the players dressed up before the game—but today it was more of a struggle than normal. Even our peppy social media manager, Tatum, couldn't get me to smile for the camera.

After practice, I went to lunch with my sister, Sloane, who'd surprised me with a text a few hours ago, telling me she unexpectedly had to come to Raleigh for work. I'd teased her and asked if she was sure she didn't miss me so much she hopped in the car to come visit, before she smacked me upside the head and told me it was too bad I didn't know some geography in that "big history nerd brain" of mine. Because, apparently, Nashville to Raleigh isn't a "hop in your car on a whim" kind of drive.

It was great to see Sloane for the first time in months and only confirmed that trying for the trade to Nashville is the right decision. But I was late getting back to the hotel for my pre-game nap, and I desperately needed the sleep after the way I'd tossed and turned last night. Then my nap was cut short by another call from Lucy after she and Abby returned from the pediatrician.

Turns out, Abby has hand, foot, and mouth disease, which was easy to diagnose because right before they headed to the doctor's office, the fever broke and she developed a rash on her feet.

Lucy was eerily chill about the whole thing, and the fact that she wasn't freaking out is the only reason I didn't imme-diately look for a flight home after tonight's game.

But I'm tired as fuck, and AJ is the last person on this planet I want to talk to.

"What?" I bark out. I don't know why I let the mere sight of her rile me up like this; it only fuels the fire.

She raises her eyebrows. "Seriously? That's how you address your GM?"

"Our history—our *professional relationship*—is too fucking long for these games, AJ. What do you need?"

"I need you to keep your team under control tonight. I don't know what got into Colt in the last two games, but it can't continue."

"Lester's still out for this game," I say, referencing the player whose nose Colt broke in Game 1 of the series, "so Colt will be just fine."

"Like in the last game?"

"Hey, that was Carolina's players coming after *him* in Game 2."

"Yeah, and tensions will *still* be high, especially now that we're in their arena. After two losses and an epic fight, their players will be out for blood. We need to be smart, not reactive."

"I'll pass your message along." My voice is flat, because even though she's right—even though I actually *do* agree with her—the thought of admitting that turns my stomach sour.

"*You* need to be the one to convince them to settle down out there, McCabe." She leans against the wall, crossing her arms under her chest. The thin white turtleneck she's wearing creases right between her breasts, a fact I wish I didn't notice—but she's got curves for days and is unfortunately attractive, no matter how much I hate her. "You're not a fucking parrot passing along my message. If I wanted it to come from me, I'd say it to the team myself. I want you to be the leader they need, and tell them to get their shit together and stop being so reactive."

Grinding my teeth together, I try not to let her get under my skin. Maybe I need to talk to someone about all this anger? Zach Reid has a sports psychologist he raves about, and Drew started working with her earlier this season, too. Maybe I should get her name from one of them?

Then again, if I'm only with the Rebels until the end of the season, I can put up with AJ for that long.

"Understood." The word comes out through clenched teeth, sounding more like a growl than any tone that would be appropriate to use with your boss.

Her cheeks grow pink, something I haven't seen happen in the six years she's been in Boston. Back in St. Louis, though, I saw that look—embarrassment mixed with anger— quite often.

Somehow, I can't make myself care that I'm seeing it again. Or rather, I can't *let* myself care. Because the last time I did, she kicked my legs right out from under me.

Turning away from her, I push through the door to the locker room, and almost run smack into Coach. "Hey. Thanks for getting us out of that lunch today."

Wilcott rolls his eyes and says, "You're so damn lucky you didn't have to be there. It was painfully awkward. But you don't need to thank me. AJ was the one who got you guys out of going. She's always looking out for you."

Well, fuck.

———

I skate back toward the crease as the ref takes the puck to one of the face-off circles in our defensive zone. "I told you before the game," I say, narrowing my eyes at Colt, "not to fucking antagonize Carolina."

I broke down and had the talk with the team that AJ asked me to. But Colt keeps chirping the Carolina players every time they say something to him, and if that shit doesn't stop, another fight's going to break out like it did in the first game of the series.

"Not my fault they keep running their mouths. It's not like *I'm* going after them. *They* keep coming at me."

"You're the one who broke Lester's nose. Of course they're pissed. He's their best player."

Colt shrugs before turning his body toward the circle where players are getting into position. "Too bad for them."

"Just fucking knock it off," I say, my tone stern. "You don't have to respond to every stupid thing they say. You're smarter than that."

I skate forward to line up for the puck drop, and when Drew manages to get possession of it and passes it over to Walsh, I skate around one of Carolina's players to surge forward. But before the puck even heads my way, I'm checked from the side, right into the glass.

As the ref blows his whistle, I calmly turn toward the guy who hit me. I don't think he even did it on purpose; I think he thought Walsh had passed the puck back to me.

"Thanks for the power play, asshole."

As I skate backward, away from him, Zach comes up on my other side. "Nice job there."

I know exactly what he means. If I'd reacted, I would have

been sent to the sin bin too, thus negating the benefits of the power play. "Thanks, I took a page out of your playbook."

Zach is known as one of the smartest players in the league. The mind games he plays on the ice are brilliant—the way he eggs an opponent on until they lose their fucking mind, but then skates away before a fight can start—and make him a formidable opponent.

We learned earlier in the season, the one and only time I've ever seen him fight in his professional career, that he avoids fights because he's actually a black belt in Aikido. The man is absolutely deadly with his hands. I'm just thankful that we're on the same team now, because playing against him is torture and, like most players in the league, I've fallen victim to his head games before.

"Fine work, grasshopper," Zach says, dropping his voice low so he sounds like a wise, old martial arts master.

Given that I've got almost a decade on him, that has me chuckling as I turn to skate back to the same face-off circle we just left. And as I get in position, my eyes flick over to the bench to see if Coach is setting up a line shift, but the woman standing directly behind him, on the other side of the glass, steals my attention. Her dark blue power suit is cut to her curvy figure, and the off-white turtleneck she wears beneath it frames her face between the jacket and her dark hair.

Even from across the ice, I can see the smug smile on her face. Her lips turn up at the corners with the self-satisfied look of someone who just got their way.

Because I just did exactly what she asked me to tell my teammates to do: I didn't react, I didn't let my temper get the best of me or let myself be goaded into a fight.

I want to tell her I did that because it was the smart choice in the moment, *not* because of what she said earlier.

I didn't do this for *her*, I did it for my *team*.

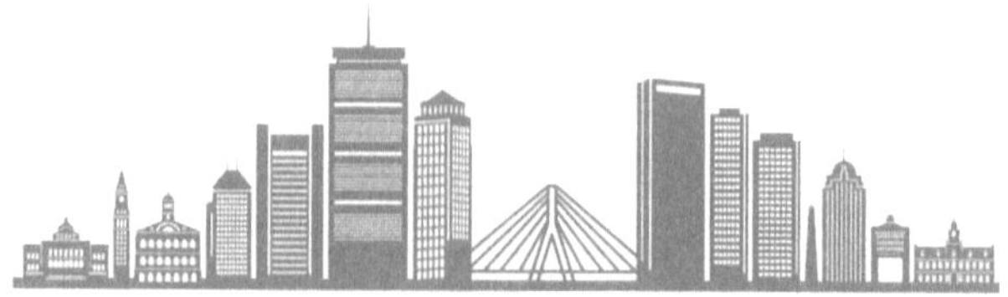

Chapter Five

AJ

"I'm so glad you ended up coming," I tell Colt's fiancée, Jules, as we stand outside the locker room after the Game 4 win. We officially won our division and are moving on to the conference finals.

She laughs lightly. "You're just saying that because he had a stellar game."

"Not gonna lie, I'm convinced he plays better when you're here."

With a teasing roll of her eyes, she brushes her long blonde hair over her shoulder. "I mean, I'm not saying I'm his good luck charm . . ." She gives me a little wink.

Jules is a complete boss, and having known her since before she and Colt were "dating," I can confidently say she's the *last* person I'd ever have expected to give someone with his reputation a chance. But a strange twist of fate has them engaged—something only her family and I know is fake— and now . . . it's starting to feel very real. Especially since she flew down here for this game to surprise him, is wearing a tank top with his name sewn over a heart across her chest, and will be coming home on our team plane.

"I know you're joking, but I'm not." I lock eyes with her so she'll know I'm 100% serious. "You may need to travel with us for the rest of the season."

Her laugh is tight. "AJ, I have a job and a life, and I'm not dropping it for a man. Not even for Colt."

"But you know how superstitious hockey players are, right?"

"Were you a hockey player?" she asks. "Because you really seem like you're buying into the idea of these superstitions."

"Yeah, I've played my whole life."

Her eyes widen. "Do you still play?"

"No, there's not really time. But I'm on the ice whenever I can be." I don't know why I admit this to her . . . it just kind of slips out. I'm normally incredibly secretive about this, using our practice rink early every morning, before anyone else is there. The only one who knows I still skate is Gerard, the morning janitor, because he's the only other person who's there that early. I'm sure if there was ever a reason to review the security footage, my secret would be out. But I've managed to keep it under wraps for years.

"That's amazing. I've never been very good at skating, I always left that to Jameson and Colt."

"Speaking of, if Colt gets it in his head that you're his good luck charm—"

"Please, *don't* put that idea in his head. Seriously. We have a waitlist a mile long at Our House, and I'm already behind because I went up to Montreal with him a couple weeks ago."

"Yeah, about that . . . Remember earlier in the season

when I was telling you I had just moved into a new place, but I wanted to live with it a bit before doing renovations . . .?" I trail off, hoping she'll jump in and offer to help, but she just told me how behind she is, so I'm not surprised that all she does is nod. "I wasn't kidding about wanting you and Audrey to work on that renovation. I *love* the idea of supporting a female-owned and operated business, and I really want it to be you two."

"How do you even know that you'd like our work?" Jules asks, her big blue eyes flicking toward the locker room like she can't wait to see Colt. And if the way he was looking at her during warmups, when she surprised him at the glass, is any indication, I'm sure he can't wait to see her too. He'll be the first one out of the locker room, no doubt, even though goalies normally take forever.

"Because I sort of stalk your social media. It's so well-done. Like it's curated enough that I have a sense of your design, but I also love that you guys post a bit of personal stuff there as well."

"That was all Morgan," Jules says.

"Lauren's cousin?"

"Yeah. She's really good at it, and neither Audrey nor I want to be responsible for it."

Morgan's in her mid-twenties and came to Boston with Lauren when she moved here a year and a half ago. Since then, she's become close to Audrey and Jules, but I had no idea she did that type of work. "I thought she was Petra Ivanova's personal assistant?"

"She is," Jules explains, "but Petra's closing her event planning business now that the TV show has really taken off, and since the studio already has a personal assistant for her, there's not as much for Morgan to do these days. She basically runs Petra's online presence, and she's started her own social media consulting business on the side."

Petra Ivanova is one of Lauren's best friends, so I've gotten to know her a bit over this past year. She's a powerhouse of a woman and the face of the award-winning talk show *And Yet We Rise*. Every week, she interviews a woman who overcame great obstacles to redefine success in her field. The show is both inspirational and aspirational—exactly the type of show I wish had existed when I was younger. It doesn't surprise me at all that it's taken off the way that it has, but it sounds unfortunate for Morgan.

"I had no idea. I should see if she can do some consulting for us. Our social media manager, Tatum, is sweet, but she's not doing anything as innovative or trendy as I see some of the other teams doing."

"Yeah," Jules says, but her head is turning away from me and her whole face lights up because Colt is walking down the hall toward us. "You should talk to her." And then she's off, barreling down the hall toward him before she jumps into his arms, wrapping her legs around his waist and nuzzling her face into his neck.

I turn away, not to give them privacy so much as to prevent myself from being sick at how in love they seem. I remember the early days with my ex, the way it felt when he walked into a room, his gaze landing on me. You could have lit the Eiffel Tower with how I radiated from his attention. And look where it got me . . . cheated on and divorced.

Not that I think Colt, or really anyone else who isn't a

narcissistic asshole, would have reacted the way Chet did in our situation. But still, seeing two people so in love, especially in the early days, still hurts.

I just want to get on that plane and sleep while we fly home. I'm always exhausted by the end of the season, but this year it feels particularly intense. I'm not sure if it's because early yesterday morning I caught a flight home for Lauren's bridal shower, and convinced Jules to come down for Game 4, before flying back last night. Or if maybe I need to see my endocrinologist about adjusting my medications?

I'm about to pull out my phone to shoot her a message when Charlie walks up. I congratulate him on a good game, and we chat a bit about what the next week should look like now that we don't have to play Games 5, 6, or 7. Round 3 of the playoffs won't start until the following week, and it feels like a gift for all of us to have a whole week without games or travel.

"The guys will be well-rested compared to either Philly or New Jersey," Charlie says, and I nod in agreement. Their fourth game finished up in Philadelphia only minutes ago, and the teams are tied 2-2 in the series, so they'll be playing at least two more games next week, if not three. Whoever wins, we'll take on in Round 3 and hopefully our week off will give us an advantage.

"I know you'll want to practice," I tell him, "but make sure not to overdo it. They need to conserve their energy."

"Exactly what I was thinking," Charlie says as we walk out into the humid evening air and across the parking lot to the bus.

I glance behind me, looking for Jules, because I'd offered her the seat next to me on the plane home. But she's tucked under Colt's arm, and I have a feeling he's not going to let her go. Turning back toward the door of the bus, I laugh to myself about how Drew, who normally sits next to Colt, is going to lose his seat. But then the laughter dries up when I realize that might mean Drew ends up next to me on this flight, as I'm the only one who normally has a free seat beside me.

Whatever, we'll all be sleeping anyway.

———

"I'm sorry, but what the actual hell do you think you're doing?" I say to McCabe as I glance up at where he stands next to me, eyeing the seat next to mine.

"Drew lost his seat to Jules, so I gave him mine," McCabe says before using one of his long legs to step right over me and toward the window seat when I don't move out of his way.

"Why would you do that?" I hiss, trying to keep my voice low, so I don't attract Charlie's attention. He's deep in conversation with our assistant coach, Larry, and I'd love not to cause a scene. "You better not be trying to talk to me about your contract." Players aren't allowed to negotiate directly with management, and I don't want it to look like anything unethical is going on here.

"Relax, AJ. I'm just planning to sleep, and this is a nicer seat than what we have." He's right; the seats up in this section are first-class, whereas the rest of the plane is retrofitted with business class seats. Ours fully recline, which is the only reason I can normally sleep on these flights.

"Fine," I grumble, pulling my Kindle out of the seat pocket in front of me.

"But I did have a question for you."

"No. No questions, McCabe—not here. If you want to talk about your contract, or this team, or anything else, drop by my office with your agent." He knows better. He knows the only conversation I can have about his contract is with his agent, and we've already agreed to wait until the season is over. Too damn bad for him if he's having second thoughts now that we're headed into the third round of the playoffs. If he hadn't wanted to wait, he should have negotiated instead of throwing out such ridiculous demands.

"Oh, so we're at the *not being able to talk without a mediator* stage?" His gruff voice has a hard, sarcastic edge like it always does now.

"No, we're at the *I'm exhausted and want to go to sleep, and not talk to you* stage."

"Fine," he says. "Answer one question for me, and then I'll leave you alone."

I roll my eyes as I glance up at him, and I'm surprised at how bright green his eyes are up close, even in the dim light. The practically permanent scowl he wears usually has his eyebrows dipping low, and his green eyes aren't really able to shine like they used to when he was a fresh, young player who I brought up to the NHL from our AHL affiliate.

Did I do that to him? Did I dim that spark when I traded him to Boston?

It's not the first time I've wondered this, but I've never had the nerve to ask. *Man up and stop being such a scaredy cat,* I hear my Dad's voice, even after all these years of trying to get him out of my head.

"Fine."

The plane starts taxiing toward the runway, and I glance down when I sense McCabe's fists tighten on the armrests on either side of him. But he's glanced out the window and I'm relieved he doesn't see me looking, both because I don't want to be caught staring at him and also because if he's scared of flying, I'd be the last person he'd want to admit that to.

He turns back toward me, and his face is a mask. There's no trace of the fear I sensed a moment ago as he asks, "What were you doing in my building the other afternoon?"

I have literally no idea what he's talking about. "Your building? Like where you live?"

He nods.

"I have no idea where you live, McCabe." Why would I know anything more than the fact that he lives in the city? Unlike some of the other players, it's not like he's hosted big team events at his place.

"That seems unlikely, since I watched you walk into my lobby five days ago."

Five days . . . My eyebrows scrunch as I do the math. Five days ago was right in between Games 1 and 2. We were at the children's hospital that afternoon, and I left right before it wrapped up because I needed to get home and order takeout before my brother and his girlfriend arrived. They tend to stay at my place when I'm out of town, both because it's more comfortable than their tiny apartment, and also so they can cat-sit my extremely unfriendly cat, Tabitha.

"The only lobby I was in that afternoon was my own," I say flippantly, as the plane takes a turn onto the runway and begins increasing speed. What is he on about?

"No, I'm pretty sure you were in *my* lobby."

We look at each other, in a stalemate of sorts, because obviously only one of us can be right in this instance. "Okay, so where do you live then?" I ask, confident I can prove him wrong.

"89 Ashburn Street."

This isn't happening. I do a long, slow blink as the plane accelerates and I feel the front wheels lift off the ground, but when I open my eyes, we're still on the plane and he's still sitting next to me. How is this my life? "Bullshit."

"I think I know where I live, AJ."

Turning my head toward him, I open my eyes as I level him with a glare. "That's where *I* live."

"Nooo." The word is a low growl coming from between his clenched teeth, and our eyes are locked like we're each trying to convince the other this isn't possible.

"What unit are you in?" I ask.

"Why? You planning on visiting?"

I huff out a small laugh. "Making sure I can avoid you, is more like it."

"1705."

I press my eyes shut tightly. This isn't possible. If this man lived across the hall from me, surely I'd have seen him sometime in the last couple of months since moving in.

"You?" he asks. His voice is tight, like it always is when he speaks to me. Grumpy is McCabe's default, but I've occasionally seen him relax enough to look like he's enjoying himself. Just never when he knows I'm around.

"1706."

I glance down in time to see his fists tighten on the arm

rests again, and now that we're airborne, I know it's not because of the takeoff.

"Well, this is awkward," he says as he reclines his seat, closing his eyes and resting his head against his headrest.

I guess this conversation is over?

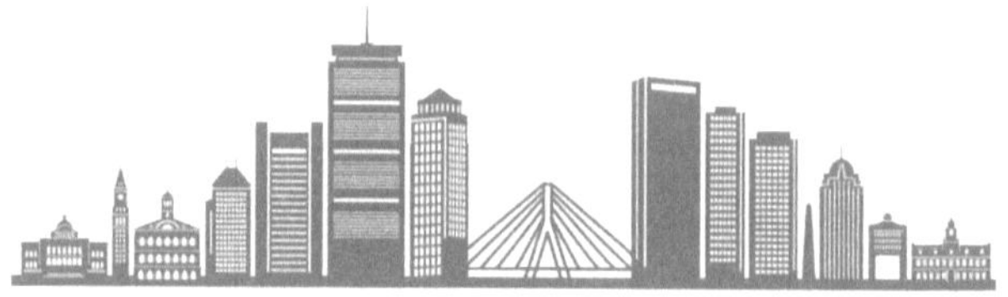

Chapter Six

AJ

Ordinarily, I can't wait to get home and into my own bed after a road trip. This return trip is different—my body is jittery with nerves as I approach my building.

I drive down the ramp into the underground parking garage and my eyes are scanning the reserved spaces for McCabe's black Range Rover. When the elevator doors open, I half-expect him to be inside. And when I walk down the hall of the seventeenth floor to my condo, my eyes flick over to his door.

How is it possible that he lives right on the other side of the hall?

I wonder if I will feel this keyed up every time I come home now, or if it's just because this is new information?

My heart races as I step through my door, and I let out a deep sigh of relief as if I narrowly avoided running into him.

Even though I've lived here for months and never seen him, now that I know that we're not only in the same building, but also just across the hall, I can't help but expect him to be everywhere.

Standing there with my back against the front door, I catch sight of my asshole of a cat, Tabitha, who hisses at me as she arches her back, her black fur standing on end, before she runs toward the doorway across from my bedroom.

Just then, my brother steps into the hallway in nothing but a pair of jersey shorts, and Tabitha snakes her way around his ankles, rubbing against him like he's her best friend. I'm not sure why she hates me, or if maybe she just prefers men?

"Shit," I say, glancing at my watch. "Did I wake you? It's not even five yet, I'm sorry." I always try to be as quiet as possible when we get home from a road trip, because the worst possible way to thank my brother and his girlfriend for cat sitting is to wake them up at the ass crack of dawn.

"I was half-awake," he says.

"Why?"

"Because Nicole had wine last night."

The laugh comes from the back of my throat and sounds almost like a snort. One of the first things Nicole and I bonded over when my brother started dating her a year and a half ago was how much we both love red wine, but how it makes us snore if we drink too much. Now that I'm not sharing my bed with anyone, it's not something I worry about, but my brother's always a little bitter when she chooses to drink it.

Taking a few steps forward while I roll my suitcase

behind me, I step out of the small entryway and into the living room. My eyes scan the space, and I can hardly believe what I'm seeing. Everything is organized, and it looks lived-in, with no trace of the moving boxes that have been my roommates for months.

"What the hell?" My gaze flicks over to my brother, where he's rubbing the back of his neck like he always does when he's nervous.

"We made an executive decision while you were gone. You've lived out of those boxes long enough. It's time you were settled."

I've been saying I'd "unpack the rest soon" or I'd "unpack once the season's over." Nicholas obviously knows me well enough to know I'd probably still be living out of those boxes next season too.

"So . . . what? You guys finished unpacking for me?"

He clears his throat as he bends to pick up Tabitha, and she cuddles into his arms, closing her one eye and letting her front leg hang over his arm. "Uh, we sort of hired a professional organizer to unpack and organize everything."

"You didn't have to do that!" As a college senior who is working as a waiter for the summer, he definitely doesn't have the money for that.

"Well . . . please don't be mad." He widens his eyes in a silent plea. "I sort of used your credit card for it."

My chest shakes with laughter. "Of course you did."

I'm not mad in the least. The lightness I feel walking into this space and not seeing evidence of all the things I have to do makes it worth whatever was spent.

"Now you can just relax when you're home."

"That's . . . really thoughtful, actually. Thank you."

"You don't even want to know what you spent on this?"

"Nope. I'm just glad it's done."

"Okay." He releases a whooshing breath. "Nicole thought you might be mad."

"Nah," I say. "I probably would have still been living with those boxes when next season starts. It takes some weight off my shoulders not to have to think about how I should be unpacking them. Plus, now when I need something, I can just hunt through drawers and cabinets to figure out where my shit is, instead of having to open up boxes."

Truth be told, when I couldn't find something I knew I already owned, I usually ended up buying a new one. Because which is easier: buying a new can opener, or rifling through five unopened boxes of kitchen stuff to find it?

I'm not normally big on avoidance or wasting money. At work and in my personal life, I'm more of a take-the-bull-by-the-horns kind of girl. But for some reason, the weight of everything I still had to do to finish moving in was crushing me. I couldn't feel settled until it was done, but I also couldn't force myself to do it. Time was certainly a factor, but it was also like I couldn't allow myself to feel settled in this new place, and I'm still not sure why.

"I'm relieved you're not upset," he says. "But you look exhausted. Did you not sleep on the flight?"

I can normally sleep in any moving vehicle, but on last night's flight—with McCabe sleeping next to me after learning that we're neighbors—I don't think I slept much, if at all. I'd close my eyes, but then thoughts of running into him in our building kept haunting me. I fell asleep at one point, because I dreamt that I was leaving very early to go to work and when I opened my front door, he opened his too and was standing there in nothing but a towel.

It was nothing I haven't seen a hundred times in the locker room. But something about that sight in my own building, and the way we locked eyes and stood there staring at each other, jolted me awake. And after that, there was no hope of going back to sleep.

I've never dreamt about one of my players before. Never allowed myself to picture any of them in a state of undress, even though it's a sight I'm so used to. I don't allow my eyes to go below shoulder level when I'm in the locker room.

I'm a goddamn professional, and there's no chance I'm ever looking at one of my athletes as anything but the hockey players I hired them to be.

So why did I dream about McCabe in nothing but a towel?

"Yeah, I had a hard time sleeping," I tell my brother. "I think I'm going to head to bed and see if I can get a couple hours in."

"You going to work today?"

"Maybe for a little bit," I say. No one expects me to work on the weekends, yet I find myself in my office most days.

"You promised you'd slow down once the trade deadline passed," he reminds me, needlessly. I'm a workaholic, and he knows that will never change. But taking care of each other is just what we do.

When I don't reply, he says, "Okay. Well, Nic and I are going to head out early because she has a big test this week, so she's going to the library all day."

"How long is this summer class she's taking?"

"Six weeks."

I let out a low whistle. "That must be intense." Nicole is a nursing major, and she's taking one class this summer while also doing an internship in the NICU at the children's hospital.

"It keeps her pretty busy." He doesn't sound resentful, just like he wishes he could have more time with her.

"What are you doing today?" I ask. "You're not working until tonight, right?"

"Yeah. I'm going to take care of some grocery shopping and errands so Nic can study in peace."

"She hit the lottery with you. You know that, right?"

He winks at me. "You trained me well."

In truth, he hit the lottery with her too. Nicole is not only naturally beautiful inside and out, she's also low maintenance, incredibly smart, and unequivocally kind. She thinks my brother walks on water, which, after the upbringing we both had, is exactly the kind of partner he deserves. He treats her like a queen, and she responds in kind. It's the partnership every woman wants, and they found it in their early twenties. I'm thrilled for them, even while I'm a bit jealous that I've never had that.

"Let's do dinner one night this week," I say, moving my suitcase in front of me. "I'll cook."

"Ugh . . ." The hesitation comes through loud and clear.

"I found a new recipe I want to try."

"Do you remember what happened last time you cooked for us?" he asks, slightly cringing.

I roll my eyes. "It was a tiny fire. Stop acting like I burned the place down." When I overheated the oil and it caught on fire in the pan, I froze for a second while trying to figure out what to do. My brother raced in and threw the lid on it, and the fire died out in seconds.

"How about you get the ingredients and I'll cook," he suggests.

"You don't even know what I want to make."

"So send me the recipe. We can make it together if you want. It's never too late for you to learn," he says, but his voice betrays him. He sounds doubtful, like he knows you can't teach an old dog new tricks.

Our seventeen-year age difference has never felt greater.

"Fine," I say. "How's Wednesday night?"

"I think we're free," he says, as I start heading across my living room toward the hallway to the bedrooms. "I'll check with Nic and let you know."

"Alright," I say. "Goodnight. Or . . . whatever time of day it is."

In my room, I fall into my bed fully clothed. The guys change into sweats or more comfortable clothing once we're on the plane, but I never feel comfortable getting that casual around them. Luckily, I've managed to find nice-looking dress clothes that are comfortable, too. And as I snuggle into my pillow and pull the blanket that lays at the foot of my bed over me, I'm so tired that changing into pajamas never even crosses my mind.

Unfortunately, thoughts of McCabe climbing into his bed across the hall, trying to get a few more hours of sleep before his baby wakes up, permeate my thoughts and keep me awake.

What the hell is happening?

I haven't spent this much time thinking about McCabe

since he punched my now ex-husband eight seasons ago, dislocating his jaw and forcing me to trade him.

And you're not going to start thinking about him now, damn it.

But telling myself that and actually doing it are two different things. It seems I can't stop my mind from racing through all the possibilities of how things could have gone between us in the past. And try as I might, I can't come up with a single scenario that doesn't end with him hating me.

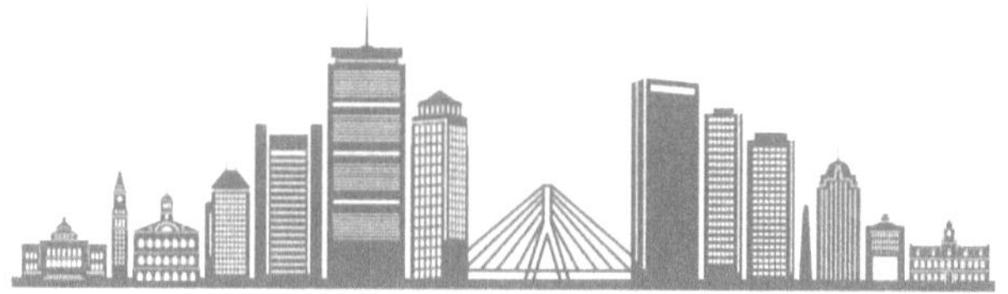

Chapter Seven

McCabe

"With the Rebels sweeping Carolina in Round 2, news of their general manager, Alessandra Jones, being voted into the top three finalists for GM of the Year, and their first game of Round 3 at home tonight . . . you've got to imagine that the team is feeling the pressure," sportscaster Ted Deveney's voice carries through my living room. I glance over at the TV from where I lie on my living room floor, flat on my back with my arms extended above my head as I hold Abby above me, flying her through the air like she's a superhero.

Her giggles almost drown out Ted's voice, but I still take note of his mention of AJ being a finalist. That shouldn't add pressure on our team, but it does. Because AJ is the first woman to hold her position, she's also the first to receive this nomination. And the fact that she's a finalist means that it's down to only her and two other men when they do the final round of voting during the Stanley Cup finals.

Despite my personal feelings about her, professionally there is not a single doubt that she deserves this award—and has deserved it for years. Everyone in the Rebels organization, from the players to the owner, wants to see her win it almost as much as they want to raise another Stanley Cup banner at Liberty Arena at the start of next season.

We all feel the need to win this next series, to prove that AJ deserves this award—that we're the team we are today because of her.

I played for the Rebels for a season and a half before she became our GM, and that team didn't have a shot in hell at the Cup. Now, we're on the road to possibly winning it for the second time since she arrived.

In those first couple of years, she hired a new coach, reorganized management, and began building our team with the exact players we needed to become a cohesive team instead of a group of hot-headed athletes that were only in it for themselves. And we've been reaping the rewards since.

"Or," his co-host, Stefanie Flowers says, "they're feeling super confident as they open this series at home. After sweeping Carolina like they did, I wouldn't be surprised if we see them come into this series with the explosive energy we saw in the last one. Especially since they've had a week off to rest, while Philadelphia was battling it out in the second round right up through Game 7."

"Maybe," Ted says. "I guess we'll find out tonight. Tune in at 7 p.m. when Boston takes on Philadelphia at home."

I glance at the clock in the corner of the TV screen, noting that Lucy should have been here a few minutes ago. *Shit. Where is she?*

While flying Abby through the air above my head, I'm

contemplating whether it was a mistake to give Lucy the week off to go to Nantucket. She was pissed she would have to miss tonight's party for his grandmother, but this way, she got to be there for the week with his family. It felt like a good compromise at the time.

Abby is teething and all that drool is getting precariously close to falling onto my face, so I bring her in for a landing that has her squealing with laughter. Setting her up with some toys on the floor, I'm hoping she'll sit still long enough for me to grab a burp cloth to wipe her face and find my phone so I can make sure Lucy didn't text me that she'd be late or anything.

Now that Abby's crawling, I can't take my eyes off her for a second—but seeing her move around on her own is also pretty amazing. I'm not ready for her to start walking yet, even though I know that's the next big milestone.

She's almost ten months old, and I'm already feeling like the old adage is true: the days are long, but the years are short. There have been days that I thought would never end, and yet, looking back, I don't know where the time has gone. It feels like just yesterday she was a newborn with diapers the size of my palm, and now she's already pulling herself up to standing. It's hard to prevent my mind from jumping to her first day of kindergarten, her first date, her wedding day.

My grandma used to tell me that I need to live more in the present and less in the future. That's never felt truer, and I've never wished she was still here more than I do now. She would have loved meeting Abby. She would have known exactly what to do in every situation, whereas half the time I feel like I'm stumbling my way through parenting with no one around to help me.

After wiping Abby's face and quickly scrolling through my messages, I see Lucy hasn't texted me since before she left for Nantucket earlier this week. There is, however, a message from Walshy in our team chat.

WALSH

Marissa thinks we should take AJ out tonight to celebrate her nomination for GM of the Year. Who's in?

Because I don't have a wife or a serious girlfriend, alternate captain Patrick Walsh's wife, Marissa, acts as the "Head WAG." She loves organizing all the wives and girlfriends, and planning things like team social events and playoff jackets. But she's never suggested a social event that crosses the line between players and management. We save that for things like team-sponsored charity events and the annual Christmas party the Hartmanns host. But taking our boss out for a beer? Never.

The enthusiastic replies of my teammates indicate that I'm the only one who has a problem with this. Which makes sense. Everyone knows AJ and I don't get along, but I've never told anyone what she did to me in St. Louis. People can love her as a GM if they want. I did . . . until she betrayed me at the worst possible time in my life.

I wish she wasn't so damn *present*, though. I wish she wasn't everywhere I turned at work. I wish I didn't now know she lives across the hall from me. I wish I could forget the moment back in St. Louis when I let my attraction to her make me act without thinking. I wish that she'd grown less attractive over the years, instead of more.

Fuck. Get it together, man.

I'm not the naive twenty-five-year-old I was then. I'm old enough to know better than to be attracted to someone so damn infuriating. Not to mention she's screwed me over once before and seems willing to do it again.

MCCABE

Sorry, I can't. Have to get home to the baby right after the game.

DREW

Don't you have a nanny?

MCCABE

Yeah, a fucking unreliable one who isn't even here yet and I was supposed to leave ten minutes ago.

God, I miss my old nanny, Stacy. She was perfect at her job, but I knew when I hired her in the fall that she was moving in May. I'm lucky I had her as long as I did, but Lucy is in no way a suitable replacement.

I sit on the floor next to Abby, and she crawls up into my lap, standing on my legs and stretching up toward my face. Tilting my head down toward her, I pucker up for what I know will be a sloppy kiss. And the girl doesn't disappoint. I have what feels like a gallon of drool on my lips and chin. A year ago, that would have made me want to throw up, but now it just leaves me with the goofy grin I can never get rid of when Abby does something cute.

A few minutes later, the grin is gone. Lucy's now half an hour late. I pick up my phone, watching Abby standing on her knees and swinging her favorite stuffed puppy around by his floppy ear as I dial Lucy.

She sounds both surprised and confused when she answers with a startled, "Hello?"

I pause, noticing the music in the background. "Where are you?" I ask the question, even though I'm afraid I already know the answer.

"I'm at Tim's grandma's party." Her voice still carries notes of confusion, like I should already know this and she's not sure why I'm calling.

"You were supposed to be here half an hour ago, Lucy. I have a game tonight."

"No, I texted you three days ago and told you I wasn't going to make it back to Boston until tomorrow. I said to let me know if you wanted me to see if one of my friends could watch Abby, and I didn't hear back, so I figured you were all set."

"What the actual fuck are you talking about?" I ask.

Lucy knows I needed her here. When I offered her the week off, I made it perfectly clear that she needed to be back here today in time for me to leave for my game. She happily agreed, and I'd been able to get a woman, Tammy, who used to watch Drew and Audrey's son, to come babysit Abby the two mornings I had practice. But since I knew Lucy would be back today, I don't have anything lined up for tonight.

"I don't understand." Lucy sounds genuinely confused. "If it wasn't okay for me to stay, why didn't you say so."

"*I did.*" The words come out in a roar that scares Abby, and her lower lip starts to wobble as her eyes fill up with tears. The last thing I want to do is upset my daughter, so I scoop her up in my free arm, holding her to my chest and giving her a quick kiss on the forehead, before lowering my voice. "I *did* tell you that. Both times you asked. And then I gave you a paid week off to make up for you having to miss tonight's party, and you agreed to that under the condition that you'd be back in time for tonight's game."

"Well, I changed my mind, and I gave you three days' notice."

"No, you didn't. And it wouldn't have mattered if you gave me three weeks' notice, Lucy! I don't have anyone else to watch Abby, and I'm supposed to be at the rink, getting ready for my game. This is a job. You don't get to just show up when you feel like it. You show up when you're scheduled to work, because that's what I'm paying you to do."

I can't even imagine what was going through her head when she made this decision. This isn't just about me and my job. Abby is a baby, totally helpless and dependent on the adults in her life to take care of her. That's when it hits me. While, legally, Lucy may be an adult, she certainly doesn't know how to act like one. And I'm at fault here because, even though I had reservations, I hired her.

In the background, I can hear someone say something to her, and Lucy hums in acknowledgement.

"I don't appreciate your tone," she says. "You're acting like I didn't tell you."

I ignore the comment about my tone because, while I think she deserves it, I've been told before that I'm way too "grumpy and growly."

"Because you *didn't* tell me."

"Hold on, I'm going to send you a screenshot of the text." There's silence for a second, and then she grunts out, "Shit!" Another pause, then she's back and tells me, "The message didn't send. It has that little failure notification next to it, which I didn't see until now."

It doesn't matter what happened; the issue is that she's not here now. "What the hell am I supposed to do with Abby tonight while I'm playing?"

"I don't know, Mr. McCabe, but I can't do anything about it from Nantucket."

I can feel my whole body tensing up, and I don't want to hurt Abby where she's snuggled against me so I force myself to relax. "Here's a piece of advice from your former employer. Next time you feel like not coming into work, make sure you get approval from your boss *before* not showing up."

"My *former* employer?" she squeaks out. Did she think I'd keep her after this stunt?

"Don't have anyone call me for a reference. And don't expect a paycheck for this week."

"But you said I could have a paid week off!" Her voice is awfully whiny when she doesn't get her way.

"I said you could have a paid week off, *as long as* you were back here for tonight's game. Which you're not. Enjoy Nantucket."

Hanging up, I look down at Abby where her big blue eyes are focused up on me. Maybe one day we'll look back on this night and laugh.

"Guess you're coming to work with Daddy."

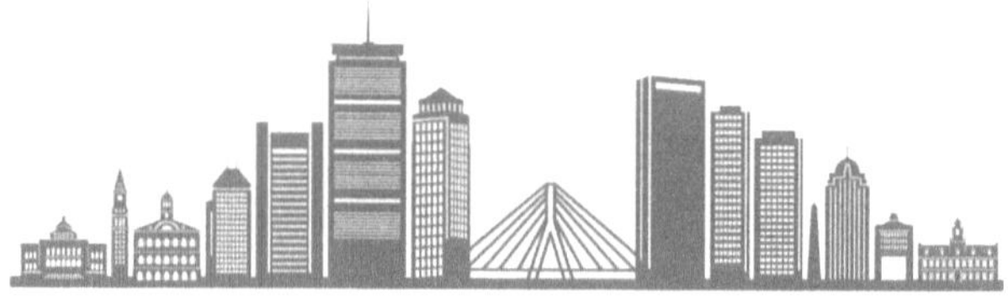

Chapter Eight

AJ

I don't know what I expected when Charlie texted me to say, "I need you in the locker room," but it wasn't twenty grown men singing nursery rhymes at the top of their lungs.

Pausing for a moment outside the door, I let out the giggles that are rising up at the horribly off-key rendition of "The Itsy-Bitsy Spider." There's no way I'm walking in there with a smile on my face—not when the team is supposed to be on the ice for warmups, but is instead . . . I don't even know? Reverting to childhood revelry?

When I push open that door, I'm greeted by the uniformed backs of my players, who are standing shoulder to shoulder in a circle. They're lightly bouncing up and down on their skates, and they're all doing the hand gestures as they sing ". . . down came the rain and washed the spider out!"

I push between two of the players, and my presence

inside the circle has a hush gradually falling over the team. The last man singing is Colt, who looks like a giant standing at least six and a half feet tall with his skates on. He's got one arm across his stomach with a baby girl sitting on his forearm facing out, and he's holding her back against his chest with his opposite hand.

The minute the singing stops, she bursts into tears.

"Ahhh, come on, AJ," Luke Hartmann says, "we just got her to stop crying."

I want to laugh at the ridiculous scene in front of me. When Charlie texted me, I figured something must be wrong. I never expected that the boys were too busy babysitting to take the ice. So I keep my voice slow and deliberate when I ask, "Why is there a baby in the locker room?"

The far side of the circle parts, and Ronan McCabe sits at his locker stall, bent over and lacing up his skates. His head snaps up, and he uses one hand to brush back the tendrils of dark hair that have fallen across his forehead.

When our eyes meet, he doesn't look anything like the angry, annoyed man I normally see. He looks more like the college kid I drafted back in St. Louis—the kid with bright green eyes and a cocky smirk, who walked onto his D1 hockey team and ended up getting drafted to the pros his junior year—than the pro-hockey player who's spent the past eight years hating me.

He looks . . . lost.

As he bites his lower lip, I can't take my eyes off him, and I can't stop wishing he hadn't just done that. I don't want to notice that full lip or the row of perfectly straight teeth sinking into it. I don't want to notice the way his eyes heat when he looks at me, or the way they sweep from my face down my body and back up again so quickly I'm not sure it actually happened. Because Ronan McCabe hasn't looked at me with this lost puppy dog look in a *very* long time, and the last time he did, it ruined my marriage and almost ruined his career.

Silence stretches on for a few seconds too long as we stand there staring at each other.

Then his adorable daughter lets out a real wail, and he stands quickly, rushing over to her. As he holds her tenderly, snuggling her against his chest and shushing her as he bounces lightly on his skates, I wish I wasn't seeing this side of him either.

Because the hard, resentful man who's played for me the past six years is easy to boss around and easy to dismiss. But seeing this human side of him that reminds me of who he used to be? This isn't going to be good for either of us.

"Again," I say once the baby has settled down. "Can someone explain why there's a baby in the locker room? And why you're all in here when you're supposed to be on the ice for warmups?"

Charlie clears his throat, but when I look at him, he's watching McCabe standing there, bouncing his baby in his arms.

As my eyes track over to our captain, he says, "My nanny didn't show up tonight."

The other guys stay silent, watching this stare down between us.

"After making you late for our flight in the last series, and now not showing up, she's sounding more and more like someone who shouldn't be responsible for a baby."

"Which is why she isn't my nanny anymore."

"So, what is the plan for your daughter during this game?" I ask, crossing my arms over my chest..

He clears his throat and shrugs. "I haven't gotten that far. But I couldn't exactly leave her home alone."

"Obviously," I say, unable to resist rolling my eyes. "Alright, give her here, and get your asses out on the ice."

"What?" His head rears back in shock, like I'm the last person he'd leave his baby with.

"I'll take care of her," I assure him.

"I'm not expecting you to watch her while I play."

"Well, someone has to," I say, looking around. "And every other person in this room needs to be on that bench tonight. So unless you don't want to play, hand her over."

He eyes me dubiously.

"Alright," Charlie says loudly. "Everyone else on the ice while McCabe and AJ work this out."

"You good?" Drew asks McCabe from beside him, which makes me wonder if he's afraid to leave the two of us alone in a room together. That thought has a laugh slipping out— because if they only knew—and twenty-three sets of eyes settle on me.

A flush creeps up my neck. "You all are acting like I can't possibly take care of a baby for the next few hours."

"Nooo," McCabe says slowly. "We're acting like it's not your *job* to take care of a baby, especially during a game."

"My job," I say, a hard edge to my voice as I lock my gaze back on him, "is to make sure my players are on the ice and ready to play. And if taking care of your baby in an emergency situation is what I need to do for you to go out there and win, it's what I'm going to do."

"On the ice, boys," Charlie snaps, as McCabe and I remain

squared off like we're ready to fight. And as everyone around us filters out of the room, we stay six feet apart, locked in a battle of the wills.

"I don't want to be that guy," McCabe says quietly before pressing his lips to his daughter's head while bouncing her in his arms.

"What guy is that?"

"The one who asks his GM, the only female in the room, to watch his kid."

Well, that's unexpectedly thoughtful.

"You're not asking, I'm insisting. And while I appreciate your attention to gender roles, in this situation it doesn't matter. I need you out there on the ice tonight. I need you to play. And if being responsible for her so you can do your job is what's needed, that's what I'm going to do. It's what any GM should do in this situation—male or female."

"You know that no one else in your position would do this, right?" he asks, voice quiet.

"Maybe not," I admit. But I'm not about to let my pride—the fact that I'm in charge of an entire hockey organization, and not a damn babysitter—get in the way of my team winning tonight. "But we need this win, which means I need you out there."

"Can't win without me, huh?" He's teasing, but I hear what he's saying—I need to sign him to a new contract. But for that to happen, he needs to compromise. Which is a conversation for another time.

"I'd rather not find out tonight. So get out on the ice."

"She can be really fussy with new people," he warns and, as if she understands him, her face scrunches up and she lets out a cry. She looks pissed off, and I can't blame her. If I'd been passed around a circle of hockey players singing off-key, I'd be pissed too.

"We'll be fine," I assure him.

"She's teething."

"Most babies do."

"It's almost her bedtime."

"She can sleep on me."

"Are you really sure you want to do this?" he asks with a subtle shake of his head. "The optics . . ."

"I don't give a shit about the optics, Ronan!" I say, and his look of surprise as I use his first name—something I haven't done in the entire time I've been in Boston—stops me for a moment. "What matters tonight, is winning. After that, we can focus on finding you a new nanny."

His eyebrows dip and he looks at me suspiciously. "Why are you doing this?"

"Doing what?" I ask on an exasperated breath. He's acting like I'm offering him my kidney, instead of offering to help him out with this baby for a few hours. I can't go out there and play for him, so I'll do everything else that's within my power to ensure a win.

"Helping me?"

"What part of *we need to win tonight* isn't resonating?" This man is infuriating. It's like he needs to question everything I say and turn every conversation into a fight, and I'm already tired of saying the same thing over and over.

He sighs so deeply it seems to physically deflate him, and then he places his baby into my outstretched arms. "Don't make me stop hating you now." His words are practically whispered as he watches me take his baby and turn her so she's facing me.

"Wouldn't dream of it," I reply flippantly as I hold his little cuddle bug against my chest. She settles immediately, no trace of the fussy baby who was being passed around the circle minutes ago. I run my fingertips up and down her back, and her head grows heavy on my breasts. "Does she have a name?"

I already know her name, of course. I take my job as GM seriously, and make sure I know my players' families. Too bad I never thought to memorize their home addresses. It could have saved me from buying a place across the hall from McCabe.

"Abby."

"Hey, Abby," I coo down at her, and her eyes flutter closed, long eyelashes resting against her chubby cheeks. I glance back up to find him watching us closely. "Do you have one of those baby carriers so I can strap her onto me?"

He presses his lips together and turns, walking over to a stroller I didn't even notice off in the corner near the door to the athletic trainers' room. Bending down, he pulls some sort of canvas backpack-looking thing from the storage space beneath the seat.

"Help me get her strapped into this," I tell him, "and then I need you out there warming up."

His eyes close briefly—a long blink that someone else might not even notice, but it says a lot to me about how hard it is for him to accept this help.

Standing in front of me, he lines the baby holder up against Abby's back and then asks me to hold it in place before moving to stand behind me. Reaching around my hips, I can sense how tense he is, how careful he's being not to touch me. But when he slips the padded straps under

Abby's legs, his forearms graze my hip bones before he brings the straps up around my waist, lifting my blazer as he clips them together behind me. There's no way for him to avoid touching me as he tightens the waist strap.

"You just need to slip your arms through these shoulder straps," he says.

"My jacket will get bunched up and uncomfortable like this," I say as I hold one arm out. "Can you pull this sleeve so I can get my arm out?"

He holds the end of my sleeve with two fingers, like he's touching trash—really, I just know he's avoiding touching *me*. And I pull my arm out, then slip it through the shoulder strap, before pushing it back into the sleeve of my blazer. After repeating the motion on the other side, Abby's secured to me and already half asleep.

"Such a fussy baby," I say, rubbing Abby's back through the soft carrier. His head snaps toward me, but his face relaxes when he realizes I'm teasing, and then his entire expression softens when he sees how comfortable Abby is with me.

I'm not sure why, but babies love me. It's a cruel trick of nature, I guess, to give a woman who can't have kids the ability to calm any baby she comes into contact with. The unfairness of it all used to get to me, but now I just embrace this gift and snuggle everyone else's children any opportunity I have.

"I'm not sure why, but she seems to like you," he says.

A laugh bursts out of me and startles Abby, her arms and legs flying out quickly. But I wrap my arms around her, shushing her and saying, "Don't let your dad's grouchiness get to you, babe. We've got this." Then I level him with a look, and using my bossiest voice, I say, "Can you please go do your job now?"

"Are you *sure* you're okay with her?"

"I'm positive."

"You'll come get me if you're not?"

"I won't be coming to get you, because we'll be fine. Now go out there and play, and don't think about us again until the game is over."

"Where are you sitting?" he asks.

"I'll be in the owners' box with the Hartmanns," I tell him. "And I'll probably stop by and see the Flynns, too."

"Behind the bench, right?" he asks, as if everyone on the team hasn't given Drew endless shit this season about the way he can't take his eyes off Audrey every single time he comes off the ice.

"Right. But for real, you don't need to check on us. *We'll be fine.* Now go do your job."

"Okay. There's a diaper bag in the bottom of the stroller with extra diapers, wipes, and a changing pad, and there's a bottle of water and formula in there too if she needs it."

It's obvious how uncomfortable he is leaving Abby with me. But he brushes his fingertips across her head before turning to pick up his gloves, and then walks out the door just the same.

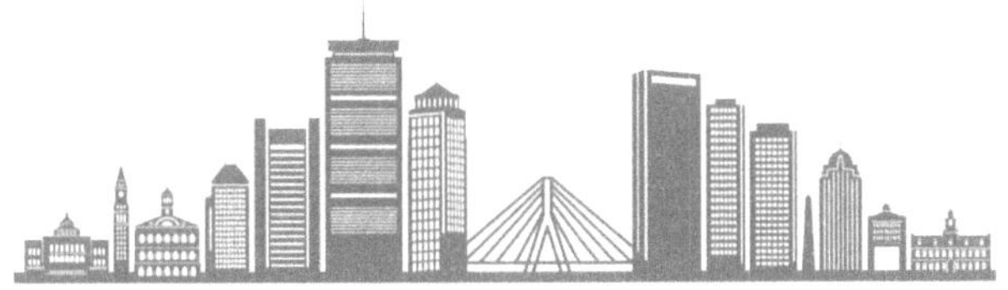

Chapter Nine

AJ

I take a moment in the empty locker room to practice walking around with Abby. I've got plenty of experience holding babies, but not while walking around a crowded hockey game in three-inch heels. Once I feel more steady on my feet, I walk out into the empty hallway, taking it slowly. The last thing I need is to insist he trust me with his child, and then have some sort of mishap.

The noise from the arena isn't that bad right now during warmups, but once they take the ice for the beginning of the game and the arena is full of screaming fans, music, and the announcers, it'll be a different story. I feel like Abby needs those little baby noise-canceling earmuffs. Then again, she probably won't be at another game, and it's unlikely this one experience could damage her ears.

Plus, I think babies tend to sleep best with noise, and he did say that it was her bedtime. With any luck, she'll sleep through this whole thing.

"Something you're wanting to tell us, Miss?" Ralph, the nighttime security guard for this floor, jokes as he sees me walking toward the elevator with a baby.

"Did you miss my whole maternity leave?" I wink at him. With my high-profile role in this organization and my no-nonsense attitude toward my job and my team, no one is going to expect to see me walking around a game with a baby strapped to me tonight.

Little do they know that, once upon a time, I wanted nothing more than to be a mother. I'd have left everything behind, scrapped my entire career, if it had been possible. But it wasn't. And that's when I learned that my husband, the same man who'd initially been attracted to my drive and ambition, basically only saw me as a vessel for his future children, which I was unable to have. It was all downhill from there.

"Whose baby you steal?" Ralph asks.

"McCabe's."

Ralph eyes me like he's about to ask why McCabe's baby is at work with him, but most players' kids come to at least the beginning of home games with their wives or nannies, or both, before going home to bed. Instead, he just nods and extends his key card to the electronic pad on the wall to call the private elevator for me.

"You have a nice night, Miss."

For the first three seasons I was here, I constantly asked Ralph to call me AJ instead of Miss. But eventually it stopped feeling like he was calling me out for being, at the time, the only woman in management, and I accepted that because my position in this organization is higher than his, addressing me with a title was just how he was raised. "You too, Ralph."

He continues down the hallway as I stand waiting for the elevator, and when I step into it, I'm surprised to find Lauren standing there. Her mouth drops open as she takes me in.

"You have a baby. At a hockey game."

I chuckle at her perplexed expression. "This is Abby."

"McCabe's daughter?" she asks, leaning in to get a closer look.

"Yep."

"Is this a kidnapping? Do I need to stage an intervention here?" She's teasing me rather than asking the question I know she's really wondering: what circumstances could possibly result in him handing over his child to his boss, a woman he so clearly hates?

"His nanny didn't show up tonight. Former nanny, I guess. Sounds like she's been pretty unreliable."

"Ahh," Lauren says, nodding knowingly. "Yeah, he had Tammy watch her this week during practices."

"Tammy, your old nanny?"

"Yeah," Lauren says with a little laugh, because she retired from being a preschool teacher, only to wind up as a nanny for Audrey and Drew's son for a few years, and then for Lauren's twins until they were old enough for preschool. "Now that she's officially retired, she had some time to help out this week while his nanny went to Nantucket."

"Sounds like maybe she didn't come back," I say as we ride the elevator up.

"Hey, speaking of McCabe, did you ever speak to him about the fighting in the crowd like Frank asked you to?"

"Shit, no. I was supposed to talk to him before tonight, since this is our first game back on home ice." I'm relieved that Lauren mentioned this before I see Frank in a couple of minutes.

Maybe he'll be so distracted by the baby that he'll forget to ask me about it. He was born to be a grandfather, but unfortunately for him, none of his boys are ready to settle down and give him grandkids—a fact he reminds them of far too often. In the meantime, he loves spending time with the players' kids and will probably already know who Abby is the second he sees her asleep on me.

"Well," she says as the elevator stops and we step out on the club level. "Let's see if he says anything."

"You're headed there now, too?"

"Yeah, he asked me to stop by before the game."

"That's weird."

"Maybe I'm getting fired?" Lauren says with a shrug, and I laugh, because we both know there's no way she's getting fired. If anything, he probably wants to give her more responsibility. If there's one thing Frank Hartmann excels at, it's the business-side of hockey—knowing what people are capable of, and making sure they're in a position to be successful. But he wouldn't do anything without telling me first, which makes me think he's just trying to get her comfortable with the idea of taking on a bigger role, so that she'll be ready when an opportunity arises.

I ignore the looks shot my way as we walk through the private floor that's only accessible to people with box seating or season tickets in the club level below the boxes. Most people around here know who I am, even if I don't know them, and I'm sure they're all equally shocked to see the GM of the Boston Rebels walking around a game with a baby on her.

For a split second, I wish Abby was my baby, because I'd love to be the one to normalize women in sports bringing their babies to work. But that ship sailed a long time ago.

———

Even though my back is killing me from carrying Abby on me for the first period, I head down the steps toward the Flynn's sixth row seats as the team skates out onto the ice for the second period. Lauren said they had an empty seat tonight, and if McCabe spends one more second of this game looking up at the stands for Abby, I'm going to fucking throttle him. He's playing okay, but he's distracted, and I want one hundred percent of his focus to be on the ice.

"Here, we left you the aisle seat," Lauren says, gesturing to the seat next to her as I reach their row.

"Thanks." I say hello to Lauren's fiancé Jameson, his sisters Jules and Audrey, and Audrey's son Graham before I sink into the cushions, thankful the seats on this club level are padded. Abby's been great tonight, as long as I've been moving. The constant din of noise hasn't bothered her at all, and she's slept most of the first period, only startling awake if there's a sudden loud sound—or if I stop moving.

But I didn't think about what it would feel like to have twenty pounds strapped to my chest for this long, while standing in heels. My lower back aches, and my shoulders and upper back are sore as hell, too. And we're only a third of the way through the game. She'll probably stay asleep if I keep patting her back like this.

I watch the players circle the ice before skating to the bench, and McCabe comes in last—probably because his eyes are cast up to the stands, and when they land on me, sitting there with Abby, they widen before the corner of his lips turn up in a half-smile. It should be illegal for a guy to have eyes that green or black lashes that long, not to mention a legendary scowl that turns into a grin that fucking melts women's hearts.

Not mine, though. Definitely. Not. Mine.

The entire crowd makes a collective "oooo" sound, and that's when Lauren's elbow meets mine, and I glance up at the Jumbotron. McCabe's stupidly handsome face is plastered there, head tilted back and his huge green eye staring up. Next to him, in big white block letters, it says, "Who's McCabe looking at?"

I glance down at Abby before the camera can pan to me, because even though I know it will anyway, I don't need to see myself enlarged up there as well. Hopefully, all they'll focus on is his baby, not me.

"All clear," Lauren whispers a few seconds later, and when I glance up, the video on the screen is showing the players lining up for the first face off of the second period.

"How long was I up there for?"

"Just a few seconds. Saved by the start of the period."

Shit. I probably should have stayed in the owner's box. Because now I see what McCabe was talking about in the locker room—his GM watching his kid during a game is likely not something that would ever have happened if I was a male.

There's no doubt it was the right call, the necessary move in the moment. But I can't help wondering how the public will perceive it, or how my colleagues will view it when it comes time for the final votes for GM of the Year to be cast.

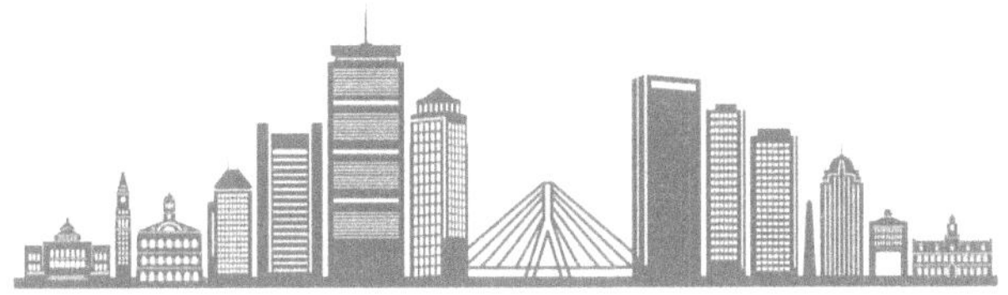

Chapter Ten

McCabe

"I need you for the press," AJ tells me when I'm walking down the hall toward the locker room after a tough loss tonight. I didn't play my best, and I know I was distracted—a point that was made abundantly clear when AJ came down to the glass before we cleared the bench at the end of the second period and read me the fucking riot act. In front of my teammates. In front of the crowd.

"Not tonight." I barely get the words out through my clenched teeth. I'm pissed—a little at her for calling me out publicly, but mostly at me for letting myself get distracted like that during a game.

She assured me that Abby would be fine with her. But I spent so much of the first period trying to get my eyes on them, to see for myself that Abby was okay, that she had to come down and sit in the stands just so I could focus on the game.

And every single time I glanced over after that, Abby was

contentedly snuggled into AJ, probably asleep. I wish I could say that I kept glancing over because I was worried about Abby, but the truth—a truth I will *never* reveal to a single living soul—is that I couldn't stop looking at *her* holding my baby.

Seeing AJ with Abby was like seeing a whole other side of her. A softer side that I hadn't seen her reveal in years. I want to forget what she used to be like, before her asshole ex-husband hardened her, before she had to seal herself off because now she's everyone's boss.

Because that version of AJ—the one I saw when she was the scout who recruited me to the NHL, and the one I still saw glimpses of after she was promoted to assistant GM in St. Louis—that's the version of her I could have had feelings for, if she wasn't married at the time.

"Listen," she says, one hand on the stroller as she pushes it back and forth. I glance down to see Abby sleeping peacefully, no trace of the fussiness she normally exhibits around strangers. "You need to be in there because there was *another* fight in the stands tonight. It's the third home game in a row that this has happened at, and it's always our fans, and they're always wearing your jersey."

"I don't have control over how the fans act, AJ."

"You have a lot more influence than you realize. And this organization needs you to say something about what's acceptable behavior for our fans, because this reflects poorly on Boston . . . on our players, our fans, our arena. Every aspect of this organization suffers from shit like this. You have to see that."

"Sure." I shrug. "But I'm not our fans' behavior police."

"I don't need you to be the behavior police. I need you,

when asked what you think about the recent fights that have broken out in the stands, to say something about appreciating the fans' enthusiasm, but that fighting's not acceptable behavior at games, except between players on the ice."

My fists clench and I pause for a brief second, wondering if she's intentionally goading me. Because the last time I got in a fight off the ice, she traded my ass so fast I was left wondering what the hell had happened.

"I don't need the fucking reminder that off-ice fighting isn't okay," I tell her, hating how I can feel my cheeks burning. I live with that reminder every day. My heart still breaks every single time I think about what I missed out on when I was traded to Boston. "But neither you nor I have control over what fans do in the stands."

"See, you keep saying that, but I don't think that's true. These are grown men who idolize you because you're living the dream they never achieved. You tell them to change their behavior, and I bet they'll fall in line."

I fold my arms across my chest. "We'll never know, will we?"

"You have ten minutes to change and be in that press-room. I'll see you there."

I glance down, wanting to stroke my daughter's cheek but afraid I'll wake her. "What about Abby?"

"Lauren's going to stay and watch her so I can be at the press conference."

"Making sure *I* fall into line?" I ask with a raised eyebrow, so she might think I'm teasing. But I'm not, and I'm sure she knows it.

"Someone's got to, McCabe."

I take a small step toward her. She's tall, but she still has to look up at me from this distance. "And you think it's going to be you?"

The question is bordering on flirting. It's the kind of thing I'd have said to her eight years ago, and I need to shut that shit down. Because no matter how attractive I find her, and it's even more so after seeing her with Abby, I know that *nothing* comes before hockey for AJ.

She not only traded me, but she demoted her own husband after that fight, sending him back to the AHL as a head coach and calling it a promotion. No one was fooled, because clearly an assistant coaching job in the pros is a step up from a head coaching job in the minors.

She squares her shoulders, and I have to wonder if the bead of sweat that falls from my hair down the side of my face is from the game I just played, or from sparring with her.

Her dark eyes narrow. "It's either going to be me, or it's going to be your next GM. I guess it depends on how badly you want to stay in Boston."

I swear ice runs through her veins, because this woman can be painfully cold. I don't know why I like that side of her so much.

"I guess we'll see, then," I say, before turning and heading into the locker room to get changed for a press conference I don't want to attend.

When I take my seat at the table in front of the microphones, Walsh on one side of me and Colt on the other, I wish we'd had time to shower. Because it's hot as hell in this small room, and even the clean t-shirts we changed into and the Rebels hats we threw on to hold our sweaty hair out of our faces are doing nothing to hide the stench of three guys who just played their asses off and still came up short.

The first few questions are about the game—about what we could have done differently, whether we got just a little bit cocky after sweeping Carolina in the last series, and what we plan to do differently when we take Philadelphia on again in two days. Our answers are the same, bland answers we always give because we can't say anything about strategy, our players' strengths, or the other team's weaknesses.

And the longer we sit there, avoiding their questions, the more annoyed I am that we constantly have to play this stupid game with the press. We're never going to give them the answers they're looking for, but we have to sit here pretending after every game. All I want to do is hop on the bike and move some of this lactic acid out of my legs, which are already starting to cramp up, and then get Abby home and in bed.

So when the question comes, I'm already in a bad mood. And even though AJ told me how she wanted me to respond —maybe even *because* she practically dictated my response and then threatened not to renew my contract if I didn't act accordingly—I do the exact opposite.

When the friendly question is lobbed my way, asking what I think about the fact that so many fights have broken out at our home games lately, I say, "I *don't* think about it."

Beside me, Colt clears his throat, clearly telling me that wasn't the right answer.

"In every instance, the fans involved were wearing your jersey," the reporter says. "What would you say to those fans? Do you condone their actions?"

My eyes flick to AJ where she's standing in the back of

the room, her face unreadable—just how she seems to like it. I don't take my eyes off her when I respond. "Hockey can be a violent sport. But being the captain of my team doesn't mean I'm in charge of the fans. So I don't have anything to say about their behavior."

I hear the low groan that rattles out from both Walsh and Colt, too quietly for the microphones to pick up, but I don't give a shit. All I care about is the fire I see brewing in AJ's eyes. I like that way more than the impassive expression she was wearing a moment ago.

"Was your daughter in the stands tonight?" The question rings out from a reporter I most definitely didn't call on, so I should probably ignore it. But when I get riled up, I have a hard time controlling my mouth.

"Why is that your business?" I ask as my head snaps to the young woman who's new this year.

"Well, when your general manager is the only female up for the GM of the Year award, but then appears to be babysitting your kid at a game"—she looks around at the other reporters—"we naturally have questions about that."

I scoff, about to respond with a very sarcastic, "Naturally," when AJ's voice takes over from the back of the room.

"I'd like to take that question, since it's about me," she says, taking the steps down the side of the room until she's on the same level as the table where we're sitting. "I was not *asked* to watch McCabe's daughter tonight; I *insisted* on it. And I don't like the implication that it's because I'm a woman."

She levels the young female reporter with a look that has her shrinking back in her seat. "When you're the general manager of a team, you make hard decisions. But helping a player out when his nanny doesn't show up isn't one of them. That decision was easy. He needed to play, and I had the power to make that happen." She folds her arms under her chest and lifts her chin as she adds defiantly, "If there's another GM in the league who wouldn't have done the same in that situation, maybe he doesn't truly have the best interests of his team at heart."

It's mayhem as everyone throws more questions out, but AJ remains eerily calm as she says, "Thanks so much for your questions, but we're going to let our players wrap up their night. See you again after our next game."

She turns and is the first one out the door, but when Walsh, Colt, and I follow her into the hall, she grasps my forearm. Looking up at me with searing intensity, she says, "My office. Tomorrow morning. Ten o'clock."

And then she's off down the hall, her hips swaying beneath her blazer in a way that has me entirely too focused on her ass.

"Shit, man," Colt says once AJ is out of earshot.

"We were even told we were getting that question ahead of time," Walsh says. "How'd you fuck it up so bad?"

"I didn't fuck it up," I tell them. "I said exactly what I told her I was going to say."

"Why are you always trying to piss her off?" Colt asks, eyebrow lifting as he looks at me.

"I'm not." It's a lie. "Nothing I said was untrue. Being the captain of the team doesn't mean I have to babysit the fans."

"Just like being GM doesn't mean AJ has to babysit your daughter," Walsh says, his disappointed dad tone ringing out in his voice. "And yet she did, because it's what was best for the *team*. Leadership requires sacrifice, my friend. It means that you put the good of the whole above any personal feelings you might have."

"I fucking know that," I say with a bite. But even as the words leave my mouth, I know that I didn't act that way tonight. I let my history with AJ get in the way of doing what the team needed me to do. Maybe I wanted to piss her off, or maybe I'm subconsciously trying to make sure she doesn't renew my contract—I don't even know. What I *do* know is that I don't think clearly when she's around.

"Do you, though?" Colt asks.

"I assume you're not coming out to celebrate AJ's nomination tonight?" Walsh asks as my head snaps toward Colt. I'm sure he's trying to interrupt what could easily turn into an argument.

Fuck, why am I fighting with everyone these days? This isn't who I am. These are my teammates. They're practically brothers to me. I need to unstress my fucking life so I'm not always so agitated.

"No. Not only do I have to take Abby home," I say as I see Lauren at the end of the hallway wheeling the stroller toward me. "But I highly doubt AJ would want me there anyway."

"Probably not tonight," Walsh agrees.

Pissing her off felt good in the moment, but it feels childish now. *Damn, this woman turns me into a fool.*

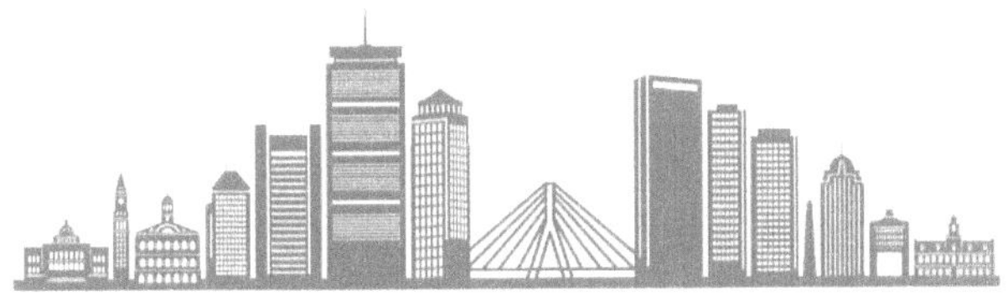

Chapter Eleven

AJ

When I get to my car after that disaster of a game and an even worse press conference, I'm still fuming.

The parking lot is mostly full, as the majority of players left their cars here when they headed out to the Neon Cactus, the unofficial bar of the Boston Rebels that's walking distance from Liberty Arena where we play our home games. I've never set foot in that bar, or gone out with the players after a game.

Walsh's wife, Marissa, has planned a little celebration tonight to honor my award nomination. I know it would be an asshole move if I didn't show up. And as hard as I'm trying, I cannot seem to muster the emotional energy to care.

I lean against the driver's side door of my car and pull out my phone. I need to make my apologies to Marissa, and also let Lauren know I'm canceling since Jameson was going to head home to the twins while she came out with me. She'll probably decide to go home with him if I'm not going out tonight.

AJ

> Hey, so sorry to do this, but I'm not going to
> be able to make it tonight. I'm exhausted
> and just don't feel up to it.

I've no sooner hit send on the text to Lauren than she walks out the side door. "Hey, there you are! You ready to go?" Her voice is so light and full of excitement.

"Uh, I just sent you a text, actually. I think I need to cancel. I just don't have the energy to go out."

She crosses her arms and raises one of her auburn eyebrows. In the yellow haze of the flood lamps that bathe this parking lot in light, her dark red hair glows a fiery orange. "Bullshit."

"No really, I'm exhausted."

"Are you sure you're not just headed home because you're pissed we lost the game and that McCabe didn't do what you asked him to?"

"I mean"—my sigh is so large it feels like it deflates me— "that's part of it, for sure. And I think all the travel is catching up to me."

I don't mention that one reason I'm exhausted is because I flew down to Carolina for Game 3, then flew back to Boston for Lauren's bridal shower, before returning to Carolina the same day, because I don't want her to feel bad. Or how that was compounded by my lack of sleep on the plane after Game 4, when I found out McCabe is my neighbor.

Lauren's one of my closest friends, but I like to keep my personal life . . . personal.

"Well, given how excited Marissa is about getting everyone together, and that Audrey and Jules are coming out specifically to celebrate you, I think you need to show up for at least one drink. Plus, Jameson left a while ago to relieve Morgan, who was babysitting for us, and she's going to stop by too. I think Jules said you wanted to talk to her about some social media consulting for the team?"

My god, those four really do talk about everything. Is that what it's like to have sisters, and sisters-in-law, and cousins? The longing for close female relationships like that hits me unexpectedly hard, like a sucker punch that has my stomach clenching in anticipation of something I've always wanted but never experienced.

"Fine, but just for one drink. Otherwise, I'll probably fall asleep at the bar." I'm not joking. The physical toll of carrying Abby for hours, combined with the emotional toll of watching McCabe self-destruct at the press conference like that, has me just wanting to crash into bed. Thanks to my messed-up hormones, my body's response to acute stress like I experienced tonight is almost always an exhaustion phase where I feel steamrolled by fatigue for a day or two.

We head over to the Neon Cactus, and I'm thankful it's only a few blocks away and that Lauren's yapping for the entire walk. My feet feel like lead and my eyes feel like if I closed them it'd be impossible to reopen them for at least eight hours. Everyone's already there when we arrive, and I'm just thankful that McCabe doesn't have childcare tonight, so I don't have to worry about him showing up.

After saying our hellos to the team, Lauren and I head to the bar to grab a drink, and I take a moment to look around. Neon Cactus is known for its variety of tequila, and I've heard you can get a hundred-dollar margarita here, but it looks like we walked into a dive bar. The walls are lacquered wood panels, with a variety of neon and metal signs covering most of the surfaces. There are Christmas lights strung up around the top of the bar like someone put them up years ago and never took them down. In the very back, there are pool tables, but the rest of the bar is full of pub tables with booths around the perimeter.

Walsh shows up next to us as we wait for the bartender to deliver our order. "Hey, boss," he says. "Just wanted to say how happy I am for you about this nomination, and how sorry I am that our captain was such a dick tonight. I'll talk to him."

Walsh is such a genuinely good guy. You'd never know it to watch him play, because he chirps the opposing team non-stop and lands a dirty hit in almost every game. But he's a leader among the players, a fantastic husband and dad, and one of those people who just seem to exude warmth and energy.

He's not originally from Boston, but he's always looking to give back to the community that welcomed him and his family with open arms years ago. If I ever need a player to show up for something, he's the first to volunteer. If I had asked him to say something at tonight's press conference, he would have done it happily. He's a team player, through and through.

He couldn't be more different from McCabe. Maybe he deserves to wear the *C* on his jersey, instead of the *A* he's sported for several years now.

"Thank you, on both accounts," I say. "But you don't need to talk to him. I've already got a meeting scheduled with him tomorrow morning."

He lets out a low chuckle. "Of course you do. Try to go easy on him, maybe? He's really struggled this season to balance being a single dad and team captain. I don't know how I'd be a parent without Marissa"—I swear his eyes do this sappy thing when he looks over at his wife, and it has me imagining cartoon hearts flying out of them—"or without our nanny, Katie. With all the travel . . . well, I don't have to tell you how hard it is."

Not every GM in the league goes to every away game, but my philosophy has always been that I need to be where my players are. If they can do the non-stop travel during the season, so can I. Besides, after playing college hockey, followed by coaching college hockey, then scouting for St. Louis, travel is just a part of my life.

"I appreciate that you're looking out for him," I say, and next to me, Lauren's rumble of laughter slips out like she already knows what I'm going to say. "But he's a big boy. He can stand up for himself."

Walsh laughs then, too. "Against you? I'm not so sure he can."

I can't tell if he's teasing me or if he truly believes that a 6'4" professional hockey player, who once beat the shit out of my ex-husband, would have a problem standing up to me. Of course, no one here knows about him assaulting Chet, so there's that.

"Lauren!" A woman's voice comes from behind us, and we turn to find Morgan barreling in our direction with Jules and Audrey right on her heels. She's visibly upset, her face flushed and her eyes full of tears.

"Oh my god, Morgs! What's going on?" Lauren asks, her expression and tone both full of worry.

Morgan's gaze shifts to me. "Hi, AJ, Walsh. I'm so sorry, am I interrupting?"

"Of course not," I tell her.

At the same time, Walsh says, "Nah, it sounds like you ladies have important stuff to talk about. I'll see you later." He turns to leave, giving Morgan the privacy she needs to share whatever's wrong.

"I just . . ." She closes her eyes and takes a deep breath, and as she does, the tears roll down her freckled cheeks. When she opens her eyes again, it's clear she's embarrassed to be crying in a bar.

"Hey, there's a free table over there," I say, nodding to a booth in the corner at the same time the bartender sets our drinks on the bar. I hand him my card and tell him to keep the tab open and then follow this close-knit group of women over to the table, feeling a bit like an outsider.

When we slide into the booth, I somehow end up sandwiched between Morgan and Lauren, with Jules and Audrey taking the seats on the outside of the rounded booth.

"Alright, what's going on?" Audrey asks Morgan the second we're all seated.

"I parked at my place on Newbury Street when I came home from Lauren's," Morgan says, "and then I was walking over here when Carter called."

I have no idea who Carter is, but Lauren, Jules, and Audrey are all nodding.

"And he . . ." she stutters as a sob wracks her body. ". . . I think he broke up with me?"

"You think?" Jules asks bluntly, as Audrey and Lauren immediately jump into sympathy mode, giving Morgan supportive squeezes and cooing their disappointment.

"Yeah . . . I don't really understand what just happened. He said he thinks I'm more into him than he is into me, and maybe we need to 'pump the brakes'"—she uses air quotes and an eye roll to emphasize his words—"on this relationship."

"Wait, this is the same guy who has been *all in* since the minute you two started talking a month ago?" Audrey clarifies. "The one who flew you to Miami with him when you'd been together for, like, three days because he couldn't stand the thought of not seeing you while he was traveling for work? The one who introduced you to his family after dating for a week? Who sent you non-stop gifts and couldn't go a night without seeing you, even if it meant staying on FaceTime with him all night?" Her voice is rising in anger with each point she recalls about their short relationship.

"What a fucking love-bombing asshole," Lauren says with a huff.

"God, it's like you just can't trust guys today," Jules adds. "Most of them just want a quick hookup, and here you found one who was all in right from the beginning, and then he pulls *this* shit?"

"You guys are so lucky you don't have to deal with this anymore," Morgan groans, folding her arms on the table in front of her, and resting her forehead against them with a loud groan of frustration. "I used to think I liked being single. But watching all my best friends get engaged has me rethinking things." She lifts her head again and glances from Audrey to Lauren to Jules. "I want what you all have."

Jules's laugh is low and throaty, her words quiet. "You know my and Colt's engagement is fake, right?"

"Like hell it is," Lauren says. "That man is down bad for you, just like you are for him. It might have started out fake, but there's *no way* you can convince us it's not real now."

"The *feelings* are real," she confirms.

"You're still wearing his ring," I point out. "You're still living with him, and you're still coming to his games wearing his name on your back." My eyebrows raise as I glance at the WAG playoff jacket she's wearing. The fact that she's even in the WAG group chat and sporting one of their jackets shows me exactly how serious Colt is about her, because players don't take that shit lightly.

"Because she's *in lovvvve*." Audrey drags out the word, playfully teasing her sister. "And besides, he said the only way this was ending was if *you* broke up with *him.* You planning on breaking up with him?"

It's a rhetorical question, asked only to emphasize that their relationship has become very real. Jules just rolls her eyes.

"I can't see any other outcome than you marrying him," Lauren adds. "He wouldn't survive without you at this point, and I've never seen you happier."

Jules sticks out her lower lip and blows out a puff of air, ruffling the waves of blonde hair that fall on either side of her forehead. "Yeah. I kind of can't see any other outcome either."

I feel Morgan's pain. Even though I'm not super close with these women, except Lauren, I've still watched as my players and my friend have fallen in love with them. I'd never begrudge anyone their happiness, but it makes me wonder if I'll ever have that kind of joy in my own life.

Of course, I'd have to open myself up to the idea of falling in love again. And I'd probably have to stop working eighteen hours a day and start dating. I've built a comfortable, safe life for myself in Boston, but it's starting to feel more stifling than safe lately.

As if she can sense my thoughts, Morgan turns and says, "What about you, AJ? Any special guy in your life?"

I snort a laugh. "I'm already married to my job. I don't have time for a man."

"You sound like Paige," Morgan says, and when I dip my eyebrows, she reminds me, "Lauren's sister. She's married to her job, too."

Lauren looks like she wants to say something, but presses her lips together. Then she says, "AJ does give excellent relationship advice, though."

My brow furrows. "I do?"

She knows about my divorce, my infertility, and that my husband cheated on me. I'm hardly the right person for relationship advice.

"Yeah. One of the first real conversations we had," she tells her friends, "was right when I found out Josh was leading a double life, and AJ popped into my office. You remember?"

She's looking straight at me. Of course I remember. It was the first time I felt like someone I worked with could also be my friend. I nod.

Lauren continues. "AJ told me that when a woman is beautiful, strong, and successful, she's a triple threat. And that weak men don't like to be threatened, so they'll find any way to undermine and invalidate you—to make you feel small, like you're nothing without them. But a strong man will encourage and support you, will want to see you shine and be successful in all aspects of your life, not just where it relates to him." Lauren pauses and laughs before saying, "And then she offered to help me bury the body if I needed."

"What body?" Audrey says with a laugh.

"I believe the offer was that if I needed to kill 'the other woman,' she'd show up with shovels."

Now I'm laughing. "Hey, we women need to stick together. Look at you all," I say, my eyes flicking to each of them. "The men in your lives are lucky to have you. And you know what the best part about that is?"

"The sex?" Jules offers, and Audrey swats at her from across the table.

"I mean, sure." It's been so damn long since I've had good sex, I can't even remember what it's like. "But I was thinking that the *best* part of it is, they all know how lucky they are."

"So it's just us with the sucky love lives then, huh?" Morgan says, leaning over and resting her head on my shoulder. I don't think she's even thirty yet, and with her strawberry-blonde hair, freckles, and cute upturned nose, she looks even younger.

I reach my hand up and pat her head. "I guess we'll just have to keep killing it with work. I hear you started your own social media consulting company?"

She sits up, clearly surprised. "You did?"

"Yeah, Jules mentioned it. I'd love to talk to you about that at some point. I think our team could use some social media advising."

Her eyes widen. "I . . . I'd love to talk more about that. But first"—she flags down a passing waitress—"I think a round of shots are in order."

Jules groans. "I'm not doing fucking shots, Morgan. How about a round of margaritas?"

As we all order another drink, I point at Morgan and tell the waitress to put an extra shot in her drink. "I've already got a tab open. Last name's Jones."

As we sit around that table, laughing and chatting in our booth, I'm shocked by how comfortable I feel around these women. We range in age by a decade and a half, but it's amazing how easily we find common ground. It makes me realize that there's something inherently freeing about having girlfriends you can talk to.

I see it in how well they know the ins and outs of each other's lives, and how supportive they are of each other. It couldn't be more different from how I saw women treat each other—the backstabbing, the jealousy, and the competition—when I was growing up.

So while I'm not necessarily spilling any of *my* secrets, it's nice to spend time with a group of women where I feel like, maybe, in the future, that could be a possibility.

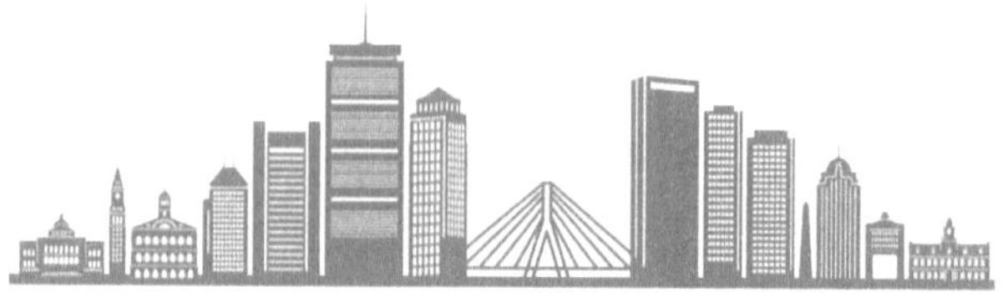

Chapter Twelve

McCabe

I show up at AJ's office the next morning with my metaphorical tail between my legs. I had a good amount of time last night—while Abby was up and fussing because her top front teeth are coming in—to think about my interaction with AJ in the hallway.

Once the infant acetaminophen kicked in, and I'd fed her a bottle and rocked her long enough, Abby fell back asleep. I wish I had as well, but my mind was spinning, wondering why I escalate every conversation with AJ into a fight. Especially after she'd done me such a big favor, and then acted so graciously about it in front of the press. She could have easily turned it back on me, about how I'd been unprepared to play or didn't do a good enough job lining up childcare for my daughter. But she didn't.

She's the consummate professional, always level-headed, impossible to rile. She faces screaming ex-husbands and irate hockey players with the same cool indifference. Maybe I just want to see her have some fucking emotions?

"Come in." Her voice has the same low, no-nonsense tone it always does. It makes me wonder if she's ever squealed in joy with her girlfriends, or what it sounds like when she drops her voice even lower . . . I bet it sounds downright sensual.

Fuck me. It's been years since I've thought about her this way. Seeing her with my kid, and her doing me one favor, shouldn't have me feeling like this—like I can't wait to see her, and don't want to see her, all at once.

"Hey," I say, pushing the door open. AJ's sitting at her desk in a pale peach wrap sweater that almost blends in with her skin, her dark hair down in waves that fall past her shoulders.

"Where's Abby?" she asks, clearly confused that I've shown up without my daughter after firing my nanny.

"She fell asleep in the car."

AJ tilts her head like she's trying to figure out if I left her there.

"Relax," I say as I shut the door behind me. "I put her car seat in the stroller and she's right outside the door, sitting next to Colleen."

"Ahh," she says with a knowing smile. "Good luck getting Abby back. Colleen has total baby fever right now."

"Baby fever?"

"You know," AJ says, sweeping her hand through the air, "like she really wants a baby. Pretty sure I'm going to lose her as soon as that happens, actually."

I take a few steps toward her desk right as she stands and

starts to move toward the chairs and couch next to the full glass wall that overlooks the practice facility.

We both glance over at the seating area, which I've always thought is far too feminine for a GM's office. There's a big off-white sofa with a coffee table in front of it, and two chairs flanking that, facing each other. There are throw pillows and decorations on the table, and it's like something you'd see in a home magazine.

"I wanted to talk to you about—" AJ starts.

"I'm sorry about last night," I say at the same time.

Her eyebrows dip and she looks like she's sizing me up, trying to find the lie. "You are?"

"Yeah. I was out of line."

"You were." Her voice is firm, but then she drops it lower, and with a defeated-sounding sigh, says, "I don't like doing this with you."

I don't know why I take a step closer. I should be keeping my distance, but somehow, I'm continually drawn to her. Like the other night on the plane, where it took everything I had to close my eyes and pretend to sleep when all I wanted to do was lean closer and ask if it was actually an accident that she moved across the hall from me. I know it had to be —she'd never have intentionally put herself in a situation where she was living next to one of her players. But my damn mind was getting the best of me, so I had to shut that down, quick.

Hating her is the only safe route.

"Doing what?" My voice is as low as hers, but whereas hers sounds downright sexy, I just sound gruff.

"Fighting with you. It's like you try anything and every-thing to piss me off."

"I'm not *trying* to piss you off. I can't help it—you're infuriating, and I just react."

Eyes narrowing, she puts her hands on her hips. "Really? Because honestly, Ronan, everyone else likes me just fine. It's only you who has a problem with me."

I make sure not to speak any louder when I say, "Yeah, well, you didn't trade anyone else as a punishment for doing the right thing, did you?"

Her voice is a little unsteady when she responds. "I thought we agreed we weren't going to talk about that again?"

"I don't know what you mean by *again.* We never talked about it in the first place. In fact, the first thing you did when you got the GM job in Boston was call me into this office"—I glance around the space, thinking about how sterile it felt before she took over—"and tell me to get over the fact that you traded me two years earlier because we were *never* talking about it."

"I—"

"But I'm *not* over it, and I'm probably never going to be." Okay, now my voice is rising, but to be fair, this is a conversation I've been wanting to have for eight years.

"Why? You're playing a hundred times better for Charlie Wilcott here in Boston than you ever did back in St. Louis. You never made the All-Star team in St. Louis, and you certainly wouldn't have been the team captain or won a Stanley Cup championship if you'd stayed there. You should be *thanking* me for trading you!"

It's the way she drills her finger into my chest as she says this that has my blood boiling. That, and the fact that she has no idea what the actual fuck she's talking about.

"I'm not pissed because of the hockey side of that trade!"

"Then what the hell are you pissed about?" she asks, dropping her hand when I step in a bit closer. She tries to take a step back, but finds herself trapped by her large desk behind her.

"I'd just put my grandma in a nursing home," I tell her, and I watch the way her eyes widen and her lips part in surprise.

Everyone knows the story of my upbringing because it was one of those "feel good" sports stories that the media focused on when I was drafted. My parents died in a car crash while our next-door neighbor—an older woman who all the neighborhood kids called Grandma, even though she had no children of her own—was babysitting my sister and me.

We had no other family. Our parents had met as teenagers in foster care, and my sister and I would have ended up there too if Grandma hadn't become our legal guardian. She didn't have the means to raise us, and we barely scraped by for most of my life. She even sold her car to pay for my hockey expenses once I was a teenager, so we walked everywhere.

When I got my first endorsement deal in college, I bought her a new car. When I signed my contract with St. Louis, I bought her a new house. There's nothing I could ever do to repay her for her kindness—the way she loved us, sacrificed for us, and gave us a better life when she didn't have to.

"She was too old to take care of herself." I continue after a moment of silence, our breaths the only sound filling the small space between us. "And my sister and I couldn't be there all the time to make sure she was safe. The nursing home was the best option. But she hadn't been there for two weeks when I got traded. And then she got pneumonia and died before I could even get back to see her. So yeah," I say through a tight jaw, swallowing my emotions. "I'm still pissed off, AJ, because you made it so that I couldn't spend Grandma's dying days with her."

Her eyes are watery, and she bites her lower lip before, "I didn't know," slips out in a voice so small and unsure that it doesn't sound like her at all.

"Well, you made your choice. And now you know the implications of it."

"I didn't *have* a choice!" A flush creeps up her neck and across her cheeks as the words ring out.

"There's always a choice."

"The *choice* was either to trade you, or your career was over."

"Because I defended you when Chet was berating you?"

Sure, he was my assistant coach, and I probably should have treated him with a bit more respect. But the way he was talking to her, telling her that not only was she a shit hockey manager, but an even worse wife . . . my temper flared so quickly I reacted without even thinking. Because she wasn't any of those things.

As our assistant general manager, we all loved her. In fact, we liked her a hell of a lot better than we liked him, which is probably why he felt the need to belittle her. And she always bent over backward to do things for him, to make his life easier, to try to make him happy. We all saw it time and time again on the road.

He didn't deserve her, and I'm glad she finally left his cheating ass.

"You didn't *defend* me," she says, squaring her shoulders. "You *attacked* him."

"I saw red. Any man who disrespects a woman like that in front of me is going to be put in his place." It's the god's honest truth, but still, I know she's right.

It was like I was looking for a reason to pummel him before I even threw the first punch. And all the others that followed. I don't think he ever got a single shot in before I was being pulled off him by AJ and security.

"You thought you were going to continue playing for him after that? You would have ridden the bench for the last two years of your contract. Career: over."

"Nah, Coach Miller loved me." Our head coach was always checking in on me when I first joined the team, making sure I was settling in, helping me learn the ropes. He had the hockey knowledge and skills—plus the desire to make his players feel welcome—that set him apart from someone like Chet, who was only in it for his own glory.

I take in the way she's crossed her arms under her chest. It's a defensive posture, but it's pushing her tits up into the V-neck of her sweater in a way that's disarming me completely. I look back at her face, but I can tell by the way she's looking at me that she noticed me checking her out.

"Miller agreed to the trade."

"Yeah, because you convinced him!" My voice carries the heavy notes of exasperation I feel. Miller told me himself that he didn't want me to go, but that AJ and Chet were right . . . I couldn't play for Chet after attacking him like that.

I'll never admit how much it stung that the choice was to get rid of me, instead of Chet, who was actually the toxic one. His ego was hurting the organization.

"It *was* what was best," she insists, pushing out a heavy breath. "For everyone involved."

I inch closer to her. "For *you*?"

My eyes focus on those full lips, and the way the tip of her tongue darts out to wet her lower lip before she pulls it between her teeth.

Goddamn. I've wanted this woman for eight fucking years, and I need to get over this. *Now.*

"Yes." She glances up, meeting my gaze. Her look is one of steely determination, the same look she wears when she's taking a player to task or negotiating a new contract, but her voice is devoid of emotion. "It was a necessary trade for me, too."

"Why?" I'm genuinely curious. But also, marginally hopeful. Could she have needed me gone because she was starting to think about me the same way I was trying so hard not to think about her?

"Because I was married, McCabe. And you wouldn't stop looking at me like I was your next meal. I could ignore that and make sure things stayed professional, but Chet was noticing. So was Miller. Your little crush was becoming a *thing*, and it had gone on long enough. It was getting in the way of my career, and yours."

It wasn't a fucking crush, I want to say. But I don't, because she's probably right. I didn't know her well enough for it to be anything but a crush . . . an attraction to not only her beauty, but her brain.

No one knows hockey better than Alessandra Jones. I'd never met a woman who knew half as much about the sport as I did, so to have her recruit me when I was in college, and then have these high-level conversations about my career and hockey strategy when she was the assistant GM . . . it was a huge turn-on.

"So . . ." I drag the word out. "Instead, you created a situation where I would hate you?"

She rolls her eyes. "Why would I do that?" Her tone is flippant, but her expression tells me I've hit too close to home.

I inch even closer, fully invading her space to see if she'll step aside to increase the distance between us. Instead, her arms move from her chest to grip the edges of her big wooden desk behind her. "I don't know, AJ. Why *would* you want me to hate you?"

She turns then, like she's going to step away, but the movement has her shoulder and arm brushing along the entire front of my body. And when her knuckles graze my dick, it has heat pooling there, then erupting into flames that lick through every nerve ending and light me up.

That's the only reason I can think of to explain the way I reach out and grab her arm as she begins to step away, pulling her back to me.

And when my mouth crashes into hers, all logical thought ceases to exist. Because the way she wraps her hand around the back of my neck and threads her fingers into the hair at my nape, the way her lips part for me and she lets me invade her mouth, the way her entire body presses up against mine in response . . . it makes no sense.

Nothing that's happening here—not the way my fingers toy with the edge of her sweater before sliding it ever-so-slowly down one shoulder, or how she snakes one of her legs around mine to anchor me to her—makes one lick of sense.

But I'm not thinking about what a terrible idea this is. I'm allowing my body to act on instinct. And my instinct has *always* told me that AJ and I together would burn hotter than the sun.

She hums her approval as my mouth travels from her lips, along her jawline, and down her throat. I lift her hips, setting her on the edge of her desk, as my mouth trails across her collarbone. And then I'm pulling her sweater aside, revealing the sheer lace of the bra she's wearing. Her nipple is stiff and pressing right against the seam of the cup, and when I brush my thumb across it, she arches into my hand with another appreciative hum.

Holy shit. She's going to be the death of me one way or another, so it might as well be through pleasure.

My eyes flick up to meet hers before I dip my head down to her breast, laving my tongue against her nipple through the fabric, and then sucking her between my lips. She moves her hands behind her back, pressing herself into my mouth as she slides both sleeves off her arms. When I lean back to look at her, chest heaving, I can't stop myself from saying, "You're so fucking beautiful. Too beautiful."

And then I slide the straps of her bra off her shoulders, and she pulls her arm out as I slide it down to her waist with her sweater. Both my hands are on her breasts, thumbs sweeping across each nipple, as she reaches out and undoes the button on my jeans.

Her hand pauses on my zipper, and I glance back up at her to find her staring at me. There's naked lust written across her face—the way her pupils have almost taken over those big brown eyes, her lips parted as her tongue darts out to lick them, her cheeks pink with an exhilaration I've never seen from her.

The thought that she's actually feeling something here, and that I'm the one causing that, spurs me on. "Go ahead. I want you to see what you do to me. And I want to feel what I do to you," I tell her as I reach down and smooth a hand up the inside of her thigh where her legs are spread for me. I keep my eyes locked on her, wanting to make sure I don't see a single trace of doubt on her face, and she nods, giving me the go ahead. So I rub my thumb along the seam between her legs. "You're fucking soaked."

In response, she slides my zipper down and reaches into my pants to grip my quickly hardening dick. My hips shoot forward involuntarily, my entire length pressing along her palm.

"So this is what I do to you?" she asks, her voice a cross between teasing and curiosity.

"Yes." It's a groan as I pump my cock into her hand, wishing there wasn't the fabric of my briefs between us. And then I lean forward to kiss her, our mouths meeting and our tongues clashing like we're both trying to assert our dominance as I hold one of her tits, running my thumb over her nipple, and slipping my other thumb into her panties where I circle it over her slick clit.

"Fuck, yes." She pulls back from the kiss and sighs the words out as she tilts her hips up to meet my thumb, over and over. "Don't stop."

She's so wet for me, and I've never felt as needed or needy as I do right now.

"I wouldn't dream of it," I tell her. She slips her hand inside my boxers and the feel of her skin on mine as she grips my shaft has my mouth colliding with hers once more.

There's nothing gentle about this kiss, and my throat rattles in response as I let out a primal growl.

The need to claim this woman, to take control of her body and make it submit to me, outweighs everything else. I think this whole building could go up in flames and I'd stay right here, appreciating the way her body responds to mine.

And then, as if the universe wants to prove me wrong, the wail of a baby cuts through the sounds of pleasure, and we both freeze.

Fuck. Another loud wail, and I turn toward the door, determined to get there before Colleen opens it to find our boss with her tits out, legs spread, and pussy on display.

I zip and button my pants on the way, then cast a quick glance at AJ over my shoulder as Abby really lets loose, one angry scream after another just as I reach the door. But AJ isn't looking at me anymore; she's too busy getting her bra straightened out and trying to pull her sweater back on.

Slipping out the door and shutting it behind me, my pulse pounding in my ears, I find Colleen bringing Abby up to her shoulder. "Pew, kiddo. I'd be crying too if I just did a stinky in my diaper like this," she says, bouncing lightly on her feet as she pats Abby on the back.

"Sorry about that." She spins in surprise, not even realizing I'd come out of the office behind her. "Here," I say, reaching out my hands for my daughter, "I'll take her."

"You're already done with your meeting?" she asks, eyebrows dipping in surprise.

"We're done for now."

And as I take Abby, holding her to me with one arm while I use the other to steer the stroller to the nearest bathroom, hoping there's a changing table in there, I can't stop the thought ringing in my head: *Holy shit, what did we just do?*

I kissed my boss. She definitely kissed me back. Clothes were shed. Her tits were in my hands, her nipple in my mouth, and her clit throbbing under my thumb. My cock was hot and hard in her hand.

How do we ever come back from that?

Chapter Thirteen

AJ

I open the door to my office, my legs still shaky and my heart still pounding in my throat, and expect to see him there with Abby. Instead, Colleen is sitting at her desk in the empty waiting area.

"Where'd McCabe go?" I ask, startling her as I come up behind her.

Did he really just have me half-naked on my desk, about to come, and then run away like a scared little boy?

"Abby had a dirty diaper, so I think he went to change it?"

And he couldn't have done that in my office?

"Is he coming back?"

"I don't know," Colleen says. "He said your meeting was 'done for now.' Do you need me to get him back here for you?"

"No . . ." I try to think of something that doesn't sound suspicious, because she does not need to know that I'm about to chase him down and demand we talk about what the hell just happened, and why it can never happen again. "I just thought of something else I need to tell him, though. Which way did he go?"

She points to her left. "I think he was probably headed to the bathroom to change her?"

"Thanks." I'm so busy trying to ignore the pit in my belly as I rush down the hall that I don't even have time to prepare what I want to say before I'm already at the men's bathroom. Perils of walking so fast, I guess.

Without giving myself time to think about what I'm doing, or whether it's a good idea to go chasing after him, I'm knocking twice and pushing the door open. He's standing at the wall of sinks with Abby's changing pad spread out on the counter and her tiny feet captured in the air in one of his huge hands.

"God, that smells terrible," I say as my head rears back. I'm honestly shocked that someone so tiny could create such an awful stench.

"Yeah, changing diapers is not the best part of parenthood. Especially once they start eating real food, and not just formula."

I cross one ankle over the other and my arms under my chest as I lean up against the wall, trying to look more composed than I feel while I watch him attempting to wrestle a diaper on his squirming baby.

"You realize this is the men's restroom, right?" he asks when I stand there staring at him long enough that he feels like he needs to say something.

I swallow down the nerves. "What just happened in my office—" I start, but he's speaking at the same time.

"I'm sorry, I should never have done that." He glances at

me in the mirror, his cheeks growing pink, before looking down at the diaper he's wrangling on.

Holy shit, did Ronan McCabe just blush? I can't reconcile that reaction with the anger he has consistently displayed since I came to Boston.

"But also," he says quietly, "why did you kiss me back?"

"I don't know," I sigh, my head shaking slightly. And I really don't. God, the way I just shed my clothes the second his hands were on me is downright shameful . . . not to mention wrong. I'm his boss, and we're in the middle of a contract negotiation. "You did that thing . . ."

"That thing?" One of his eyebrows is raised as he glances up at me in the mirror again. I hate the way I'm standing off to his side, with him turned away from me, as we're having this conversation. But we need to talk, and Abby needs a diaper on her, so it is what it is.

"Yeah, like that thing where you go from scowling to smirking."

"That's *a thing*?"

"You must know it is."

"I don't spend a lot of time analyzing my own facial expressions, Alessandra."

No one calls me Alessandra. Not anymore.

"Maybe you should, because then you'd know that you're always scowling."

"I'm not *always* scowling." His voice is still quiet, but not defensive. I think maybe he's teasing?

"Pretty sure you are."

"I wasn't scowling when you were kissing me."

I roll my eyes, and a little voice at the back of my head

asks, *What if he only kissed you as a last-ditch effort to persuade you to renew his contract?*

I know that this kind of thinking—the assumption that everyone's trying to manipulate me—is a function of my upbringing. My formative years were spent watching my parents barter, like *If I go to this gala with you, then you need to make an appearance at the club's golf fundraiser next month.* My relationship with my ex-husband was much the same.

It wasn't until I entered therapy after my divorce that I learned not all relationships are transactional like that. And since then, I've had the privilege of seeing some wonderful relationships, like the Hartmanns, who are still very much in love, even after almost forty years of marriage.

But sometimes, old habits die hard.

"Yeah, about that. It can't—"

"Happen again. I heard you the first time." He puts Abby's shorts on over her diaper now that it's secured, and as he does, he glances at me in the mirror again and lifts an eyebrow. "And remind me why not?"

I take a few seconds to study his face . . . the razor-sharp cheekbones with dark stubble almost covering his skin below, the full lower lip, the straight nose with a small scar along one side, and those bright green eyes framed in dark lashes. His eyes were the first thing I noticed about him when I scouted him years ago.

Some might describe his eyes as piercing, but I thought they looked hungry. Hungry for success, for victory, for the NCAA championship he was striving for. I wanted that kind of hunger in a player . . . the kind that would keep them going when things got tough.

But once he was playing for me, there was an unmistakable, different type of hunger in those eyes—the kind that couldn't hide that he wanted me. He never took a single step out of line, never said or did anything inappropriate. He knew I was married, and he respected that.

Until he walked in on Chet berating me. I doubt he heard enough to know why, but the fact that his first instinct in hearing me disrespected like that was to lay my husband out was proof enough of his feelings. I didn't mistake them, and unfortunately, neither did Chet.

Not that I ever would have done anything about that back then—not when I was married, and his boss, and he was still practically a child. And I shouldn't do anything about it now, either.

He's still younger than me, and I'm still his boss.

But standing here looking at him, watching the heat in his eyes and the open desire in his gaze, has the part of me that should stay frozen melting for him instead.

"Because I'm your boss and we're in a contract negotiation. It's not just inappropriate, it's unethical."

As if she agrees, Abby lets out some fussy sounds, kicking her feet and clearly wanting to be held.

"Here," I say, reaching my arms out, "give her to me."

His eyebrows pinch, but when he lifts her and Abby reaches her arms out to me, too, he hands her over.

Holding her facing out, so she can see him, I dip my head toward hers. "See that scowl, baby girl? You're going to need to learn how to ignore it when your daddy does that."

I glance at him in time to see the way he bites his lower lip like he's trying to hold in a smile.

"I'm not scowling," he grumbles as he gathers up the changing pad and wipes, tossing them in the bottom of the stroller before he puts Abby's diaper in a small bag, ties it off, and tosses it in the trash. It's all done with practiced efficiency, and before I know it, he's nodding his head toward the door.

I lead the way, with Abby in my arms and him following behind with the stroller. And when we exit into the hallway, Ralph is walking toward the bathroom and giving us an inquisitive look.

"That was a nasty diaper change," I tell our security guard. "I wouldn't go in there if I were you."

"There's not even a changing table in there." He looks at McCabe. "Why would you—"

"Don't you dare ask why a man would need to change his baby's diaper," I say. "The better question is, why aren't there pull-down changing tables in the men's bathrooms like there are in the women's?"

He holds his hands up. "I wasn't saying . . ."

"It's a problem that will be rectified soon enough." I turn back toward my player, my voice oozing professionalism. "McCabe, let's finish that conversation in my office. Now."

———

"So that's your solution?" McCabe says, sitting across from me while I hold Abby, lightly bouncing back and forth where I stand behind my desk. The six feet of distance and a baby between us have kept things professional, but there's no doubt we're more familiar and friendly than we would have been before he had me naked. "You think your brother would be a more reliable nanny than the one I just fired? Even though he's the same age she is, with even less experience?"

"Like her experience did you any good" I give him a pointed look. "Besides, Nicholas is like me with babies."

"And how's that?" he asks with a curious tilt of his head.

"Babies love us." I don't know why we are both so great with kids, given our upbringing. "Plus, he's studying child psychology, and he volunteers at the NICU where his girlfriend interns. He's dealt with much fussier babies than this perfect angel," I say as I look down at Abby gnawing on her fist, and kiss the top of her head. She's still got that baby scent, and if I had functional ovaries, I'm sure they'd be exploding with the desire to have a baby just like her someday.

"But has he ever spent a long period of time with a baby? Holding them for a couple hours in the NICU is . . . really nice of him . . . but it's not exactly the same as taking care of a nine-month-old."

"I think he could handle it. And he lives with his girlfriend, Nicole—"

"Wait, so their names are Nicholas and Nicole?" He lets out an amused chuckle.

"Yeah, and they're stupidly cute together, and super easy to get along with. Anyway, she's getting her nursing degree, and interning at the NICU, and taking a summer class, so that all keeps her pretty busy. He's just waiting tables for the summer and could easily switch to watching Abby instead."

"I'd only need him until the playoffs are over," he says. "Would it really make sense for him to quit his job for what could be . . ."

He doesn't say it. He doesn't mention that this could all

be over next week if we don't win four games. No hockey player is going to jinx it like that.

"I'm pretty sure you're going to need him well into June." I'm confident these men can take us all the way to the finals, and I'm looking forward to watching them do it.

"Why would a college-age guy want to watch a baby for the summer?"

"For the same reason a college-age girl might, I suspect: it's a job. With better pay than waiting tables. And like I said, babies love him." He's come over to Lauren and Jameson's with me before, and Lauren's twins treat him like he's their own personal jungle gym, which, somehow, he seems to love. "I'd have to double-check with him about this, but I know my brother pretty well, and I think he'd be up for it."

"Even with all the nights he'd have to stay at my place with Abby?" He sounds like he can't imagine a college kid who doesn't want to go out partying every night.

"He's kind of a homebody. Plus, he and Nicole stay at my place when I travel with the team, so he's already used to being there while we're gone. Staying at your place to watch Abby wouldn't be that big of a difference." As if she recognizes her name, she kicks her feet excitedly. "See how excited she is about this?"

McCabe unfolds his arms from their resting spot across the t-shirt that's stretched over his chest, and drapes them along the arms of the chair instead. "Why do they stay at your place when you travel?"

"I have an ancient cat who hates people but also goes crazy and pees on the rugs and tears apart the furniture when no one's around. I assume she's confused and thinks she's a dog."

A small smile graces his pale pink lips, pushing his cheeks up and making the angular lines of his cheekbones soften. He looks good when he smiles. Not that he ever *doesn't* look good . . . but he looks *better* happy.

"What?" he asks, studying my face.

I lift my eyebrows and put a neutral expression on my face, afraid to let him know how closely I was watching him. The only time I should be watching him that closely is on the ice.

"We still haven't talked about the press conference," I say, as if that was the thought running through my head a moment earlier.

His expression goes hard again as he bites the inside of his cheek. "Let's not forget that I already said I was sorry, before—"

"Let's skip right over that to the conversation we *should* have had. The one we were supposed to have after that stunt you pulled last night." I pace back and forth behind my desk, bouncing Abby in my arms. She's not heavy, but I can tell my arms would easily tire from holding her like this for too long. My eyes flick to McCabe's muscular biceps, the lines of which I can see even while his arms remain motionless.

"I know I was in the wrong," he says, his voice placating. "I shouldn't have said exactly the opposite of what you asked me to."

"Why did you?" The question feels loaded as it comes out of my mouth. As if we're not just talking about this specific instance with the press, but the way he constantly tries to piss me off.

His eyes trail down, focusing on Abby, like he can't possibly look me in the eye. For a moment, he looks like he might open up and give me a real reason. And then he says, "I don't know."

"But we cleared the air about what happened when I traded you, right?" I push down the guilt I feel now that I know about his grandma.

"Cleared the air? I'm pretty sure you just told me what I already knew, adding in, 'but I didn't have a choice.'"

"McCabe, I had *no idea* about your grandma, and I'm really sorry for the role I played in that. You didn't deserve to get traded, especially because you were standing up for me. But it wasn't a punishment. I didn't do it because I was mad that you beat the shit out of my husband. I did it because my hands were tied. Now I'm hoping we can at least work together in a less hostile way."

He gives a small shrug of his shoulder and looks at me with a smirk. "Yeah, maybe."

My stomach flips. "But maybe not?"

"I don't know, AJ. I think a lot of things that happened as part of that conversation . . . changed things. But it's not something I can talk to you about while you're holding my daughter in your arms."

My chest shakes with silent laughter, and Abby kicks her feet harder, like she thinks we're playing a game. "You know she can't understand whatever it is you want to say, right?"

"Okay," he says, huffing a laugh, "maybe I don't *want* to talk about it while you're holding my daughter."

"And why not?" I press, unable to stop myself from taunting him a bit.

That smirk is back already as he comes around my desk, leans in, and plants one hand on the bookcase behind me.

His eyes focus on mine, his pupils dilating until there's only a sliver of green surrounding them.

Ohhh. He still wants me.

My heart pounds against my ribcage so powerfully I'm sure he can feel the vibrations from half a foot away. Why does my body have this reaction to his?

"Because the feelings I'm having about what just happened aren't something I can explore with her in the room."

"Like I said before," I steel my voice even while my body wants to press forward into his. "That can't ever happen again."

He pushes off the bookcase, giving me some room to breathe. "If you say so." His gaze is still locked onto me, like he's challenging me to prove him wrong.

Done. Because if there's one thing I excel at, it's compartmentalizing my feelings and prioritizing work over everything else. And that's what this relationship is—work. He's the captain of the team I manage, and there is no situation in which it would be okay for me to have anything other than a purely professional relationship with him. No matter how tempting it is, it wouldn't be worth the fallout.

"I do say so."

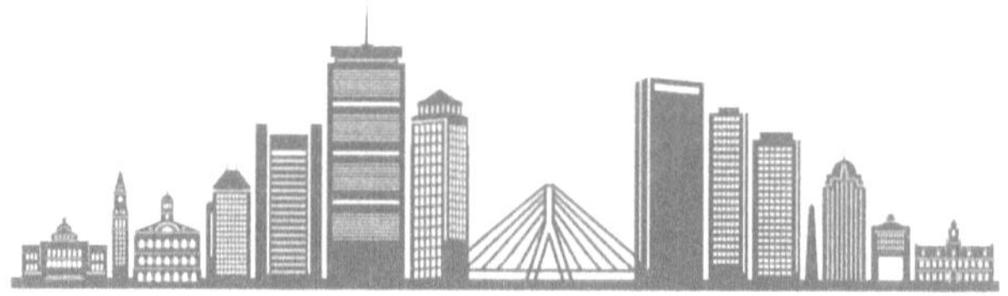

Chapter Fourteen

McCabe

The knock on my door startles me, even though I was expecting it. I don't know what the fuck is wrong with me—I'm so damn jumpy today. It's like the thought of seeing AJ outside of work has me on edge.

"Let's go meet the guy who might be your new manny," I say to Abby, kissing her on top of her head as I pick her up from where we were playing with some big plastic cars on the floor of the living room.

I don't know for sure whether Nicholas is going to be the right choice, but we have a game tonight and I still don't know what I'm doing with Abby during it. The agency I used to find my past nannies said it was unlikely they'd be able to find someone for at least a few weeks, so he's my only option for the short term.

The minute the door opens, Abby reaches her arms out toward AJ, who gives her a sweet smile as she takes my daughter from me without a second of hesitation. Maybe it's the way her dark hair is back in a ponytail with some tendrils left down framing her face, or that she's in leggings and a tank top, but the woman standing in front of me is not the same woman I work for. She's . . . casual, and far softer and more feminine than I'm used to seeing her.

"You must be Nicholas," I say, extending my hand toward the young man standing next to her. Unlike AJ, he's got light hair and sun-bronzed skin. But their big brown eyes are the same, and he's got the same wide mouth as her. That's where the resemblance ends, though.

"Yes, nice to meet you, Mr. McCabe."

"Ronan, please," I say.

"Okay," Nicholas says with a slight laugh as he drops my hand. "That's going to take some getting used to."

"McCabe is a hockey thing." In the hockey world, everyone calls me by my last name as if it were my first name, so it's always weird to hear someone call me Mr. McCabe. And honestly, I prefer it when people use my first name . . . I don't even know how it happened that I became just "McCabe," but I never fought it, so it's just kind of stuck.

"Noted," he says, and the clip of his voice reminds me of AJ's all-business tone.

"Come on in." I invite them into the entryway, shutting the door behind them. "Living room's that way." I gesture past the kitchen, and both he and AJ laugh.

"We know," she says. "Your place is a mirror image of mine."

"Good to know," I say, following them into my condo and trying to convince myself to stop staring at the way her ass looks in those leggings. The last thing I need is a hard-on while talking to her brother about watching my daughter.

I'm starting to wonder why I can't control the way my body reacts to hers. I've always been attracted to her, but it was never like this—the physical pull toward her whenever she's around, this fucking *yearning*. It's like long-buried feelings are resurfacing. Now that she's no longer married and my reasons for hating her are mostly invalidated, it's harder to resist her than it ever was before.

I sit across from AJ, far enough that I hope my body will stop reacting to hers. But watching her play with Abby, bouncing her up and down on her knees while holding her hands and quietly singing a nursery rhyme, is doing something entirely different to me. I don't even know how to explain what exactly it is, but it has my heart feeling like it's turning to goo right inside my rib cage.

Fuck, no. She's my boss—a fact I've had to keep reminding myself of over the last twenty-four hours, but I just can't seem to make that fact matter as much as it should.

Nicholas and I chat for a while about his experience with kids, what he's studying in college, whether he can really commit to this position for the next week or month, depending on how we do. He's easy to get along with and seems just as reliable as AJ said he'd be.

Most importantly, Abby seems drawn to him in a way she never was with Lucy. His voice is soothing, and eventually Abby crawls from AJ's lap over to Nicholas's. I'm shocked at how easily he can carry on a conversation with me while also playing with her, making her feel comfortable and cared for. It's a skill I don't think I've mastered. I never feel like I can do anything else when I'm with Abby, and I feel guilty if I give her anything less than my full attention. But he's a natural at balancing everything, much like his sister yesterday in her office after Abby's record-breaking diaper change.

"Has AJ already shared with you the schedule for this round of playoffs?" I ask.

"Yes, and the morning skate schedule for the home games. There's nothing that I couldn't cover, except for tonight's game. My girlfriend Nicole has a tenuous relationship with her mom, and she's in town right now . . . staying with us. We're taking her down to Newport for dinner tonight as soon as Nic's off work, and I can't cancel on her—both because she doesn't drive, and also because I just can't leave her and her mom alone together for that long without some sort of huge relationship-ending fight," he tells me, and I can't imagine why she'd want to have a relationship with her mom if things are actually that bad. "But her mom will be gone by the time you leave for your away games in a few days, and if you have anything you need to do before you leave, I can be around to watch Abby for whatever times you need during the day."

"Okay." I explain my commitments coming up over the next few days, and then sit back in my chair, looking over at AJ. "I still don't know what I'm going to do about tonight. Tammy can't watch her, and Walsh has a call in to his nanny to see if she knows anyone who could babysit, but if she doesn't, I'm fresh out of options."

AJ glances down at her phone. "It's fine, I can take her."

"I wasn't asking you to do that," I say, even though I know I probably don't have any other options.

"It's fine. Lauren can help me out if I need it, and Abby will probably just sleep on me most of the game anyway."

"AJ, you can't do that again. Once was enough . . . The optics are just not—"

"I don't give a shit what the optics are, McCabe. I need you to play. In exchange for me watching Abby, feel free to score a hat trick tonight." Her lips curve up at the edges as she nods her chin at me. "It's been a while."

Part of me is tempted to tell her I'd be more inclined to score if she'd renew my fucking contract, but the other part of me knows that kind of sarcastic remark is both uncalled for, and just not true.

Plus, I don't want her to renew my contract. I want to become a free agent so that Nashville can pick me up and I can move closer to my sister and nieces. Don't I?

———

There are only two minutes left in the third period when I score my second goal of the night, and before my teammates surround me in celebration, my eyes fly up to exactly where I know AJ is sitting, right next to Lauren, six rows behind the bench.

She's got one arm wrapped protectively around Abby as she stands up from her seat in excitement, and her other arm in the air, her fist curled triumphantly. Her smile is wide as we lock eyes, and she mouths, "Good job!" before Lauren takes her hand mid-air and AJ turns toward her.

Walsh is the first one to crash into me where I've come to a stop at the boards near our bench, but he's followed closely behind by Drew—our line is on fire tonight and we're completely dominating this game against Philadelphia.

Some angry shouts in the stands quickly drown out the

noise from the cheering, and all three of us turn our heads toward the ruckus. From the ice, I can see that a few Boston fans in the row behind AJ, and Philly fans in the row in front of her, are hurling insults at each other. AJ keeps her arm wrapped around Abby as she turns and looks up, shouting something at the Boston fans behind her while Jameson moves down the row, trying to position himself between the two groups and protect AJ and Lauren. But he doesn't get there in time, and I watch in horror as one of the Boston fans leans down to push one of the Philly fans, but his shoulder connects with AJ, and she goes toppling over backward with my daughter attached to her.

My stomach drops and I don't think, I just react. I skate to the glass in front of them as quickly as I can, banging on the glass to get their attention. "Hey!" I yell, my voice so loud the fans in the first few rows go silent. "Fucking stop this shit right now!" The security guards moving down the aisle toward them catch my eye, and I flag them down. "Help AJ first," I call out. "She has my daughter!"

I watch helplessly from the other side of the glass as three security guards reach the row, one of them holding the Boston fans back and the two others helping AJ up. It looks like she fell backward, landing on the seats two rows down, and as the security guards get her back up on her feet, it's clear she's injured. Abby is screaming, but it's impossible to tell if she's in pain or if it's because she was jolted awake while falling.

I rush over to the bench, hopping the boards and striding straight down the row. "I'm out for the rest of the game," I tell Wilcott as I move past him. "And if AJ or Abby got hurt just now, heads are gonna fucking roll."

With my heart racing, I don't stop to listen to his response. I just run into the tunnel, trying to figure out where security will take them. They're probably on the next level up, so I step into the elevator, and as I ride it up to the Club Level, I glance down at my stick still in my hand and my skates still on my feet.

And sure enough, as I exit the elevator, AJ is standing with two security guards and one of our team doctors. AJ is patting a still-crying Abby on the back with one hand while cradling her other arm up against her shoulder like she's trying to avoid Abby accidentally kicking it.

"It's fine," AJ insists, shaking off the doctor as she tries to examine her wrist. But the grimace on her face gives her away—she's not fine, and we can all see it. Glancing up at me as I approach, her brow furrows as she asks, "What are you doing up here?"

"What do you think I'm doing here?" I step closer to her. "You and Abby were just attacked. Did you think I'd still be down there playing?"

Everyone stares at me like I'm crazy, and that's when I realize my mistake. I didn't say I was up here for my daughter. But fuck it if I'm going to pretend that she's not one of the reasons I walked away from my job tonight, especially since she was hurt trying to protect my baby.

"I'm fine," she tries to assure me. "And so is Abby."

I hand my stick to one of the security guards as I unhook the top of the baby carrier. "I'm going to take Abby out. Can you move your hand behind your back so she doesn't hurt you more than you already are?"

"I'm fine." The words come out between gritted teeth, but she bends her arm and moves her hand behind her back.

Abby's face lights up as I lift her out of the carrier, and she snuggles into my chest pads, unphased with everything going on around her.

"The EMTs will be here in about three minutes," one of the trainers says as he runs up to Dr. D'Angelis. "They're coming to the door in the back parking lot, so we can get them out without walking through the main entrance to the arena."

"We don't need to go to the hospital, Olivia," AJ says to Dr. D'Angelis, using that bossy voice she does so well.

"I disagree." Dr. D's voice is equally firm, and she crosses her arms over her chest the same way AJ does when she's putting her foot down about something. "And I won't clear you to come back to work until that hand is X-rayed and we make sure you didn't sustain any other injuries. We need to make sure the baby wasn't hurt in the fall either."

Abby has stopped crying, so I know she's not in pain. Her cries were probably more from fear than anything.

"Stop questioning the team doctor, AJ," I say. "This is literally her job."

"Olivia," she says to the doctor, eyebrow raising, "I'm not one of the players."

"And yet I still won't clear you to return until you're checked out." Dr. D's face and voice both soften when she says, "Let me do the job you hired me to do, AJ."

AJ lets out a dramatic sigh, but doesn't say anything. There's no chance she and Abby aren't going to the hospital right fucking now, and there's even less of a chance that I won't be with them.

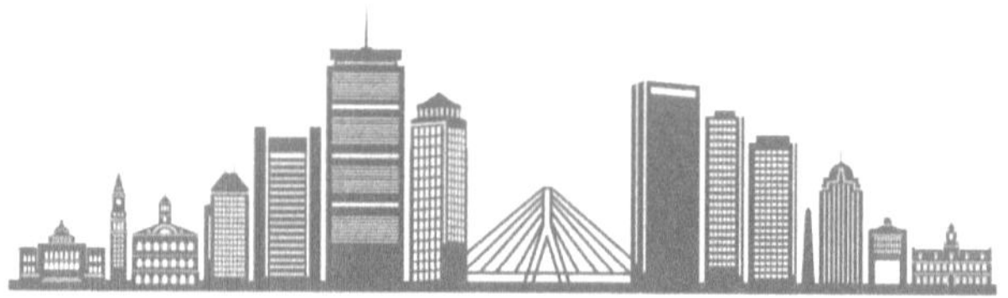

Chapter Fifteen

AJ

"Most people wear clothes in the hospital, you know," I say, in pain and annoyed at everything about this situation, and apparently deciding that verbally sparring with McCabe is the best way to get out my frustration.

He turns from where he was standing next to the plastic bassinet on wheels that they brought in for Abby when he'd asked if there was somewhere she could sleep.

Taking the few steps across the small ER room, he says, "I hope you know I like it when you're feisty." That damn smirk that drives women crazy graces his lips.

I never understood why anyone would go for the whole grumpy, growly bit . . . but maybe I'm starting to get it?

"Can't you, like, find some scrubs or something?"

My wrist is in so much pain, and so far, all they've given me for it is some ibuprofen. Something about not being able to give me actual narcotics until they know if I'll need surgery?

Screw surgery—we're leaving for an away game the day after tomorrow, and there's no way I'm missing it. Especially not after the way Philadelphia came back in the last minute of tonight's game to tie it up, and then won in overtime.

Now we're 0-2 in a series that should have been 1-1, and probably would have been if McCabe had stayed. Not that I blame him for wanting to make sure his daughter was okay. Plus, I'm sure the EMTs wouldn't have let her go to the hospital without her dad coming along, anyway.

He steps closer to my hospital bed, wearing nothing but the compression shorts he had on under his uniform. I get why he wanted to take his uniform and pads off, especially with how sweaty he was by the end of the game, but he's dried off now, so couldn't he at least slip his jersey back on or something?

"Does it bother you seeing me half-dressed? Because you've been in the locker room plenty and it never seemed to bother you before."

I hate the way my stomach flips at his gravelly voice, the way those words seem to reach out and caress my skin, making it prickle with goosebumps.

"Ronan . . ." I warn, before glancing over at the bassinet. Even though we turned off the overhead lights and he's playing some sort of white noise app on his phone, I still don't know how Abby fell back asleep after that fall. I don't think I'd ever close my eyes again if I was sleeping peacefully on someone's chest and then found myself upside down.

Thankfully, as I was pushed backward, I was able to hold

on to her with one arm and break our fall with the other. The impact on my wrist when the heel of my hand connected with the cement step of the row below us, however, was excruciating. The way my ribs crashed into the tops of the seats and my head collided with the shoulder of the person sitting in the row below is also going to leave some bruises.

It could have been worse, but as my wrist throbs in my lap, I realize it could have been a whole lot better, too.

The important thing is that the doctor already confirmed that Abby was unharmed—a fact her father hasn't let me forget. He's been looking at me like I walk on water, like I'm some sort of angel that saved his kid instead of a woman who did what any normal person would do in the situation.

He could have taken her home already, but he refuses to leave until he knows that I'm okay, too. It was much easier to ignore the tension in the room when we were both so focused on Abby. Unfortunately, now that she's asleep, all his attention is on me.

"Careful, *Alessandra*," he says, practically purring my name like it's some sort of exotic foreign word as he stares down at me from the side of the bed. "You wouldn't want someone to overhear you calling me by anything but my last name."

He's right. I make sure to maintain the strictest professional boundaries with my players. It's a hazard of being the only female GM—people always seem to want to put me, and everything I do, under a microscope. So I make sure that my image is as squeaky-clean as possible.

It's yet another reason why yesterday's activities in my office can never happen again.

I open my mouth to respond, but he leans forward, planting one hand on the mattress behind my head. With my bed inclined to a sitting position, he's only partially leaning forward, giving me a good look at those pecs up close.

I don't understand how a man with such thick almost-black hair on his head, and a perpetual five o'clock shadow even when he's freshly shaven, has so little body hair. Aside from a smattering of hair across his chest and, I note as my eyes glide down his abdomen, a trail of hair from his belly button down into his compression shorts, the rest of his abdomen is hairless. With my eyes now focused on his crotch, I don't miss how his dick stirs in those tight-ass shorts.

With a gulp, I glance up quickly, but his eyes are amused when they meet mine, and my cheeks flush when I realize it's because he knows I was just checking him out.

What the hell is wrong with me? We're in the hospital because I'm hurt and his daughter was nearly injured too, and like two horny teenagers, we can't keep our eyes off each other.

"I—" I start to say, intending to respond, but finding that I've completely lost track of what we were talking about.

The knock on the open door has both of us turning our heads. I'm expecting to see the doctor, but instead Lauren stands there, holding a big Rebels duffle. It's too small to be a hockey bag, so I assume it's some piece of swag she snagged from the marketing offices.

"Hey," I say quietly, noting how she looks worried that she just interrupted some private moment between the two of us. "Come in. We're just whispering so we don't wake Abby. She's not hurt or anything, just sleeping." I nod toward the bassinet against the wall.

The grunt McCabe lets out is half-laugh, half-sigh.

"I brought you some clothes," Lauren tells him, "since you left in your uniform. And some shoes, because Olivia said you left in your socks?"

"Yeah, I took my skates off, but there wasn't really time to change."

"Yes, there was." I roll my eyes. "You could have changed and then driven yourself to the hospital. You didn't need to come in the ambulance."

There wasn't even room for him in the back, especially not with all his pads on, so he sat up front with the driver.

He rolls his eyes right back at me before reaching out for the bag and mumbling his thanks. And when he heads over to the chair next to Abby's bassinet to rifle through it, Lauren steps up to the bed, taking the seat next to it. "You okay?"

"I've been better. I just need the orthopedist to look at the damn X-rays so I can get out of here."

Lauren glances down where my lower arm rests in my lap, splinted with an ice pack on either side of my wrist. "Do they think it's broken?"

"Yeah. They also took some X-rays of my ribs to make sure they're okay. I definitely feel like I pulled some muscles in my back, or bruised it badly or something. But I think it would hurt worse if I broke any ribs," I explain, then quickly change the subject to what I'm most interested in knowing. "So, what happened after I left? Did they kick those fans out?"

"Yeah, security took them out and had the police waiting for them. It was mayhem for a couple minutes there. It's a relief you and Abby weren't more seriously hurt, but I'm sorry about the outcome of the game."

"Were the guys distracted? Like by me getting hurt, or McCabe rushing off the ice like that?"

"I mean . . ." Lauren pauses, her eyes flicking over to where McCabe stands, his back to us as he steps into the sweatpants he's pulled out of the bag. "I'm sure that's not why they lost."

I press my lips together and nod, but I know she doesn't actually believe that any more than I do. Part of the game is tuning out any distractions, but this wasn't just something that happened in the stands; their captain rushed off the ice and out of the game.

I'm not blaming him—it is what it is. But it's silly to pretend like there was no impact. I glance back at Lauren. "I guess we'll never know."

"We'll get them in the next game, AJ." McCabe's low voice carries across the room.

Just as I'm about to respond, there's another knock at the door and the doctor's back, with a clipboard in hand and a nurse following close behind him.

"Well," he says, "you got lucky."

My heart soars with hope. Maybe the pain and the swelling will subside and I'll be good as new!

"You've got a distal radial fracture," he tells me, slapping the X-ray film up to a light box on the wall. Pointing to the lower part, he traces his finger across the image as he says, "What that means is, your radius—this bone that runs along the inside of your lower arm from your wrist to your elbow —was broken in the fall. But the good news is that it's only a fracture, not a clean break. You won't need surgery to repair it. We'll splint it for now, and you'll need to be very careful with it so you don't aggravate the injury. When the swelling goes down in a week or so, we'll put your arm in a cast to let it fully heal."

Thinking about what my life will be like with my right arm in a cast, I ask, "*That's* getting lucky?"

"Since the alternative would have been a much worse break, and surgery with 6-12 weeks of recovery time . . . yeah." The last word is clipped, and I can tell he's annoyed that I'm not happier about this news. But unlike me, he isn't thinking about what it'll be like to live on my own with an unusable right hand—the one I use to do everything. How will I dry my hair? Do my laundry? Shift while I'm driving? Actually, do I know how to do *anything* one-handed?

"What about her ribs?" McCabe practically growls at the doctor.

"They're not broken, and the X-rays don't show bruising on the bones either. You'll probably get a fair amount of superficial bruising because of the impact, but again, you're lucky because the fall didn't damage the bones. Jenn will go over your care plan with you." He continues, nodding toward the nurse at his side. "And then we'll get you discharged, and your husband can take you home."

A laugh bursts out of me as he glances over at McCabe, whose face is an unreadable mask, where he now stands at the foot of the bed. The pain that shoots through my back as I laugh has me wincing, instead. "He's . . . not my husband. We just work together."

The doctor must not be a hockey fan.

"Okay, so who is taking you home and helping you out for the next week or so? You won't be able to do much of anything without help. Even things as simple as getting dressed will be a challenge, and you'll need help managing everything. You need to keep your wrist totally immobile until it's casted—treat it like it's glass—or you risk worsening the fracture and needing surgery instead."

"Uh . . . I can just ask my brother to stay with me, I guess," I say tentatively.

McCabe presses his lips together, but doesn't call me out on my lie. He knows that Nicholas can't stay at my place right now because Nicole's mom is here and staying with them. Even as much as my brother loves me, he's not going to risk World War III by leaving Nic and her mom alone. And we're leaving the day after tomorrow for our away games. There's no chance in hell I'm not going to those games, and Nicholas can't come with me, because by then he'll be staying with Abby.

"Alright. Which of you," the doctor asks, nodding back and forth between McCabe and Lauren, "is taking her home tonight?"

"I can do it," McCabe says quickly, and Lauren's eyes basically pop out of her head as she glances over at me in surprise. "We live near each other."

I appreciate the way he doesn't say we live across the hall from each other, since I haven't mentioned that fact to Lauren yet.

The doctor nods, and as he turns to say something to the nurse, McCabe tells us, "I'm going to Uber back to the arena and get my car, since we'll need it for Abby's car seat. Are you two okay here with her until I get back?"

"I brought your car, actually," Lauren says, pulling her long red hair back into a ponytail. "I hope you don't mind. Your keys, phone, and wallet are in the side pocket of that bag. Basically, everything that was in your locker. And Abby's car seat is in the back seat, and her stroller is in the trunk."

His jaw drops open. "Thanks?"

I'm a little shocked that he doesn't sound more appreciative, but then he shakes his head and says, "I . . . I would never have expected someone to do that for me."

There's a small tug at my heart when he admits that. I mean, I don't have a huge network of people in Boston, but I've got my brother and Nicole, Lauren and Jameson, and I'm getting closer to Jameson's sisters, Audrey and Jules. But still, I wouldn't be shocked if any of them, or anyone I work with, for that matter, stepped up to help me in this situation.

"It was no trouble," Lauren says with a soft smile. "And it was Colt's idea, actually. He was going to swing by with your stuff, but he had to hit the bike and shower first, so I offered since I could come right away."

"So, your discharge plan," the nurse says, handing me a whole stack of paper as she launches into the aftercare information for managing the pain and swelling. When she finally takes a breath, Lauren excuses herself and says that Jameson is waiting downstairs in his car for her, and they have to get home because their babysitter needs to leave.

McCabe offers to head down with her so he can grab Abby's car seat, while the nurse gives me some additional information about scheduling a follow-up appointment with the orthopedist and reads me the riot act about not using my right hand to do *anything*. By the time she's helped me out of the gown and back into my sweater, McCabe is walking back into my hospital room with an empty baby carrier in his hand.

He says nothing about my lie regarding Nicholas staying

with me until I'm seated in the front of his SUV and we're pulling out of the parking garage. As we turn onto the dark, empty street to head away from the hospital, he says, "Don't for one second think that I'm letting you stay at your place without someone to help you."

"Yeah," I say with a small scoff, "because I have so many other options for people to just move in with me."

"You have at least one other option."

"Oh yeah? And what's that?"

"You're moving in with me."

My laughter rings out sharply, filling the silent car, and for a second, I'm afraid I'll wake Abby where she's sleeping in her car seat behind me. "Yeah. Sure."

"You can't live by yourself," he says. "Doctor's orders."

My entire body tenses at the thought of being in that close proximity to him, even if just for the next few days. "I'll get a friend to stay with me, then."

"Fine. Until a friend shows up to stay with you, you can get settled at my place." He knows he's calling my bluff, because I literally just told him I didn't have any options.

I want to ask if he's always this bossy, but instead I say, "There's no way I'm staying at your place."

"Well, there's no way you're staying alone. And it feels like it would be a lot easier for you to move into my guest bedroom for a short time than for Abby and me to move in with you. But whatever you prefer." He says it so casually as he makes the turn into Government Center that I have to wonder if he's kidding.

"I'll be fine."

"Yep, my place is very comfortable," he says.

"I meant I'll be fine on my own."

"Over my dead body."

"Easily arranged," I mutter under my breath.

He chuckles, and as I glance over at him, I can't help but notice how that smile lights up his face. Even though his eyes are trained on the road and I can only see half of it, I can still tell how different he looks. How relaxed. Happy even.

"I'd like to see you pull off this one-handed murder," he says, and I bite the inside of my lip to stop myself from smiling. It's better for everyone if I seem unaffected by his charm.

He shouldn't be this comfortable with me. He shouldn't be driving me home, joking around with me, or offering to take care of me. He definitely shouldn't be insisting I move in with him. But somehow, I still like it that he's doing all of these things.

"I'm not moving in with you."

"Okay." He shrugs. "I'll probably have to take Abby's crib apart to move it into your place, but it shouldn't take that long."

I groan. "You're not moving in with me."

"So you'll stay with me. Perfect."

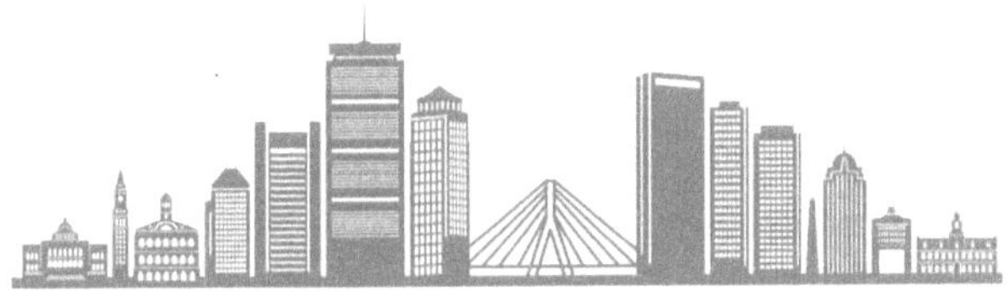

Chapter Sixteen

McCabe

Early the next morning, I sit in the kitchen feeding Abby some rice cereal mixed with sweet potato for breakfast, when I hear a grunt of pain from the guest bedroom. It's all the assurance I need that forcing AJ to stay with me was the right call.

I'm pretty sure the only reason she relented was that she needed to pee badly when we got back to our building, and didn't have time to fish out her key and open her door left-handed, so she agreed to use my bathroom. When she was unable to redo the button on her pants left-handed, I think she finally realized that living on her own with her dominant hand immobilized wasn't possible. At least not yet.

"You okay?" I call out, thankful the guest bedroom is the closest to the kitchen so she can hear me.

"I'm fine." Her words are grunted too, because she's most definitely not okay.

Goddamn, this woman is stubborn. "Do I need to come in there?"

She clearly doesn't miss the amused tone, because she calls out, "Don't even think about it."

I'm guessing she's trying to change her clothes without help—exactly what the doctor and nurse told her she couldn't do. Now the images of her undressed body are filling my head, which is just so wrong, given that I'm sitting right across from Abby. Still, I can't stop my brain from going there.

"Oh, I'm thinking about it!" I call back.

Reaching forward, I tickle Abby under her chin to get her to open her mouth so I can shovel in another spoonful of rice cereal. It's not that she doesn't like it. It's that she wants mealtimes to take as long as humanly possible, and I'm not going to lie . . . feeding her is kind of boring. I'm committed to avoiding distractions while doing it. I don't go on my phone or watch TV while I do anything with her because we don't get that much one-on-one time with my travel schedule, and I want to make our time together count. But the sooner she eats, the sooner we can move on to something more fun.

"Dada," I say, pointing to myself.

"Daaaaaaa," she repeats.

She's so close to stringing multiple syllables together, and I'm pretty damn determined that "Dada" is going to be her first word.

"Shit!" The yelp of pain accompanying the curse has me setting the bowl on the table and handing Abby the empty rubber spoon so she can chew on it in her highchair while I investigate what's going on in the guest room.

I knock twice before I enter, and when she spins around, it's clear why she's in pain. She'd insisted on sleeping in her clothes last night because she didn't want me to help her get undressed, and now she's decided to take matters into her own hands. As a result, she's got her good arm out of her sweater, but her splint has snagged inside it.

"Can I help get you untangled?"

"I'm freaking undressing. Why are you barging in here?" She's annoyed and feisty, and I don't know why, but I really like that. Still, I don't want to be a creep and make her uncomfortable.

I hold up my hands and look at the ground. "Because you're not supposed to be doing that by yourself. It's why you're here, and not across the hall in your own place."

She makes a sound that's like a growl rattling around in the back of her throat. "I hate feeling helpless like this."

"You're not helpless," I say with a sigh, "you're injured. Come here. I'll help you get out of that sweater, and I promise I won't even check you out while I'm doing it."

"Oh yeah, because you're such a gentleman."

"I am, actually," I tell her, not even chuckling at the slicing glare she sends me in response. "Come here, let me help." I don't move toward her. She needs to make this decision because she's willing to accept my help, not because I'm standing over her and demanding it.

"Fine." Her chest deflates with a big sigh as she steps toward me.

Reaching inside the arm of her sweater where it's tangled around her shoulder and biceps, I spread the knit fabric enough that she can pull her splinted arm out without snagging it. Then I reach down and grab the t-shirt I'd offered to help her put on last night where it sits on the dresser, and hold it out with my fingers spreading the shirt sleeve so she can slide that arm in first, before I pull it over her head and she slides her other arm through.

"You going to put the shorts on too?" I ask.

"Yeah. I hate hard pants."

"You . . . what now?" I ask with a laugh as I grab the pair of boxer shorts off the dresser.

"Hard pants. You know, like with zippers and buttons and stuff."

"As opposed to soft pants?"

"Yeah, like leggings and sweats."

"Huh. Yeah, me too, I guess." I never thought about it that way, but it makes sense.

She reaches down with her good hand and lifts the front of the t-shirt to undo the button and zipper of her navy-blue dress pants with her other hand, while I stand there wondering why she almost always wears trousers to work if she hates the feel of them.

"Can you pull these off for me, please?"

Squatting, I grab the fabric at her knees and gently tug down until the pants pool at her feet. It's not until I look up at her that I notice my face is right at the level of her crotch. I know I said I was a gentleman and all, but that doesn't mean I don't imagine this scene playing out differently—me lifting that t-shirt and sliding her thong down her legs before tasting her.

But because I'm not a creep, and because I can hear Abby babbling away in the next room, I hold the boxers out at AJ's feet so she can step into them, and then pull them up to her knees, letting her take them with her good hand.

"I'm going to finish feeding Abby breakfast. Are you hungry?" I ask, turning away so she can get the boxers on under the t-shirt without me watching.

"I don't eat breakfast. But I'd kill for a cup of coffee."

"All this talk of killing people last night and this morning . . . I didn't know you were so violent," I tease.

"That's because you don't know me, McCabe." Her voice is hard, and I can feel her trying to put distance back between us . . . the kind of distance that should exist between a general manager and her players, yet seems to disappear when we're alone.

I should let those walls go back up. Nothing she told me the other day about her reasons for trading me changes anything. I still missed out on the last couple of weeks of my grandma's life because of her.

By the time I got the call that Grandma was sick and I needed to come home, she was already on a ventilator . . . and she never came off. I never got to tell her how much I loved her. How she saved my life and gave me a future, all because she was so wonderfully selfless.

I should have been there for her at the end, when she was sick but still lucid. And I would have been, if I'd still been playing in St. Louis. I would have been able to stop by every day we weren't on the road. But instead, I was in Boston.

And yet . . . I can't bring myself to blame AJ anymore. Because she's right—*I'm* the one who beat the shit out of her husband right before the trade deadline, and there was no way I was going to play for him after that. I didn't leave the team much of a choice but to trade me.

I turn back toward her, happy to find that she's managed to get those shorts on under the t-shirt. Not that she even needed them, since my shirt comes down to her mid-thigh. "I'll go get you some coffee. Still like it black?"

Her tongue darts to the corner of her mouth as she scrunches her face up. "Why do you know that?"

I shrug and give her a wink before I turn to head back to the kitchen, where I can hear Abby getting fussy in her highchair.

She follows me into the hallway, walking beside me. "Just because you know my coffee order doesn't mean you *know* me, McCabe."

"If you say so."

I'm a quiet guy by nature, reserved in a way that has people thinking I'm grumpy or pissed off. But it's not because I don't like people, it's because I'm fascinated by how much you can learn about others when you simply shut your fucking mouth and listen.

The world is full of people who just want to talk, who aren't comfortable with silence and want to fill every moment with conversation—usually about themselves. I prefer to observe, and to speak only when I actually have something worth saying.

One of the reasons I was first drawn to AJ is that she does the same thing. She has an ease around people that I don't have, but she leads quietly. Unlike a lot of people in her position, she's never been self-aggrandizing. Her predecessor here in Boston thought he walked on fucking water, which he most definitely didn't, and he never let you forget it. AJ isn't like that.

She puts her head down and does the work, and attributes any and all successes to the team, not to herself. That's why people here like her. She's the kind of GM that makes you want to put in the effort and do your damn job the best you can, just so you can earn her approval.

Despite everything that happened between us in the past, even when I hated her, I never stopped observing.

"Good," she says, plopping down in the seat across from Abby and making faces at her before she turns toward me where I stand at the cupboard about to get her a coffee mug. "So stop trying to act like you know anything about me."

"You always get punchy and defensive like this when you're afraid someone might be getting close? Might actually see you as something more than a woman in charge of an entire hockey organization?"

The whoosh of breath that leaves her as her jaw falls open tells me I've hit a little too close to the heart of the matter.

"But no," I say with a healthy dose of sarcasm as I pull a blue Boston Rebels mug off the shelf. "Of course, I don't know *anything* about you."

She turns her attention back to Abby, covering her face with her hands and popping up from behind them, saying, "Peek-a-boo!"

Abby shrieks with delight each time, and I can't help but smile as I listen with my back turned to them while pouring AJ a cup of coffee.

"Here you go," I say, crossing the kitchen to hand her the mug. I've got it cupped in my hands, holding it from the bottom, so she can easily grab the handle with her left hand. "I'll take over with her so you can drink your coffee."

"Pfft." She lets out an adorably dismissive snort. "I can drink my coffee and chat with Abby at the same time." Then she turns back toward my daughter, and her voice completely changes. She's practically cooing as she tells

Abby, "Girls are excellent multitaskers. You'll see. Besides, we're going to be good friends. And when you're older and your dad is being a grouch, you can sneak across the hall, and we'll have juice boxes and watch *Barbie* movies together."

I know she's just babbling to keep Abby entertained, that she doesn't really plan on developing this relationship with my daughter. She's probably just trying to annoy me by making me think she and Abby are going to team up against me someday.

But for reasons that don't even make sense, that thought doesn't annoy me at all. In fact, it has the opposite effect. It makes me think of my own parents, and how much I've always wanted what they had. The teasing and the laughter, but also the deep trust, respect, and affection.

That's not something I can ever have with AJ—not only because I'm probably moving, but also because, even if I stayed, she'll always be my boss.

And she's made it clear that's a line she won't cross again.

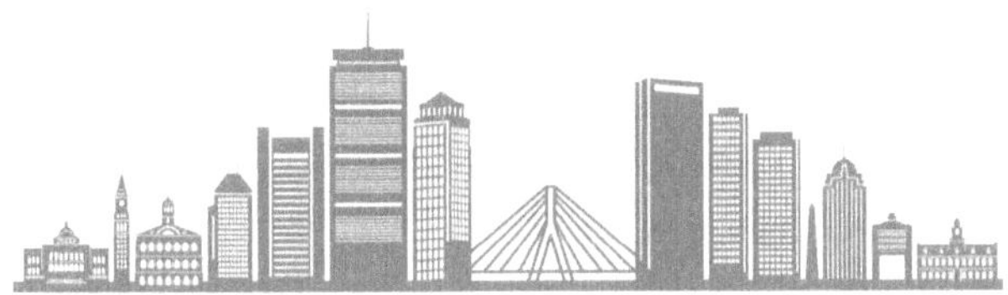

Chapter Seventeen

AJ

"You sure you're doing okay?" Frank asks after we wrap up our weekly check-in. Normally, I love that he's the type of owner who's around and available, but today, I'd really prefer he was sitting somewhere else counting his billions instead of asking me personal questions.

Sitting in McCabe's kitchen early this morning, I thought I was doing okay, all things considered. But my body has gotten progressively more sore as the day has gone on and Frank obviously hasn't missed how I've been shifting in my seat, trying to get comfortable.

"I'm fine. Just tired. I don't even remember what time it was when we got back from the hospital last night—"

"*We?*" Frank moves his bushy eyebrows up and down in a way that draws a laugh out of me. He probably thinks I'm seeing someone, and as much as I'd like an excuse to avoid all the men he tries to set me up with, I don't want to risk stirring up any rumors.

"No, don't get your hopes up. It's not like that. McCabe gave me a ride home after Abby and I were cleared by the doctor." At the beginning of our meeting, I'd given him the brief rundown of my experience with the fight and the hospital visit—which had led into a conversation about how this is exactly why McCabe was supposed to tell the fans that the fights needed to stay on the ice in the first place.

Would things have turned out differently if he'd reacted differently at the press conference? I don't know. But when Frank showed me footage of last night's fight, there was no denying that the Boston fans behind us were responsible for what happened. And they were both wearing McCabe jerseys.

"Speaking of, you'll talk to him about that again, right? I need him to make a statement or something about what happened," Frank says.

"I'll talk to him. But you saw what happened last time. I don't know what his deal is," I admit. "His agent is making outrageous demands—"

"Which we're not agreeing to."

"I know. And McCabe knows what our salary cap is. I don't know why he's getting greedy all of a sudden, but I wonder if his refusal to speak out about this at the press conference is because he's pissed about the negotiations breaking down?" It's incredibly frustrating that I can't just talk to him about this directly, but management can only discuss contracts with the player's agent, not the players themselves. "He's acting like he has one foot out the door already."

"Well, as long as he plays for us, he needs to act like a Rebel. I wish he'd said something before his daughter took a tumble and you got hurt, because now his statement will look reactive, like he only cares *now* because his daughter was involved."

Frank's right, but maybe emphasizing that bystanders were hurt will be even more effective?

"I'll talk to him t—" There's a split second where I realize I'm about to say *tonight*, and I consider being honest with Frank about the fact that I'm staying with McCabe. But as much as he's like a father to me, there's only one outcome that could result from telling him—he'd remind me how inappropriate the situation is, and that given my position and this award nomination, I'm already under a microscope. Both of which I already fully understand. Besides, tonight's the last night I'm staying with him, because tomorrow we're on the road. So there's no reason to say anything. "—tomorrow before the flight."

"Let me know what he says. And if you need to drop my name in there to get him to cooperate, you can."

"I won't. He's going to do this because it's the right thing to do, not because I had to bring in the big guns to get him to comply."

"*You* are the big guns, AJ," Frank says with a laugh.

"Yeah, but *you* write their paychecks."

He gives me a quick chuckle before he returns to that concerned look he had a few minutes ago. "And you're sure you're okay to travel with the team tomorrow? No one is going to question it if you stay home."

I stand, hoping that I can relieve some of the pressure on my right hip and stop my back from knotting up. I wasn't bruised when I looked this morning, but I'm afraid of what my body might look like now. Plus, I need this meeting to end because McCabe texted to tell me he was picking me up at six, and not to be late. The painkillers and my injury mean I can't drive myself, but when I tried to tell him I'd just book myself a ride home, he was having none of it. Now, I've got less than five minutes to get down to the parking garage. Hopefully, everyone else has left for the day and no one sees me leaving in his car.

"I'll be on the plane," I tell him with a nod. "I'm fine."

"You keep saying that," Frank says, "and somehow, I still don't believe you."

———

"I didn't really picture you as such a good cook," I tell McCabe as I blot some of the pasta sauce I can feel coating my lips with my napkin. I don't normally eat this late, but McCabe whipped this up after Abby went to bed, and it smelled so good, I agreed to have some. The sandwich I'd had in the late afternoon before my meeting with Frank didn't exactly feel like it was going to tide me over for the night.

His eyes flick up from his plate, and his lips quirk at one corner in that goddamn smirk that does things to me I wish it didn't. "Oh yeah, so how *did* you picture me, then?"

"I guess I just assumed you probably ordered out more than you cooked."

"You sound like you've given this some thought?" One eyebrow lifts, like he's trying to get me to admit that I spend a lot of my time thinking about him. Which is not the case, at all.

Or at least, it wasn't until the other day in my office. Now I feel like I keep reliving that moment over and over, and it's doing funny things to my body, my mind, and my moral compass.

Unethical. That word bounces around in my head, even though I know there's nothing in my contract about being involved with a player. It's probably not something anyone would have thought necessary with a male GM. Though, let's face it, that shouldn't be off the table either.

Regardless of what my contract says, I'm still his boss. The power dynamic is still there, even more so due to the new contract we're trying to work out. *No one* would look at what happened in that office and think it was okay. Not even me.

"The only time I spend thinking about you is when I'm trying to figure out why you're so obstinate."

"Ohhh, pulling out the big words now, aren't we, Sunshine?"

My laugh escapes like a snort. "Sunshine? What the fuck, McCabe? I may not be as grumpy as you are, but no one has ever accused me of having a sunny disposition." I'm far too much of a realist for that.

"Nah, I think it fits. You don't know what this organization was like before you became GM." He tears off a piece of his bread and uses it to mop up some of the pasta sauce on his mostly empty plate. "It's like you brought the light with you."

"That's . . ." I lick my lips as I think about what he means, my chest warm and tingly. ". . . oddly sweet."

He shrugs and reaches for his water glass. "Just telling it like it is."

Releasing a breath, I try to change the subject. "In any event, back to you being obstinate—"

He rolls his eyes. "Of course. You can't just let me distract you with a compliment?"

"Not gonna happen, McCabe. You had the opportunity to say something at that press conference about the fans leaving the fighting to the professionals on the ice, and you didn't. In fact, you said it was not your place to have an opinion on that. So now that I was injured and your daughter was almost hurt as well, what's your plan?"

"Have someone ask me again after our next game."

"After the way you responded last time?" I ask with an incredulous laugh. Like I'd trust him again. I'm not even sure I want him in front of the media after what happened in the pressroom a few days ago. But, as team captain, it's kind of expected.

"Trust me," he says, as if such a thing was possible. "Have someone ask me again."

I press my lips together between my teeth, wondering if it's worth the risk. The right statement from him could help, but if he goes off script again . . . "Not unless you get some coaching on what you're going to say first."

"I don't need fucking coaching on what to say." Letting out a huge sigh, he sits back in his seat.

I follow suit, but the second my shoulder blade makes contact with the back of the seat, I wince. I try to hide it, but he's quick to ask what's wrong.

"Just sore," I say breezily.

"Are you bruised from the fall?"

"I don't know. It's not like I've looked at my back since getting dressed this morning."

"You weren't bruised then," he confirms.

"I thought you said you were keeping your eyes closed?" He'd promised he wouldn't look at me while he helped me get my dress on today. It had been easy for me to get into the short-sleeved dress; he'd just needed to zip up the back for me.

"I said I wouldn't look while you were putting the dress on. I didn't say I was going to zip it up with my eyes closed. Anyway, I didn't see any bruises, but the dress was covering most of your back." He stands, rounding the table toward my seat. "Let me check."

"What?" I shrink back in my chair, which is foolish because the minute my full back hits that seat, I yelp in pain. "No."

"Why not?"

"Because there's no need." I keep my words breezy so he won't notice how my entire body is heating up at the thought of his hands on me. I need to keep the boundaries between us clear—something he doesn't seem to know how to do.

"I'm going to have to unzip your dress later on so you can change, anyway," he says. "You're done eating, so why not now?"

"Because . . ." I say, but I can't think of any good reason except that I can tell there's bruising and I don't want him to see it. He already has some sort of a martyr complex about helping me recover since I saved Abby from injury. I don't need that complex to get any stronger when he sees what shape my body's in after that fall.

"Stand up, Alessandra, before I haul you out of that chair."

His words are low, but they're not threatening. They're a caress, a promise that he'll get his way but he'll be gentle in doing so.

"You wouldn't."

He puts his hand on the back of my seat, easily turning the chair so I'm facing him. "I would. So I highly suggest you stand on your own, or you're going to end up over my shoulder."

I'm so tempted to test him, to sit here stubbornly, just to see if he'd actually do it. But that feels like a line I'm not willing to cross, so instead, I stand.

"There, happy?" I huff.

He looks down at me, and there's a heat in his eyes that shouldn't be there. His voice is low and raspy as his breath coasts along the top of my head. "Good girl. See how easy it is to do what you're told?"

I close my eyes, gulping as I tilt my head down, away from the sound of his sexy-as-hell voice. There's no reason those words should have my underwear already damp, but that's what's happening. I should be telling him to check himself, but my body is having an entirely different response.

Stop it right fucking now, I tell myself, willing my good sense to return. Whatever it is he does to my senses, and the way my body responds to him . . . it needs to stop.

"Just unzip me, McCabe. I can look at my own back in the mirror in the bathroom. I don't need your help," I say, too quietly, and he looks at me like he knows I'm trying to hide from him even while we stand toe to toe.

He brings his knuckles under my chin, tilting my head back so he can see my face, and goosebumps erupt along my chest and down my arms. "What is it you don't want me to see?"

Me, I want to scream. Because right now, with him staring down at me, this whole situation feels too raw, too vulnerable. Like not only will he be able to see how bruised and battered my body is, but maybe he'll even be able to see that my heart is in the same condition.

"I'm your boss," I say, because I feel like maybe we both need that reminder.

"Like I could forget," he says, eyes searching mine. "But you're also the woman who saved my daughter from getting injured, and I'm going to take care of you until you're recovered."

I exhale, relieved that's all this is to him—he's only taking care of me because he feels obligated, given that I protected Abby.

"You don't need to do that. I'm *fine.*"

"Really? Then let's see." He rests his hands on my shoulders tenderly, like he knows I'm in pain and wants to make sure he doesn't hurt me, then turns me so my back is to him.

I suck in a breath when his fingers skim the skin over my spine, and exhale slowly as he grips the fabric at the top of my dress with one hand, then slowly pulls the zipper down with the other.

When I feel the zipper pass my bra, I try to step away, knowing I can unzip it the rest of the way one-handed. But his palm snakes around to the front of my neck, pulling me back to him gently. This beast of a man is cradling my body in his—his rock-solid chest barely touching my shoulders, one arm wrapped around me and cupping my neck in his hand—and I can't fucking breathe from how turned on I am.

I try to exhale to make room in my lungs for new air, but it comes out sounding a whole lot like a moan.

"You're going to let me see what's going on with your back." His words are a low caress. "So are we doing this the easy way, or the hard way?"

While I know the easy way is to just let him look, my imagination is captivated and my body thrums at the idea of finding out what the hard way looks like. But my confidence fails me at that moment.

"Easy," I squeak out.

His hips settle against my lower back as his hand trails around to the nape of my neck, then down the bare skin along my spine. Knuckles pressing against me, he slides his hand into the dress and holds the fabric together as his other hand tugs the zipper the rest of the way down in one fluid motion.

He dips his head so his lips are right next to my ear. "Good girl. Now show me where it hurts."

My entire core clenches in need, my hips flexing back against him without my permission. *What the hell was that?*

I've never in my life wanted to be treated like someone's fucking pet. Yet here this man is, his deep, gravelly voice melting me with his words of affirmation.

With my left hand, I slide the dress off my right shoulder, and he sucks in his breath so sharply it sounds like a gasp.

"What the fuck is this?" He pulls the dress farther down my arm to bare more of my back to him, and then traces his fingers ever-so-lightly across the tender flesh. I all but stop breathing, but it's not because of the pain. It's because of how this gruff man is so tender when he's touching me.

"I'm fine," I assure him.

"Like hell you are. I want this dress off so I can see what else is hurt."

My shoulders shake with laughter. "Yeah, sure that's why you want this dress off."

"There is no question that in other circumstances, I'd want your dress off for other reasons. But right now, I honestly want to see how badly you're hurt. Nothing more."

The erection he's pressing against the curve of my spine says otherwise.

"I'm not taking my dress off in the middle of your condo," I say, nodding my chin toward the walls of windows at the corner of the room, which are uncovered. Outside, the light is fading fast as we approach sunset, and anyone in one of the surrounding buildings could see in here.

"Fine. My room, then." With his hand on my lower back, he steers me toward the hallway to the bedrooms. "I'm just going to double check on Abby first."

Earlier tonight, while I was across the hall feeding Tabitha and packing the suitcase he'd laid out for me on my bed in preparation for tomorrow's trip, he put Abby down to sleep and made us dinner. After collecting my suitcase and bringing it over to his guest bedroom, he fed me.

I don't know who this man is—I want to think that this caretaking side of him is only because he feels guilty and wants to make it up to me, but what if this is just who he is? And worse, what if I like this side of him a little too much?

"Fine," I say with a sigh. He's not letting this go without seeing what condition I'm in, and after that huge pasta dinner with the carb-loading hockey player, I'm getting tired. I just don't feel like fighting him on this. I'll show him my back and my hip, and then call it an early night by retreating to the guest bedroom.

That feels like a safe plan.

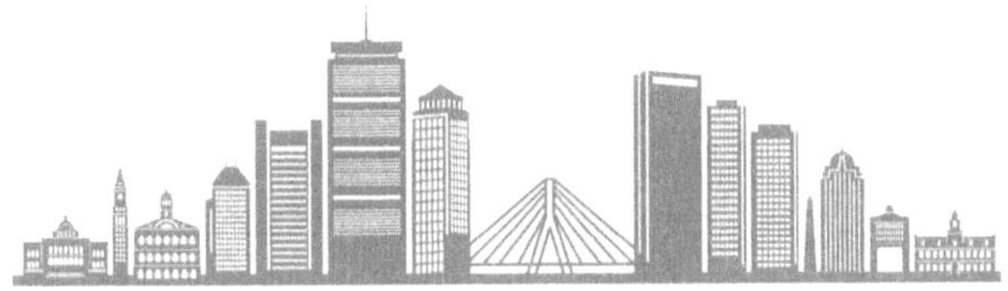

Chapter Eighteen

McCabe

As I expected, Abby is still fast asleep, but her pacifier is on the floor so I place it back in her crib, hoping that if she wakes up tonight, she'll use it to self-soothe. Like some sort of a miracle, that worked last night—when I heard her fussing and grabbed the video monitor to take a look, she was chewing on her pacifier and then she popped it in her mouth, rolled over, and went back to sleep.

She's sleeping through the night about fifty percent of the time now, but I'd love to get to that being the norm every night—I'm a much better dad when I'm not sleep deprived. I hate being away from her when I travel, but at least I get to catch up on sleep when I'm on the road. My teammates all think I've turned into an old man since Abby came into my life, but the ones with little kids understand.

It's only been a minute when I get to my bedroom, and

I'm surprised to find AJ standing there in the middle of the room, looking lost.

"I thought I told you to take that dress off."

She puts one hand on her hip while her injured arm hangs limp at her side. "I'm not going to stand around in nothing but my underwear. Besides, I wasn't sure how to close your shades."

"Here." I step over to the wall of glass doors that lead out to the same balcony that runs across my living room, and pull back the curtains to show her where the remote is mounted on the wall.

"Oh, fancy," she says as the light-filtering shades descend. "I should get some like this. I don't love having my curtains closed during the day because then it's dark, but I also hate the thought of people in other buildings being able to see into my bedroom."

"Same," I tell her as the shades hit the lower lip of the sliding glass doors. "Now let's see those bruises."

"It's not that big of a deal," she says as she turns her back to me. "I'm only letting you look because I don't feel like fighting with you. Take a quick peek, and then I'm going to sleep."

"It's nine o'clock."

"And I'm exhausted. I don't even remember what time we got back from the hospital last night."

"Like 2 a.m.," I say as I hook my thumbs under the neckline of her dress, and watch the shiver run down her spine.

Sliding the shoulders of the dress down each of her arms, I let it stop at her waist. The right side of her back is covered in angry purple bruises. Her entire shoulder blade is a grayish purple color, and it extends over to her spine. There's a fainter line of bruises, not quite as bad, leading from her shoulder blade down to her waist. I push the dress down, exposing the curve of her ass, and in the relative silence of the room, I don't miss the way she sucks in a breath as my fingers trace the dark line that runs horizontally from her sacrum over to her right hip, directly below the strand of lace holding her thong in place.

In the pattern of bruises, I can see exactly how she landed—her hip and ass connecting with the back of one row of seats, and her shoulder blade and spine connecting with the next row down. It's amazing she didn't break her back, along with her wrist.

My hands rest lightly on each of her hips, but it's like I've been immobilized. I stand there, forcing myself to breathe as I look at her battered body, while every cell inside me is threatening to explode—from both anger and gratitude. I'm angry at the fans who started this fight, yes, but I'm also angry at myself. Maybe I couldn't have stopped this from happening, but I could have done more to prevent it—I could have just done what she'd asked, and spoken out against fighting happening in the stands.

We're so lucky that she wasn't hurt worse, and I'm immensely grateful that she was able to prevent Abby from injury. I can never repay her for the way she kept my daughter safe.

I'm such a jumbled mess of conflicting emotions right now.

"So?" she asks, breaking me out of my trance.

I rest my forehead on the crown of her head, and breathe in the sweet scent of her shampoo. "Fuck, Alessandra." I breathe out her name reverently. "I'm so sorry this happened."

My fingertips move to connect over her abdomen so my hands are practically circling her waist. All I can think about is that I want to kill whoever caused her this pain. But then my fingers meet stickiness.

"What's this?" I ask, pulling my fingers free where they're lightly stuck to the sticky spots on her skin.

She tilts her head down to look at her stomach, and that's when her dress falls past her hips and pools at her bare feet. My god, she has a delicious ass—rounded and muscular, sitting atop absolutely ripped thighs. Her body is all hard lines and flat planes . . . and I'm left wondering how she's so muscular. It's like she's curvy, but it's all muscle.

There's not an ounce of softness anywhere on her body, which is kind of perfect because there's not an ounce of softness in her personality, either. Except when she's with Abby, and then it's like seeing a whole different side of her.

"It's from those sensor things they stuck to me yesterday when they were running some tests," she says, then looks over her shoulder and catches me staring at her ass.

"Eyes up here, buddy," she says, her voice sarcastic. She doesn't sound mad that she caught me checking her out.

"Sorry," I say as I lift my chin to look her in the eye. "But I mean, you're standing in front of me in a tiny thong, so you can't blame a guy for looking."

"I can, actually," she says. "You said you wanted to see the bruises, not check me out."

"Hey." Reaching out, I cup the side of her face, pulling her toward me in a way that gives her no choice but to turn around. I keep my gaze locked on her face when I say, "I'm sorry."

She rests her cheek in my hand, and I stand there wondering what it means that she hasn't pulled away.

"You haven't showered." The words are out of my mouth the second they're in my head. "No wonder you have sticky spots"—I look down at her abdomen, trying to ignore the curve of her breasts, covered by the thin fabric of her bra.—"all over you."

"How would I shower?" she asks, her voice dripping with sarcasm. "I can't even use one of my hands, and I'm not allowed to take this splint off."

I try to picture how she'd squeeze the body wash onto a bath sponge, or shampoo or conditioner into her hand. It would be impossible to do that one-handed.

"C'mon," I say, nodding my chin toward the ensuite bathroom.

Her eyebrows dip. "What?"

"I'll help you."

Her laughter is the awkward kind that bubbles up when you don't want it to. "I'm not showering with you."

"I'm not offering." Not because I don't want that—fuck, my body wants that so badly I'm about fully hard just thinking about it—but because I know *she* doesn't want that. "But I'll draw you a bubble bath, so you can rest your splinted arm on the rim of the tub. And once you're settled, I'll come in and wash your hair for you."

"You . . .?" She shakes her head, and with her lips parted and her eyebrows still dipped in confusion, she looks like she can't make sense of anything I'm saying.

"C'mon, Sunshine, think how good it'll feel to be clean. When's the last time you took a shower?"

"Yesterday morning."

I guide her into the bathroom with my hand resting lightly on her lower back, taking care to avoid the bruised side. And as she stands on the tiled floor, she turns so her back is to the huge, framed mirror that runs above the vanity, and looks over her shoulder. "Yep," she sighs. "It looks about how it feels."

"I can't believe you went to work today," I say, turning on the tap and letting the water run into the tub. When I get it nice and warm, I flip the lever next to the spout to close the drain.

"I never even considered staying home," she admits quietly, and I get the sense that this is an important realization for her.

"Why not?" I keep my eyes focused on the tub that's slowly filling with water. I'm avoiding looking at her in that sexy thong and bra, trying to stop wondering why she's wearing sexy lingerie to work, because I need this fucking hard-on to disappear before she notices it.

"I don't know. Work is sort of . . ." There's a long pause, and I don't fill the silence. I want to know what she's thinking, and I sense that she's working it out in her own mind. Getting to hear her thought process feels kind of like an unexpected gift. ". . . what I do."

I pick up the bubble bath sitting on the ledge above the big freestanding tub. "What do you do besides work?" I ask as I squeeze the liquid into the tub.

"Why do you have bubble bath?" she asks with a laugh,

like the fact that I said I'd draw her a bubble bath didn't actually register until she saw me pouring it in.

"Abby loves bubbles. I hope you won't mind smelling like coconut?"

"Love coconut. I actually have a candle in my living room called *Beach Day*. It smells like coconut-scented sunscreen, and I burn it all summer long."

There are so many questions surfacing . . . things I want to know about her everyday life. But I shouldn't be trying to figure out what her life is like outside of work, and she was the first to remind me of that by the way she tried to change the conversation when I asked.

"You want to feel the water and make sure it's the right temperature?"

"Sure," she says, stepping toward the tub. I stand and move away, otherwise her tits would be right at eye level and there's no way I should be looking at her like that. But I do glance over as she bends to test the water with her good hand, and that's a mistake. Because Alessandra Jones bent over in that sexy thong is a sight that has me just about ready to come in my fucking pants like some sort of middle school boy.

"I'm going to give you some privacy so you can get in the tub when there's as much water as you want," I say quickly, turning away so that she won't be able to see the enormous boner I'm sporting if she looks back at me. "Call me once you're in."

And then I rush out the door, and when it's shut, I rest my hands on either side of the frame, taking deep breaths and reminding myself that no matter what I want to happen, she wants to keep things professional.

Trying to convince myself that I'm not just respecting her boundaries here, but that I actually don't *want* anything to happen either, doesn't pan out. *You don't even like her*, I remind myself. But is that really true? The years I spent holding that grudge about the trade feel like wasted energy.

The unmistakable sound of sloshing water as her body sinks into the bath has me picturing the scene clearly in my head, which is doing nothing to help the situation in my pants. I try anything that might help . . . I think about my high school gym teacher who liked to bite his nails and spit them at us if he thought we weren't doing sit-ups fast enough, I remember the time in elementary school when I didn't notice the maggots in my box of raisins until I started popping them into my mouth, I think of all the gross shit I've seen in locker rooms over the years. And then, with those memories and mental images circulating in my brain, I take a lap around my bedroom, walking back and forth, again and again.

"Alright," AJ calls from the bathroom. "I'm in."

God, even the sound of her voice does it for me. How did I go so quickly from hating her for years, right back to this crush I once had?

But as I walk toward the bathroom, I realize that's not what this is. This isn't the pathetic crush of a guy in his early twenties, lusting after the powerful but married woman who he knows he can't have. That crush was safe—or so I thought, until it ended my career in St. Louis.

But this . . . the way I can't stop thinking about her? The way I moved her into my condo with a flimsy excuse the second I saw the opportunity? The way she is with Abby? All of it makes me want *more*, and *that* is the part that's dangerous.

It could ruin her career, make her a laughingstock among her peers, and ensure that she doesn't win an award she more than deserves.

And for me? She's already made it clear she's not trying to keep me in Boston next season. So getting involved with her? Or worse—letting myself fall for her? That would be the most wildly stupid thing I've ever done.

But do I let that stop me from walking into that bathroom? Sitting on the edge of the tub and noticing how she's arranged all the bubbles in the middle to ensure she's covered under the water? No, I sure don't.

Do I let it stop me from dipping the bath sponge into the water, then adding some body wash to it? Nope.

And when she leans forward so I can wash her back for her, do I stop myself from slipping my hand along her neck and brushing her hair to one side before I move that bath sponge along her shoulders, careful not to put too much pressure on any of the bruised parts? Not a chance.

Because even though I know she's right, that nothing *should* happen between us, I don't think there's anything I could do to stop this. There's no way I'm not taking care of her while she's hurt. And when she's recovered . . . well, we'll see.

"I think you're going to need to dunk under the water to get your hair wet enough for me to wash it," I tell her.

"Alright." The word is spoken so softly. "Will you just hold my arm up here." She nods her chin toward the opposite rim of the tub where her splinted arm rests. "I don't want the splint to get wet."

"Sure." I lean over, cupping my hand where her elbow sits against the porcelain tub, and she sinks into the water. Trying to remain a gentleman, I keep my eyes focused on the frosted window that takes up the wall space above the tub.

She resurfaces a moment later, using her good hand to wipe the water from her eyes. When I lather up my hands with shampoo and sink my fingers into her hair, I try to focus on how I'm helping her rather than on how intimate this is. As I massage her scalp, she tilts her head back into my hands, letting out a breathy and contented sigh.

The way she's both tentative about accepting help, but then laps it up when it's given . . . it has me wondering so many things about her previous relationships.

After working the shampoo down to the ends of her hair, I gently tilt her head back so her hair's in the water and, holding the weight of her head in one hand, I use my other to work the suds out of her hair, before sitting her back up.

"You're remarkably good at this," she says, still not looking at me. "Do this often?"

I've never washed a woman's hair before. Never shared this type of intimacy with someone. Shower sex? Sure. But nothing like this.

"Only for Abby," I tell her. "Though . . . her bathtime is . . ." I clear my throat. ". . . not this."

Her shoulders shake with a silent laugh, and I reach across the tub to the ledge under the window and add a few pumps of conditioner to my hand.

"Why do you have shampoo and conditioner over here? Besides Abby's, I mean." She nods her chin to where the baby shampoo sits next to my bottles.

"Uhh." Is this a trick question? "For when I take baths?"

"You take baths? And use conditioner?"

"Why do you sound shocked? I'm sure you can imagine how sore and stiff my muscles get after practices and games. Sometimes, a hot soak is as necessary as an ice bath. And yeah, of course I use conditioner." My hair isn't long, but it's long enough that it gets tangled if I don't condition it.

The "hmmmm" that rattles around in her throat gives me no indication of what she's thinking, so I work the conditioner through her hair in silence, before tilting her head back again to work the lather out of her hair with the water.

"Do you want me to use the sprayer to get this out of your hair? Or . . ." I'm about to ask if she'd rather do it herself, when I realize how difficult that would be for her.

"Sure," she says. "I'll just sit up with my back to you so my hair's all the way out of the water?"

"Sounds good." Why does it sound like I have a frog in my throat?

I busy myself with turning on the water to the handheld sprayer, and making sure it's a good temperature while she turns to sit facing the window. "I need to pull the plug and let the water drain a bit or we'll overflow it with this new water."

"Kay." The answer is clipped, and she sounds . . . nervous?

I have her tilt her head back and use the sprayer to work any remaining conditioner out of her hair until it's squeaky clean, and then I hold her hair up and rinse off her upper body. "How do you want to . . . rinse the rest of yourself off?"

There's no way I can rinse her off without her standing up and being fully naked in front of me.

She clears her throat, but her voice is still thick when she says, "I think I can do it one-handed. And then get myself dried off."

"Alright." I lean down to put the sprayer in front of her where she can grab it with her left hand. "There are towels right on the shelf there." I point toward the wall above the faucet. "Just call me if you need anything."

And then I head out, shutting the door behind me, feeling like I'm barely breathing as I remind myself that there's nothing physical going on here. I'm only helping her because she's hurt. It's nothing more than that, and she doesn't want there to be.

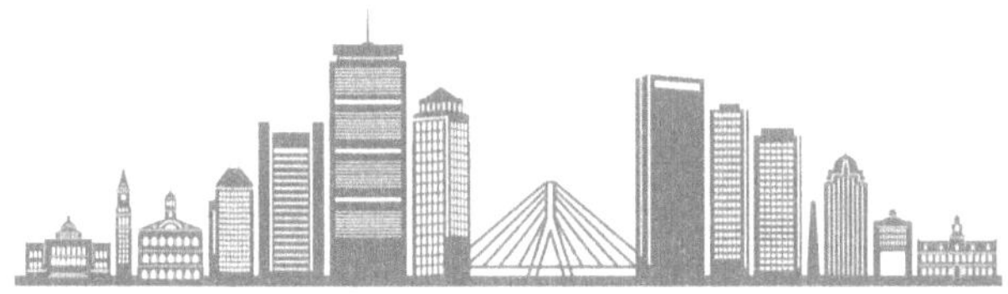

Chapter Nineteen

McCabe

"You gotta stop following her around like a goddamn puppy," Colt says, turning his head back to me as I follow him onto the plane.

"She shouldn't be carrying a suitcase with a broken arm."

Maybe I shouldn't have rushed over to AJ when she got out of the private car she insisted on taking to the charter jet terminal our plane is leaving from. She can't drive herself right now, and she said it would be way too suspect if we arrived together, so she wouldn't let me drive her either.

"Pretty sure she has two arms," he replies.

There was no way I was letting her roll that big-ass suitcase over to the luggage cart, or lug her carry-on suitcase up those stairs to the plane. Not when she's injured.

Colt drops his voice lower and says, "Never thought I'd see you go from hating her to hovering like this. Is this all because of the way she protected Abby the other night?"

The silent "Or . . .?" at the end of the question hangs there heavily.

"Yeah, I feel kind of indebted to her now. And Abby adores her, so that's kind of softened my stance on her, I guess." I try to play it off like this is just about Abby, and hope he buys it.

"Good, maybe she'll renew your contract if you stop being such a dick."

I laugh, and Colt's eyebrows shoot up in surprise. "I'm not a dick. She just pisses me off."

"She gave you your first contract in the NHL a decade ago, and took Abby *twice* so you could play the first two games of this series. Maybe whatever happened in that time between those two things doesn't matter that much?"

After eight years of playing with Colt, I don't know why it still surprises me that there's more to him than the fuck-boy image he portrayed for so long. He's so much more perceptive than he wants people to know.

"Maybe," I grunt out as we take our seats—me in the aisle across from Colt, and him next to Drew.

"So . . ." Drew leans forward, looking at me. "You got your childcare all worked out?"

"Yeah. Found a *manny*, actually."

"Like a guy who's a nanny?" Colt asks, scratching at the back of his neck like the thought of having to spend four solid days with a baby is making him break out in a rash.

"Yep."

"How'd that happen?" Drew asks.

"Little brother of a friend. He's getting his degree in child psychology and loves kids. It's only working because it's just a summer gig for him. But at least I think he'll be reliable through the rest of the season."

Colt chuckles. "A college guy who's watching a baby for the summer. Hope he's not like either of you guys were in college."

Colt came straight to the NHL, whereas Drew was drafted after his senior year of college, and I left after my junior year for the pros. But he's right. I was definitely not the kind of guy you'd leave in charge of a baby back then. And after the way Drew accidentally ghosted Audrey post-senior year and missed the first five years of his son's life as a result, I don't think he was responsible enough either.

"Stop trying to make him worry," Drew says, elbowing Colt. "The last thing we need is for our captain to not have his head in the game."

"Abby's going to be just fine with Nicholas," I say, praying I'm right. I have such a better feeling about him than I ever did about Lucy. And the fact that he showed up ten minutes early this morning only confirmed my intuition.

My phone pings with a text, and I glance down quickly, relieved that Hartmann isn't in his seat next to me yet, because no one needs to see AJ's name popping up on my screen. I quickly go to her contact and change her name so that I don't risk one of my teammates seeing that she's texting me.

SUNSHINE

Stop treating me like I'm made of glass. I
can roll my own damn suitcase.

MCCABE

You had two suitcases and one good hand.

SUNSHINE

And yet you insisted on taking both my
bags.

MCCABE

What can I say? I'm a gentleman.

I'm pretty sure I hear her scoff from the front of the
plane, where she sits twelve rows in front of me.

SUNSHINE

Sure you are.

MCCABE

I was a PERFECT gentleman last night,
wasn't I?

SUNSHINE

That's debatable. But you were helpful, so
there's that.

MCCABE

I'll take helpful.

For now.

SUNSHINE

What do you mean, FOR NOW???

Do I type out a message and delete it five times, simply
because I like picturing her biting her lip as she watches those
bubbles pop up while she waits for my response? Yes, I sure do.

I quite like the idea of making her squirm a bit . . . I just
wish she was squirming right over the top of my—

"Dude, who are you texting?" Hartmann's voice cuts into
my thoughts. Glancing up to where he stands looking down

at me, I almost fumble my phone in the rush to put it in my pocket before he sees AJ's name at the top of the screen. Then I remember that I already changed her name.

"Just the new nanny."

He purposely presses his ass into my face as he steps over me to get to his seat, like an impatient teenager who can't be bothered to wait two seconds for me to get up and let him pass.

"I can't fucking wait for Renaud to get back next season," I grumble. "You're a shitty seat mate."

Aidan Renaud has been my closest friend for the past few years, but an injury this past summer sidelined his whole season, and he's spent most of this past year back in the beach town he grew up in.

Hartmann just laughs. "So, this new nanny. She hot?"

"Relax, Lover Boy," I use the nickname Walshy gave him when he joined our team earlier this season. "She's a he."

"Your nanny is a guy?"

"Yep."

"None of my nannies growing up were dudes," he says, his face getting serious, like he's really considering what it would be like to have a male nanny. "That's so badass. I bet a guy would have been so much more fun."

I roll my eyes. "You know Abby's an infant, right? It's not like they're out playing baseball together."

"Still, it's cool for him. He can put her in the stroller and walk around the city, and I bet he pulls so many girls that way."

I never feel older than when I spend time around some of these younger, single players. Was I like this before Abby came into my life? Hopefully, I'd long since grown out of that phase.

"He has a girlfriend."

"Hmm. What a waste for him. A guy with a kid is a total chick magnet."

Is that so? Because that hasn't been my experience. Only one woman in my life has ever seemed at all comfortable with my kid. Of course, it's the one woman I can't have.

And. Don't. Want! I practically scream the reminder in my head, but it's useless. I'm not delusional enough to believe myself. I do want her. Whether she wants me is an entirely different question.

————

SUNSHINE

Any chance you're free right now?

When the text comes through, I'm half asleep on the bed in my hotel room after a particularly heavy pasta dinner with the team put me into a carb coma. The recap of another hockey game is playing on my TV, but the volume is so low that I can't even hear what the sportscasters are saying. Doesn't matter, I'm not watching for their commentary. I just want to see what the competition is doing.

MCCABE

Depends.

Her reply comes back almost immediately.

SUNSHINE

On what?

MCCABE

On why you're asking.

I'm not sure why I like to be difficult when it comes to her. I could have just said "yes," but where's the fun in that?

SUNSHINE

I happen to be on FaceTime with Nicholas,
and Abby is trying to walk.

I fly off the bed, grabbing a shirt off the chair as I frantically type out my reply.

MCCABE

What's your room number?

SUNSHINE

Oh, nowwwww you decide to be direct? No
leaving me hanging without responding for
hours . . .

Shit. I scroll up on the screen and see that she's right. I got distracted with my teammates on the plane and I never actually sent a response to her earlier message.

MCCABE

Room number.

Now, AJ.

I'm not missing my daughter's first steps
because you're pissy I didn't respond to
your text.

I'm going to assume she's just teasing me, because I don't think she's actually the type of person who would make me miss a milestone like this out of spite.

SUNSHINE

407

No. Fucking. Way. What kind of trick is the universe trying to play on us?

MCCABE

Open your door so I can slip in without anyone seeing me, please.

SUNSHINE

How soon?

Grabbing my key card off the dresser, I shove it into the pocket of my shorts as I crack open my door, peeking out into the hallway to make sure no one is around. It's empty.

MCCABE

Now.

Her jaw drops when she swings her door open to find me standing in my open doorway across the hall.

"No fucking way," she says, and I chuckle as her words mirror the exact thought I just had. "Did you arrange this?"

"Yeah." Sarcasm drips from my tone as I take two steps across the hall and into her room, quickly shutting the door behind me. "Just like I arranged for you to move in across the hall from me at home."

Abby's gurgling baby sounds draw me into the room, where I find AJ's phone propped up on the dresser against the TV.

"I muted myself because she was getting distracted any time I said something to Nicholas," she tells me, grabbing the phone off the dresser and handing it to me as we sit on the bed next to each other so we can watch my daughter.

Abby is standing with both hands on the long bench-style ottoman I now use as a coffee table because it's padded and she can't hurt herself on it.

"Hey, Abby." Nicholas must be sitting on the floor below his phone, because I can just see the top of his head at the bottom of the screen.

Abby's head turns toward him, and he holds up her favorite puppy, making it dance around in the air in front of him. Abby takes a tentative step, still holding on to the ottoman with one hand for balance. I've seen her do this a bunch of times, but so far, she's never let go of whatever she's holding on to. I know she'll get the hang of walking soon, and part of me hopes it's right now on camera so I don't miss it. The other part of me hopes she waits until I get home.

Nicholas makes pretend barking sounds, and Abby giggles in response. She steps one foot toward him, and her free arm flies up to help balance her. I can tell she's not ready for multiple steps, but she might actually take one.

The puppy claps his paws together as Nicholas says, "Good job!" And then lets out another little puppy bark.

Abby laughs again, and leans toward him like she's thinking about taking a step.

We lean toward the phone, both of us holding our breaths as if breathing might cause us to miss one second of this. And when Abby brings her back leg forward to take a step, she teeters a bit but is able to right herself. She's standing, all by herself. I can feel my eyes filling with tears as I watch her take one more step toward Nicholas.

That's when AJ's hand finds mine, our fingers intertwining tightly as we both take a sharp, excited breath. "Oh my god," she whispers.

I clear my throat. I'm not going to fucking cry in front of her.

As Abby reaches out to try to grab her puppy, she falls forward onto her hands and knees and crawls the rest of the way. Nicholas must pick her up then, because her head pops up next to his and her eyes light up when she sees the phone.

"Da!"

Tapping the button to unmute the video, I say, "Good job, boo!"

"Da!"

This is all happening so fast. A few months ago, she couldn't even sit up on her own, and now she's almost walking and talking. There's a lump in my throat so thick that I'm not sure I can swallow it down.

Then Nicholas is turning and picking up the phone, holding it out so I can see both him and Abby where she stands on his thigh. She's got one hand on his shoulder, and is holding the top of his head with the other.

"Alright, we need to start getting ready for bed. I let her stay up a little late," he says, chuckling. "She got this random spurt of energy and was bouncing all over the place."

"Yeah," I say, then clear my throat again because it still feels clogged with all the emotions. "That happens sometimes. Reading her a few books while rocking her before giving her a bottle usually calms her down. Her favorites are in the stack I showed you—"

"On top of the nightstand," he confirms with a nod.

"But sometimes when she gets worked up, you have to rock her until she falls asleep; otherwise, she just stands up in her crib and yells at you until you come back."

Nicholas smiles as he looks over at Abby. "Yeah, I could see you doing that, cutie."

The whole scene . . . him playing with her on the floor, getting her to take steps, not balking at the idea of rocking her until she's too tired not to sleep . . . I'm just so damn relieved that he's there with her, rather than Lucy.

In the corner of the phone screen, I note how AJ's turned toward me, watching me closely.

"Alright," I say, "we'll let you go."

He says goodnight and Abby blows some raspberries at the phone, and then the call disconnects.

Unable to look at her when I'm this emotional, I lean sideways, resting my cheek against the crown of her head. "Thank you."

"For what?" Her voice is quiet, and with the sun low on the horizon, the room is quickly darkening.

"For making sure I got to see my daughter's first steps."

"I didn't know they'd be her first when I texted you." She pauses for a beat and says, "And I wasn't threatening to keep you from seeing them when I was like, *Oh, nowwww you respond . . .*"

"I know," I say.

"Do you? Because I really want to make sure you know that I'm not the kind of person who would do that. That kind of emotional manipulation . . ." She sighs, the motion deflating her whole body so that I have to sit up or I'll fall over onto her. In response, she looks away, out the window.

"AJ." My knuckles graze the underside of her jaw as I turn her toward me. Her dark irises blend in with her enlarged pupils so that her eyes are practically black, but it's not a look of longing. She looks . . . sad. "Finish that sentence."

"I don't . . . I'm not really sure what I was going to say."

Like hell she doesn't. I stroke her jawline with my thumb. "You know you can tell me, right?"

She closes her eyes, but it does nothing to break the moment. It just gives me a minute to study those pouty, wide lips, the ridge of her cheekbones, and the laugh lines at the corners of her eyes. Her hair is pulled back into some sort of messy bun secured with a clip, and I assume it's the best she could do with one hand.

When she opens her eyes again, she presses her lips together and shrugs. "I spent basically my whole life being emotionally manipulated. I wouldn't do that to someone else."

"Tell me more." I lean back on one elbow, hoping she'll get comfortable too. Because this tense posture she's adopted as she sits there with whatever's going through her mind has her looking like a statue.

She groans and falls back on the bed, looking straight up at the ceiling like she's afraid to let her eyes dart over to where I'm poised looking down at her.

Which is just as well, because the last thing she needs to see is the way my eyes burn as they take her in, lying in bed next to me. It's not a sight I ever let myself believe I'd see.

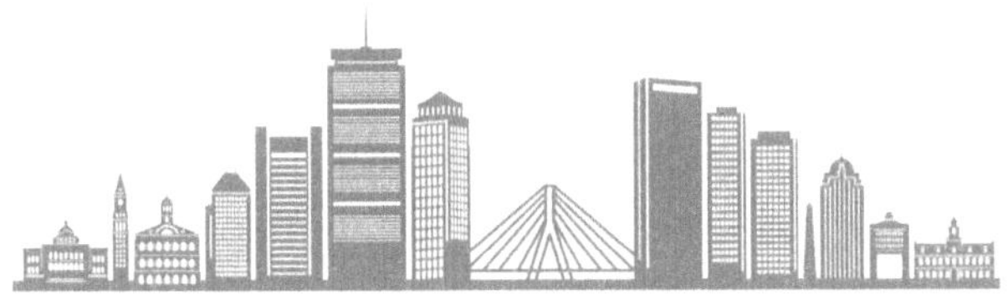

Chapter Twenty

AJ

I close my eyes and take a deep breath, wondering why I'm even contemplating sharing *anything* with him, much less giving him such personal details.

"This isn't . . . something I talk about."

"With anyone?" I ask.

"With anyone who isn't Nicholas."

"You two are really close, huh? Even despite the age difference."

It's hard not to laugh at that, because I'm old enough to be his mom. "Yeah, well, my parents treated him like the accident he was, so I had to step in."

"Shit." He breathes the word out on a long exhale. "Maybe it's because both my parents grew up in foster care, or maybe it's the way my ex so easily gave Abby up, but there's something about parents abandoning their kid that never sits right with me."

"My parents weren't . . . terrible to him. They didn't

abandon him; they were just neglectful. I was a senior in high school when my mom got pregnant, and it was obviously not planned. They'd always wanted more kids, but by that point, they'd long ago accepted that it wasn't going to happen. And then it did. I missed most of his early years because I was at college . . . "

"Too busy captaining a championship hockey team?" His voice is teasing. This isn't something we've ever talked about, so the fact that he knows I was the captain of my two-time NCAA winning women's hockey team means he's looked into it.

"But I moved back to St. Louis when I graduated so I could be closer to my family. I didn't want to not have a relationship with my little brother. That's where I coached a D1 women's team while getting my MBA," I say, thinking about how back then, there was no path for women playing hockey beyond college, so I moved into coaching and earned that business degree so that eventually I could get into the management side of the sport. "And as busy as I was, I still managed to spend exponentially more time with Nicholas than my parents did. I was absolutely appalled at how he almost didn't exist in their lives."

"How's that possible?"

"They just left him with a nanny all the time while they went about their lives. International travel, full days of golf followed by dinner at the country club, weekends away . . . he was never part of any of it."

When I glance over at him, his eyes are full of sympathy. Normally, I hate the thought of anyone feeling sorry for me or my brother. But with McCabe, it feels maybe more like empathy—like he can relate, somehow. Not because his parents were neglectful, but because he lost them when he was still so young.

He turns onto his side, elbow bent so he can prop his head up and stare down at me with that intense green gaze. "Was it like that when you were younger too?"

"No . . . my mom was never super maternal. All she ever wanted to do with me was take me shopping, go to high tea at fancy hotels, go to brunch at the country club, that type of thing. But I was never interested in any of that. I had much more in common with my dad. He spent every spare minute with me, shaping me into the hockey playing son he wished he'd had . . ."

McCabe's low rumble of laughter shakes the whole bed, and when I dip my eyebrows in confusion over his response, he says, "Sorry." His eyes slip down my body and then back up to my face. "I just have trouble imagining you as someone's son."

"You know what I mean. It was no secret that my dad wanted a boy, so I put tremendous energy into connecting with him in the same ways he'd have connected to a son. It's probably the only reason we had a relationship."

What I don't say is that it took me years of therapy as an adult to finally realize that my compulsive need to be the best at everything stems from the years of trying to live up to what my dad wanted me to be—which was someone else.

I got lucky in that I really did develop a true love of hockey, but I do sometimes wonder who I'd be if I hadn't been trying so hard to fit a mold of someone else's creation.

Maybe I'd be the same me, but maybe I'd be someone entirely different?

"He wasn't like that with Nicholas, though?"

My single shot of laughter is bitter. "No, once he finally got the son he'd always wanted, it was like he was no longer interested in being a dad. He was more like a grandpa . . . the kind that spends all day on the golf course with friends, but comes by for dinner and slips you a twenty-dollar bill as he pats you on the head on his way back out the door."

He lets out a *humph* that's half laugh, half contemplation. "I guess I just don't have any experience with parents who are so rich they spend all day shopping and on the golf course. What did your parents do for work?"

"My mom's family owned one of the largest department store chains in the Midwest, and my parents inherited it and then sold it for a fortune right before the advent of online shopping." The whole company went bankrupt within a few years after the sale, but my parents and their shareholders made out like bandits before its demise. I'd like to think I get my business sense from my dad, who saw which way the wind was blowing and made a calculated decision.

"So they were what . . . retired by the time Nicholas was born?"

"I guess I'd say they were so independently wealthy that work wasn't really a consideration. At that time, I was working hard to carve my own path. I probably should have taken over caring for him when I finished my MBA, but I was too focused on getting my foot in the door in hockey. I don't know how I would have managed also being a mom to him."

"How *did* you end up making the switch from coaching a women's college team to working in the NHL?"

I bite the inside of my cheek as I study his face, only a foot or so from mine. His voice is soft and coaxing, and it hits me that either he really doesn't know, or he wants to know if the rumors are true. And suddenly knowing which one makes all the difference.

"What have you heard?" I whisper.

He presses his lips together, then twists them to the side like he's deep in thought. I don't know if it's because he's trying to remember, or trying to decide how—or what—to tell me.

"Only the shit Chet said when he was running his mouth."

Fire runs through my blood at the thought of my ex-husband talking about me to his players. "Yeah? What did he say?"

"You were there." He reaches over, resting his forearm along my breastbone as he cups the side of my face in his hand.

Ohhh, so that time in the hallway.

"He said a lot of shit that day." I focus on my breathing, because it's still hard not to be upset when I think about everything that happened—everything that changed—in those few minutes in that hallway.

"If I remember correctly, he said you slept your way into your position."

"Ah, yes. One of his favorite lines." I roll my eyes to hide how much that still hurts.

"Why did he think that?"

The laugh that bursts out of me is probably the healthiest response I could have to that question. "Because he got me my first job in St. Louis."

His thumb strokes my cheek as his eyes skim over my face. "Yeah?"

"We'd been dating for a while, and a job in operations

opened up. With my experience in hockey and my degree in business, it was a perfect fit. I'd wanted to apply on my own, but he insisted on putting in a good word for me. At the time, he said he'd do anything it took to help me achieve my dreams. Now, I think he just wanted me to feel beholden to him."

"I'm inclined to think that you'd have gotten the job with or without his recommendation," he says, tilting his head with a pensive nod. "And you clearly didn't sleep your way to the top once you were there. You *earned* all of that. So what I'm hearing is, either he was jealous that you were more successful than he was—"

"Exactly."

"—or he was so insecure he actually believed the only reason you were with him in the first place was to get a job in the NHL. He wasn't worthy of you, so it wouldn't surprise me if that were true, too."

That thought had never crossed my mind. The idea that his own insecurity was what triggered that behavior would make a lot of things make a lot more sense. McCabe is still staring down at me, but the look on his face has changed.

It almost looks like he's proud of me? I'm not sure how I feel about that, but I feel myself softening a bit more toward him.

"I'm not sure. His whole attitude toward me changed so much that season—" I stop myself somewhat abruptly because, holy shit, was I about to just tell him the most private thing about me? Something that no one else outside my family knows?

His fingers tighten on my jaw as I try to look away, and

he angles my face back so there's no option but to look him in the eye.

"What happened?"

"It's nothing."

"If he hurt you . . . if he laid a single finger on you . . ."

"Trust me," I say, "the abuse was entirely emotional."

His entire body stiffens. "I'm going to need you to say more about that."

Tell him it's none of his business, my brain insists. But somehow, the gentleness I've seen from him the past couple of days, combined with his possessive and protective side, makes me want to spill all my secrets.

Don't do it . . .

I press my lips together, but even as I do so, I know I'm going to tell this man everything, even as I wonder why I can't stop myself . . . even as I warn myself that it's safer if he doesn't know.

Maybe there's a little part of me, some sick, twisted part, that needs to know if he'll have the same response Chet did.

"That was the year I had my uterus removed."

His thumb strokes my cheek, wiping away a tear I didn't intend to let loose.

"What happened? Are you okay?"

The absolute care and concern with which he asks those questions guts me. It couldn't possibly be more different from Chet's response.

"Yeah, I'm okay. I suffered from uterine fibroids, starting in my mid-twenties. Sometimes they're painless and people don't even know they have them. But I had . . ." I consider how much I want to tell him about my symptoms, and decide he doesn't need to know everything. " . . . significant side effects."

His thumb wipes away more tears, and he nods like he wants me to continue.

"I had two surgeries to remove them, but both times they came back within a year. My doctor said that after coming back twice, it was likely that would keep happening every time they were removed. Apparently, having fibroids the size of grapefruits lining your uterus will make you infertile, which meant it was unlikely I'd ever be able to have kids." I take a deep breath. "And given how painful they were, and that I'd be facing multiple surgeries in my future to keep removing them, I made the decision to have my uterus removed instead."

His scent, a combination of something earthy like wood, and fresh like laundry detergent, engulfs me as he leans down and brushes his lips across my forehead. Curling his arm next to my head, he uses it as a pillow so he can lay there, facing me.

I shouldn't turn on my side to face him fully. I shouldn't let him wrap his other arm around my back. I shouldn't continue my story. But when he asks what happened next, I find that I just want to keep talking.

"Chet didn't support my decision. He couldn't let go of the idea of us having kids one day and was convinced the next fibroid surgery would be successful."

"Please don't tell me you had them removed a third time."

I think back to the month-long recovery that sidelined me for a third summer in a row. "I did."

"And they came back?"

"Of course they did."

"Was he more reasonable about your choice after that?"

I can tell how sad my smile is by the way his lips turn down at the corners in response. His face keeps changing expression, and I wish I could hear the thoughts in his head.

"So what happened then?"

"I went ahead with the partial hysterectomy the following summer, even though he still didn't want me to." I watch his jaw tic. "And then once it was done, he had this whole narrative about how I always knew I wouldn't be able to have kids and I'd trapped him. I know he just wanted to put the blame on me, because he'd look like the asshole if he left me after all I'd gone through."

"He was already an asshole, either way," McCabe says with a humorless laugh.

"He put on a good show at the beginning. We were married for years before I started seeing his true colors. Honestly, I didn't even know that having kids was that important to him. I don't think it was, actually, until it was something I couldn't give him."

The way McCabe's hand is sliding down my arm, smoothing out the shiver that's rippled through my body at all these memories, has me practically melting into these sheets.

Why am I so relaxed around him? Why do I want to tell him things I've never told anyone outside my family?

"Is that where your marriage fell apart?"

"Yeah, that was kind of the nail in the coffin, so to speak. My hysterectomy was the summer before your last season in St. Louis. What you walked into in the hallway that day, it was one of the many fights we'd been having about me not being able to give him children."

"Did you guys consider adopting?"

I make the fakest shocked face I can as I say, "And ruin his perfect pedigree? The horror." I release a heavy sigh. "I even suggested a surrogate, since I'd had eggs removed and frozen during my last surgery, but he wouldn't hear of it."

In reality, I think I'd wanted kids more than Chet did. He just wanted something to hold over my head. I'd been angry at myself for years after I finally figured that out. But now, I just feel sad that I wasted so much time and emotional energy on him, and on trying to save our sham of a marriage.

"And you wanted kids?" He asks the question tentatively, like he knows the answer but wants to make sure he's not making assumptions.

I didn't intend to tell him any of this. It feels way too personal to share with someone I hardly know. Lying here with him, while the light has faded and the moon has risen, makes it feel like we're in our own little world—one where I'm not his boss, and he's not a hot-headed hockey player I don't even like. Instead, we're just two people connecting on a deeper level.

I gulp, trying to push down all the emotions rising to the surface. "More than anything."

His gaze searches mine, brow pinched slightly. "How did he not see how much you were hurting, and support you through that?" He shakes his head before adding, "How do you treat someone you love that way?"

"I'm pretty sure that the only person Chet loves is himself. You want to know the real kicker in all this?"

He sighs, and his warm breath mingles with mine in the small space between our bodies. "Please don't tell me it gets worse."

"The day you walked in on us fighting . . . I'd just found out he was cheating on me. With a woman who had a kid. And after I kicked him out, he went running straight to her. Ended up marrying her and adopting her daughter." I swallow down the thick lump in my throat and press my hand to my chest to relieve some of the pain that's gathering there. "It wasn't that he didn't want to adopt, he just didn't want *me*."

McCabe scoops me into his arms, pulling me against his body so quickly I barely move my right hand out of the way before it would have been crushed between us.

"He's a fucking idiot, Alessandra," he murmurs into my hair. "Don't convince yourself that this had anything to do with you. This was him, desperately trying to have the upper hand when he realized he'd married someone who was better than him in every single way imaginable."

With my eyes closed and my forehead resting against the hollow space at the base of his neck, secure and warm, wrapped in his arms, I feel like a weight has been lifted. I feel like I can breathe again.

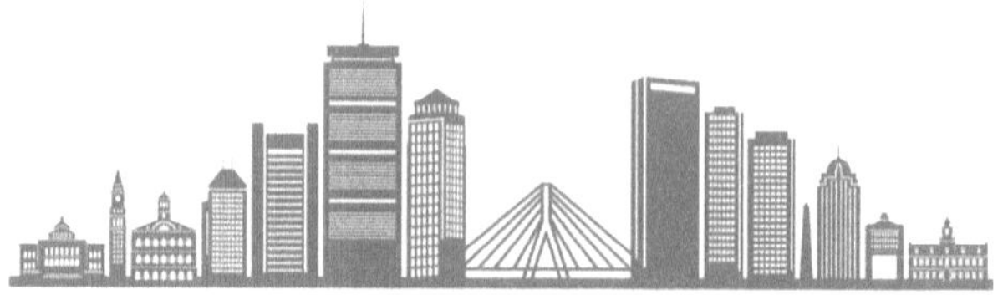

Chapter Twenty-One

McCabe

When I open my eyes, AJ's still wrapped up in my arms where we must have fallen asleep last night. But now she's got one leg slung over my hip, and in my sleep, my body must have felt hers pressed up against me, because I'm fully hard in a way that has my dick screaming to be taken care of.

Frozen in place, not wanting to wake her up, I take a few minutes to study the light smattering of freckles dusting the tops of her cheeks, right under her eyes. I'm guessing they're normally covered by makeup, but with the bright early morning light streaming in the windows, I can see them now, where last night's low light hid them from me.

I'm trying to determine the best way to extricate myself from her embrace without waking her, so I can figure out what time it is and how soon I need to leave for morning skate, when I hear banging in the hallway.

"C'mon, McCabe, we don't have time for this!" Walsh's voice carries into AJ's room.

I press my eyelids together. *Fuck, this can't be happening.*

He bangs a few more times on the door across the hallway, which has AJ stirring. Holding a finger to her lips before she can speak, I sit up, looking for my phone. It's behind me, face down on the bed, where it must have landed after falling out of my pocket.

When I tap the screen, I have a dozen texts and two missed calls from Walsh. Fuck, I fell asleep and didn't turn my ringer on last night, like I always do when I'm on the road in case there's any kind of emergency with Abby.

I shoot off a quick text.

MCCABE

Sorry. Went on an early morning run and lost track of time. Just got back. Give me two minutes. I'll meet you downstairs.

WALSH

Fuck that. You're already ten minutes late.
I'm waiting at your door so I can make sure
you get down to the bus.

Shit. I need him out of this hallway so I can get over to my room without him seeing me coming out of AJ's room.

MCCABE

Just go downstairs. I swear I'll be two
minutes behind you.

WALSH

Well you need to think up a better excuse by
the time you get on that bus, especially after
you were late to the plane last week.

I glance at AJ as she sits up next to me.

Fuck my life. I wouldn't trade last night, and having her fall asleep in my arms, for anything. But why couldn't I have remembered to set an alarm? Or even just woken up fifteen minutes ago?

"I'm so sorry," I whisper, in case Walsh is still in the hall-way. "I overslept and the team is waiting for me to go to morning skate."

"You'd better go, then." Her words are kind, but emotion-less. I can't tell at all how she's feeling. She doesn't look worried that I'm late, or sad that I have to go. But she also doesn't look like she regrets the conversation we had last night or the way we fell asleep together, so that's a plus, I guess? God, I wish she was easier to read. The aspects of her personality that make her so good at her job are the same ones that make her impossible to figure out.

You don't want to get close to her. You want to move to Nashville.

At this point, reminding myself of these things feels a little ridiculous. Yes, I want to live closer to my sister, but that doesn't in any way, shape, or form, mean I don't also want to let myself grow emotionally and physically closer to AJ.

In fact, I don't want *any* boundaries between us at all. I want to know her inside and out. I want to be there for her like no one else ever has. I don't even know what that looks like; I've never had that type of relationship with anyone. But I want to, with her.

"I know," I say. But I make no move to get up.

"McCabe. *Go*. And when you get down to that bus, please have an excuse for being late that doesn't involve accidentally falling asleep in my bed." A small smile plays at the corner of her lips, and I've never felt so relieved in my life.

"I went on a run this morning and lost track of time. Got back to the hotel late." I shrug. "Oops."

She puts her hand on my lower back and pushes. "Hurry the hell up."

"Fine," I grumble, standing and then turning to look down at her. I bend to kiss the top of her head, then say, "Don't think we're not finishing that conversation from last night."

She looks down at the floor. "There's nothing left to say."

Tilting her chin up so she's looking at me, I take in the worry in her eyes. "Like hell there isn't. But I have to go before I get fined for being late." I couldn't give a shit about the fine, but I do care about playing tonight and don't want to be on Coach's bad side.

"Good luck tonight," she says, putting a hand on my hip and pushing me toward the door.

I glance over my shoulder as I walk away, trying to memorize what she looks like sitting there in her shorts and a Rebels t-shirt, hair a mess and still looking half-asleep. God, I could get used to this view.

When I peek through the viewfinder, I don't see anyone, so I pat my pocket to make sure I still have my room key, then crack the door open and peek out. Walsh definitely isn't standing there anymore, so I swing the door to AJ's room open and take a step across the hallway to my door. And as I hold the keycard up to the reader, I peer down the hallway by the alcove for the elevators—and that's when I see Walsh, standing there watching me.

I sink into a stretch on the ice right next to Walsh. Too close to him, if I'm being honest, but I'd like our conversation to remain private. "That wasn't what it looked like, this morning."

Around us, the stands are starting to fill in with the fans here to watch warmups. I've been trying to talk to Walsh all day, but he's clearly avoiding me. He's like our team dad, and I hate feeling like I've disappointed him.

"Oh yeah? What did it look like?"

"I'm not sure, honestly. Probably like I was shacking up with some chick in the hotel last night, and that's why I was late for practice?"

He gives me the side-eye but doesn't say anything.

"That's not what happened," I insist.

"So what did happen, exactly?"

I thought long and hard today about what I wanted to tell Walsh, and Grandma's words kept running through my mind: *Oh, what a tangled web we weave, when first we practice to deceive.* I can't be fully honest with him, but the less I lie, the easier it will be to keep track of my story. Still, that doesn't mean I have to tell him everything.

I glance around to make sure we're not within earshot of anyone else. "First of all, that was AJ's hotel room."

His mouth hangs open, and he seems to have forgotten how to form words.

"Again, it's not what it looks like."

"Good to know. So, what *is* it then?"

"I'm just helping her out because she hurt herself

protecting Abby at the last game. With her dominant hand unusable, there's a lot she can't do. Like lift and open her suitcase, for example. Since I happened to be across the hall from her, I was just helping."

"Oh yeah, and what did she need this morning?" he asks. The tone of the question implies that he doesn't believe that whatever's going on is platonic. Which is fair, since from my perspective, anyway, it's not.

"She couldn't get the ironing board set up with one hand." This feels like a realistic reason she'd need someone with two functioning hands to help her, and it's a small lie that I can keep track of.

"Who uses a fucking iron these days?" Walsh asks with a laugh.

"You've seen her, right? I assume that's why her suits look that crisp even on the road."

"I can't even imagine seeing her not looking all buttoned up," Walsh says. Until a few days ago, neither could I.

She's such a rock-solid figure in this organization. But I'm learning that her tough exterior isn't all there is to her. Now, I practically live for those moments where she's casual, relaxed, and more open than I'm used to seeing her.

And then, there was last night. Holding her while she cried after opening up to me about her failed marriage—it broke something in me, too.

If the feeling was just physical attraction, I could deny myself what I want with her like I've always done. But now?

Now that I know she's not just stunning and great with my daughter, but she's also vulnerable—she's suffered, loved and lost and, most importantly, is willing to be open with me about it? Whatever lock I was keeping on my feelings has fully broken open.

"Yeah," I say, the word clipped. "It's hard to imagine that she doesn't wake up with her makeup on and her hair done, and wearing a perfectly pressed suit. Maybe she's human after all."

Walsh's laugh is more like an annoyed huff. "Given the way you've always treated her, it's not a huge surprise that you thought she was some sort of professional robot or something."

I'm about to ask what the fuck that's supposed to mean when I realize that he's right. I never hid my dislike very well. "Yeah, well, I can admit when I'm wrong."

Walsh nods as he rises so that he's standing over me. "Good. Now let's try to win this game without you rushing off the ice at the end." He pokes me in the shoulder with his stick and gives me a nod of his chin to indicate he's just giving me shit. "Okay?"

"Yeah. It's time we turn this series around." And when we head back to the locker room after warmups, that's exactly what I tell my teammates. I say all the things I should have said last time AJ asked me to talk to them. I give them the pep talk they need from their captain instead of the few grumbled words I normally say.

I lead by example, not just in the locker room, but when we take the ice. It's a textbook-perfect game on my part, and after my hat trick—the one that AJ had said it'd been too long since she'd seen—I look for her in the stands and find her standing right behind the bench like she so often is.

She's not celebrating like she was when I scored in the

last game. Instead, she's narrowing her eyes on me, like she's trying to figure out why I'm on fire tonight.

I raise both eyebrows at her and think: *Maybe I just found my good luck charm.*

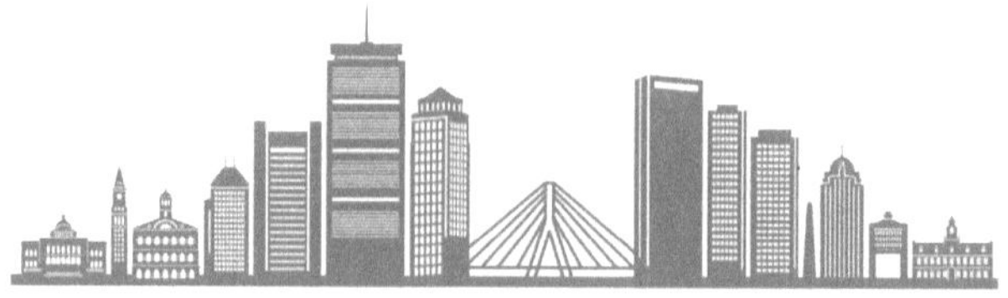

Chapter Twenty-Two

McCabe

I'm nursing my third and final beer of the night, when AJ finally responds to the text I sent her an hour ago.

MCCABE

You doing okay? Need anything?

SUNSHINE

I'm fucking fantastic.

I tap on the photo that comes through. It appears to be a glass bottle, shattered in a puddle of liquid on a tile floor.

SUNSHINE

How about you?

MCCABE

What happened?

SUNSHINE

I was trying to open this bottle of makeup
remover one-handed, and it slipped and
broke. Now I'm cleaning it up with a towel.

MCCABE

Need help?

SUNSHINE

No, I've got it. I'm just frustrated that I STILL
can't use my damn hand.

MCCABE

It's been three days. You heard the doctor,
you need to give it time to heal.

SUNSHINE

Easy for you to say. You're not the one trying
to do everything one-handed.

I glance up then, and the entire table of my teammates are staring back at me.

"What?"

"Dude," Zach laughs. "Everything okay?"

"Yeah, why?"

He and Drew exchange a glance. "You were just so lost in whatever message you were sending that when the waitress came up and asked if you wanted another beer"—he nods toward my almost empty pint glass on the table—"you didn't even acknowledge her."

"So, who's Sunshine, anyway?" Walsh asks from beside me.

Have we always been this fucking nosy about each other's lives? Thank god I changed her name in my contacts, because if I'd just been that lost in a texting conversation with my boss, there'd be a lot of questions.

"It's my nickname for Abby," I say, while mentally chastising myself for the lies. If I keep piling them on, it's going to be hard to remember them. "That's just a text thread with her nanny. He was updating me on the day."

They don't need to know that I already talked to Nicholas when he FaceTimed me earlier this afternoon so I could see Abby before I left for my game.

Walsh nods, but from his expression, it's clear he doesn't believe me. Drew, Zach, and Colt look less suspicious.

"Anyway, I have to go. He needs to talk to me about . . . an appointment she has tomorrow." I scoot out of the booth and say, "Let me know what I owe for my drinks, and I'll send someone the money."

———

She leans against the partially open door, her arms crossed over her stomach, as she asks, "What are you doing here?"

"Well, that's one way to congratulate me on the win tonight." I hold up the pharmacy bag with one hand and push the door open with the other. "I got you something."

Backing into the room as I step inside, AJ looks up at me with a lifted eyebrow. "I don't remember inviting you in."

"Seemed prudent not to stand in the hallway where anyone could see me." As the door clicks shut behind me, I hand her the paper bag.

She reaches into it and pulls out a small glass bottle. I'm not one hundred percent sure it's the same one she had, but it's a glass bottle with a black lid like the one I saw in the picture.

"You . . . got me makeup remover?"

Is it my imagination, or does she sound touched? That thought pisses me off, because replacing something she accidentally broke feels like such a minor thing—yet I don't think she's ever had someone to do that for her. Not a guy, at least. I've never wanted to punch Chet in the fucking face more than I do right now, and that's saying something.

Setting the bag aside, her eyes meet mine, and I see the war raging in her gaze. She doesn't want to want me here, but she does.

I understand the feeling completely.

I shouldn't want her. I shouldn't be here with her. It makes every single thing about my life more complicated, and I don't do complicated. But no matter how hard I try, I can't seem to convince myself that I don't want her.

And now, I've decided to stop trying.

If she doesn't want me in return, she can be honest about that, and I'll respect her decision. But I'm pretty sure we're in the exact same boat here.

"Would you like me to leave?" I ask her.

She works her lower lip between her teeth like she's considering my question, and I step closer.

"You need to stop doing that." My voice is low, almost feral with the longing that courses through me at her proximity. No one else has ever made me feel so damn needy, so desperate for her attention and affection. I would have thought I'd hate this feeling, but I don't hate it. Not at all.

Her look is coy as she releases her now-glistening lower lip. "Doing what?"

I turn toward her, and she takes a step back, right into the wall behind her. The quick grunt of pain she lets out as she winces reminds me that her entire back is bruised.

"Fuck, I'm sorry," I say, pressing my hand against the wall next to her head as I lean in. "Are you okay?"

"McCabe." Her voice holds that warning tone that turns me on. "You shouldn't . . ."

"Be here. I know." My throat bobs as I swallow, and her eyes focus on the motion, but she doesn't respond. "Tell me to leave."

As she glances up at me this time, her tongue darts out, running along the line of her upper lip, but still, she says nothing.

I lean in closer, my face a breath away from hers.

"You smell like beer," she says.

"That's because I just had a few with the guys to celebrate our win." I trail the bridge of my nose along her cheek until my lips reach her ear, relishing the way her breath catches. Dropping my voice even lower, I say, "Tell me to leave, AJ."

Her responding whimper has my entire body wanting to press into hers. But I'm not going to kiss her up against a wall without an open invitation to do so.

Not even when her hands rest on my chest before sliding up to my shoulders. Not even when she toys with the hair at the back of my neck. Not even when she parts her lips and sighs as she meets my gaze.

"Or tell me to stay."

One way or another, I need this woman to put me out of my fucking misery.

"Stay." The word is so quiet it's practically inaudible.

"Say it again, Sunshine. Nice and loud, so we're both clear that you want me here."

"Don't be a dick," she says, her fingers tightening in my hair and holding me in place when I try to step away.

"I'm not being a dick," I assure her, as I wrap my hand around the back of her neck while my thumb strokes the space where her jaw meets her ear. "I want to make sure that there's no miscommunication at all. Because *once is an accident*, but if I stay here with you again tonight, it's not an accident, and it's not a mistake. *It's a choice.*"

Her sigh is stuttered and halting, like the magnetic pull we're both experiencing makes it hard for her to even exhale. "We shouldn't . . ."

"I know we shouldn't." Dipping my head back toward her, I graze my lips over her forehead. "But are we?"

She tilts her head back against the wall and focuses on my face. The pink spreading across her cheeks, the ragged breathing, the way her eyes are practically black with desire . . . everything I'm seeing tells me she's feeling exactly the same way I am.

"Yes."

I don't know who moves first—we're tangled together so quickly it's impossible to tell. But her lips part instantly as she lets me invade her mouth, her tongue slanting against mine with utter possession. This is no languid kiss; this is the release of pent-up longing that's been locked away for far too long. I know how long I've wanted her, but this makes me wonder how long she's wanted me back.

She moans into my mouth as she presses forward, her entire body flush with mine. Bringing both my hands to her waist, I anchor her against me, pressing my cock into her stomach as my fingers slide up her sides under her shirt. I run my thumbs along the waistband of her shorts, while the tips of my fingers toy with the seam of her bra.

I'm so keyed up I feel like I might explode as she moans into my mouth again. When I pull back, breaking the kiss and giving my body a few inches of distance from hers, her eyes widen. "What are you doing?"

My voice is raspy when I say, "I need a second to breathe, to collect myself, or I'm not going to be able to take it slow."

She lets out a small huff of a laugh. "What in the world would make you think I wanted you to take things slow?"

"AJ . . ." I move my hand so I'm cupping her face in my palm as I give her the reminder we both need. "You're injured. The last thing I want to do is hurt you more."

"How about you let me be the one to decide what kind of pain I can endure? Because sometimes . . ." Reaching down, she cups her hand over the zipper of my pants, and as my balls tighten up, I'm afraid I'm about to embarrass myself. ". . . a little pain is . . . just . . . fine."

Holy shit.

"Well, I was going to take it easy on you, but sure, we can do things your way . . ." I slide my hands under her ass and pick her up so fast she gasps, laughing and wrapping her legs around me as I step into the bathroom because that's got the closest horizontal surface.

She's always beautiful. But a *laughing* Alessandra Jones? She's unbelievably gorgeous.

I set her on the counter, next to the sink, then step between her legs as I unbutton my dress shirt. In the pale glow of the light emanating from behind the large mirror, she watches my every movement carefully, like she's trying to memorize everything about my body the same way I did with her this morning while she slept.

When I toss my shirt on the floor outside the bathroom, she reaches out to undo my belt, then shakes her head when she remembers that one of her hands is splinted. I take that arm by the elbow, raising her hand to my lips. "I'd never have wanted you to get hurt like this. Never. But is it wrong that I'm the tiniest bit grateful that it led us here?"

"I don't know yet," she says, her voice breathless. "Why don't you take your pants off and make it worth my while?"

My chuckle fills the entire bathroom as I set her hand back in her lap. "You literally can't wait to get me naked."

Defiance takes over her face. "Don't tell me the same isn't true for you."

"Oh, Sunshine, I've been waiting for you for a fucking decade. I could wait longer . . . I *would* wait longer, if I had to."

Her lips part with a soft sigh. "Why do you have to keep saying things like that?"

"Because they're true."

"Ronan . . ."

God, I fucking love it when she uses my first name.

She stares up at me like she doesn't know what she wants to say next, so I plant my hands on either side of her and lean in close.

"Yeah, Sunshine?"

She clears her throat, and whatever sentimental thought she was having disappears. "You're wearing entirely too many clothes."

"As are you," I say, then grasp the hem of her t-shirt, lifting it over her head and carefully sliding it over her injured arm after she's pulled her head and her other arm through. Beneath it, she's wearing a nearly sheer bra with underwire cups. There's a ribbon of lace that runs from the center, across each breast, to the strap, and beneath it, her nipples are so hard they're pulling the lace away from her skin.

Hooking my thumbs under the fabric, I slide the cups down under her breasts so those pretty pink nipples are exposed, rubbing the rough pads of my thumbs up and over them. She's biting her lip as she moans out her pleasure, and her legs come around behind me, circling my waist and pulling me to her.

Dipping my head, I trail my tongue across one of her nipples while I continue toying with the other, then suck it into my mouth with a long pull that elicits another deep moan. Moving to the other side, I repeat the motion as she tilts her hips up, grinding her center right along my cock.

"Fuck," I groan as I pull back and take her in—how her nipples are wet and glistening where I hold her tits in my hands, the way she's anchored herself to my dick, how she's panting with longing. "You look good when you want my cock."

She glances down at where our bodies meet. "And you'd look a lot better without those pants on."

I unbuckle my belt slowly, watching her face as she focuses on my hands. I wonder if she even realizes how she's licking her lips in anticipation? I kick my shoes off, then hook my thumbs in my waistband, sliding both my pants and boxers down my thighs and letting them fall to my feet, where I kick them out the door into the hallway.

"Is this more to your liking, Sunshine?"

She drags her gaze up to mine like it's taking a lot of effort to tear her attention away from my cock, but the small smile on her face lets me know she likes what she sees. "I guess that depends."

"On what?"

"On what you plan to do with that thing."

I step back between her legs until my thighs hit the countertop and my dick is pressed up against her stomach. "Alessandra." Leaning in close, I cup her breasts in my hands again, sliding my thumbs over her nipples and making her squirm as I say, "My plan is to ruin you for every other man, forever. You just have to ask."

There's a momentary look of doubt that passes over her face, like I've pushed her too far and she's unwilling to ask for what she wants. And then it occurs to me that maybe no one has ever asked her what she wants. Maybe sex has never been about pleasing *her*. I hope that isn't the case, but given some of the things she opened up about last night, it wouldn't surprise me if that was true in her marriage, at least.

"I want you to make me feel good. I want to forget that my wrist hurts and that my ex-husband was a spineless dick and that we're still down one game in this series." She reaches up and presses her good hand to my breastbone before trailing her fingers down between my pecs and along the groove between my abs straight down to my waist. And when she wraps her fingers around my throbbing hard cock and runs her hand up and around the head before sliding back down to the shaft, my eyes roll back. I have to force myself to take a deep breath through my nose before I fucking pass out. "Go ahead." She nods and raises her eyebrows like she's challenging me. "Ruin me."

My mouth crashes into hers with a tortured moan and, like always, she meets my energy. But the long pulls of the kiss, the soft and eager sounds escaping her throat, combined with the way she's working her hand up and down my shaft, have me way too close. So I pull back, lifting her hips and sliding her thong down her legs, then dropping to my knees on the cold tile floor.

She lets loose a hiss that turns into a sigh as I bring my arms under her thighs, smoothing my hands over her hips and then resting my palms on her lower abdomen as I use my thumbs to spread her pussy open in front of me.

Her silky pink skin glistens with her arousal, and when I lean in to taste her, she releases a shuddering breath. As my tongue works circles around and over her clit, she gasps once and then once more before sinking into the sensation, her hips beginning to move to the rhythm I'm setting. A small moan escapes her parted lips, and when my eyes flick up to hers, she clamps her lips between her teeth like she's embarrassed by her reaction.

"No way, Sunshine," I tell her. "Those sexy moans belong to me. I'm working for them, and I want to hear them. I need to know what this does to you, and you're going to tell me . . . or I'm going to stop."

"Oh my god," she says on a gasp as she leans back, resting her shoulders and head against the mirror. "Don't you dare fucking stop."

"Then don't hold back." I lean forward again, licking her from the bottom of her pussy up to her clit, and back. "Tell me what you like."

"This," she pants, and I return to lavishing her clit with my undivided attention. And when my chin is soaked with the evidence of her arousal, I change the angle of my face so I can press two fingers to her entrance.

Her gasps and moans, her sweet scent, the warmth of her body—they all consume my senses, and I swear I've never been more turned on by a woman in my life. I think I might die if I don't get to see her come undone for me.

"Yes," she encourages, looking down at me. "I want to feel you inside of me."

I slide my fingers into the tight space, and the way her pussy clenches has me moaning, too.

"Fuck yes," she says, then whimpers, "I'm so close. Oh my god . . ."

She's meeting my fingers thrust for thrust, the silky walls of her cunt clamping down on them so hard that I can't wait to know what she feels like on my cock. But first, I want to know what she feels like coming on my fingers and my face, so I curl my fingers inside her slightly, feeling the telltale ridges that I know will give her even more stimulation while clamping my lips around her clit and sucking her against my tongue.

"Oh fuck! I'm . . ." she trails off, words lost as she cries out while her muscles contract against my fingers and her legs shake where they rest over my shoulders. The almost inhuman sounds coming out of her mouth while she rides the waves of her orgasm have me on the verge of coming, but I hold back because there's no way I'm not feeling myself slide into her after this.

When she's done, her back slides down that mirror and her hips press forward into my face. It's like someone's taken all the bones out of her body, and she chuckles in response, saying, "I can't move. I think you broke me."

I rise, standing between her legs and leaning over her where her back and head now rest against the deep counter atop the vanity. "I'm pretty sure you're not broken. Seems like you work just fine."

I wrap one hand beneath her neck and my other arm beneath her lower back so I can bring her up to sitting. Moving my hand from behind her neck to cup her jaw, I say, "Kiss me. I want you to taste yourself on my tongue."

"What?" The word barely squeaks out as her eyes widen.

"You've never tasted how sweet you are?"

"No. That's . . ." For a moment, I think she's going to refuse me, but then she wraps her hand around my neck, pulling me to her. The kiss is tentative, like she's not sure what she's going to find when her lips part and she meets my tongue with hers. But I deepen the kiss, holding her against me, rubbing my cock along her abdomen and feeling the way her nipples scrape along my ribs. And when she wraps her lower legs around mine, her calves pulling me into her even harder, that's when I know she still wants more.

Tilting her head back, I break the kiss and enjoy her resulting whimper. Her face is pouty, like I've just taken away something she wants. I'm living for this side of her— where she's not trying to hide how she feels about me.

I lift her hips, setting her on the tile floor and turning her to face the mirror. Standing behind her, I move her hair off her back, sliding it over her left shoulder so I can dip my head down to her ear. Without breaking eye contact in the mirror, I ask, "Have you ever watched anyone fuck you?"

Her jaw drops open slightly, and then she glides her

tongue along her upper lip. Out of pure instinct, my fingers curl around her hip bones as I press my cock into her lower back.

"Because I want you to see how fucking magnificent you look when you come."

Her eyebrows scrunch in question, creating an adorable divot between them. "But I already came."

"And you're going to come again, this time on my cock."

The vibrations of her shaky exhale ripple against me, and I press my hips forward into her again.

"I can't . . ." she pauses, and I wait her out. ". . . come that way."

"You've *never* come that way, or you *can't*?" I ask, but either way I'm determined to prove her wrong. She can, and she will.

Her eyes lock with mine in the mirror, and with a roll of her eyes, she says, "Same difference."

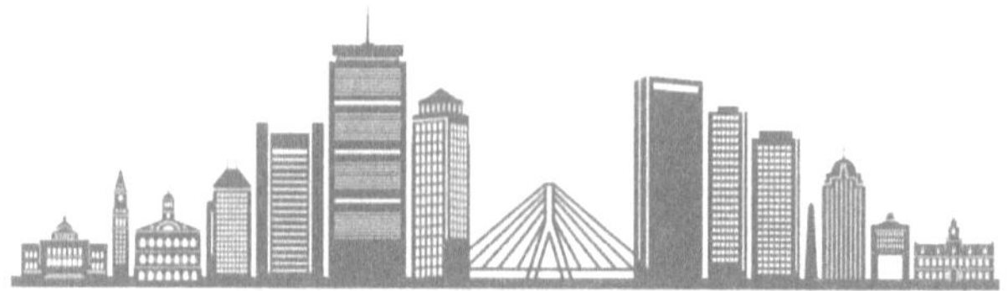

Chapter Twenty-Three

AJ

"No," he says, his voice hard as he grinds the words out between clenched teeth. "It's not."

I hate the way my cheeks turn pink as I watch us in the mirror, so I turn my head away as I explain, "Lots of women can't have an internal orgasm."

His hand slides from my hip up my abdomen and between my breasts, his forearm grazing my nipple, before he settles with his hand around my throat. I like the possessive feel of his hand there—hell, the feel of his hands *everywhere*—maybe more than I should.

With his palm still cupping my throat, he uses two fingers on my jaw to turn my head so I'm facing the mirror again.

"Just because you can't have an internal orgasm doesn't mean you can't orgasm during sex," he says. I know my face conveys my confusion because he shakes his head and adds, "My god, has no one ever taken care of you?"

There's a lot of emotion in his words, and I wish I was

better at reading him. I can't tell if he's mad at that idea, or sad about it. My mind runs through all the ways *he's* taken care of me in the past few days—physically, emotionally, and sexually. Before him, though . . . not so much.

He presses a kiss to my temple. "You're going to come on my cock, and it's not going to be a one-time thing. Do you trust me?"

In the quiet bathroom, my gulp is audible, and I watch myself give him a single nod. I don't know why I trust him, when all the men in my life disappoint me.

That's not true, I remind myself, instead focusing on the positive relationships I have with men who don't suck: Nicholas, Jameson, Frank. There are plenty of guys on the team who are good, standup men too. *Don't let your father and Chet destroy your trust in half the species.*

McCabe said he was going to ruin me for all other men, and after that earth-shattering orgasm he just gave me, I believe him. Clearly, he's a man of his word. If he makes me come again, *during* sex, he truly will have achieved his goal, because no one else has ever done that for me.

But since I can't be with him in any other way than these stolen moments, ruining me for anyone else feels like maybe I'm inviting a lifetime of sexual frustration?

"What's going through your mind right now?" he asks, and that's when I realize that even though I gave him the go ahead, he hasn't moved. He's still got one hand wrapped around my throat possessively and his lips pressed to my temple.

In the mirror, I watch the way my chest heaves, certain he can feel the thumping of my heart beneath his forearm where it's pressed against my breast.

"Nothing," I whisper.

"Don't fucking lie to me, Alessandra. Not when you're standing here naked, wrapped in my arms. If you've got any doubts about us having sex, we'll wait."

I'm shaking my head before he's even finished. "It's not that."

His other hand comes from my hip to toy with the ends of my hair, the backs of his fingers moving against my breast where it lays. "What is it, then?"

How do I tell him that I'm afraid sex with him will be too good? That instead of getting it out of my system so I can stop thinking about him, it'll make me crave him even more?

"When you said you were going to ruin me for all other men, forever? I'm afraid you might not have been exaggerating."

His chest shakes against my shoulders with a low rumble of laughter. The timbre of his voice is a soft caress when he says, "I wasn't exaggerating. Why? Do you *plan* to sleep with other men after me?"

My gaze locks on his in the mirror, breath catching as I take in the vulnerability in his eyes. "How could this ever work between us?"

Without breaking eye contact, he presses another kiss to my temple. "How could it not?"

It's a crazy thing to say.

Isn't it?

Because there's no way this can work, and we both know why. But at this moment, I'm having trouble recalling all the reasons. They feel like a problem for future me to deal with, because the way his hard cock is pressing into my back and his hot breath is warming my skin, the way he's cradled my entire body in his embrace—the only thing I feel . . . is safe.

This is a man who will take care of me. And after a recent injury and a lifetime of mediocre sex, I could use a man who knows how to make me feel good.

My hips arch back into his as longing ripples through my core, and I take his hand that's toying with my hair and move it to the apex of my thighs. And when the pad of his finger ghosts over my clit, still swollen and sensitive from my last orgasm, my entire body shudders.

"Taking care of your needs feels like the bare fucking minimum, Alessandra. And if doing that ruins you, then prepare to be spoiled senseless."

I want to ask him what he means, because this is just sex. But the way he's dipping his finger inside me and using my cum as lubricant to slide his finger over my clit has my good hand flying to his forearm, grasping it as I press my head back into his chest and look up at him with wide eyes. How am I already turned on again this quickly?

He presses his lips to mine in a firm kiss, and then asks, "Do you want me to use a condom?"

He knows I can't get pregnant—something no guy I've slept with after my ex-husband needed to know, because I never let a relationship get serious enough that I'd share that information.

"Are you positive you're safe?"

"Yeah," he grits out as he flexes his hips forward, his cock sliding along my lower back. "But if you'd prefer, we can use one. I've never not."

My eyes search his. How is that possible? "But . . . Abby?"

He shrugs his shoulders. "Sometimes condoms break.

And I've been tested, just in case. But again, we can use one if you're more comfortable."

His finger is still gliding over my clit, slowly working me up, and I press my teeth into my lower lip as I try to think clearly.

"Goddamn, you're so sexy when you bite your lip like that. You do it all the time, and it drives me fucking insane."

Letting go of his forearm, I slide my hand between us and grip him firmly, enjoying the grunt of pleasure he lets out as I move my hand up and over the fat head of his cock. I'm honestly not sure how this thing is going to fit inside me, but I'm looking forward to finding out.

He slips two fingers inside me and says, "Or we can do it this way. I'm pretty sure I'm going to last about two seconds anyway. I've got a fucking decade of pent-up sexual frustration when it comes to you, and you've already got me so turned on I'm about to explode."

"I want to feel you inside me." I give him a sassy little wink as I add, "I think you promised to make me come on your cock?"

"Put your hands on the mirror." It's a demand, not a request.

I lick my lips as I lean forward, putting my good hand against the mirror and resting my splinted hand on top of it. And then I look over my shoulder at him and say, "Don't make me wait."

He presses harder against my clit, and a strangled moan escapes from the back of my throat as I watch him spread his legs to line himself up with my entrance. "Tell me if I'm hurting you."

I'm so worked up I can only nod in response. And when

he notches his cock at my entrance, sliding in slowly, I straighten my good arm and push myself back onto him, gasping as he stretches me. I'm so fucking full; every inch of space is filled with him until I feel like I can't breathe.

"You're doing so well. We're almost there."

Almost? What the hell is this man talking about? There is no room for any more of him.

He bends forward, trailing kisses along my shoulder. "C'mon, you can take all of me. Just relax."

"I. Am. Relaxed," I grit out between clenched teeth.

"Listen, Sunshine," he says, pulling out slightly and then sliding right back in. The sensation of his length gliding along my inner walls eases some of the pain from being stretched so full. "I wanted to take this slow. You're the one who decided to impale yourself on my cock." He plants one hand next to mine on the mirror, and wraps his other around my hips, anchoring me to him. "So why don't you let me take over here?"

My eyes widen at his domineering tone, as I meet his lust-filled gaze in the mirror. "Don't be condescending when you're inside me."

He tilts his chin down, his lips resting right against my ear so his words are like a low growl flowing into me. "I get that you like having control, that you're used to being in charge." He pulls out and slides back into me again, and my eyelids flutter shut for a moment as my lips part, because the feeling is just too good. "But for once, I need you to let me be in charge. I promise, I will take very good care of you."

My whole body relaxes, like it realizes it can trust him. And now that my shoulders aren't so tense, it allows my back to arch more and my hips to loosen.

"Such a good girl," he says, straightening up and using his hand to trace patterns around the bruises on my back. His touch is feather light, so instead of causing me pain, it makes me shiver.

And then he's slowly moving inside me, setting a pace that only makes me want more. The drag of his skin against mine, the crude sound of our bodies slapping together, his soft grunts and my quiet moans—it's the sexiest fucking thing I've ever experienced.

"Look at you," he murmurs, staring down at where our bodies meet. "Taking me so well, just like I knew you would."

I rock myself back onto him, trying to increase the pace because he has me feeling like I can't get enough of him. I can't get enough of him being inside me, but I also can't get enough of the way he's looking at me—it's hunger and adoration combined. He's worshiping my body as he moves his hand from my hip back down to my clit, gently pressing as he moves his finger over it again and again. It's then I realize that he'll do whatever it takes to make me feel good.

And that realization is the thing that allows me to finally let go. To give up any control I'm clinging to, to bring down any barriers I've put up, to fully enjoy the moment without worrying about what it means or what comes next.

"That's right," he praises, his teeth clenched and the words barely audible over my moans of pleasure. I watch my breasts bouncing as I sink back onto him, his one hand focused on my clit as he brings the other to the base of my neck, squeezing just enough to give me a thrill.

I'm panting and needy, letting out more sounds I don't recognize each time he bottoms out in me, letting the sensations roll through my body as he fucks me in a way I didn't know was possible—in a way that's all about my pleasure.

There's an ache building inside me, an electric feeling I've never experienced before. And as if he knows exactly what I need in order to turn that current up all the way, he brings his hand from my neck to my breast, rolling my nipple between his fingers. Sparks shoot through me, like lightning in my veins, until I'm practically screaming.

He reaches over and slams the bathroom door shut right before I tip over the edge, moaning out his name and god's name, plus several expletives, interchangeably, as he buries himself deep inside me. With the sexiest groan I've ever heard, I feel his release shooting against my inner walls as he comes, because there's no room for it inside me. And as he pulls out and presses back in one more time, his cum runs down my leg.

It's the most erotic and dirty thing that's ever happened to me, and I know without a doubt that I need this again. I had no idea sex could be like this, and I need more of this—more of him—in my life.

His upper body falls forward, his hand bracing him above me as he kisses the crown of my head before whispering reverently, "You're fucking spectacular, you know that?"

"That *felt* spectacular," I murmur, closing my eyes because I'm absolutely spent.

He gathers my hair in his hand and presses a kiss on the back of my neck. "You didn't do what you were told, though."

"Oh yeah?" I ask, in a daze.

"Yeah. I told you to watch, so you could see how you look when you come. But you closed your eyes when you got there."

"I couldn't help it." I'm still unable to open my eyes or lift my head. "I was . . . overcome."

"Next time," he says, leaving more sweet kisses on my skin, "I want you to watch."

"Next time, huh?" My words are teasing, but we both know there will be a next time. How could there not be when it feels that good?

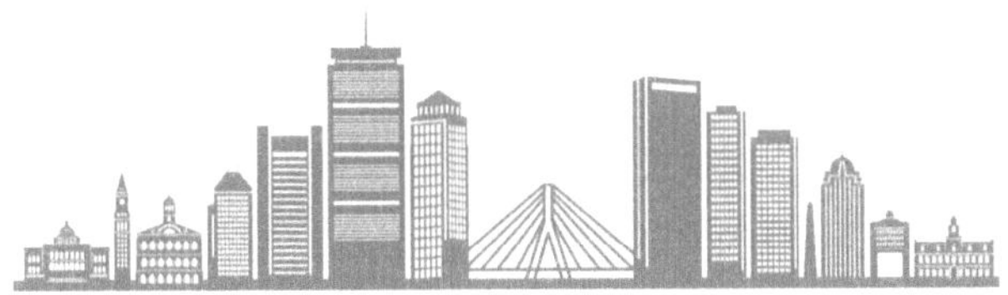

Chapter Twenty-Four

McCabe

My heart pounds so hard and fast I can feel it rattling against my ribcage. My breath is coming in short, deep pants, and my entire body is on high alert as the blood races through my veins.

"Hey," a sweet, soft voice soothes as I feel a warm hand press against my cheek. "Hey, it's okay."

What the hell?

I open my eyes, and even in the darkness, I can see AJ lying next to me, her face only inches from mine. She swings her leg over my hips, pulling me to her in a full-body hug.

"What . . .?" I exhale.

"You were having a nightmare."

And then it all comes tumbling back—standing on the ice, the glass separating me from the crowd as I watched AJ get pushed forward with Abby strapped to her.

"I . . . In my dream, we were back at that game when the fight broke out in the stands, but instead of you falling backward, you fell forward and landed with Abby underneath you." I woke up right as they hit the seats in front of them, but my body's reacting like I just watched my child get crushed between the hard seat backs and AJ's body.

Realistically, I know she might have been able to break that fall without injuring Abby because her hands would be in front of her, but all I can picture in my mind is Abby getting crushed. That fall could have had a catastrophic outcome, and my mind clearly can't let go of that, even though Abby is safe and AJ's injuries were much less severe than they could have been.

Leaning forward, she kisses my forehead while smoothing the furrowed line of my brow with her thumb. "Everything's okay. Abby's just fine."

"Yeah, but you're not," I say, running my hand down her arm until I get to the splint that's around her wrist.

"I'm fine, really." Her voice is vulnerable in the quiet, and it's such a turn-on to see this other side of her, when she's not wearing the armor she shows up in every day. "The swelling has mostly gone down, and when we get back to Boston, they'll put a cast on. I'll be good as new once it's healed."

I'd traced the bruises on her back last night while buried inside her, thankful she wasn't hurt worse but also feeling the double-edged sword of guilt, knowing that if she hadn't been injured at that game, then we probably wouldn't be here, together.

Or maybe we would be? This thing between us was set in motion when I kissed her in her office, but her injury definitely accelerated things—gave me a reason to see her more, gave her less of an opportunity to push me away.

My voice is still gruff from sleep when I tell her, "It shouldn't have happened in the first place. I should have spoken up about the fans' behavior when you asked me to—"

"I doubt that would have prevented what happened."

"We'll never know because I didn't do what I should have. But I will. You just need to have someone ask me about the fighting again." There were no questions about it after last night's game, which could mean a lot of different things—either people have already forgotten about it, or the reporter who asked at the home game wasn't at our away game, or AJ meant what she said about not asking me again until I'd gotten some coaching around what to say.

When I ask her about it, she says, "I think that you need to talk to someone in PR about this before you're asked again."

Pulling her tight against me, I kiss her forehead. Outside, I can hear the low thrum of a city on the verge of waking up, while the soft orangey light of sunrise filters through the slit where the heavy hotel room curtains meet.

"It's early. Let's go back to sleep and we can talk about it later."

She murmurs her agreement and rolls over, snuggling her back into me so I'm spooning her. I lie there, my thoughts still running wild as I listen to her breathing slow and become more rhythmic, until I'm certain she's sleeping.

My body is often restless when I first wake up, like it can't wait to start moving again. I know there's no way I'm falling back asleep, so I cuddle her until I can't stay still any longer. When I roll away from her and stand up, she doesn't move. So I pull my clothes back on quietly, grab my phone off the nightstand where I left it last night, and slip out of her room almost silently.

I'm thankful it's early enough that I don't run into any of my teammates in the hallway. I bet most of them are sleeping off the partying from last night. With a big win yesterday and no practice today, everyone celebrated—even Colt, Drew, Zach, and Walshy, who rarely go out after the games except to grab some dessert.

I change and then shoot her a text so she'll know why I'm not in her bed when she wakes up.

MCCABE

I couldn't fall back asleep, so I'm going to the hotel gym. If you don't have plans today, don't make any.

I'm half an hour into my workout when Colt and Drew amble into the small exercise room in the hotel. They're mid-conversation as they open the door, chatting about Colt and Jules's engagement, and freeze when they see me.

"You're up early," Colt says as he takes the bike next to me, while Drew heads to the treadmill. Running is my nemesis . . . something I do only when forced to.

"Couldn't sleep," I say, but as I reach for the towel hanging on the handlebars and bring it to my forehead to wipe away the sweat dripping from my hair, I catch a whiff of AJ's scent—sweet but musky—on my hand. I press down the memories of last night that resurface at the smell of her, and focus on the way Colt is rambling about how he can't sleep anymore without Jules.

"Oh, how the mighty have fallen," I joke.

"You'll see," he says. "Someday, you'll meet that person

you can't live without. Everything changes then, and you'll wonder how you survived before."

I glance sideways at him, afraid to turn toward him because I'm not sure what he'll see on my face. Because in my head, I'm thinking: *Is AJ that person for me?*

For as long as I've harbored this attraction to her, I never truly envisioned a scenario where things could work out for us. Not until recently.

Suddenly, I don't want a life where I don't get to see her chatting away to Abby in her highchair in the morning while she sips the coffee I made her, where I don't get to bury myself inside her every night while telling her how fucking magnificent she is.

But I don't know if that's what she wants.

"Dude," Colt laughs, the low rumble rolling out of him from beside me. "Something you want to tell us?"

I glance up, and though the treadmill is facing the wall, Drew's watching our conversation in the mirror with interest. That's when I notice his headphones are still around his neck, so he's clearly listening as well. Thank god Walshy isn't here, because given what he knows about AJ and me, it would be easy for him to assume there's something romantic going on.

I bark out a laugh, like the idea of me having feelings for someone is ridiculous. "Yeah, like I have time to have a woman in life."

"You dated that chick, what's her name . . . "

"Annabelle," Drew chimes in, and I'm not even sure how he knows that.

"Yeah, that's the one. You dated her in the fall," Colt reminds me.

"Which is when I realized the only girl I have time for is Abby."

What I actually realized in dating her was that most women aren't interested in a guy who already has a kid with another woman.

Colt looks like he's holding in a laugh as he nods. "Okay. Sure."

"You know you could tell us if you were dating someone, right?" Drew says.

"I'm not dating anyone."

"Yeah," Walsh says from the open doorway, and our heads all swing toward him. How is he so fucking stealthy? "McCabe has too much on his plate right now for a relationship."

But from the look in his eyes, I can tell that he's starting to connect the dots. *Fucking hell.*

"Speaking of," I say, glancing at the clock on the wall. "I'm supposed to check in with the nanny before he takes Abby to the sing-along at the library this morning."

Hopefully, none of them knows that the library doesn't even open for a full hour. But given that Walsh has several kids, I'm sure he suspects I'm just trying to get out of this conversation—and out of this room—as quickly as I can.

***

"I never in a million years would have imagined that this is how I'd be spending my day off," AJ says, pulling her sunglasses onto the top of her head as we come to a stop on a covered bridge. When I told her to be ready for a day of sightseeing, I neglected to mention that we were leaving the city in a rental car, or that it was a convertible. She's wind-blown and her cheeks are pink, even after spending the last hour walking through the mostly shaded trails of Valley Forge.

"Sorry, I'm a bit of a history nerd and a national park enthusiast."

Her shoulders shake with laughter. "Yeah, I got that from how riveted you were by the intro video we watched at the welcome center. And then the way you dragged me through several historical buildings, looking like a kid in a candy shop."

"Hey," I say, stepping up behind her and fully boxing her in against the low wall of the bridge as she looks out at the creek below us. It's quiet at the park today. We've barely seen anyone on the trails leading from one site to another, probably because it's a weekday. "You can take the history nerd out of the classroom . . ."

"I forgot that's what you were studying in college." Looking up over her shoulder at me, her eyes search my face like she's running through the memories of when she scouted me all those years ago. "Didn't you say that if hockey didn't work out, you wanted to get your PhD and become a professor?"

"Yep. Why do you look so amused by that idea?"

A scoff rattles around in the back of her throat. "I can totally imagine how packed your classes would be . . . all those girls wanting to fulfill their history requirement with the hot, grumpy professor who growls at them when they don't know the answer."

My bark of laughter echoes against the hillsides. "So you think I'm hot?"

She chuckles. "I think that's your only saving grace, given the less charming aspects of your personality."

The smirk gracing her lips lets me know she's teasing, so in response, I trail my fingertips up her thigh under her dress, pressing her back into me so she can feel how I'm already growing hard from just her proximity. When I reach her waist, I toy with the top seam of her underwear. "Really? That's my *only* saving grace?"

She drops her voice even though no one is around. "I mean, I guess you give me decent orgasms as well."

I let my fingertips creep along her skin until I can feel the curls right above where her legs meet. "Decent, huh?"

Pressing her head back against my shoulder, she whispers, "We can't . . ." and then takes a gasping breath when I slide two fingers over her clit and slip them into her. "We can't do this here." She's panting as I work my fingers inside her and she lets me continue just long enough that I don't think she's going to stop me.

"No, really," she says, her hand flying to my arm. "I want to. But I can't. Not out in the open like this." She pulls my arm away from her so that my fingers slip out.

I hold her tighter against me, lowering my voice. "This morning at the gym, when I went to wipe my face with my towel, I found I still had the scent of your cum on my hand." I press my now rock-hard cock into her lower back. "All I've wanted to do since then is touch you again . . . make you come so hard you forget how to speak."

She reaches her arm up, sliding her hand back around my neck and pulling me even closer. Then, in a low, sultry voice like the one I dreamed she might have, she says, "You don't like it when I talk?"

I tilt my head to the side so I can meet her gaze as she looks up at me over her shoulder. "Let's get one thing straight. I think you're fucking brilliant, and I love talking to you. But I love it even more when I've brought you so far over the edge that the only word you remember is my name. And I'm going to take you over that edge again, ideally right fucking now."

"If we're caught . . ." I can tell her eyes are darting back and forth to the paths that lead to either side of the bridge.

"We've hardly seen a single person out here."

"Yeah, but if we *did*. I don't have the luxury of being wanton like that in public. If I'm caught, I could lose every-thing—the reputation I've built, the award I'm nominated for, and possibly even my job."

I let her words sink in, let myself fully understand her worries. She's worked so hard and broken every stereotype to get where she is in this industry and with this team. I don't want to ruin that for her. But I also don't miss how "every-thing" for her is really just work.

"Come here," I say, taking her hand and leading her across the bridge.

"Where are we going?" She's struggling to keep up with me in her cute little fashion sneakers. I didn't tell her we'd be hiking, but to be fair, I didn't know at the time. I thought we'd stop by the visitor's center and see some of the histor-ical buildings. I didn't realize I'd be so desperate to be alone with her that I'd suggest we "take a walk" on what turned out to be actual hiking trails.

"There are some ruins up this trail," I tell her. "I suspect we can find somewhere more private."

"You really can't wait?" Her voice is teasing, but also, she sounds surprised. She deserves to feel wanted, to know what it's like to have a man in her life who's desperate to be with her. And the fact that she's been married—and yet hasn't experienced that before—pisses me the hell off.

I spin so I'm facing her and pull her toward me, my eyes scanning the trail below to make sure there's no one within earshot. And then I take her good hand, bringing it between us and pressing it against my cock. She sucks in a breath when she feels how hard I am.

"Does it feel like I can wait, Sunshine? Because I feel like I'm about to die if I don't get to touch you again right now. And from the way you were dripping all over my hand, I'm thinking you don't want to wait, either."

She lets out a small whimper of longing while she strokes me, and I take a small step backward, breaking contact.

"Oh my god." The words are practically a whisper as they fall from her lips, and the way she's looking at me with those glassy eyes, dark with desire, there is no doubt that she wants me as badly as I want her—even though we're in the middle of a national park.

"But if I'm wrong, and you want to wait, we will." I hold my hands up in mock defeat.

A strangled gasp leaves her—as if she now can't stand the thought of waiting, even though a few seconds ago, she was suggesting it—and she steps toward me. Raising onto her toes, she wraps her arms around my shoulders and kisses me, right in the middle of the path. And my mind races, considering the quickest way to get her alone and naked, before determining that my suggestion of the ruins is, in fact, probably the best option.

"Come on." I nod my chin up at the hill. "Let's find somewhere more private."

As soon as we crest the top of the trail, the stone walls of the old bottling factory come into view. I recognize it from the video at the welcome center, and I'm even more thankful that I paid attention.

We take the stone steps up, and AJ murmurs, "Are you sure we're supposed to go in here?"

"The 'watch your step' sign makes me think it's okay," I say. "But hopefully no one else wants to explore this area for at least the next five minutes."

She snorts a laugh. "Only five minutes, huh?"

"We're going to have to be quick," I tell her, keeping my voice low because I know how sound can carry through the valleys carved between these rolling green hills.

"No multiple orgasms this time?" Her whispered teasing makes me wish we had all the time in the world, but I'm not willing to risk getting caught.

"I'm going to make you come so many times tonight that you'll lose count. But today, I'm going to fuck you so hard and quick you'll come faster and harder than you ever have."

"Jesus." She exhales the word with a sigh, and when I look over my shoulder at her, I'm captivated by the swell of her breasts in the scoop neck of her black tank dress, and her pebbled nipples showing through the thin fabric as she stands there at the top of the steps.

I pull her around a corner and against a solid stone wall so we're blocked from the view of any hikers on the path.

AJ's hands are already on my belt, unbuckling it and then working on my button. "Hey, you shouldn't be doing that with your hand hurt like it is," I say, bringing my hand over to cover hers. I'm thrilled that she's not in so much pain that she can't use her fingers, as was the case a few days ago, but I also don't want her to do any damage. Instead, I undo the button and zipper, sliding my pants down my hips and letting the waistband rest on my thighs where they'll be out of the way just enough.

I don't expect her to drop to her knees while telling me to pull my boxers down, but the sight of her there removes any lingering concerns I have about what we're about to do.

Because watching Alessandra Jones take me in her hand while she circles the head of my cock with her tongue before wrapping her lips around me and taking me all the way to the back of her throat is one of the sexiest things I've ever seen. The quiet gagging sound she makes, and the way she pulls back and then takes me even deeper so I'm sliding into her throat, has my balls already tightening up.

"AJ," I hiss on a pained whisper, because if she doesn't stop, I'm going to come right down the back of her throat—and as much as I love that idea, I want to feel her coming on my cock even more.

She tilts her head up to look at me while she works her hand around my shaft, but she says nothing, instead raising one eyebrow like she wants me to continue.

But words are failing me, so all I manage to grit out is: "Up. Now."

A small smile plays on her lips. "Yes, sir."

Oh, fuck me. Is there anything in the world hotter than the most powerful woman in hockey calling me *sir*? I think not.

When she stands, I slide my hands up her thighs, curl my fingers around the thin straps of lace, and jerk my hands apart quickly. The ripping sound of the fabric is barely audible above the rustling of the leaves in the gentle breeze and the birds chirping in the dappled sunlight.

Jaw dropping open in surprise, AJ stares at me with those huge brown eyes. I could get lost in the kaleidoscopic of browns, amber, and gold I see there. But I won't, not now anyway. Because I'm too busy bringing that thong up to my nose, inhaling her scent as I tell her, "I fucking love the way you smell when you're turned on."

"Holy shit," she whispers before licking her lips and leaving them parted like she can't breathe without her mouth slightly open.

I stuff her underwear in my pocket before I pull her dress up around her waist, slide my hands around the back of her thighs, and lift her up against that stone wall. I don't even check to see if she's ready for me; I just assume she is, and as I step forward, lining my cock up with her entrance, I'm met with the signs of her arousal. "I love the way you're always dripping wet and ready for me, Sunshine."

With a moan, she closes her eyes and leans her head back against the stone wall.

"I want access to your tits."

"Jesus, Ronan," she says, as she moves her hands from my shoulders to the straps of her tank top, pulling down and to the sides so her breasts slip out. The way they're held there by the bra and the edges of her top have them pushing together, looking bigger than they actually are.

She's a perfect handful, and that's all I need, but the slit of her cleavage where they're pressed together has me telling her, "Someday, I'm going to fuck these breasts."

Her eyes fly open at my words, and I tilt my hips up, notching into her sweet, hot pussy.

"God, you're so fucking wet for me."

"Only for you," she says sweetly, bringing her hands back to my neck. She threads her fingers into my hair, giving the strands a tug. "Now fuck me, please." As she drives her hips down, I slide into her a bit more. "Don't make me beg."

"The thought of you begging me to fill you . . ." I groan, pushing into her another inch. ". . . has me harder than you can even imagine."

"Please, Ronan."

And that's it. The sound of my name rolling out of her with a breathy sigh has me pulling her down onto my cock hard and fast. Pinning her against the wall, I rail her while I dip my head forward and suck one of her nipples into my mouth, circling it with my tongue and taking a few long pulls that have her moaning.

I look up at her, and pull back enough to say, "Quiet, Sunshine. You don't want us to get caught, do you?" And then I scrape my teeth lightly around her nipple before sucking it back into my mouth, testing her ability to hold back her pretty sounds.

Her lips are clamped together now, but the groan that rasps in her throat as I slip into her over and over, combined with the delicate drag of my cock against her inner walls and the crude sound of slapping skin every time our bodies meet, has me on the edge of coming.

"I need you to touch yourself," I tell her, and she brings two fingers to my lips. I pull them into my mouth, running my tongue along and around her fingertips, loading her up with my saliva. If I weren't so close, I'm confident I could make her come without the additional help. But that will have to be a goal for another time. Right now, we need to finish before anyone else wanders up this path.

She sucks her stomach in to make room for her hand between us, which has her pussy clamping down on me even more. "Fuck," I whisper. "This is too good."

Biting down on the corner of her lower lip, she smirks at me. "Too good will be when you make me come."

"Try to be quiet," I say, and then I take her other nipple, drawing it into my mouth with a not-so-gentle suck that has her hips pushing forward to meet mine while she chants "Yes, yes, yes" on whispered sighs.

She increases the speed while she uses her good hand to circle her clit and rests her splint on my shoulder in order to tug at my hair. The slight amount of pain pushes me closer, and I feel the telltale signs of my orgasm. But I don't want to come before she does.

"Now, Alessandra," I growl between clenched teeth.

"I'm not there yet," she says breathily.

"Like hell you're not." I pull her nipple back into my mouth roughly, sucking hard and leaving her moaning. Then I adjust one of my hands that's holding her up and press my middle finger against the opening of her ass. I meet her gaze as I apply a light pressure, not entering her, but wanting to make sure she's okay with being touched there.

Her mouth parts with a sharp inhale, her eyes widening as she stares down at me. As I press a bit harder, her eyes widen even more. She's breathing hard, her hips moving into me at a frantic pace, and she gives me a little nod. So I slip my finger into her, just barely, and her mouth drops open as she pushes her head back into the stone wall so hard her back arches. I feel her pussy clamping down on me as a choked cry escapes her, her muscles moving in rhythmic waves as my orgasm simultaneously moves through my body and nearly has my legs buckling from the intensity.

Faint voices ring out in the distance, and I lift my head, taking her mouth in mine and kissing the hell out of her as she works through her climax. Not only do I not want to risk her making a sound, but also, I'm feeling emotions I've never felt before.

It's not just the desperate need to be with her, to be inside her. It's also the realization that I never want to feel this with anyone else. And that thought is both terrifying and reassuring at the same time.

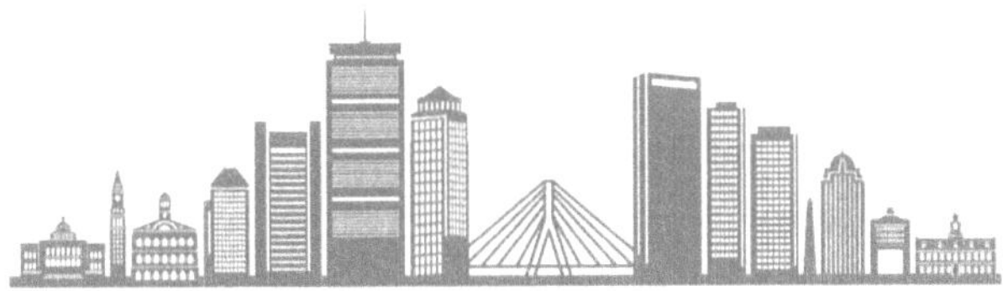

Chapter Twenty-Five

AJ

Nicholas's name pops up on my caller ID right as we're driving back into Philly. I debate not answering it, but I don't want him to think anything's wrong.

"Hey, what's going on?" I ask, pressing the phone to my ear so I can hear his response over the noise of the traffic and the wind whipping around us.

"Nothing. Abby's down for a nap, and I just wanted to see how you were doing."

I glance at McCabe, who's focused on the road. With his aviator sunglasses on and his dark hair blowing in the wind, he's relaxed in a way I rarely see. Is this just a side of him I haven't seen because of our boss-employee relationship, or is he loosening up and showing me who he actually is?

"I'm doing great. Big win last night, which we really needed," I say, and next to me, McCabe chuckles. He's probably thinking about *after* the game because getting me to come with him inside me, after also giving me a mind-blowing orgasm with his mouth—that was a *big win* too. "And then I did some sightseeing today."

"Oh yeah, where'd you go?"

"Valley Forge. There's a national park there, so I walked around for a bit. And then I stopped at a huge mall near there and did a little dress shopping." I still can't quite get over the mental image of McCabe following me around, holding all the gowns I picked out to try on. He didn't complain once, not even when I'd loaded him down with twenty different dresses. And then he humored me when I wanted to buy Abby some adorable pink high-top sneakers that we saw in a shop window, helping me find the right size so she could wear them now.

"You're really going to go to the gala?" Nicholas asks. His voice is disapproving at best.

"I mean, I kind of have to."

"No, you don't. There's no need to spend one second with those assholes, especially since you know Chet is going to be there."

My childhood was far from perfect, but it was still much better than what Nicholas got.

"It's more work to *not* go, you know? I can suck it up and show up for two hours since I'm going to be in St. Louis anyway—"

"Oh, you're *that* confident about this series?" Nicholas teases. Yeah, we're down 2-1, but we plan to rectify that tomorrow night. We're a better team, and I'm confident we can beat Philadelphia in the end. I'm equally confident that St. Louis is going to win their current series, given their current standings, which will put us in a position to be playing them two weeks from now.

"Pretty much. If I'm there anyway, what's my excuse for not going?"

"Work. It's your excuse for everything else." There's an edge to his tone that has the hair on the back of my neck standing up.

"What's that supposed to mean?"

Next to me, McCabe reaches over and rests his hand on my thigh. I know he can only hear my side of the conversation, but I appreciate that he recognizes my defensiveness and the subtle way he tells me he's here for me.

His palm presses into me, his fingers giving me a supportive squeeze along my inner thigh—right where we'd had to use my thong to wipe up his cum as it dripped out of me only an hour earlier. The memory has me letting out a sigh, forgetting I'm even on the phone.

"You don't need the big sigh, AJ," Nicholas says into my ear, jolting me out of my stupor.

That jerky movement has McCabe chuckling next to me again, like he knows exactly what his touch does to me.

God, this relaxed version of him—the way he takes things in stride, the smile he reserves only for me— he's like an entirely different person, and it's addicting. *He* could be addicting.

"I just meant," Nicholas continues, "that you've used work as your excuse to get out of things you didn't want to do plenty of times before."

"Do you feel like I've used it to get out of doing things with you?" I ask, concerned about that edge I hear in his voice.

"No. You've always made time for me when I needed you."

I hear what he's saying, and previously that would have been enough for me.

"What about when you didn't need me?"

Nicholas's voice is softer, quieter, when he asks, "What's going on with you? You don't sound like yourself."

"I don't know . . ." I look up at the sky as we take the offramp from the freeway to head into the city. "I guess I'm just re-evaluating my priorities?"

What I'm really wondering is whether working this hard to get where I am—literally devoting every waking moment of almost every single day to hockey—was necessary to end up here? Or was it an excuse to get out of having an actual life? Was I singularly focused on taking professional risks so I didn't have to take personal ones and risk getting hurt again?

"This feels like . . . a shift," Nicholas says, and when I glance over at McCabe while we wait at a stoplight, he's looking at me with the same curious gaze I imagine my brother is probably wearing right now.

"Nah, just the musings of a middle-aged woman," I joke, swallowing roughly. "Anyway, I've got a few extra seats at my table. I'd offer them to you and Nicole, but you'll be watching Abby." Not like he'd want to come. Since he was still a kid when we lived in St. Louis, he's never had to attend these kinds of events that make up a significant portion of my family's social life.

"You bought a whole fucking table? For your own family's charity event?" Nicholas's full-bodied laugh makes me pull the phone away from my ear.

"Seemed like the safest way to avoid sitting with Mom and Dad."

"Must be nice to have money to throw away like that."

"Hey, you can't put a price on sanity," I say, chuckling. "And I'm bringing Frank Hartmann with me, so he can serve as a buffer."

"Ah, Second Dad will be there? I love that guy!"

"He really is the best," I say as we pull through the intersection. In front of us, there must be someone double-parked or something, because suddenly there are horns honking and people yelling out their windows.

"Where the hell are you?" Nicholas asks.

"In a car coming back from shopping. There's something going on up ahead," I say as a driver lays on his horn and doesn't let up. "I better go."

"Alright, see you tomorrow night when you get home."

"See you then."

I set my phone down in the cupholder, not missing how McCabe's hand still rests on my thigh, his thumb still stroking the skin there. Closing my eyes, I lean back against my seat.

"You want to talk about it?"

"Talk about what?" I ask, not bothering to open my eyes.

"Whatever this gala is with your family, and why you need to bring Frank with you as a buffer?"

"It's nothing, just an annual charity event . . ."

McCabe huffs a laugh and asks, "You go to a lot of those?"

"Not as many as I used to." I think back to the years when I still lived in St. Louis and my social calendar was peppered with these types of events.

I had a charmed life growing up, from the outside

anyway. But the mansion and the cars and the fancy vacations didn't offset the emotional toll of being raised by parents who wanted me to be someone I wasn't.

The constant pressure to be successful, combined with never living up to the socialite my mom wanted me to be and the son my dad wished I was, gave me a serious type-A personality and a work ethic that's turned me into a perfectionist driven to succeed at any cost. And no amount of therapy to help me understand the root causes of my issues has allowed me to change these ingrained parts of my personality.

"You don't want to go, though?" His concern is evident in the tone of his voice.

"Not particularly. Chet's going to be there—"

"Why the fuck is your ex-husband going to be at *your* family's event?"

I love that he's angry on my behalf, but my laugh lacks humor when I tell him, "He's the one they kept in the divorce."

McCabe takes a sharp turn onto a side street, brakes squealing as he slips into a parking spot, the quick action making my stomach flip. He turns toward me, his face all hard lines. But that look warms me, because he cares enough to be pissed.

"What the fuck do you mean, *he's the one they kept?*"

I shrug and look down at my lap. "Chet's a family friend. His dad and mine have been golf partners my whole life. We grew up together . . ."

He reaches across the space and uses his fingertips to gently turn my face toward him. "You didn't answer my question."

"My parents wanted me to look past his cheating and stay married. In front of my parents, Chet was begging me to forgive him, promising to do anything to make it right. I knew there was no way I'd ever get past what he'd done, but my parents acted like this was just a part of marriage and I needed to get over it."

It was enough to make me wonder if that was part of their marriage too—not that I'd ever ask. Those were not the type of things that were discussed in the Jones household.

"The fuck?"

I appreciate how taken aback he is, because it lets me know that I'm not crazy for refusing to give Chet a second chance. For a long time, my parents were big on gaslighting me—trying to convince me that I was the problem. It's a relief to have an outsider confirm that I made the right decision in leaving.

"Yeah. So that kind of tarnished our relationship—you know, even more than it already had been because of Nicholas. When I threatened to sue for custody of my brother on the grounds of neglect, that was the nail in the coffin of our relationship."

"You did what, now?" His brow pinches as he searches my face.

"When I started talking to Frank about the GM position in Boston, I realized I didn't want to leave my brother in St. Louis without me. So I looked into boarding school options here. Initially, they didn't want him to go—though I still have no idea why. It's not like they ever spent time with him, unless it was to show him off at some social function."

"So you brought him to Boston with you?"

"Yeah, I mean, he went to boarding school, but he was

only like half an hour outside of the city. And he's lived here ever since. St. Louis really isn't home for either of us, anymore."

His thumb slides along my cheekbone, and that's when I realize he's still holding my face. He's eyeing me like I'm someone he needs to fix.

"Don't look at me like that," I tell him, feeling uncommonly vulnerable.

His voice softens. "Like what?"

"Like I'm broken."

"I don't think you're broken. If anything . . . I'm looking at you with admiration. It's like the person I see in front of me now is completely different than the person I thought you were. And I *really* like who I see."

"You're just saying that because now, every time you look at me, you're thinking about what I look like when I come."

I don't know why I feel the need to take this moment and make it into a joke. But there's a heaviness to his words that has my belly flipping over. There's a seriousness that terrifies me. I excel at holding people at a distance, and I don't know how he keeps breaking through my barriers.

His fingers tighten on my jaw. "No, I'm saying that because you keep surprising me in the best ways. I'm kind of in awe of you."

I try to gulp down my emotions, to hold my thoughts in, but somehow, he always disarms me. Maybe it's that fiercely protective look in his eyes, or the way he keeps telling me how he feels. Maybe it's that I've never had a truly healthy relationship with a guy, and the way McCabe validates me and supports me like a friend would, while worshiping me sexually, has me wanting to share parts of myself with him I've never shared with anyone else.

I don't break eye contact when I tell him, "You keep surprising me in the best ways, too."

He leans forward, pressing a kiss to my forehead. "At some point, we're going to need to talk about what to do with this relationship. It's getting harder to hide."

"Harder to hide?" I laugh. "You mean since last night?"

He chuckles, shaking his head. "No. I mean since I kissed you in your office, and since you moved into my place, and since Walsh caught me coming out of your hotel room, and since the guys were ragging on me at the gym this morning, wondering why I looked like a lovesick fool."

A lovesick fool?

"That's . . ." I gulp, racking my brain for the right way to explain how I'm feeling, and coming up short. ". . . new information."

"Yeah, well, I can't stop thinking about you, and the guys are starting to notice. I get why we need to keep it a secret for now, but eventually, we're going to need to talk about where this is going. Us together is a *challenge*. Us sneaking around and potentially getting caught is a *problem*."

"Uhh . . ." What is he talking about? We flirted until the flames of sexual tension turned into an inferno . . . but that doesn't mean this is . . . whatever he thinks it is? "I meant what I said last night. I don't see how this could ever work."

I at least halfway believe what I'm saying.

He clicks his tongue in disagreement. "And *I* don't see how it could ever *not*."

"You really think that a relationship between a player and his GM is ever going to fly?" There's no way. It's a level of unprofessionalism that I can't even fathom myself, much less expect anyone beyond the two of us to understand.

"I don't give a shit what anyone else thinks, AJ. And the sooner you can let go of maintaining this perfect image, the sooner we stop sneaking around. I want a shot at a real relationship with you."

My mind races at his declaration. This is too fast. This is too sudden. How could this ever work?

"But . . . it's been, like, two days . . ." I stumble over the words.

His eyes narrow, like he's reading my mind and knows I'm wrong. "Have you ever in your life connected with someone like we've connected over the last few days?"

I close my eyes, hoping that if I can't see him, I'll be able to lie to him. To tell him, *sure, all new relationships are like this.* But it's just not true.

"No." There's almost no sound as the word rolls off my lips, but I know he hears me, because when I open my eyes, he's looking at me with the self-satisfied smirk of someone who thinks he's won. "But that doesn't mean this can work."

"Of course it can. We just need to figure out how."

Chapter Twenty-Six

AJ

AJ

I'm exhausted, so I'm going straight to bed.
Let's make plans for dinner one night this
week.

I shoot the text off to Nicholas as I ride the elevator up to my floor, feeling anything but exhausted. There's excitement, because after another win tonight, we've tied our series 2-2. And there's the thrill of seeing McCabe again once Nicholas leaves.

I click over to my text thread with McCabe and read the messages we exchanged on the plane.

MCCABE

You're coming over tonight, yes?

AJ

Is that an invitation, or an assumption?

MCCABE

Yes.

AJ

You're getting a little cocky, assuming that I
can't go a night without you.

MCCABE

If there's one thing I am, it's a realist.

AJ

Is that so? Maybe what you REALLY need is
a night alone, then?

MCCABE

Don't threaten me, woman. I'll text you when
Nicholas and Nicole leave.

AJ

I'm too old for booty calls.

I threw the "old" part in there because maybe we both
need the reminder that I'm much too old for him—yet
another reason why we shouldn't be thinking about anything
long term.

MCCABE

You're not too old for anything. Stop that
shit right now. And if you don't come over
after Nicholas leaves, I'll just come over and
drag you back to my place. Benefits of living
across the hall.

AJ

How very caveman of you.

MCCABE

You love every minute of it, don't lie.

I wanted to argue with him about that, but he's not wrong.

AJ

> We'll see how I'm feeling once I'm home. I
> might be tired.

MCCABE

> After a win like tonight's? Not likely. But if
> you're tired, we'll sleep. I sleep better when
> you're in my bed.

AJ

> I'm not sleeping at your place when I live
> across the hall.

With my wrist feeling better each day, it's not like I need his help to do simple things like getting dressed anymore. So there's no excuse not to stay at my own place. Maybe I'll let him give me another orgasm or two, because the one he gave me in the shower this morning feels like way too long ago, but I'm not spending the night. That screams *relationship*, and I keep telling him we can't have that.

We can't. I have to keep reminding myself too, because when I'm with him, I start wanting things I know are impossible.

MCCABE

> We'll see about that.

When I walk into my apartment, Tabitha lifts her head and hisses at me, then goes back to sleeping on my couch. I just laugh, because she really is ornery.

The anticipation of knowing I'm going to see McCabe in private in only a few minutes, after a long day of having to act like there's absolutely nothing going on between us, has all my senses heightened.

The whizzing of my suitcase wheels across the hardwood floor, the drag of clothes as I shed them and leave them on the floor of my bedroom, the pounding of my heart as I walk into my closet naked, trying to figure out what to wear over to his place . . . it has me feeling antsy, like I could crawl out of my skin. Normally, when I'm feeling like this, I pull out my very lifelike vibrator. Tonight, though, I have the real thing.

I never, ever thought I'd be the kind of person who could barely make it twelve hours without being railed by a well-endowed hockey player. Yet here I am.

I chuckle to myself as I glance in the full-length mirror. My body isn't what it once was, but I've worked hard to maintain my physique. I can't wait to get back to skating every morning. The first thing I'm asking the orthopedist when I see him in two days is how soon I can lace up my own skates. I'm not worried about falling and hurting myself on the ice, but I know my hand isn't in any condition to tighten laces, and since no one else knows about my morning skating sessions, it'll have to wait until I can do it myself.

I've just slipped on some satin sleep shorts and thrown a tank top on when his text comes through, letting me know that Nicholas and Nicole have left. I glance in the mirror again, taking in my wild eyes and the way my nipples are already hard from their contact with the fabric of the shirt. I'm so turned on I can barely stand it, and teasing him feels like a brilliant idea.

AJ

I fear I may need another minute.

MCCABE

Why, what are you doing?

I slide my hand down the front of my shorts and find that I'm already soaked just thinking about him. After my hysterectomy, the doctor warned me that vaginal dryness might be a side effect. Turns out, all I needed was a hot younger guy to solve that problem for me.

MCCABE

AJ?

What are you doing?

Collapsing back onto the ottoman in the middle of my small walk-in closet, I spread my legs wide so the fabric of the shorts doesn't impede my access.

AJ

I'm so turned on I can hardly move. I need to
take care of myself before I come over there.

MCCABE

Walk across the hall right now, or I'm going
to come bang your fucking door down.

Giggling to myself, I run my finger over my clit, knowing that it would feel better if he was doing it with his tongue, but suddenly, even waiting the thirty seconds it would take me to get to him feels impossible.

My phone rings with an incoming video call.

"What are you doing?" he all but growls when I hit the button to accept the call.

"I already told you." My voice is breathless as my fingers swipe through the slickness between my legs and then circle my clit, lips parting on a gasp at the contact.

"Fucking hell, AJ," he says with a sigh. "You look so hot right now. Pull the phone back. I want to see you touch yourself."

I do as he says, not because I think it's a good idea to be fingering myself on a video call, but because I'm so turned on, I'd do just about anything to take the edge off.

When I slide my fingers over my clit again, my entire abdomen clenches in longing. "God, I want you."

"I'm right here. Get up and walk across the hallway, and I'll take care of you."

"But . . ." I lose my train of thought as my fingers move faster. I should have just gone over, because the pressure is building and my pussy is pulsing, and there's an emptiness inside me I know he can fill. I'm too far along to stop now, though. "I . . ."

"Holy shit, woman," he groans, then sets his phone on his bathroom counter, propped up so I can see him. "Do you want to see what this is doing to me? How my body is reacting to this torture?"

"Yesss." The word is a hiss, and I close my eyes as I throw my head back while a wave of longing courses through me. When I open my eyes again, he's standing with one hand braced on the counter in front of him, and his dick in his hand. The sight alone has my hips grinding up into my hand.

"This is what you do to me," he says, sliding his hand up until it looks like he's choking the swollen head of his cock.

"You make me so hard I can't fucking think straight." As he strokes himself a few more times, I circle my clit harder and faster. "I want to be inside you right now. I *always* want to be inside you." He growls out the last sentence like he's mad about it. "Do you know how fucking hard it is to pretend like nothing's going on between us when we're working? Like at tonight's game?" With his hand moving faster, he grunts out the question.

I lift one eyebrow as I watch the way he's jerking himself off in quick, angry strokes. "Pretty hard, by the looks of it."

"You should be here right now." He circles the tip of his cock and slides his hand back down his shaft. "It's like you're punishing me . . ."

I dip two fingers inside myself and use the heel of my hand to rub against my clit with each stroke. "Ever heard of delayed gratification?" I'm teasing, but now that I'm this close, I'm frustrated with myself. I should have just gone over, because this would feel so much better if he was the one making me come.

"I'm going to teach you all about delayed gratification," he grits out. "And trust me, it'll feel like punishment, just like this does."

I don't know why the thought of that turns me on so much, but his words bring me so close to the precipice that I can practically taste my orgasm before it hits me—it's a metallic tang on my tongue as goosebumps ripple across my skin.

My moan of pleasure has him encouraging me, telling me about his plans for my body. And the visions of him buried inside me, edging me toward release and then holding me back, has me tipping right over into ecstasy. He follows my lead, letting out a string of expletives mixed with my name as he comes into a hand towel he's holding in front of himself.

And when I fully finish and lie back on my ottoman, my phone drops to the ground. I feel like I'm liquid. I'm completely unable to pull myself together.

Until his voice rings out, filling my entire closet with his growling demand. "Get. Your. Ass. Over. Here. Now."

Chapter Twenty-Seven

McCabe

Standing in the door frame of my open front door, waiting for AJ to come over, gives me a minute to collect my thoughts after that unexpected little phone sexcapade we just had.

It was hot, but it would have been better in person. And the fact that she didn't come over when I asked has me worried. I know that what's happening between us is more than just sex, but still, she holds back.

What I'm wondering right now is if we can figure out a way to make this actually work—not just sneaking around and having sex whenever we can, but actually making a relationship work. She wavers between wanting that, and not, sometimes even within the same minute.

AJ opens her door a crack and slips out, turning and shutting it quietly behind her. She's wearing super short sleep shorts that barely cover her ass, and a thin tank top with no bra beneath it.

"You look like you're sneaking out."

She gasps as she turns toward me, clutching her chest as she says, "Holy shit. I didn't see you standing there."

I cross my arms over my bare chest and lean against the door frame. "That's because you were looking over your shoulder like you were afraid your parents might catch you."

"I was trying to make sure my evil cat wasn't going to attempt an escape."

"Maybe she's evil because you're holding her captive?" I wink.

"When I rescued her, she'd been living on the streets. She had a horrible eye infection," she says, stepping toward me, "and the vet had to remove it. She also had a terrible case of fleas and was so emaciated you could see every rib."

"No wonder you wanted her," I tease.

Secretly, I love that this tells me a little more about her. She collects strays, I think. She stepped up as her brother's caregiver when she saw how their parents were neglecting him, and took in this cat no one else would have wanted. Under all that armor, there's a soft heart, and I'm embracing the glimpses of her true self that she shares every once in a while.

"Yeah, well, she seems to hate me for it. Like, what does she want? To be back on the streets, starving and in pain? Plus, with only one eye, she's not great at seeing things coming at her from her left side, so she could never be an outdoor cat."

"Sometimes we want what we want, even if it's not what's best for us."

Am I even still talking about her cat at this point?

She looks up at me, like she's wondering the same thing.

"I'm not going to turn her loose on the streets, so I guess I'll have to endure her hissing at me every time I walk past. Kind of like I endure you growling at me when you don't get your way."

Reaching out, I grab her hip and pull her against me. "That wasn't me not getting my way. That was you keeping literal walls between us when you didn't have to." I press my lips to the top of her head when her arms circle my waist. "And we're going to talk about why you keep doing that."

I walk us backward into my entryway and shut the front door behind her, before pushing her back against it. Her chest is heaving, and as I slide my hand up her neck, I can feel her pulse thrumming beneath my fingers.

"You like the excitement of this," I say as I hold her in place with my fingertips anchored firmly on her jaw.

It's not a question, but still, she responds with a breathy "Yes."

I hook the thumb of my other hand into the waistband of her shorts. "You like the orgasms."

"Yes." The word is a whispered pant, and her pulse increases.

"You like spending time with me, and you tell me things you don't tell anyone else."

She steps out of her shorts after I use my free hand to slide them past her hips and drop them to her feet. "Yes."

When she lifts one leg to step out of the shorts, I grab her knee and bring it up to my hip as I press myself against her. I'm not sure how, but I'm already growing hard again.

"And yet you hold me at a distance."

Staring down at her, I wait for her to admit this, too. But she seems to have run out of "yeses."

"If all you want from me is orgasms, that's a very different conversation than the one I want to have about where this relationship is going." My thumb strokes her knee where I'm holding her leg in place. "*Is* that all you want?"

"I . . ." She licks her lips, and then closes her eyes as she rests her head against my door. "I don't know what I want."

Dropping to my knees in front of her, I hold her leg up and then loop it over my shoulder as I lean in and taste her. "Oh yeah?" I look up at her. "So what's holding you back from knowing?"

"I can't . . ." She lets out a shaky breath. "I can't talk about this when you have me this turned on."

"Why?" I ask, before using my tongue to circle her clit. "Afraid you'll be too honest with me?"

Another labored breath, and she says, "Yes. No. I don't know, I can't think straight. Every time I'm with you, all I can think about is how much I want this. And then reality sets in and I realize it could jeopardize one, or both, of our careers."

With another swirl around her clit, I apply more pressure as I run my thumb along her opening. "I bet we can find a way to work it out."

She releases a sigh mixed with a groan as she pulls her tank top over her head. "How?"

"Well, first, you need to renew my contract. Because if I go to another team, I don't see how this could work long distance."

Her eyes flare, and I know she doesn't want to have this conversation. "I can't talk to you about this. Not without your agent."

Hmmm. The murmur of acknowledgement rattles in the

back of my throat as I clamp my lips onto her, and the vibrations against her clit make her entire body shake with need.

"If we can come to an agreement about me staying in Boston," I say, gazing up at her and noting the conflicted look on her face, "are we making this work between us?"

It's not that I'm desperate to put a label on this; it's that I need to know she's at least open to the idea.

"I . . . I think we need to talk about this later. I can't make important decisions in the midst of . . . you know." She closes her eyes as she rests a hand on my head and threads her fingers through my hair, tugging me closer.

Nodding, I slide two fingers up into her. "That's fine, but we will be talking about it. Right after I punish you for that stunt you pulled in your closet." I flick my tongue over her clit, pressing hard even though I know she'll be sensitive after coming only a few minutes ago. She cries out in surprise, and then sighs with pleasure.

"If this is my punishment," she says with a sly smile, "please continue."

I can't help but smirk as I curl my fingers inside her while I continue pushing her closer to her orgasm. She rocks her hips against my face, increasing the pace until she's panting and telling me how close she is.

And that's when I stop and peer up at her again. "You want to come?"

"Yes."

Pulling my fingers out of her, I stick them between my lips, sucking them clean. Then I drop her leg from my shoulder as I stand and put one hand on either side of her head, boxing her against my front door.

"What . . . what are you doing?" she asks, her voice wavering.

"Delivering your punishment."

"By withholding an orgasm from me?"

"No," I say, wrapping one hand behind her neck and pulling her close to me. "By using you every way I want to before I let you come again."

Her tongue darts out, licking her lower lip before she bites down on it like she's trying to hold in a smile. "Sounds just terrible. Such a horrible punishment."

Oh, this is going to be fun.

Gripping the back of her neck, I kiss her hard. She gives it right back to me, standing on her toes to meet me while she threads her fingers through my hair again. I don't know why I like that edge of pain when she tugs on my hair, but I do. It pulls a sound of longing from my chest, and I half-groan, half-growl right into her mouth.

"So needy," she teases, pulling back to smirk at me.

"Yes, I'm *quite* needy. In fact, right now, I need you on your knees."

She drops immediately to her knees with that same smirk, showing me this isn't a punishment at all.

"Take my pants off."

"Yes, sir." Her chest shakes with silent laughter.

"You're going to think that's a lot less funny when you're gagging on my cock," I say, just to see what her reaction will be. I've never talked to a woman this way, but I get the sense she's enjoying it as much, or maybe even more, than I am.

In response, she slides my sweats and boxers down my legs. "We'll see."

After I kick my pants off, she stands up on her knees, so

her face is right at my waist, and takes my cock in her hand. I'm not fully hard yet, so she strokes me with long, hard pulls as she trails her tongue around my head. The blood rushes to my dick so quickly I have to put my hand on the wall behind her because I feel lightheaded.

This woman will be the death of me. I've never been more confident about anything in my life. Now I'm just trying to figure out whether it's going to be a slow, torturous death, or whether we'll go down in an explosion together.

I'm throbbing and hard as steel in her hand in no time, and she hums her approval against the head of my cock, making my hips thrust forward as I slide into her mouth. The way her head bobs as she takes me to the back of her throat has me pulling out and pushing back into her, grabbing her hair and twisting my hand so it's wrapped around my fist. Her eyes flick up to me with a brief flash of panic when I hit the back of her throat and she gags, so I take my other hand and brush the underside of her chin, telling her, "You're doing so well."

Her moan reverberates along my shaft and my mouth drops open with a quick exhale as my abs clench. Eyes still focused on me, she takes me deeper.

"Touch yourself," I demand, and her splinted arm reaches down between her legs. "Show me how wet you are." She holds her fingers up for me to see. "Now smear your cum on your nipples."

Another moan around my cock, and I feel like I'm about to pass out. As I watch her circle each of her nipples before demanding she touch herself again, I'm not sure which of us is more aroused. Her hips are rocking to the same rhythm we've set as she takes my cock into her throat, and she starts making desperate sounds that are about to make me come.

"Now stop touching yourself."

She whimpers in response, but does what I say, looking up at me as she pulls me out of her mouth, lightly dragging her teeth around the head of my cock and sending an electrical current across every cell in my body. Holy shit, I've never felt anything like that before.

"I didn't tell you to stop."

"We both get to feel good, or neither of us does," she says with a little shrug, doing nothing to hide her sass. I know she's just pushing me, trying to get to whatever punishment I've promised.

Game on.

I tug on her hair, pulling her up to standing, and then spin her around so I'm behind her. Taking her good hand, I place it low enough on the door that she's bent forward a bit, and then I rest her injured hand on top of it, just like I did in the hotel bathroom the other night. Hovering over her, I trace the curve of her ear with my lips before sucking her lobe between my teeth. "Are you going to be a good girl for me, so you get to come?"

"We'll see," she hums.

I let go of her hair, bringing both my hands to her breasts, toying with her nipples until she's pushing back into me and sliding along my cock. Straightening, I still roll her nipples between my fingers as I reposition myself, guiding my dick between her legs so that as she moves she can rub her clit along my shaft. Every time she gets to the head, she circles her hips before sliding back.

I can feel her coating me—a combination of her cum

from when she pleasured herself in her closet, and new arousal from being here with me—as she grinds herself against me, seeking friction.

"Your greedy little pussy is soaking me," I say, looking down at the view of the shiny pink skin between her legs. "Tell me what it needs."

"Youuu," she moans. "Please."

"Please, what?"

"Please fill me," she begs, and the sound of it has a new wave of longing coursing through me. "Please make me come."

I grab my cock, holding it in place as I press the head of it against her clit, rubbing it back and forth over her as she moans again. "Please."

Pulling back, I slide into her in one swift movement that takes her breath away and has me groaning in relief. I bring my hands back to her nipples, pinching them lightly as I roll them in my fingertips and slam into her over and over.

Her moans escape on exhales every time I bottom out, until she's a frantic mess beneath me. "Touch me," she begs.

"I am touching you." I know what she wants, but I continue working her nipples.

"My clit. Please, I'm so close."

"Oh, Sunshine," I say, making a tisking sound with my tongue. "How's it feel to be so close, and not get what you want?"

Her only reply is the sound of her panting as I work her closer to coming on my cock.

"Does it feel like a punishment?" I taunt.

"Please, Ronan," she grunts out my name as I bury myself deeper inside her.

I lean forward so my lips are right next to her ear. "I like it when you beg, especially when you use my name. What I don't like is when my body is craving yours, and you spread your legs and show me your pussy over a video call where I can't touch or taste you."

She turns her head slightly, rubbing her cheek along mine. "It seemed like a good idea at the time."

Chuckling darkly, I reach between her legs, sliding my finger over her clit until she's chanting "Yes" over and over. And when I stop, pulling my hand away suddenly, she groans in frustration.

Holding her hips as I return to standing, I pull her back on me, hard. "How's it feel to want something that's just out of your reach?"

The way I've been edging her, I'm confident her orgasm is going to be earth-shattering as soon as I let her have it. But in the meantime, I'm enjoying holding her off, knowing that this "punishment" is going to be more than worth it in the end.

"I hate you."

I trail my tongue up the side of her neck and enjoy the way her whole body shakes with a shiver before I press my lips to the space where her earlobe meets her jaw, and then whisper, "No, you don't."

"I *want* to hate you."

"That's not even close to the same thing," I grit out as I bury myself in her again.

"Why do you have to be so damn perfect for me?" she mumbles, her voice barely audible.

"I could ask you the same thing." I could ask her so many things, like why she's letting her fear get in the way of this amazing thing that's developing between us, or what she thinks is the worst thing that would happen if people found out about us? "Maybe instead, if you ask me *very* nicely, I'll let you come."

"Please, Ronan . . . please make me come."

"Look at you begging," I practically purr into her ear.

I trail my hand down her abdomen and press two fingers onto her clit. With my other hand, I pinch her nipple, rolling it between my fingers. In response, her hips move faster, taking me harder and deeper as she lets out soft moans and grunts of pleasure.

"Such a good girl."

Pressing with more intent on her clit, I work her up into a frenzy until her legs are shaking and her movements are erratic. And as I tilt my hips to change the angle, I can tell I hit the perfect spot inside her, because the walls of her pussy are squeezing me, rhythmically moving along my shaft in a way that has the first feelings of my own orgasm snaking through my body.

She cries out as her climax rips through her, and my hand shoots up to her mouth, covering it. "Quiet, now," I say through gritted teeth as I try to hold back from coming until she's done. "Let's not wake the baby."

Turning her head, she looks over her shoulder at me as she bites into my palm while she rides out her pleasure. And that edge of pain as her teeth sink into my skin has me coming so hard my vision is blurry at the edges until all I see is her face, and those wide, dark eyes staring into mine. I think I could handle anything life threw at me if I got to end each day with her, like this.

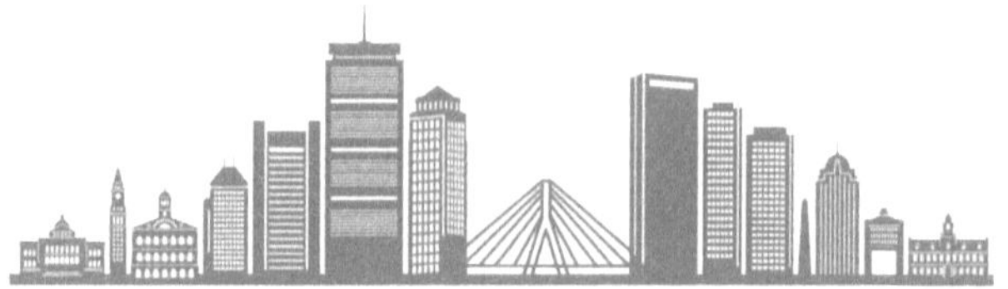

Chapter Twenty-Eight

McCabe

When we're both spent, I scoop her into my arms. I'm fairly sure her legs wouldn't work if I asked her to walk, so I carry her toward my bedroom. "Let me clean you up."

She opens her mouth like she wants to say something, but no words come out. Then she closes her eyes and sighs, her lips curving up in a way that makes her look totally content.

Laying her on my bed, I head into the bathroom and wet two washcloths. After I quickly clean myself off, I bring the other washcloth back to the bedroom. AJ hasn't moved from where I set her down, lying on her side, facing the bathroom, eyes closed, like a picture of serenity.

"You alive?"

She doesn't open her eyes, just mumbles, "Barely."

Taking her knee, I lift, rolling her onto her back so her legs fall open. I'm looking down, focusing on what I'm doing as I use the warm washcloth to gently clean her, but I can feel her gaze on me.

"I'm just going to . . . rest here for a minute," she says. "Then I'll head home."

"Stay with me tonight." After three nights of sharing a bed with her, there's no way I want her across the hall when she could be here.

"No, it's okay. I can find my way back to my place."

I lie on the bed next to her before she can get up, my arm tightening around her ribcage, and pulling her so she's cuddled into me. "That wasn't a request."

Her chuckle is low and sultry. "So now you think you're giving me orders?"

"I answer to you in every way, AJ. This is the one and only place where you can let me be in charge, and I suggest you do if you want me to continue providing you with orgasms."

"This was supposed to be a one-time thing."

"And yet you came back for seconds, and thirds, and fourths . . ." I tease.

Her annoyed expression only makes me smile. "I'm going home now."

God, I love it when she's feisty.

I pull her back to me before she can get up from my bed. "Over my dead body."

She tilts her head to look at me, a wild glint in her now very awake eyes. "If you insist."

She's so cute when she starts making threats. "Maybe you should climb up here and sit on my face . . . try to suffocate me while I give you yet another orgasm."

Even though she's shaking her head, she can't seem to stop herself from smiling. "You're incorrigible."

"Maybe so, Sunshine," I say, gripping her hips in each hand as I lift her up and set her with one knee on either side of my head. "Better sit on my face and teach me a lesson."

There's a moment of hesitation before her smile widens and she reaches forward for the headboard. And when she slides her knees farther apart so she can sink onto my face, I'm pretty sure that if she actually tried to kill me right now, I'd go happily—so long as I died with her cunt spread above me like this and my tongue gliding over her clit.

Because the sounds she's making as a result, and the way she breathes out my name as she gets closer, is exactly the soundtrack I'd want to hear in the afterlife.

———

I'm surprised to find my bed empty and the sun streaming through my windows when I wake up. I didn't set an alarm last night because we don't have practice today, and I knew Abby would get me up at 6:30 in the morning. She's like clockwork in that way.

But when I grab my phone off my nightstand, I'm shocked to find that it's an hour past her wakeup time. And when I glance at the video monitor, her crib is empty.

In a panic, I jump out of bed. My feet are on the floor and my heart is pounding in my throat before it occurs to me that Abby can't get out of her crib, and so AJ must have her. But how did I sleep through that?

When I pad out to the kitchen in nothing but my sweats, AJ and Abby are sitting on the living room floor. I watch from the doorway between the two rooms as AJ stacks soft, colorful blocks on top of each other, and then Abby pops up onto her knees and knocks them over, laughing. I'm sure I'm grinning like a lunatic as I watch them repeat the process several times—especially when AJ laughs and tickles Abby under the chin, calling her a "little monster."

I don't know what's wrong with me. It feels like there's some sort of vise around my ribcage, making it hard to breathe, hard for my heart to keep beating. But . . . this scene. This fucking scene is just so domestic, so perfect. And it hits me then that this is what I want for Abby and me—and I want it with AJ.

I must let out a sigh or something because Abby's head shoots up, looking for me, and AJ's back stiffens.

"Da!" Abby yells before crawling around AJ and toward me. I pick her up and give her a big hug, kissing the top of her head when she snuggles into my shoulder. I expect she'll want to stay there for a while because she's normally pretty clingy on my first day home from a trip, but after hugging me, she's leaning down and whining. Squatting to set her on the floor, I watch as she crawls right back over to AJ, who's staring at me with some sort of apologetic look on her face.

Moving closer, I sit down next to her. "Hey, what was that look?"

She glances back toward Abby, refusing to meet my eye. "What look?"

I put my hand on her lower back, rubbing circles there as she leans forward to rebuild the tower of blocks so Abby can knock it down again. "The one where you looked like you were . . . I don't know, apologizing?"

"What would I be apologizing for?" Her tone is dismissive, like she's trying to find a way out of the conversation.

After Abby knocks the blocks over and AJ claps for her,

telling her what a good job she's doing, I reach over and turn her face toward mine. I hate that I can't read the look on her face. It's like she's put those walls back up, and I just want to crash through them. "What's wrong?"

Her gulp is audible. "Nothing's wrong."

"Don't lie to me, AJ. That's not what we have here."

She takes a deep breath. "I need to go."

My hand clamps down on her thigh, trying to anchor her here so she doesn't get up and leave. "What? Why?"

"I just . . . I have things I need to do today. I need to stop by the office—"

"On a weekend?"

She looks away, and it feels like she's avoiding my gaze so she can lie to me—and possibly herself—more easily. "Yep. There are things that I need to take care of before this week starts."

There's a hard edge to the way she's speaking, and I know I should let her go. I should give her some space and time to work through whatever complicated emotions she's having about our developing relationship, spending the night here, being part of this domestic scene this morning.

But I don't want her to go. I don't want her to have space or time, because I'm fucking terrified that if she walks out that door, she might not walk back through it again. I don't know if making her talk about this right now is the right thing to do, or if I need to pause and leave the ball in her court.

I opt for the latter option, even though it goes against every instinct I have. I'm acting like a stage-five clinger, and I need to stop.

"Alright," I relent, as she stares down at my hand where

my fingers are curled into her thigh. I relax them, and she glances up at me. "I don't want you to go. But if you have to, you have to."

The impassive look on her face—the one I usually see at work but not in private—softens. "I'm sorry. But I do have to."

I swallow and give her a nod while I sit there wondering what the hell is happening. I keep following my heart instead of my head when it comes to her, and it seems like it's causing AJ to pull away. As I watch her run out the door without so much as a goodbye, I have to wonder if distance actually *is* what she wants?

"Thank you so much," I say, handing Nicholas the baby monitor. Abby's fast asleep, and hopefully she won't wake up while I'm gone. "I really won't be gone for too long, maybe a couple hours at the most."

"It's fine," he says. "Nicole's at the library tonight studying for a test, so I was just hanging around anyway."

I've almost forgotten what it was like to have free time, back when my life wasn't ruled by the whims of an adorable ten-month-old tyrant. Not that I'd want it any other way now that I have Abby, but sometimes, I do miss just being able to walk out the door when my teammate calls me about getting a beer, instead of having to scramble to find a babysitter. Thank god I have Nicholas, for now.

As I head out my door, I can't help glancing at AJ's. I wonder if she's home? And if so, how long ago did she come back? Is she planning to reach out? Is she coming over tonight?

The thought of not having her in my bed is painful.

I'm not just desperate for her physical proximity, for the way we make each other feel when we're together, but also for the way she opens up with me, the way she shows me who she is and how she feels in a way that she doesn't do with anyone else.

It's not just the sex. I want her. *All* of her.

I want her to keep talking to me, to feel safe and comfortable enough that she keeps revealing parts of herself that no one else knows. I want to tell her about my sister, and how earlier today she texted me a listing for a house in her neighborhood, with the message, "Want to live on my street?"

I want to talk about why she's refusing to renew my contract, when I'm barely asking for more money than I'm currently making. I know what the salary cap is. I know what she's already spending for next year. That's why I initially told Trevor to be reasonable in the negotiations, but then AJ refused even a tiny pay increase despite my stats line and the fact that I'm the team captain.

The *not knowing* is killing me. Not knowing whether I'm staying in Boston. Not knowing how she's feeling about us, beyond the amazing sex. Not knowing if she'll ever want more than sneaking around.

I know I fucked up last night. I can't demand we talk about my contract while I'm licking her pussy, driving her toward another orgasm after watching her make herself come. In fact, I shouldn't be talking to her about it at all. That's exactly the type of unethical shit she was worried about. But in that moment, I felt so desperate for her to know that I *want* to stay. That I *want* to work things out between us.

I don't care that she's my GM, but I know she cares. She's poured everything she has into her career. She's forsaken a lot in other areas of her life to be successful in her role. And I understand her fears about how she'll be perceived by her peers, her employees, her players, and the media if this all comes out.

But I don't give a shit about what anyone else thinks about this relationship, and I wish she didn't either.

I'm so lost in my own head, trying to figure out what to do next, that I don't see Walsh sitting at the bar until I've almost passed him and he reaches out to punch my arm.

"Shit. Sorry, man," I say as I pull out the seat next to him. Unsurprisingly, the bar is pretty empty on Sunday night.

"You look exhausted," he says. "Abby keep you up all night?"

"No, she let me sleep in, actually," I tell him, feeling guilty because of course I look exhausted—I've stayed up late the last few nights with AJ. And the only reason I got to sleep in this morning was because AJ got up with Abby.

"Then why do you look like shit?"

"Pint of Guinness, please," I tell the bartender as he slides a coaster onto the bar in front of me, taking the opportunity to avoid answering Walsh's question. Finally, I say, "Didn't know I looked like shit. Thanks."

Walsh takes a sip of his beer, eyes focused on the game on the TV, then glances over at me. "You look like a sad puppy that just got kicked to the curb. This about AJ?"

I glance at Walsh, wondering if I can trust him. It would be great to have someone to talk to about this, and I know this is the real reason he called and said we should grab a beer. As team captain, I'd have done the same thing if I thought any of my teammates were stepping over a line like this.

Keep your fucking mouth shut, I tell myself.

Coming here was a mistake. I should go home and call Renaud, who is supposed to be my best friend. But I've hardly talked to him this season while he's on the IR. And the only person Aidan Renaud worries about is himself—so I don't know how much he'd be able to help in this situation. He'd probably tell me not to tie myself down in such thorny circumstances, give me some advice about getting back out on the dating scene and finding *any* woman who isn't my boss.

I decide to risk confiding in Walsh, instead. "Can I trust you to give me good, and confidential, advice?"

It's not that he's not a trustworthy guy—he's one of the best. But his sense of right and wrong is so black and white; I worry that he won't be able to see into the gray areas of this situation.

"Yes, you can trust me not to tell anyone, and to give you my honest opinion."

I mull over his offer as I take a long gulp of my beer, draining half the glass and hoping that the alcohol will smooth out the erratic beating of my heart and relax my overly tense muscles. Instead, it loosens my tongue.

"I think I'm falling for AJ."

Walsh doesn't say anything, but his jaw tenses. Then he picks up his pint glass, tilts it toward the bartender and calls out, "I'm going to need another," before he drains it.

With my heart still pounding, I take another sip of my

beer, directing my gaze to the TV where St. Louis is crushing the third game in their series, while I wait for him to respond.

"So the other day when you said it 'wasn't what it looked like' and that you were just helping her iron her suit, that was . . .?"

"A partial truth. A couple weeks ago, we realized that we actually live across the hall from each other—"

"How the fuck did you not know that?"

"Because I'd never seen her in my building. I guess she moved in a few months ago, but I think she's *always* at work. And it's not like my schedule has a consistent pattern either. So anyway, when she got hurt and couldn't use her right hand, I was helping her out a lot."

I don't mention how I moved her into my place, helped her get dressed, took her clothes off to look at that bruise on her back, bathed her, and then fucking jerked off in my room thinking about how she was just down the hall. Because looking at it from his perspective, I know there's no way *any* of that wasn't crossing a line.

"Um hm," Walsh says, like he knows exactly where this is going.

"And she helped me out by getting her little brother to be my nanny until the end of the season." That wasn't exactly the order of things, but he doesn't need to know that.

"Your *manny* is her brother?"

"Yep. And the night before you saw me coming out of her hotel room, she'd texted me to tell me she was on FaceTime with him, and that Abby was trying to take her first steps. So I rushed over there so I didn't miss it, and before you ask, no, we didn't realize our hotel rooms were across the hall from each other until then."

"The universe has a funny sense of irony," Walsh says, chuckling.

"You're telling me." Slightly relaxing, I take a sip of my beer. "Anyway, we were chatting and eventually we fell asleep. Nothing happened. I wasn't lying about that."

"Yeah, because people *always* fall asleep chatting when they're not already laying down together."

He has me there. "I already feel bad for your kids when they're teenagers. Nothing gets by you."

Lifting an eyebrow, he turns to take his second beer from the bartender. "So then . . .?"

"So by then, I was getting to know her. Not just the side of her she shows us when she's at work, but the real her."

"There's another side of her?" He asks the question ironically, calling me out for previously thinking she was a one-dimensional person.

I dip my head and laugh into my beer as I bring it to my lips. He does *not* want to know about the sexy side of her that I've explored, and I'd never tell him anything personal about her past that she's shared with me. "Yeah."

"So...what? You guys are seeing each other?"

"I mean, it's only been a few days. Maybe a week if you count the few days before we went to Philly, when I was seeing her a lot more than normal."

"Are you sleeping with her?" he asks, and my stomach twists.

"I'm not going to answer that."

"But you're falling for her?"

I lick my lips as I try to think of how to explain it. "When you and Marissa were first together, what did it feel like?"

He tilts his head as he assesses me, and I know he wasn't expecting me to compare my feelings for AJ to his for his wife. "Like I wanted to be with her every second of every day. She was oxygen and I needed her to breathe. Gotta be honest, still feels like that."

"All these years later?"

I don't know if the thought of always feeling this addicted to AJ is appealing, or fucking terrifying. All I know is that it doesn't matter, because there's no way I want to live without her in my life.

"Yeah," Walsh says. "Even after all these years. I think that's how you know you have a good thing, because even though life changes, you still love being with that person."

"I think . . ." I press my eyes closed, before admitting, ". . . I think AJ is my person."

Walsh scoffs. "I never, not in a million years, thought I would *ever* hear you say that."

Our eyes lock, and we both laugh, because there's no getting around it. She and I are quite possibly the world's most unlikely pairing. And yet somehow, it just works.

"So what are you going to do about it?" Walsh asks, eyebrows pinching.

I pause, thinking about what my options are. "I don't know. Everything feels so uncertain at the moment. Like, I don't even know if she's going to renew my contract."

"You guys haven't talked about that?" Walsh asks.

"That would be unethical. Not only because she's not supposed to talk to me about stuff like that without my agent present, but also because I'm not using this relationship as a bargaining chip. I want to stay in Boston," I tell him, wondering exactly when that changed, and realizing that I need to have a conversation with my sister about that. And I should probably let my agent know. "But ultimately, it isn't up to me."

"I'm not sure how the guys are going to take this news. Are you planning on telling people?

"I don't know," I say. "I have to talk to AJ about it. I don't even . . . I don't even know for sure that she feels the same way."

"Shiiiiiit." Walsh grinds out the word. "You're talking to me about it and you haven't even talked to her?"

"Oh, she knows how I feel. But every time I try to talk to her about where this is going, she shuts the conversation down. She's convinced that there's no way this can work."

"And you're convinced there's a way it *will* work?" The doubt in his voice says a lot.

"It can't work the way that it is right now, with us sneaking around all the time. But also, I can't imagine a situation in which it *doesn't* work out in the end. So we have to find a way."

"And what does that way look like?" Walsh asks, sounding more curious than doubtful this time.

"I still have no fucking idea."

"You guys have to figure this out before everyone else sees what's going on here. You're lucky it was me you ran into in the hallway, and not someone with a bigger mouth."

"I know," I tell him, pressing my lips together. "And I appreciate your discretion while we figure this out."

"Are you prepared for . . ."

"Spit it out," I say when he trails off.

"Are you prepared for the reality that she might not want to go down the same path you want to go down?"

"I don't know," I tell him, trying to imagine how I would feel if AJ doesn't want this. A wave of nausea rolls through me.

"This is a dangerous game, and she's the one who stands to lose the most in this situation. You need to *seriously* consider whether this is worth it. Because if you get in any deeper and she isn't in it with you . . . dude, you're going to be wrecked. You're already so fucking far gone over her," he says, a breath whooshing out of him. "And as much as I like her, I don't want to see her ruin you over this."

I huff out a laugh, but we can both tell how fake it is. Because he's right. If this doesn't work out, I'm going to be a fucking mess.

Is pursuing a trade actually the smartest option? Maybe she's right, and this can't work out while I play for the team she manages. Maybe the only way I can have her is if I don't play for the Rebels. But how would it possibly work out if I lived halfway across the country?

I'm starting to see why she thinks our situation is hopeless.

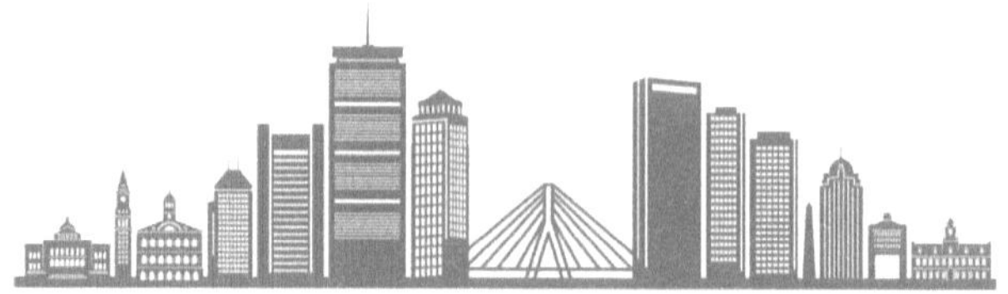

Chapter Twenty-Nine

AJ

"Are you positive you're okay?" Lauren asks.

I glance over to her from where I've been staring out the wall of windows along one side of my office, overlooking the practice rink. Below us, the players are on the ice, getting ready for tomorrow night's game when Philly comes to Boston.

I've been so focused on McCabe that I've literally lost track of our conversation. I'm too busy worrying about how he's dealing with me walking out yesterday, and not responding to his text last night asking if we could talk.

As I watch this practice, it's clear that something's off with him. And the way Charlie's arms are flying and his mouth doesn't stop moving while McCabe stands there hanging his head, I'm worried about whether it will affect his game, too.

"Yeah," I say with a small laugh and a shake of my head. "I guess I'm just thinking about our next game."

Lauren eyes me skeptically, like she knows I'm not telling her the truth. "What's really going on, AJ? You're not yourself."

Shit. And here I thought I was doing such a good job hiding my feelings, but I guess I'm not. "Nothing's wrong."

"You're never distracted like this," she says. "You've had this vacant look on your face half the time we've been chatting. Like, you're physically here, but your mind is elsewhere."

Laughing to myself, I'm thankful I'm able to hold it in because, yeah, my mind is certainly elsewhere. Mainly thinking about all the ways in which I've probably already screwed up this thing with McCabe.

Yesterday morning, I rushed out of his condo because I was overcome with emotion. The way he was looking at me while I sat on the floor playing with Abby, and the way my heart ached for a life I once thought I could have—a life full of children, a loving husband, and something to fulfill me besides my work.

It was just too much, because that's no longer my reality.

Sitting there on that floor, though, with Abby on one side of me and McCabe on the other, I had this moment when I wondered if that life was still a possibility. If maybe I was being given some sort of a second chance? A do-over?

But I needed space so I could figure out if the complexity of our situation is too much of an obstacle to overcome.

"AJ." My name is a sharp reprimand coming off Lauren's lips. "You're scaring me right now."

It's only then that I realize I haven't even responded to her. "I'm sorry. I really am just lost in my head."

"Are you sure you don't want to talk about it?" she asks.

God, do I want to talk about it.

And while I know that I could tell Nicholas and my secret would be safe with him, I also know that the advice he would give me might not be as right for me as the advice Lauren could give. As an employee here, she will understand the nuances of this situation more than Nicholas would. As a woman who decided to take a second chance on love after roiling from the turmoil of betrayal, she'll understand why I'm so hesitant to believe that this could work.

"I *do* want to talk about it," I say with a sigh. "But the problem is, Lauren, I can't."

"Why not?" Her eyebrows dip with confusion and concern. "Is it too personal to share?"

I take in the way she looks a tiny bit hurt at that idea. Like she thought we were close enough that I would confide in her, but is now realizing we're not. And I don't want her to feel that way, because that isn't accurate. She knows all about my struggles with infertility, Chet cheating on me, and our divorce. She knows how distant I keep myself from men now, so that I can never be hurt like that again. She's the best friend I have, and I trust her implicitly.

"No," I tell her, "it's not that. It . . . it has to do with work and it's highly confidential."

"Well, if you change your mind, I'm happy to keep your secret. I think you know you can rely on me not to say anything to anyone. Especially not here at work."

I think about how I once offered to bury a body for her, and I'm sure she'd do the same for me. If I can't even talk to *her* about this, how could I ever go public with our relationship?

The reason I'm so fucking conflicted is that yesterday,

after I woke up from some of the best sex of my life and I sat playing with Abby on the floor, McCabe came in with his hair all disheveled from sleep and that dreamy look on his face as he stood there in nothing but his grey sweats . . . looking at me like I was exactly where I was supposed to be.

I've never wanted anything more in my entire life.

A man who listens to and respects me, who delivers orgasm after fucking orgasm, who takes care of me when I'm hurt, who has a child I adore, who's life I fit into so easily and naturally that it's hard to picture myself walking away.

I don't want to walk away.

"Do you swear you can keep this secret, Lauren? Because it's a big one."

Her eyes widen, like she really didn't think I was going to confide in her.

"Yeah, of course," she rushes out, a small smile playing on her lips. "I can keep your secret."

"Okay, so here's what's going on . . ."

Ten minutes later, I'm trying my best to hold back the tears and she's sitting next to me, clasping my hand and looking at me like she doesn't even know me.

"AJ, you *really* have feelings for him, don't you?"

"Yeah." The word is an admission that comes out with a laugh. Because this is the most unlikely thing that ever could have happened.

"Why is there even a question in your mind, then?" Lauren asks.

"Because how could it *ever* work out? How could I ever be with him when he works for me? How could I ever be with him without ruining everything I've built for myself? You have to admit, I'll become a laughingstock as a GM if I'm dating one of my players."

"Will you?" she asks as she pushes her red hair behind one shoulder. "Or are you just *worried* that you will?"

My eyes narrow. "I'm worried because I *know* it will happen."

She just gives me a small smile and questions me once more. "Do you?"

"Lauren, what do you think is going to happen? You think I'm just going to tell the world that I'm dating our team captain, and everyone's going to be like, 'Cool, cool. Yeah, that seems appropriate?' I've spent my whole life carving space in this sport for women. I've made this team into what it is, staked my reputation on honesty and transparency, and I've never once even *thought* about crossing any kind of a professional boundary. I've made sure that I've brought on players who are not just excellent at their sport but are also good people, because I never want to work with an asshole like Chet again."

"So you're telling me, that even though you've done *every-thing* you possibly could to prevent yourself from having feelings for one of your players, McCabe still managed to sneak right past all of your defenses and make you fall for him?"

"Yeah, I guess that is what I'm saying."

"And you're telling me," she says, looking at me pointedly, "that you don't know if *that's* worth fighting for? This person who knows you, who you've confided in, who's obsessed with you and has told you he wants more than just sex, and you don't think *that's* worth fighting for?" The pitch of her voice raises with each question. When she puts it like that, it does sound like maybe I'm focusing more on the obstacles than the possibility, and perhaps I'm not trying hard enough to find a solution.

"I just don't see any way it can work out . . ."

"No, you don't see any way it can work out without some discomfort. But is that really the worst thing? So people talk. So people question whether it's appropriate. If you know in your heart of hearts that this is good and right, why does any of that matter?"

"I never wanted to be a public figure," I say with a little laugh.

Lauren gives me a smile. "Perils of breaking the glass ceiling, I guess."

"Mmhmm. I just never envisioned a downside to this work. Hockey has always been the singular focus of my life," I tell her. "And I love that Frank gave me a chance in this organization. And I love that the team has stood behind me every step of the way. And the thought of anything that I've built here being called into question, of my ethics being called into question." I have to stop because my throat is thick, and the tears are threatening to fall.

"Yeah," Lauren says, squeezing my hand. "People might call your ethics into question. But you know that there's nothing to question. And I know it, and Frank will know it, and every single person in this organization will know it. And isn't that what really matters?"

I think about what she's saying and realize that there's a lot of wisdom there. It's exactly what McCabe has been saying. His words from our conversation in the car in Philly keep going through my head. *I don't give a shit what anyone else thinks, AJ. And the sooner you can let go of maintaining this perfect image, the sooner we can stop sneaking around.*

"I guess I can kiss that GM of the Year Award goodbye," I say with a watery laugh. I don't know why I'm crying. I resigned myself years ago to the fact that I was never going to get that award, but with this year's nomination, it felt so close . . . so possible.

"Maybe," Lauren says, "but maybe not. You never know, AJ. People might surprise you."

I swallow down the lump in my throat, wishing that we lived in a world where there was any chance of that happening. "Yeah," I sigh. "I don't think that will be the case."

But when I really stop and think about it, does it even matter? So I don't get this award. I've never been the kind of person who needed an award to tell me I'd done a good job. The satisfaction is always in the work itself, in winning on the ice. Does not getting an award negate any of the success I've had here?

In the end, what's going to be more fulfilling? Twenty years from now, am I going to say to myself, *Thank God I gave up on that relationship, but at least I got that award?*

"I think you know what you need to do," Lauren tells me.

"Yeah." I nod, taking a deep breath. "But I don't even know where to start."

"Might I suggest that you start by talking to Frank?"

"The thought of telling my boss that I'm sleeping with one of my players has me about to throw up."

"Maybe it's time you stop letting fear rule your decision making."

I chuckle at her kind critique and how she winces slightly as she says it.

"Yeah, maybe. But first, I think I need to talk to McCabe. If this were any other new relationship, we wouldn't need to go public about it like this. I hate that we can't keep this private and see where it goes."

"AJ, if this were any other relationship, there'd be no reason to keep it private. The only reason you're scared for people to find out is because he works for you."

"And because I'm terrified by how quickly and completely I'm falling for him. This is all happening so fast."

She gives my hand one last supportive squeeze, like she's trying to tell me she believes I can do this. "Fast doesn't mean bad. Let me know how it goes with both those conversations." As she stands, she turns back to me. "Oh, what are you doing tomorrow night? Paige is finally home from her last business trip, and we're going to go out for dinner. Morgan might come too. You want to join us?"

"I'd love to," I tell her. I could really use more girl-time in my life, and I haven't seen Lauren's sister, Paige, in months. She's a business consultant who travels all the time for work, but we have a ton in common and I really like her. "But I already told Nicholas he could come over for dinner."

I'm always happy to see my brother, but I feel a pang of regret that I can't take her up on her offer. In my entire adult life, I don't think I've ever had girlfriends I could trust and talk to until now.

Part of that is my fault. My move back to St. Louis after college, dating Chet, and ultimately getting my first job in the NHL—in those years I was either surrounded by the backstabbing social elite I'd grown up with, or hockey men.

When I moved to Boston, I was so focused on my career that I didn't make time for friendships, or any kind of nonbusiness relationships. I was too busy making sure my brother was adjusting to boarding school but still knowing that I was here for him, and rebuilding this team into what it is today.

Immersing myself into work was the easiest way to avoid thinking about how shitty my parents and my marriage both were. Instead, I'd focused my attention on the fact that I had broken Nicholas and myself free of their toxic generational cycles. And I'd relished those victories so much that I'd inadvertently made work my entire personality.

But the way Lauren has worked to fold me into her friend group over the last year and hasn't given up on me even when I'm always working or traveling; the way she knows that female friendships are hard for me, but doesn't let me pull away; the way she shows up for me, like I showed up for her a year ago when she discovered her late husband had a whole separate life she didn't know about—it makes me realize that maybe work isn't "enough."

Maybe my life would be far more fulfilling if I focused more energy on relationships outside of work.

"You're cooking?" she asks, like it's the most preposterous thing possible, more so even than me being in a relationship with McCabe.

"He's cooking, just at my place."

"Okay, well, tell him and Nicole I said 'hi.' And if anything changes, please come out with us."

"I will. But if not this time, next time, for sure."

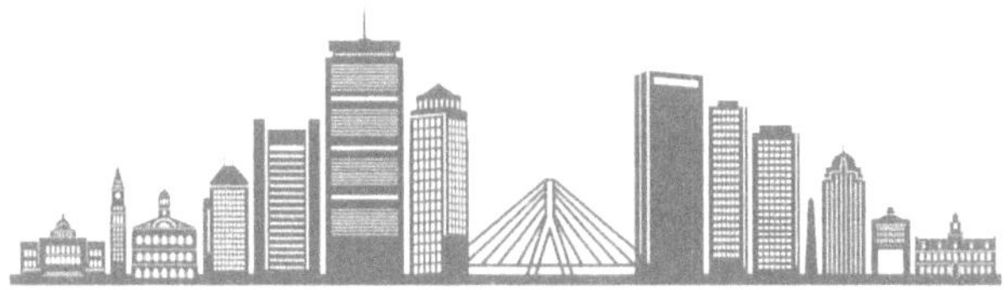

Chapter Thirty

AJ

I'm standing outside the locker room after practice, chatting with one of the equipment managers, Tim, when players start filing out. I'm not sure what's going on—they're not chatting with each other; everyone has their heads down like they're trying to mind their own business. The vibe feels off, and I don't like it.

I'm trying to pay attention to what Tim is saying about the new supplier for next year's jerseys, but I'm highly distracted by whatever just went down in that locker room.

"That sounds great," I say to Tim, not even entirely sure what he just said.

"Perfect, I'll drop a sample by your office tomorrow."

"Thanks," I tell him, right as McCabe walks through the door, his bright eyes locking onto mine as he looks at me with such naked longing it's impossible to miss.

I clear my throat and he looks away, thankfully before

Tim notices him staring. "Hey, McCabe," I call out. "Can I talk to you for a minute?"

"Sure." The word is gruff and borderline hostile, just like it would have been a couple of weeks ago. It's wholly unlike how he's spoken to me recently. *What the hell?*

I turn toward Tim. "Is there somewhere down here McCabe and I can chat privately?"

"Yeah, the stick room is right there." He nods his chin at the labeled door. "Everything's been put away already, so no one will need that space."

"Thanks. Looking forward to seeing that jersey," I tell him as I start walking toward the metal door labeled "Stick Room." I can feel McCabe hot on my heels, and as soon as I reach for the door, he's reaching past me, pushing it open for me to walk in.

The minute I step inside, I know this was a mistake. Because there are sticks lining three walls, and as he steps in behind me and closes the door, I realize there's barely enough room for the two of us in here.

"You wanted to talk, Boss?" He leans his back against the door like he's trying to give me space, but crossing his arms over his chest like he's pissed.

"What the hell is that tone?" I ask, eyes narrowing on his.

His jaw tics. He keeps his words quiet when he says, "I don't know how I'm supposed to talk to you right now, AJ. One minute, you're chanting my name while coming all over my face, and the next thing I know, you're running out my door and not returning my texts. So please, tell me what tone, *exactly*, would you like me to take?"

Pressing my lips together, I close my eyes and take a deep breath. Which is a mistake, because the only thing stronger than the epoxy smell of the carbon fiber sticks and the earthy, almost leather-like smell of the grip tape, is *him*.

He smells like soap mixed with something more masculine, something woodsy and musky. I didn't even realize I knew his scent until I was away from him. I step toward him, letting my head fall forward so my forehead rests on his chest. "I'm sorry. I'm just trying to figure my shit out."

"We all have shit we're figuring out, AJ," he says, but his voice has lost its hard edge, and his arms drop so he rests his hands on my hips. My body relaxes at that simple touch. "That doesn't mean we run away when things get . . . I don't even know, because I don't know what you're running away from. And since you won't talk to me about it, I'm left guessing."

"I just needed some time to think," I admit.

He dips his head, his lips pressing into my forehead at my hairline, as he asks, "About what?"

"About where we should go from here."

"Doesn't that seem like it should be an *us* decision?" He brings one of his hands to my chin and tilts my head back so I'm looking at him.

"Probably. Yesterday morning I got spooked, I guess."

"Why?" His gaze searches my face, like he's hoping to find the answers there.

"Because I don't know what to do with these feelings!" I'm trying to keep my voice low so no one walking by outside will hear us. "I've spent the last eight years learning to be okay with being alone and coming to terms with the idea that I'm never going to have children. And there you were, standing in the opening to your living room, looking sexy as hell and staring at me like I belonged there. Like I was meant to be in your and Abby's life . . . not just while my wrist heals, but . . . for real."

I swear his eyes turn a softer shade of green, the color of a vibrant grassy hillside as the bright sun goes behind a cloud. "Maybe you *are* meant to be in our lives." He brings his hand up and his knuckles glide along my cheekbone, making me feel cherished by the way he's looking at me and touching me. "I know it feels impossible, given that you're my boss. I understand what's on the line for you. But I'm not convinced that makes this whole thing hopeless. I have to be honest . . ." He tilts his head down so his forehead rests against mine, and I wrap my arms up over his shoulders so I can play with the hair at the base of his neck, which is easier to do now that my doctor put my new cast on this morning. I've missed him so much in the past day and a half, but instead of letting that realization scare me, I finally let it convince me that it means this—us together—is right. ". . . now that I've had you, I don't think I can let you go."

"Now that you've *had* me?"

He can't mean just the sex?

As if he knows exactly where my mind just went, he says, "Now that I've had you in my life, in my bed when I go to sleep at night, and playing with my daughter when I wake up in the morning . . ." he trails off as his lips brush along the bridge of my nose. "It's not about the sex, Alessandra. It's the way we fit into each other's lives so naturally, like it was meant to be."

"Just because it's easy, doesn't mean it's right." Even as I say the words, I know they're a lie. It might be wrong for me to date one of my players, but nothing about *us* together is wrong. In fact, nothing has ever felt so right.

"How could anything that feels like this, anything that we both want so much, be wrong? I'm not giving up unless you tell me you don't see any chance of a future between us." With his gaze locked on me, his lips meet mine tentatively, like he's giving me a chance to pull away. But if the last thirty-six hours have shown me anything, it's that I don't want any more distance. Before I can really kiss him back, he lifts his head. His green eyes shine between those dark lashes as he asks, "Is that what you want?"

It hits me then that I can keep trying to back away, but he'll just keep finding me, pulling me back to him. He's not going to let me ruin this for us.

"I *want* to see a future between us."

"Good." Then, he invades my mouth and we're a mess of clashing tongues and tangled limbs. We devour each other like we're both starved. Like it's been two months instead of less than two days since we last had sex.

His hands work to undo the buttons down the front of my blouse so quickly that he's got open access to my breasts in no time, and then they're spilling out as he pulls the cups of my bra down so he can run his thumbs across my nipples. The sensation travels straight through my body like an electrical current, pulling a moan out of me as my core clenches in need.

"Shhhh," he whispers against my mouth, and it's only then that I remember we're at work, that anyone could walk through the door behind him and catch us.

As he drops to his knees, telling me to put my hands against the door while he undoes the button and zipper on my pants, I find that I'm less worried about that than I should be. Besides, with me leaning up against the door like this, and him on his knees in front of it, it's not like anyone could push it open.

He drags my pants and underwear down my legs, and I step out of them with one foot so I can spread myself open for him. When his hot breath meets my clit, he glances up at me and whispers, "Tell me to stop."

I press my tongue against the top row of my teeth, then use it to wet my lips. I feel desperate and out of control, and I know this is probably a bad idea. And yet I can't make myself care.

Trailing a finger along the seam between my legs, he brings the moisture there up to my clit, lightly circling it with his finger. All I want is more pressure, more friction.

"Tell me to stop," he says again, "and I will. But if you don't, I'm going to make you come, and then I'm going to fuck you like I'm furious with you for the way you walked out on me yesterday."

"*Are* you furious?"

"What do you think?" His finger pushes back, sliding right into my slick entrance, and there's a dangerous edge to his voice that I find thrilling.

"Don't stop," I plead as he dips his face forward so that his tongue meets my clit, and he adds a second finger as he works himself deeper and harder, stroking me in a way that has me nearly breathless.

It seems like only seconds have passed when I feel the telltale signs of my orgasm—that tingling ache that radiates out from my clit through the rest of my body, the pulsing that's starting deep within my core, the clamping of my muscles around his fingers as he hums a growl of approval against my clit intensifies everything.

"Fuck." The hushed word escapes on a pained sigh. I don't want to be quiet right now, but I want to get caught even less. "Oh god, don't stop . . . I'm so close."

And when he pulls my clit between his lips with a soft sucking motion, I know that I'm coming undone for this man—not just in the way the waves of my orgasm ripple through me, but also in the way my heart pounds like it only wants to beat closer to his, the way my body curls forward, my hand wrapping his jaw in my palm like he's a cherished object, the way my mouth wants to utter promises of a future together that I'm not sure are possible. When he looks up at me, meeting my gaze, I see the same feelings mirrored back at me.

I could spend forever with this man.

But if this relationship doesn't work out, it could actually break me.

The minute my orgasm subsides, he's lifting me, spinning to pin me against the door with my legs wrapped around his hips, and sliding into me. He sets a punishing pace, fast and hard as he fills me until I feel like I can hardly breathe.

He nips and kisses up the side of my neck until his lips meet my ear, where he murmurs, "I once thought that raising a daughter by myself would be the hardest thing I'd ever do in my life. Turns out, pretending I don't have feelings for you is, by far, the hardest thing I've *ever* done. And I don't want to pretend anymore."

I lean my head back against the door as he kisses his way back down my neck and to my breasts, teasing one nipple with his mouth and the other with his hand, working me into such a frenzy that I'm not sure I can hold my own thoughts in, either.

"I want this, too, Ronan. I really do. But . . . we need to figure out what a relationship between the two of us can even look like." I'm breathing hard, almost unable to form words. Which is probably for the best, because I don't want to make promises to him while he's buried eight inches deep inside me . . . I want to make them with a level head and a clear heart.

"We will," he assures me, the whispered words warming my breast. "First, I'm going to give you another orgasm, like only I can. And then we're going to figure out a path forward."

He changes the angle of his hips, and the delicate glide of his skin against mine, the sound of our bodies meeting, the thin sheen of sweat across his forehead and temples—this whole experience has my emotions overtaking me, right as he says, "Because I don't want to do this life without you in it."

My whole body warms, stomach fluttering. "Yes," I hiss out the word as I chase the second orgasm that no one but him has ever been able to give me. "We'll find a way."

That promise has his mouth claiming mine, kissing me like he's trying to brand me while his hand dips between our hips. With his palm pressed flat against my abdomen, his thumb finds my clit.

As he works me closer to that orgasm, he rests his forehead against mine, and with eyes locked on me he says, "God, I just want to possess you. I want to worship you and own you at the same time. I want to respect you at work and disrespect your body at home. I want every last one of your orgasms, and I want your heart. But I want you to give it to me willingly, once I've shown you that you can trust me with it."

My physical and emotional feelings are all-consuming, and then I realize that he's moved his hand to the base of my neck, pinning me to the door. The thrill that the feeling of not being able to breathe brings on—the spike of panic, calmed immediately by the knowledge that he'd never hurt me—has my release starting deep inside me and spreading so quickly I feel like I might explode. I clamp my legs around him even tighter, holding his hips in place so he's barely moving as I feel my muscles working his orgasm out of him.

He lets go of my neck and kisses me through our shared climax, like he's worried I'll scream his name if he doesn't prevent me from doing it. He might be right.

When every last sensation finishes flowing through me, leaving my body buzzed and sated, I wrap my arms around his back, pulling him tighter against me as I cling to him. "We'll figure this out," I assure him.

"How?" The word is whispered and vulnerable.

"I'm going to talk to Frank."

His head rears back and he looks down at me. "You're sure you're ready for that? You don't want to wait until the end of the season?"

I hear what he's not saying: *After the GM of the Year award is announced.*

"Maybe that's what Frank will think is best. But I need to tell him about us, and officially recuse myself from your contract negotiations. I *still* won't be able to talk to you about that, but at least there will be no concern about me giving you some sort of preference in the negotiation process."

He snorts in response, but it's not the sound of him trying to hold in a laugh. No, this is a fully derisive sound.

"What?" I ask, suddenly uneasy.

"Not only have you *never* shown me any kind of preference throughout this process, the contract negotiation thus far made it pretty clear that you don't want me back on this team." His words are measured, but I hear the sadness and the anger behind them, and that confuses me to no end.

I made a perfectly reasonable counter to his agent's ridiculous request, offering him an increase and another three years in Boston. "What are you talking about?"

"I mean that refusing even a small increase in my pay and saying that you wanted to see how the playoffs went before you committed to renewing, was a *huge* slap in the face. And that's the only reason I asked Trevor to start looking into Nashville. Well, that, and my sister's there."

Alarm bells are going off in my head . . . not the warning kind like you might hear after opening your front door before putting in the alarm code, but the loud, intrusive ones you'd wake up to during a break-in in the middle of the night. The kind where the police respond, because the threat is real. *Emergency*, my brain screams at me.

I put one foot on the floor and tell him to finish taking his boxers off so we can use them to clean up. I am *not* having this conversation while he's still buried deep inside me and his cum is dripping out onto my ass. And when I'm done wiping myself up, I hand him his boxers so he can do the same, while I get my clothes straightened out.

Tense silence blankets the space as I wait until our hormones have calmed down before saying anything, because nothing about this situation is okay—neither the sex in the stick room, nor the mention of his contract—and I need to walk us back before we fully cross an unethical line.

When we're clothed, I finally meet his eyes and say firmly, "I think you need a new agent. Call Jameson Flynn and tell him I told you that you need new representation. We can talk more tonight."

Then I turn and slip out of the door, thankful to find the hallway completely empty because I have no doubt I'm wearing my emotions on my face right now. Not the gooey, love-filled feelings I was overcome with in that room while we had sex, but the rage I feel at knowing that his agent has been lying to both of us.

It's one thing to drive a hard bargain when trying to get your player a better contract—I'd expect nothing less. It's entirely another to lie about what your client wants, and then to lie to your client as well. And something like this has clearly happened, because the story McCabe is telling himself about his contract negotiation is not at all what really happened.

Suddenly, this feels like the most important issue to address. I've been telling myself this can never work between us because I was sure he was intent on leaving Boston, and it turns out that isn't what he wanted at all.

Chapter Thirty-One

McCabe

When I wake up, AJ's not in my bed. Again.

We'd spent most of last night talking and coming to the conclusion that what's developed between us is far more serious than either of us had planned—but that we both want to stick with this relationship and see where it leads.

Even though we'd broken off the conversation about my contract in the stick room, we agreed not to discuss it further last night. She insisted that Jameson would understand what happened and be able to explain it when I meet with him later today, and as much as I hated not hearing it straight from her, I had to respect those professional boundaries.

Her meeting with Frank is today, too, which makes me feel like this is a big day—for me as a player, her as GM, and us as a couple.

So the fact that she's snuck out this morning has me a bit

worried. I reach over, resting my hand on the indentation in her pillow, and the warmth there tells me she just got up. Slipping my shorts on, I note that it's still before six in the morning, and pad down the hall, hoping to find her in the kitchen. Instead, I find her about to walk out my front door.

"Hey," I say, my voice still scratchy from sleep. "Where are you running off to?"

"I need to head into work."

I clear my throat. "It's not even 6 a.m."

"Yep."

"AJ." I say her name like I've just caught her doing something wrong and need her to level with me.

"Yes?" Her reply is far too sweet to be sincere.

"Why are you really rushing out of here so early?"

"I really am going to work," she says, but her voice wobbles, betraying her.

I lift an eyebrow. "Who goes to work this early?"

She sighs as she crosses her arms over her chest, showing off her new cast. "I like to skate for a little bit before anyone gets there."

"What?" I don't mean for the word to come out sounding so harsh, but the woman has a broken arm, and she thinks she's skating?

"Hey, my orthopedist told me at my appointment yesterday that, now that I have the cast on, it's okay to skate. I just have to be extra careful not to fall."

"Did you tell him no one else would be there or even know that you're skating? That seems like an unnecessary risk."

"Really? Would *you* be okay not skating for months?"

"That's different."

"Why?" she asks, and I find that I don't have a good answer. "Skating is how I start almost every single day. For me, it's part of staying physically and mentally healthy. The rink is where I do my best thinking, and given that I have that meeting with Frank later today, I really need to think through what I want to say."

Last night, she wouldn't tell me exactly how she planned to approach the conversation with Frank. Now I'm thinking that maybe she's still not sure how to tell him.

"How are you going to lace your skates up with that cast? There's no way you'll be able to get them tied tight enough without hurting your wrist." The force she'll have to put on those laces as she tightens them could potentially exacerbate her injury. "And if your skates are too loose, that'll be dangerous. Let me come and help."

"What about Abby?" she asks.

"Abby normally wakes up around now anyway. I can get her up and dressed while you go change, and I'll bring her breakfast to the rink. She can eat while you skate."

"That doesn't make any sense. You have to be there in a few hours for practice. Why would you drive there, and then have to bring Abby back here to meet Nicholas, just to turn around and have to return to the rink again?"

I level her with a look. "Because then I can be there for you, too."

Her whole expression softens. "You'd go to all that effort just to lace up my skates for me?"

Driving halfway across the city to make sure she's safe while skating seems to me like a very small sacrifice, yet she clearly thinks it's a big deal. Just like when I brought her the new makeup remover in Philly.

Why is she so shocked when people genuinely want to help her? Every time I realize just how low of a bar Chet set, it makes me want to punch him in the fucking face again.

"I'm not sure there's anything I wouldn't do to keep you safe," I say, because I'm afraid that what I really want to tell her, that there's *nothing* I wouldn't do for her, would freak her out.

"Fine," she sighs. "I hate to inconvenience you like that, but I *really* want to get back on the ice. I feel like part of me is missing when I can't skate."

"How did I not know that you still skate?"

"I keep it pretty well hidden."

"Why?"

"I don't know." She shrugs, leaning toward the open door like she's about to slip out. "I guess when it comes to work, I keep most aspects of my personal life private. That, and I wouldn't want you guys to feel bad when I skate circles around you."

I let out a hearty laugh at the thought of her skating circles around a bunch of NHL players. Then I realize that because she's smaller than we are and led her college team to a D1 championship, she might not be exaggerating. "Wait, you're serious, aren't you?"

"Dead serious." And with that, she says, "Alright, I'm going to get dressed and pack my work bag, and feed Tabitha. I'll be back in ten minutes or so."

———

I should have left already. If anyone sees me here watching AJ skate before 7 a.m., this whole charade would be over.

But the way she's zipping around the ice, and how she easily handles her stick, even with her cast on, has me mesmerized. Every single thing about this woman has me in a state of awe: how she looked snuggled into me last night before she fell asleep, the way she kept turning around to talk to Abby as she babbled away in the back seat on our drive over here, and the way she's proving to me that she probably *could* skate circles around everyone on our team.

Or is it the way my daughter is standing on the wooden ledge at the top of the boards, wearing the pink high-tops AJ bought her, jumping up and down in excitement while I hold her waist to keep her upright, and yelling "Ay Ay" so that her name ricochets across the ice and off the glass on the other side?

Even though she's correctly used "Da" to identify me, Abby still hasn't put two syllables together to say "Dada." So the fact that she's already trying to say AJ, and is coming so close to getting it right, has a lump in my throat. Her first word is going to be AJ, and I'm as thrilled about it as if she'd just said Dada.

AJ speeds by, giving Abby a tiny poke in her belly as she does, and Abby laughs. It's the kind of guttural baby laugh that would have everyone else laughing along, if there were anyone here but the three of us.

Being here, simply watching AJ do something she loves . . . it brings the kind of quiet contentedness that has a smile permanently etched onto my face. I can't wipe it off—I'm trying, I really am.

Is this . . . joy? I can't remember the last time I felt like this. Have I ever felt like this?

It makes me imagine AJ being the one to teach Abby to skate, and to play hockey. It's been less than a year since I found out I had a child, but in that time, I've never once imagined a future that wasn't just the two of us. I'd worried about raising a daughter on my own, and I'd never been able to picture someone else walking that path with me. Until now.

———

"The good news," Jameson says as he hands me a bottle of water and drops a copy of my contract on his desk before sitting in his chair across from me, "is that you have a termination clause in your contract. Otherwise, there'd be no point in us talking."

"Meaning that I can back out of my contract with Trevor and hire you instead?" I ask dryly. I love that his first order of business was to check that my contract wouldn't prevent me from hiring him.

"Meaning that we can chat about your situation, and you can determine if you want new representation. Doesn't have to be me. But I'm not the kind of person who'd go behind another agent's back and talk to his client if the player's contract didn't allow for it."

I unscrew the cap on the water bottle. "Fair."

"So tell me why AJ thinks you need a new agent."

I give him the details of Trevor's negotiations with AJ before the trade deadline, and his eyes narrow. "That makes no sense."

"I know. I couldn't understand why she was digging her heels in like that—"

"Yes," he cuts me off. "That's the part that doesn't check out. AJ is extremely reasonable and she's a smart businesswoman. She wants another Stanley Cup. Hell, she doesn't just want *one* more, she wants one every year. And getting rid of you would make it more difficult for the team to achieve that goal."

"Trevor said my proposed contract would put her over the salary cap. So I could either take a one-year extension at exactly what I'm making this year, or leave."

"I've negotiated . . . " He pauses, and his eyebrows dip as he thinks. " . . . at least ten contracts with her in the time she's been here. I can't see her making that offer, not with your stat line and her goals for the club."

I want to push back and tell him that my agent was the one who was there, so he'd know. But that's when it occurs to me that maybe *this* is why AJ suggested I talk to Jameson— because he knows her better than any other agent does.

"Are you suggesting that what Trevor told me about their negotiation is . . . untrue?"

Jameson chews on the inside of his cheek as he leans back in his chair, crossing one ankle over the opposite knee as he rolls up the sleeve of his button-down shirt. "I don't want to step on Trevor's toes here. But I will tell you that in all the time I've known AJ, I've never seen her be unreasonable like that. And I've never seen her make a move that would hurt the team. Sure, as GM, she has to make hard decisions, but keeping you seems like an easy one."

I exhale a relieved sigh and take another sip of my water.

"If you're thinking you want new representation, we can

talk about that. But, if you want it to be me, I'm going to need you to level with me about something."

"What's that?"

"Why did AJ know what Trevor was telling you?"

I look at him in confusion, and as I watch his eyes narrow on me, that's when I realize . . . *Shit.* Obviously, the only way she'd know that is if we were discussing my contract, which is expressly prohibited.

"Can I assume that whatever I tell you will remain entirely confidential?"

"Anything you tell me as a *client* would be confidential, but since you're not a client yet . . . whatever. I can keep my mouth shut."

For a second, I wonder if I should insist on an NDA or something, but then I realize that it probably doesn't matter. AJ is talking to Frank right now, and after that, it's all going to come out one way or another. And if he's going to be my agent, Jameson needs to be prepared so he can help me navigate the publicity aspect of the situation.

"So . . . AJ and I are seeing each other," I force out, wondering if it'll ever get easier to admit that I'm dating my boss.

His mouth drops open, and he says nothing. Jameson's the kind of guy who chooses his words wisely, but I've never seen him speechless. Not even when he's dealing with some of the shit that Colt, his best friend and most lucrative client, has done.

Skepticism fills his voice when he asks, "And she discussed your contract with you in that capacity?"

I can tell just by his tone that he doesn't think she'd do

that, and he's trying to decide if he's just lost all respect for her or if I'm lying.

"No, we didn't discuss it. She's steadfastly refused to discuss my contract with me—"

"As she should."

"—but I made an offhand comment yesterday about how her refusal to consider even a modest increase in my next contract was a huge slap in the face, like she was making it clear she didn't want me back on the team next year."

"And?"

"And the look on her face was . . . confusion? I don't know, maybe it was anger? And then she told me I needed a new agent."

"So she told you to call me, because she knew I'd be able to put the pieces together," he says, like he's working it out in his head. "Okay. And how are you guys handling this relationship? I assume no one else knows at this point?"

"I mean, a few select people know. And she has a meeting with Frank Hartmann about this today. I know she wants to be recused from any part of negotiating my salary."

He hisses out a low whistle, but then looks almost pleased as he sits back in his chair and says, "This is going to be a total shitstorm. The media's going to have a field day over this, and your teammates are going to be up in arms."

"Yeah," I agree, wishing that this was easier, even while I'm willing to walk through this shitstorm if that's what it takes to be with AJ.

He rubs his hands together. "Well, this will be fun."

"Fun?" I must be looking at him like he has three heads.

"Yeah. Now that Colt's turned into a respectable human being, I haven't had any crises to deal with in a while."

"And that's your idea of fun?"

"Getting ahead of the story and outsmarting every-one . . . yeah. That's fun."

I let out a low rumble of laughter. I played with Jameson for a year before he retired and became an agent, but I've never really seen this side of him. "I'm glad one of us is looking forward to it."

"Want me to have my assistant draft up a letter for Trevor, letting him know you're releasing him from your contract? And get a new contract drafted up?"

"Yeah, I think the sooner we do that, the better."

"You know there's nothing I can do to speed up the contract process, though, right? Until the playoffs are over, we can't negotiate anything."

"Yeah. I know. But I do want to stay in Boston, and at this point, I'd settle for that one-year extension at my current salary if that's the only thing possible. I'm just not ready to walk away from the team, or from her, unless they don't give me a choice."

He shakes his head, and with a chuckle, he says, "Man, you're down bad."

"Yep." I don't even try to hold back my smile.

"We're going to need to figure out a plan for when and how the news of your relationship is going to come out. I'll talk to her publicist and the Rebel's PR Team to make sure we've coordinated everything."

"Okay. I'll mention that to her."

He nods. "I do think we can get your contract settled before the July 1st deadline when you'd become a free agent. And I'm not going to mention your desperation to stay, because I think you deserve a better contract than that. But

I'll be completely honest with you about what they're offering."

"Why do you think Trevor would lie to me about this in the first place?" I ask.

"My guess is that he thinks he can get you a much more lucrative contract elsewhere, and since he stands to make a percentage off whatever you make, it's in his personal interest to negotiate a better contract wherever he can make that happen."

Anger flares through my chest when I consider that the man who's been my agent since I entered the NHL has betrayed me. "I thought he was supposed to be doing what was in *my* best interest."

"He is. But did you indicate that you'd be willing to go elsewhere?"

"Yeah, I guess maybe I did. My sister and her kids are in Nashville, and since I've had Abby, I've been feeling like it would be nice to be closer to my family."

He glances out the window, then looks back at me. "Speaking from experience, there's the family you're born with, and there's the family you choose. Sometimes the two overlap, and sometimes they don't."

"I guess that until AJ was in my life," I say, wondering why I'm admitting this to someone I hardly know, "I didn't really feel like I had family here."

"Not even among your teammates?"

My teammates are great guys, but I've always held myself at a distance. I guess I never saw myself as a family man, like Walshy and some of the other married guys, and yet never saw my teammates as my brothers, either.

"Nah, not really. I mean, I was always close with Renaud,

but because he's been out this year, I don't really have my person, you know?" Honestly, Renaud's not really the kind of guy who'd have any idea what to do to help me with a kid or give advice about this relationship, anyway.

"I do, actually," he says. "Before Lauren, I always had Audrey and Jules, but that relationship was different because I was almost like a dad to them."

"Yeah, but you've also got Colt."

Jameson snorts a laugh. "Until recently, that was almost like having another kid."

I chuckle in response. "Yeah, he's grown up a lot this season."

"Listen to you, old man."

"I'm starting to feel old," I admit.

"So are you thinking this is going to be your last contract?"

It's amazing how much more at ease I feel now, knowing that it's Jameson who's going to be negotiating my contract. He's shrewd, but he's loyal.

"I don't know," I say, even though I do know. I know it in the way my body aches at the end of games now, and the way I hate being away from Abby when we travel. "Maybe?"

"Let's make sure it's a good one, then, yeah?"

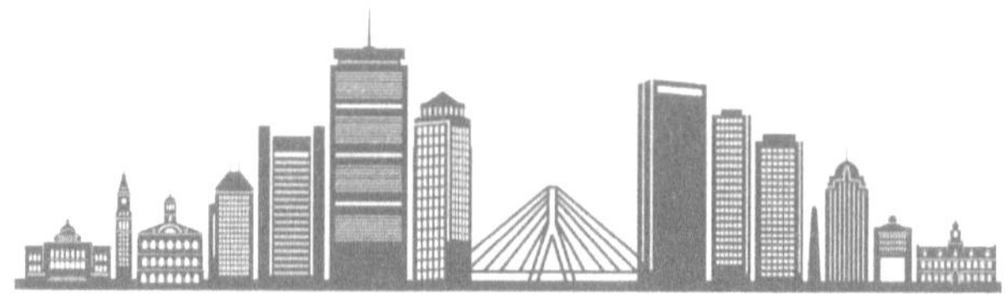

Chapter Thirty-Two

AJ

"**Y**ou've got to be kidding me," I say to Frank, my jaw falling open.

"No, I'm entirely serious." Frank's bellow of a laugh echoes around in his small office. I've always liked that, despite being a billionaire and the owner of this club, he keeps his space here small and unassuming, just like his presence in running this team.

"You don't look like this news is sitting well with you. I thought you'd be positively giddy."

"When have you ever known me to be giddy?" I ask, trying to stall the conversation, because discussing the bomb he just dropped is making me nauseous.

"Fair enough," he says with another laugh. "But the pool of candidates for GM of the Year just got smaller, and you moved right to the top."

I'm not sure what to say in response. Here I was, planning on telling him about McCabe and me, and he goes and sidelines me with the news that another GM was just forced to withdraw his nomination for the award after he was suspended without pay pending an investigation into unethical conduct for inappropriate and unwanted advances toward his assistant.

And while, logically, I know that my situation is totally different, I can't help but wonder if anyone else will make the same distinction.

"I—" I pause, not quite sure how to tell him, but knowing that I have to. "I actually called this meeting because I wanted to talk about a . . . situation."

I pause, not quite sure how to proceed after his stunning news. I don't necessarily think Brett Ivers is a good guy, or deserves this award for that matter. But the irony of Frank telling me about this situation right as I come to talk to him about my own relationship with an employee? It's just too much.

"A situation . . .?" he asks, indicating that he wants me to fill him in.

"Yeah, a situation involving my own love life."

His eyes widen. As much as Frank is constantly telling me that he wants to see me happily settled down, even going so far as to try to set me up with one of his sons, I've never indulged him by talking about that aspect of my private life.

"So . . . " I hedge, "this is going to come as a bit of a shock to you, just like it came as a shock to me. And I don't know any way to phrase this that's going to lessen that shock, especially given what you just told me."

Worry lines crease the corners of his eyes, replacing the curiosity on his face from a few moments ago.

"Believe it or not—" I gulp down the lump in my throat.

There is nothing wrong with you being in a relationship with McCabe, I tell myself. "There's something going on between me and McCabe."

Now it's Frank's jaw that falls open.

"I know that it seems entirely unlikely," I continue, pushing through the awkwardness, "but we both have feelings for each other and those feelings are becoming impossible to ignore."

"You're shitting me," Frank says with an uncomfortable laugh. "McCabe?"

He sounds like I just told him I ate roadkill for breakfast, and my stomach flips over in response. "No, I'm not kidding. I was coming to talk to you about this today because I want to be transparent about it. I don't want to do anything to jeopardize the club's reputation. It's entirely consensual and there's been absolutely nothing unethical about our relationship," I tell him, but even as I say it, I wonder if the times that McCabe brought up his contract with me over the last couple days blurs that line. But even if it did, I did nothing that was unethical. I didn't negotiate with him. I didn't even tell him that his agent is a fucking liar. I sure as shit hope that Jameson is giving him some good counsel right now.

"I know how much you value your privacy, AJ. But I'm going to need you to say more about this. Do I need to call HR in here for this conversation?"

I press my lips between my teeth. "Yeah, you probably should."

I've looked at my contract and I know there's nothing in it specifically about being in a relationship with a player. But there is an ethics clause, and all it would take for me to have violated it is McCabe saying my advances were unwarranted.

I know he wouldn't do that, but HR needs to know this is going on so that we can figure out the best game plan.

A few minutes later, our HR Director, Sarah, is sitting next to me in Frank's office. The small, cozy feeling of the space is now replaced with my cold dread. Suddenly, this all feels so real, and so wrong.

"Alright," Sarah says, "why don't you start from the beginning?"

I spend the next few minutes giving them the watered-down, sanitized version of how I grew closer to Ronan over the last few weeks. Sarah's eyes flip between Frank and me when I'm finished. She gives one long, slow blink like she's trying to steel herself from my reaction before she says, "I'm so sorry, but I have to ask, is this relationship sexual in nature?"

"Yes." My response is concise, hopefully inviting no further discussion.

She glances down at her lap, scanning a printed page before her, and then tells me what I already know. "There's nothing in your contract that expressly prohibits you from being involved with anyone working for this organization. But AJ, I have to tell you, this doesn't look good. I wouldn't be doing my job if I didn't try to protect this organization from threats of sexual misconduct or unethical behavior."

"I know that," I say, anxious for her to understand that I don't want to get in the way of her doing her job, but also hoping she doesn't ask me not to move forward with Ronan —because that's not happening. "And I respect that you need to do your job without me trying to interfere. But I also need you to know that I have been incredibly careful never to let anything that was developing between us cross over into any sort of gray area. I know he's in the middle of a contract negotiation, but I have only negotiated his contract with his agent. And even though I know that technically I am his boss and therefore in a position of power, I was not the one who pursued him. In fact, I did everything within my power to try to prevent myself from having feelings for him, because I would never want my actions to reflect poorly on the club."

I pause and sigh before I add, "But also, I think I deserve to be happy. I think I deserve to have a relationship that's built on mutual trust and respect, even if he and I happen to work for the same team. And the reason I came to talk to you about this today"—I turn toward Frank—"is because I don't want to hide it anymore. I want to recuse myself from negotiating his new contract, and I want to officially hand over any aspect of managing him, as a player, to Jim."

"Jim hasn't even started yet," Frank reminds me. Our new assistant GM was only hired a month ago and won't start until his current team's season is over.

"Then I'm sure you can handle McCabe until Jim starts. Or," I say, nodding toward Sarah where she sits next to me, "have HR be in charge of him."

"This is a tough spot, AJ," Frank says, looking at me like I'm one of his kids who's found herself in a tough predicament. "On the one hand, I'm happy for you that you're happy. I really am. I think you know how much I've always wanted you to find a fulfilling relationship. I just never dreamed it would be with one of our players."

"That makes two of us," I say quietly.

Frank relaxes his lower lip and lets out a sigh that ruffles his gray mustache. "But I'm sure you can see how, especially given what I just told you about Ivers, this could reflect poorly on the organization."

"That's why I want to be honest about it. I don't want this coming out like we're sneaking around and trying to hide it."

"The thing is," he says, shaking his head, "there's no way this isn't going to tarnish your reputation. *Even* if you're honest and transparent, and *even* if nothing unethical happened, people are going to take one look at the situation and judge you. It's not fair, but it's the way it is."

"I know."

"You go public with this, and you can kiss that award goodbye."

I swallow. "I know."

"I don't want that for you, AJ. You have worked your ass off to build this team into what it is today. As GM, you've made improvements in every aspect of this club."

I want to bask in his praise, but I can already sense the enormous *but* that's coming.

"Nothing that you've told me makes me think you deserve this award any less, and I want to see you receive it."

"You know I won't get it once people find out about me and McCabe."

"Which is why I think we shouldn't say anything about it until the season is over."

"What?" Sarah and I ask in unison.

"I think Sarah should do whatever she needs to do to accurately document this situation, immediately. I want her to have your statement and McCabe's on record, separately. I want us to have a game plan for how we'll make this information public. But I don't think we should do it until the season is over. You deserve that award, AJ. Our team deserves for you to get it. And they deserve another Stanley Cup, and I'm afraid that the news of you and McCabe would just distract them. It would bring up questions about the timing of this relationship and his new contract negotiation, and it might cause tensions in the locker room that we don't want. We can deal with this after the playoffs."

He does make a good point about the potential for this to be divisive in some way among the players. Is the fact that this never occurred to me an indication that I'm too focused on myself and McCabe, and not focused enough on the success of the larger organization?

He brushes his hands together over his round belly, and then stands like he thinks this conversation is over.

"Frank," I say, rising to my feet so we're eye to eye. "I'm not sure this is the best course of action."

"Good thing *I'm* sure, then," he says with a decisive nod. "I'm not letting you lose this award, and I'm not letting the news of your relationship cause rifts among the players. We still don't know if McCabe is going to be reasonable and accept our perfectly good offer, so this may be a non-issue once we hit July 1st."

The free agency date hangs there in the air, and a knot forms in my stomach as I worry about whether I should tell him that I don't think McCabe even knows about our perfectly good offer. Ultimately, I decide that this is something for him and Jameson to handle as part of the contract negotiation, which I'm no longer involved in.

"Not disclosing this relationship makes it seem like we have something to hide," I say.

"No, not disclosing it is doing what's best for the team. The playoffs will be over in a few weeks. Please don't tell me that you can't put off announcing your relationship until then."

It's not a question. He's not asking, he's telling me that this is what we're going to do. And even though the whole thing makes me uneasy . . . maybe he's right? Maybe this is just a small sacrifice for the greater good, because I certainly don't want to be the cause of any divisions within the team. And I'm pretty sure McCabe wouldn't want that, either.

"Of course I can," I say, because Frank just came up with the only thing that could convince me we should keep hiding this. Not because it's wrong, but because it could be a distraction for the team, and the last thing a GM or a team captain would want right now is *anything* that has the potential to distract the team from winning.

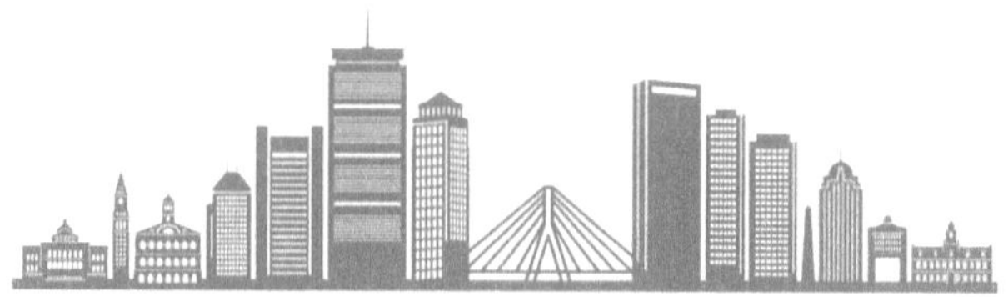

Chapter Thirty-Three

AJ

"I still don't think you should go," Nicholas reiterates as he stands from his seat at my small kitchen table and clears our plates.

"She's heard your argument and made her decision," Nicole says, looking up at him with a sympathetic smile. She's still in her scrubs from her shift in the NICU, and her blonde hair is pulled back into a sleek bun.

Nicholas looks down at her fondly, presses his lips together, and nods before looking over at me. "This is one of those situations where you aren't looking for any more input, huh?"

"Yes, and it's not as big of a deal as you're making it out to be."

"But Chet's going to be there," he says, exasperation ringing out in his tone. "And you haven't seen him since the divorce."

The last conversation I had with Chet was almost seven

years ago, when we were in the middle of divorce proceedings and I was still the assistant GM in St. Louis. I called him into my office, along with the GM, Joey Connelly, to let him know that our AHL affiliate needed a new head coach, and we were "promoting" him.

No one in the room believed that going from the NHL to the AHL was a promotion, even if it was for a more impressive title. And Chet showed his true colors, yelling and berating me, saying that this was all revenge for him cheating on me and because he'd forced my hand in trading McCabe.

Joey hadn't known about the cheating before that meeting. But after Chet acted like a goddamn toddler and talked to me like I wasn't his boss, Joey dismissed him, then looked at me and said, "You're too good at your job to be here."

"What the hell does that mean?" I'd asked, worried that he was firing me.

"Even with Chet leaving, there's too much emotional baggage for you ever to reach your full potential here." Joey had laid out reasonable arguments for me to consider looking for other opportunities: he was nowhere near retirement, which meant there was no room for me to grow professionally in St. Louis; my years with the organization would always be colored by the fact that Chet had gotten me my first job there; McCabe's trade had been a mess; and my marriage had disintegrated through it all.

He wasn't wrong. He also wasn't pushing me out. He was encouraging me to spread my wings, which I appreciated. So I'd used the rest of that season to put out feelers with other teams, and ultimately I'd ended up coming to Boston.

And I haven't seen or talked directly to Chet since then.

"I'm not worried about seeing him, Nicholas."

I get why he thinks it's better that I avoid my parents' annual fundraiser as I have every year since Chet and I split. But now, if I'm in St. Louis and I don't go, it feels like I'm hiding. And I'm done doing that.

He and Nicole both narrow their eyes at me, then glance at each other.

"Someone's bringing new energy," my brother says, raising his eyebrow before he turns and sets the dishes the sink.

"I like it," Nicole adds.

I've always done everything in my power to avoid running into Chet, including not going to family functions since my parents had kept *him* in the divorce, instead of me. I guess our family's social connection with his family ultimately meant more to them than their relationship with me.

That realization should have been shocking, but it wasn't—not even back then. And for the past six years since Nicholas and I moved away, we'd done our best to maintain our distance.

I hadn't had to worry about running into Chet during the season because he'd stayed in the AHL—until this year. For reasons I am obviously not privy to, Joey brought him back up to coach for St. Louis midway through the season. If we play them in the finals, I'll be seeing Chet anyway.

"Is there something you want to tell us?" Nicole asks, her voice taking on a singsong quality, like she's trying to cajole me into divulging secrets. Behind her, Nicholas is rummaging through a drawer for the right sized container for our leftovers.

"Besides the fact that I'm over my ex-husband?" I ask, while I mentally debate what—if anything—to tell them about McCabe and me. He said he didn't want to hide this, but Nicholas currently works for him, and I don't want to make anything awkward between them.

But it's not just how things have developed between us that is making me feel more resilient. It's my friendship with Lauren, and how she's brought me into her close-knit friend group with her sister, Jameson's sisters, and Morgan. It's the way I'm at ease now with the team, no longer feeling like I have something to prove. It's the way I'm letting go of my need to control every aspect of my public image. I'm actually looking forward to being able to be open about my relationship with McCabe, once the playoffs are over.

I'm still contemplating whether it's better if I don't say anything to Nicholas and Nicole until I can talk to him about it, when there's a knock on my door.

In the months I've lived here, not a single person other than Nicholas or Nicole has ever knocked on my door. And I gulp, because I know there's only one person it can be.

Nicole presses her lips together like she's stifling a smile when Nicholas asks, "You going to get that?"

There's a second knock, while I sit there staring at them. Shit. They damn well know there's only one other person in this building who I know, and there's no good reason he should be knocking on my door at seven o'clock at night.

"Or would you like me to answer it?" Nicole asks, amusement in her voice.

"No." I shoot out of my chair, turning toward the entryway. If I don't open the door all the way, and if I can stop him from saying anything, I can probably play it off like it was a food delivery to the wrong condo.

But when I pull open the door, he's standing there in

shorts and a T-shirt, barefoot, holding Abby, who yells "Ay-Ay," and reaches her arms out to me. I can't help but melt at the sight of them, and the way that Abby's now saying my name.

"We missed you," he says, his voice gruff like always, but with that undertone of affection he seems to reserve for me. And as he hands me Abby, he leans forward and kisses my forehead while pushing open my front door. He steps back quickly, with a strangled, "Oh."

"Might as well come in now," I say, knowing full well that Nicole and Nicholas are gawking at us.

"Uh . . ." He stands there, frozen, and I hold in a laugh.

"We already knew!" Nicholas calls out.

"What the hell?" I mutter under my breath, turning and carrying Abby back into my kitchen. "How did you know?"

"Well, we were suspicious when he came over to your hotel room to see Abby on a video call the first night you guys were in Philly," Nicole says. And though she wasn't there while we were on the phone with Nicholas, I'm sure he told her later that same night.

"Oh, hello," McCabe says from behind me, and when I turn to see what he's talking about, Tabitha is rubbing herself up against his ankles. I'm just about to remind him that she's evil, when he bends to pick her up. She goes willingly into his arms, snuggling against his chest and purring.

What the actual hell? If I had tried to pick her up, I'd be covered in claw marks.

"Oh my god," I say with a laugh. "The world's grumpiest cat has found the world's grumpiest man, and it's a match made in heaven."

"I'm not grumpy," he all but growls, but there's a heat in

his eyes that I don't miss. I wonder if he's still thinking about our little tryst in the stick room yesterday like I am?

"And see," Nicole says, "that right there? The way you just looked at her like you'd devour her if we weren't standing here, and how you're practically eye fucking him, AJ? You guys think you're not obvious?" She lets out an easy laugh, because apparently we're ridiculous for trying to hide this.

"It's possible that we're picking up on things because we already knew for sure," Nicholas tells her.

"Right," I say, narrowing my eyes. "Back to how you already knew?"

"The night you guys got back from Philly, Nicole and I were already suspicious. So we decided to wait down the hall to see if you snuck over to his place after we left. We waited, like, ten minutes, and you didn't come out, so we thought maybe we were just imagining things. So we went around the corner to the elevator and we were still waiting for it when you finally did head over."

I rack my brain, trying to remember how incriminating that conversation in his doorway was. Did he mention the phone sex before we shut the door? Didn't he say something about punishing me?

"You're really cute when you blush like that," McCabe says from beside me.

"This is humiliating," I mutter, hugging Abby to me a little tighter and raining kisses down on her head to avoid looking at my brother and Nicole. In response, she wraps her tiny fingers around a piece of my hair and snuggles her cheek into my chest.

"It's not like I didn't know you've had sex before," Nicholas says with a roll of his eyes.

"I don't want to talk about our sex life," I rush out, nodding at McCabe, "any more than I want to talk about your and Nicole's."

"Why?" Nicole teases. "We have a very healthy sex life."

"This is not the kind of thing I need to know about your relationship," I say.

Even though we're super close and Nicholas is in college now, it's hard to step back from the active role I took in raising him. Coaching him through his first heartbreak, teaching him to drive a car, covering his boarding school and college tuition . . . those are just a few of the ways I've assumed a parental role over the years. He's not technically my kid, but in a lot of ways, it feels like he is.

"Sooo," Nicholas says as he stands at the kitchen counter, putting leftover food into the large plastic container. "I assume if you two haven't told me, it's not public knowledge. Who else knows about this?"

"Walsh and Jameson," McCabe says. "But I need to tell my sister, too."

He hasn't told me a ton about Sloane, except that they were really close when he lived in St. Louis but that she moved to Nashville after he moved to Boston, and she has two kids of her own. I don't know whether she's married or not, just that he started considering going to Nashville because she's there.

I probably should have asked more questions when he mentioned that yesterday in the stick room, but I was too caught off guard when I realized that fucking Trevor had lied to both of us. I needed to get out of there before I broke down and told him things about his contract that I'm not ethically allowed to share.

"Lauren and Frank," I add.

"Frank knows?" Nicholas asks, his eyebrows practically hidden under his messy crop of hair that hangs over his forehead.

"Yeah. The fact that we work together makes things more . . . complicated."

McCabe quirks an eyebrow at me, and I'm wishing I could have told him about my conversation with Frank before having this conversation in front of Nicholas and Nicole.

"But Frank's okay with it?" Nicholas asks.

"Yeah, but . . . you know what? I just talked to Frank this afternoon. And we . . ." I nod at McCabe, ". . . haven't really had a chance to catch up about that discussion yet. How about I update you guys later, after we've talked."

"Of course," Nicole says, standing. "Let's get going."

"But there's still all this cleaning up to do," Nicholas says as he puts the container of leftovers into the refrigerator.

"You cooked, so I'm on cleanup duty," I remind him, taking a few steps toward him so I can literally usher him out of my kitchen. "I've got it."

"But . . ." he starts, and Nicole widens her eyes at him, indicating that he needs to take the hint and leave. I wink at her. Sometimes he can be oblivious to subtle social cues like that.

"Let's go, hon." Her voice leaves no room for argument, and he follows her as she heads toward the door, only stopping to give me a quick kiss on the cheek and turning to McCabe, confirming what time he'll be back in the morning to watch Abby.

When they're gone, my condo suddenly feels small. I

don't know why I'm nervous about telling him what Frank said today, but suddenly my throat is tight.

"Why do you look worried?" he asks, stepping toward me. But with Abby in my arms and Tabitha in his, we're farther apart than I'd want us to be for this conversation. "Is Frank *not* actually okay with this?"

"He is, but he thinks we need to keep this under wraps until the season is over. I'm pretty sure *he* wants this GM of the Year award more than I do. He also made some compelling arguments about how our relationship might distract the team, potentially causing rifts at a time when you need to be as united as possible—"

His brow creases. "He thinks that my teammates won't support us?"

"I think he's concerned that not everyone will. And since it's a contract negotiation year for you, some people might . . ."

". . . think I'm taking advantage of you? Or of this situation?" He fills in when I pause.

"Yeah."

"You know, that thought never actually occurred to me," he says, his tone bitter. "The idea that my teammates might think I'm the kind of person who'd get into a relationship with my boss for financial gain . . . " He trails off before he lets out a huff of a laugh while rolling his eyes. "I didn't know they thought that poorly of me."

"I'm sure they don't." Reaching out, I run a hand along his bicep before returning to rubbing Abby's back. "I'm sure Frank is just trying to anticipate any and all potential issues."

His throat bobs with the effort of swallowing down his

pride. "Yeah, I guess waiting until the season is over probably makes the most sense, then."

I note the way his words and his tone don't match up. And how his teeth are clenched, like it's taking a lot of effort to be okay with this. He has that hard, jaded look I seldom see anymore. Yesterday, he said he thought we should wait until the season was over. But maybe now that I said I don't want to hide this anymore, he started to . . . hope?

Is that what pretending does to him? First, pretending like he didn't have feelings for me. Now, pretending so no one finds out how real those feelings actually are?

"I don't want to," I say.

His eyebrows shoot up in response to my curt response. "What?"

"Keeping this a secret," I say slowly, working my thoughts out in my mind at the same time the words tumble out of my mouth, "only makes it look like we have something to hide. Maybe in the long run, that would make the situation worse with your teammates than if you were upfront about it from the beginning?"

"Maybe," he agrees. "But that doesn't change the way this will impact your reputation. Frank's right that you deserve that award, and I don't want to be the reason you don't get it."

"So then waiting would make sense, if the only thing I was worried about was my reputation. But it's not the only thing I'm worried about."

"It's not?" The question is so raw, and so vulnerable, it makes me wonder if he doesn't trust me not to break his heart.

"No. I'm also worried about how it will make you feel if I

have to hide this relationship like there's something wrong with us being together—"

"There *is* something wrong with it," he reminds me. "The power dynamic is off. You're my boss. Legally, this puts you at risk of someone claiming this is sexual harassment."

I tamp down the laugh that bubbles out of me, so instead it comes out like a low rumble. Not because there's anything funny about sexual harassment, but because this so clearly was not that.

"Yeah," I tease, "but if anyone is guilty of sexual harassment, it's you."

"Me?" He sounds affronted.

"I mean, you did maul me in my office, then come to my hotel room uninvited . . ." I give him a wink to make sure he knows I'm teasing. Then I say, "For real, though, Sarah from HR will get statements from both of us, showing that this is a relationship we've both entered willingly. And I've already recused myself from your contract negotiations, forever. I literally have no power over you."

"That's not true, and you know it. Your influence extends beyond contracts."

I step closer, continuing to rub Abby's back as her head grows heavy on my chest. It must be her bedtime by now, and she's clearly tired. "I've already given up any and all professional control I have over you. I've handed all management of you over to Jim."

"The new assistant GM, who hasn't even started yet?" he confirms.

"Yes."

"Thus making you appear to be ineffective as a GM?" His eyebrows dip. "Nah. If that comes out, even without any details as to why, it'll just give those assholes a reason to not give you an award you deserve."

"The other GMs wouldn't be assholes to question this. You know Brett Ivers?" I ask.

"Chicago's GM?"

"Yeah. It's going to come out, probably later tonight, that he's been put on administrative leave. And he's lost the nomination for GM of the Year because of it."

"What did he do?"

"Sexual misconduct, it sounds like. Unwanted advances toward someone who worked for him."

McCabe's chuckle has his shoulders shaking as he steps closer and drops his voice to say, "Nothing about this is unwanted, Sunshine. And I'm happy to tell that to anyone who asks."

"Sarah *will* be asking. She'll need you to make a statement on the record, so that there's proof that this is consensual."

He leans in to kiss the crown of my head, and Tabitha uses the proximity to rub her head up and down Abby's back, right next to my hand.

It's the same motion as when she runs the top of her head along a piece of furniture, like she's scratching an itch. But it seems so affectionate compared to how she acts when I try to touch her. And here she is, *still* in McCabe's arms, while I've never been able to hold her without her immediately struggling to be free.

We stand there, with a child and a cat pressed between our bodies, and it feels like we're a family. It feels like everything I ever wanted . . . which both thrills and terrifies me.

"I'll be happy to tell her just how consensual this is." His voice is raspy as he talks quietly, probably not wanting to wake Abby. "How much detail should I give her? Do you want me to tell her *everything*?"

I know he's joking, but just to be clear, I say, "Let's not mention *any* specifics. We'll just tell them this has been developing for a few weeks, that it's consensual, and that we don't want to hide it anymore."

"It feels a bit weird to think that Frank knows we're sleeping together."

"Why is that any weirder than anyone else knowing?"

"Besides the fact that he signs both our paychecks? Maybe because you two have always seemed to have a bit of a father-daughter relationship."

I tilt my head as I study his face—his bright green eyes half hidden behind those dark lashes as he gazes down at me, with the look of affection he wears so openly now.

He gives me a little smirk. "Do I need to go ask him for your hand or something?"

His tone is sarcastic, so I playfully retort, "You planning to marry me?"

"Someday." There isn't an ounce of lightness, as though he wants me to know he's dead serious.

A boulder drops on my stomach so fast that the sensation pushes the air right out of my lungs. "Excuse me?" I squeak.

"Which part of that is unclear?" he asks as his eyes search my widened ones.

"The part where we've been developing feelings for each other over the past few weeks and you're already talking about marriage?"

"I already can't imagine myself with anyone but you, Sunshine. You've infiltrated every part of my soul and overrun all my defenses. There's no part of me that doesn't want to be with you. It's okay if you're still worried about how this will work, or if you're not thinking far enough into the future to know for sure that everything will work out. I'm optimistic enough for the both of us."

I huff out a laugh. "You're optimistic? Since when?"

"I'm optimistic about *you*, and that's all that matters. Look at you, standing there holding my baby, and looking at me like you've never wanted anything more than this. Us, together . . . it's so easy. It's like it was meant to be. And if you'd stop fighting it, you'd see that too."

I gulp, before saying quietly, "I'm not fighting it."

"Maybe not now. But until yesterday, all you could focus on were the reasons this wouldn't work."

I close my eyes, relaxing into the moment. "I'm sorry."

"You don't have to be sorry," he says, peppering a trail of kisses across my forehead. "There are real obstacles that we'll need to overcome, and that part won't be easy. But I don't think it's a reason to give up on us."

"I wasn't trying to give up on us," I tell him.

"What were you trying to do, then?" The question is asked with open curiosity, rather than the sarcasm I would have expected given the situation.

My words are small, reflecting how I feel having to admit this. "Protect myself."

He stiffens slightly, but one of his hands slides to my hip, then rests on my lower back. "From me?"

"From being hurt again." Though right now, with Abby asleep on me and Tabitha purring in his arms, his lips on my forehead and his voice quiet, I don't feel in danger of being hurt. It feels . . . perfect.

"At this point," I continue, looking down at Abby's

cherub-like face, "I'm sure you know me well enough to know that I've avoided relationships since my divorce. I've avoided everything but work, and Nicholas."

"So that you don't get hurt?"

"Yes. In my experience, relationships are messy and painful. I never wanted to feel that again. I told myself I was never going there again."

"There?"

"I was married before—"

"To an asshole."

"Ronan," I say, looking up at him pointedly, "not too long ago, I thought *you* were an asshole."

A thin smile graces his lips as he lifts his hand and strokes my jaw with his thumb. "Maybe your judgment's impaired. It would explain how you thought Chet was a good guy in the first place and were confused about me being an asshole until now."

"Was I confused? Or were you an asshole until we talked about why I had to trade you?"

His smile widens. "Perhaps a little of both."

I shift because Abby's dead weight is hurting my back and arms. The cast on my right arm means my left is bearing most of her weight, and those muscles are clearly not up to the task.

"C'mon," he says, nodding his chin toward my front door. "Let's go put Abby to bed so we can finish talking about why I'm not going to let you close yourself off from being happy."

I glance back into my kitchen at the dishes in the sink and realize that I don't care about leaving a mess behind. Everything I care about is right in front of me, heading out my door, and I'm going with them.

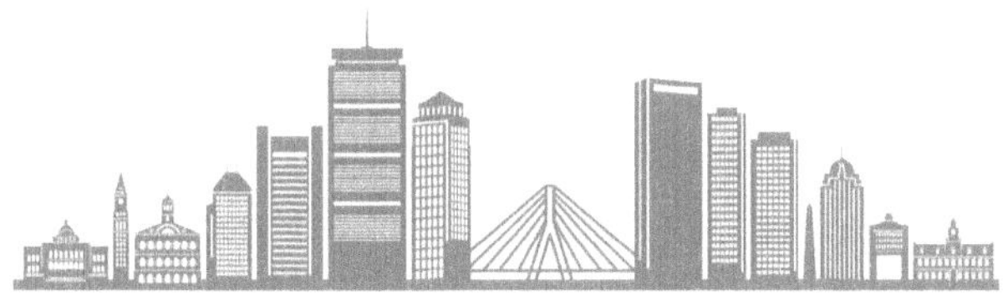

Chapter Thirty-Four

McCabe

Our third win in a row puts us up 3-2 in this semifinal round of the playoffs. The celebration in the locker room after our first win on home ice this series is dying down, and most of us are showered and dressed, but the music is still pumping and people are yelling back and forth over each other. Hartmann's on one of the benches in the center of the room, trying to prove he can moonwalk, while our unimpressed teammates jeer.

The party doesn't stop when AJ strides through the door, and yet everything in the room fades away when I catch sight of her. She gives me a subtle nod, our eyes connecting for the briefest moment, and then she's turning to talk to Coach Wilcott.

Walsh elbows me, and grits out, "You trying to get caught?"

I'm fucking tired of hiding this, that's for sure. "No."

"Then stuff those fucking heart-shaped googly eyes back

into your head before someone else sees you looking at her that way."

I turn to face him, taking in the hardened look on his face. Luckily, we're off to the side of our teammates, so no one can hear our conversation.

"When did you become the asshole here?" I ask.

"When my team captain started a relationship with the only person in the world he absolutely shouldn't be dating, and I had to start worrying about anyone else finding out. Just stop being so fucking obvious about it. At least until the season is over."

It's exactly what Frank told AJ, and I'm sure he's saying it for the same reason. And as she and I finally agreed the other night, it's the right approach—after the season is over makes so much more sense. There's no reason to risk causing issues within the team when we're so close to making the finals, or to jeopardize her chances of winning a well-deserved award. Two or three more weeks, at the most. I can keep this on the down-low that long.

But god, it fucking *hurts* to hide how I feel about her. It hurts when every fiber of my being wants to reach out to her, wrap her in a hug, and give her a celebratory kiss. Instead, I get a nod of acknowledgement.

I watch her turn and head out the door. "I'll be right back," I tell Walsh.

He grabs my forearm as I turn to go, and when I pause and look back toward him, he just says, "Be careful."

I'm not sure exactly what he's warning me about—getting caught, getting hurt, or hurting her?

Without responding, I glance around to make sure no one's focused on me, and then I follow AJ out the door. She's not in the main part of the hallway when I exit the locker room, so I follow it toward the elevator she probably used to get down here. And sure enough, I find her waiting in the alcove for the doors to open.

"We're going out tonight to grab a beer and celebrate." I keep my tone casual, in case anyone's in the hallway and can overhear me. "You should come, too. Jules and Audrey will be there."

"I can't." Her eyes meet mine as she drops her voice lower and tells me, "You know that."

"Why would I know that?" I ask quietly, moving toward her until there's barely any space between us.

"Ronan," she says in warning. I'm so used to her only saying my name in private, and usually in the bedroom, that a low hum of desire rumbles in my chest. I take in the slender column of her neck above the lapels of her suit coat.

"I hate it when you wear your hair up," I tell her, leaning my head down even closer.

"Not feminine enough for you?" She sounds surprisingly defensive, even while I watch goosebumps erupt on her skin as my breath caresses her.

"No . . . " I say, trailing my finger from the edge of her collarbone up the side of her neck and stopping right behind her ear. I'm counting on my large frame blocking the view if anyone passes in the hallway behind me. "I hate it when you wear your hair up because all I can think of is what it would be like to taste your exposed skin."

I dip my head then, my lips gently brushing down the side of her neck as she sucks in a surprised gasp, when my lips meet her hard, tense muscles. I want to dig my fingers into her shoulders, massage them until she's loose and relaxed. But I can't. So instead, I let my tongue do the teasing, enjoying the way it draws a shiver from her. I stop when I reach that hollow between her collarbone and neck, and then, realizing how dangerously out in the open we are, I pull back.

"Fuck, AJ. You're going to be the goddamn death of me."

"I doubt that," she says with an air of nonchalance, but her cheeks are flushed and her breathing is ragged.

"Trust me," I tell her. "I've never felt so close to spontaneously combusting. I have to go out with the guys, but I'll be home after one beer. I can't wait to get you alone tonight."

A needy sound rasps from her throat as she looks up at me with those big brown eyes. "Drink fast."

"This is why we should just find a diner or something like we do when we're on the road," I say after we send away another group of women who have approached our table at the Neon Cactus. I get it, we're a table of five guys having some beers, and none of us is wearing a ring . . . yet. But Drew and Colt are engaged, and Zach's so far gone over Ashleigh that he might as well be. Only Luke Hartmann and I are available—at least as far as my teammates know. "Or somewhere with a VIP section."

"Nothing wrong with women hitting on you," Hartmann grumbles, like we just took away his dessert.

"There is when you're taken." Colt rolls his eyes. "Our better halves will be here soon, and then hopefully this won't be an issue."

I wish AJ were coming. Not that she could slide in the

booth next to me so I could wrap my arm over her shoulder like my friends can do with their girlfriends and fiancées. But just being able to see her, meet her eye across the table . . .

Zach sighs. "Ashleigh can't come tonight. She has to be at her internship really early tomorrow."

"Remind me where she's interning," Drew says.

Ashleigh is studying to become an aerospace engineer, and Zach talks a bit about the defense contractor she's doing a paid internship with this summer. The way he describes her role on the project oozes with pride.

"Man, you fell for her fast," I say. They met at a diner in Seattle where she was waitressing about six months ago.

Colt scoffs. "You should see how fast I fell for Jules." The way Drew side-eyes him makes me wonder if my suspicions about their engagement are right. He's been telling everyone they've been secretly dating since October, but I have a sneaking suspicion that it's more recent and there's more to the story.

"Hey, when you know, you know," Zach says, smiling.

"That's how it was with Audrey, too," Drew adds. "Like the minute she was back in my life, I knew I wanted so much more than just to co-parent with her."

"How did you know it was love, though?" I ask, looking around the table, clearly asking all of them the question.

Four pairs of eyes focus on me like I just said something incredibly revealing. And maybe I did. Maybe even asking the question makes it obvious that I have a vested interest in the answer? But I have nothing to go on here. I've never been in love, and while I'm pretty sure that's what I'm feeling here, I don't have anything to compare it to.

I press my lips to the mouth of my bottle and tilt it back, taking a long pull of beer and hoping that they're not still staring at me when my head comes forward.

No such luck.

"Oh shit," Colt says with a laugh, and then falls uncharacteristically quiet.

"Are you seeing someone?" Zach asks.

I snort a laugh to show them how ridiculous that idea is. I don't date, and they know that. I swore off dating after Jenna and I broke up, and that was before she showed up with my baby. The one time I broke that rule was a disaster.

Besides, I wouldn't call what AJ and I have "dating." It's more like . . . I don't even know. What do you call it when you're sneaking around with your boss, and are so desperate to be with her every available second that you move her into your place even though she lives across the hall? That you stay in her hotel room on the road?

"I'm not *seeing* someone," I say with an eye roll and a shrug, but the added signs of indifference don't seem to dissuade them.

"Oh, so you're just asking about how to know if you're in love for . . . what? Research purposes?" Drew asks, his voice so full of sarcasm I want to throat punch him.

"I'm asking because I have no idea . . ." I draw out the words like it's painful to talk to these idiots. I hope they're buying the attitude, rather than sensing how eager I am to know their answer. Because I've never actually felt so entirely consumed, I've never been in a situation where I couldn't picture my life without that person. ". . . and you're all so *stupidly* in love with your women, I was curious how you knew it was love and not just like infatuation or something."

"Remember in the fall when we all met for dinner, back when I was trying to figure out how to convince Audrey to trust that I wanted, and was ready for, a real relationship with her?" Drew asks me.

"Yeah." I huff out a laugh, remembering how we all offered ridiculous advice before Walshy started dropping truth bombs.

"Walsh told us that the secret to a successful relationship was that you need to complement each other, to balance each other out," Drew says. "And when that happens, when there's that perfect sense of symbiosis, and you realize that you're happier with that person than you could ever be without them—that's how you know."

I think about what he's saying, and about how easy and natural everything is with AJ. But more than that, I think about how much I crave her company, how life just feels incomplete when she's not around.

"Doesn't that get hard, feeling like you can't be happy when she's not around?"

There must be something in my tone, because four sets of eyes are back on me. "He didn't say you couldn't be happy without her," Colt says. "He said you're *happier* with that person than you could ever be without her."

The realization hits me, harder than it has before: I could never be happy without AJ.

"You sure you're okay?" Hartmann's eyebrows dip as he looks at me.

"Yes, Lover Boy, I'm sure. Why? Are you in love, and we don't know it?" Am I an asshole for deflecting this conversation back to him? Quite possibly. Do I care? Not at the moment.

His cheeks pinken, because Hartmann's still got a bit of a baby face and is like a goddamned golden retriever—happy and wagging his tail one minute, then talking shit and irritating me the next. It's hard to imagine Lover Boy ever being serious enough to fall in love.

Because if there's anything this relationship with AJ has taught me, it's that love *is* serious—it feels an awful lot like taking a vow, risking being torn apart, inviting pain.

These feelings I'm having don't make me proud or gooey, like my teammates sound every time they talk about their significant other. And they don't necessarily make me feel happy. They make me feel clingy, like I can't live without her. Like I'd do anything to protect her, give up *everything* just to be with her. And yet, there's a lightness I feel when I'm with her that I've never felt before—a confidence that everything will be okay in the end.

It has to be love. I don't know any other way to describe how I feel about her and the sacrifices I'd be willing to make to be with her.

"Ooooooo," Colt says, his attention averted just as I intended, "you got something to tell us, Hartmann?"

He rolls his eyes as he chuckles. "I don't do relationships, so, no."

"Why *is* that?" Zach asks.

"Why is what?" Hartmann responds.

"Why don't you do relationships?"

There's a moment when a look flickers across his face, which I have no doubt we all just noticed, before he says,

"There are way too many women in the world to settle on just one."

Zach opens his mouth to respond, when Audrey and Jules show up at our table. I drain the last few sips of my beer, then push my chair back, seeing my opportunity to leave. I can't fucking wait another minute to get back to AJ.

"Here you go." I gesture at my chair. "Someone can have my seat. I need to go home so my nanny can leave." And then I'm out of there before anyone can even say goodbye.

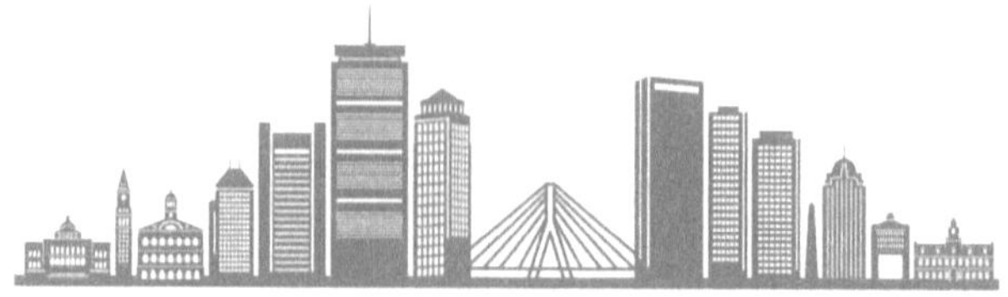

Chapter Thirty-Five

AJ

With forty-eight seconds left in Game 6, we're tied 1-1. Hartmann's exuding shitloads of nervous energy in the crease, and I'm sitting up in the luxury box with his family and some of the WAGs, wondering if he needs to be pulled. I took a big risk bringing him to Boston against his father's wishes. I know he's going to be a great goalie one day, but I fear that today might not be that day.

Relax, I remind myself. *Trust the process.*

I've hired the best coaches and players I could, and now I need to trust them to do their jobs like they've trusted me to do mine.

Next to me, Frank's hand finds mine, and he squeezes. I look down and see that his other hand is holding his wife's, so with my opposite hand, I grasp Marissa Walsh's since she's next to me. I know what it would mean to her to see her husband go to the finals again. She lives and breathes hockey and has been one of the most avid supporters of this team through the years. She squeezes back, and looking down, I watch her grab a hold of Audrey's hand, who grabs Jules's, until we're a united line standing at the front of this luxury box.

I take a deep breath as one of Philly's forwards, Mackenzie, takes a shot. It goes wide, and Zach snags the puck before he's checked into the glass. He doesn't go down, though. Instead, he bounces back and elbows Mackenzie off him, gaining control of the puck and passing it up to Walsh, who somehow manages a breakaway.

We're yelling and screaming as he speeds up the ice, across the blue line, with two of Philly's players trying their best to catch up. The nerves have my stomach in knots as their goalie moves up to challenge Walsh, but he quickly slaps the puck between the goalie's legs and our fans erupt when the puck meets the back of the net. The home crowd is booing loudly as we hold our arms up in celebration, our hands still connected, cheering our team on.

Twenty-three seconds left. Two shots on Hartmann, both deflected. And then the final buzzer sounds to end the game, and our players fill the ice while Philly's fans stand there, stunned. After coming on so strong in the first two games, they just lost four in a row to send us to the finals. It's the most satisfying, perfect end to this series and I could not be more ecstatic.

Everyone in our suite is jumping around and hugging each other, and all I want to do is get down there and congratulate our players, so I slip out through the throng of people celebrating, thanking everyone who congratulates me. And then I'm running toward the one elevator that will take me down to ice level, flashing my badge at the security guard, and impatiently tapping my foot as I wait for the doors to open.

JULES

AJ, you're coming out with us tonight, right?

Normally after an away game, especially one so close to home, we'd be on a plane home immediately. But tonight, we're staying over. Given the importance of this game and the likelihood that it would be the one to send us to the finals, combined with most players' wives and girlfriends being here, the team needed a night of celebration. Our flight tomorrow morning isn't even at the crack of dawn, like they often are.

AJ

Thank you for the invite, but I don't normally do things outside of work with the guys. It feels inappropriate.

I laugh to myself when I think about all the inappropriate things I've gotten up to with McCabe recently. Jules and Audrey are going to give me so much shit when they find out. I'm actually kind of looking forward to that. It's nice to have women in my life who aren't intimidated by me, who treat me like a friend, instead of like their boss.

JULES

But you came out to the Neon Cactus with us a couple weeks ago.

> **AJ**
>
> That was different. The team kind of insisted
> I come out to celebrate my award
> nomination.

I try not to think about how everything would be so much easier if that award wasn't a thing. *Two more weeks, at the most. You can do it,* I tell myself.

> **AUDREY**
>
> It's Marissa's birthday. Maybe you can come
> out for one drink to celebrate?

> **AJ**
>
> Shit. I wish you'd told me that before I sat
> next to her for half the game!

How did I not know? I'm so good about things like that. Except lately, my free time has been spent with McCabe, not planning out ways to make sure my players and families know I care about them. I wonder if they've noticed the difference.

> **JULES**
>
> You could just come tell her happy birthday
> in person

> **AJ**
>
> Well now I feel like I have to!

> **JULES**
>
> Yes!!! My work here is done. Here's where
> we're going . . .

A link appears on my screen, taking me to the map app that shows a bar only a few blocks away from the arena.

The elevator doors open, but by the time I make it down

through the tunnel and to the ice, our players are heading out of the box and toward the locker room. Sweat drips off them as they carry their sticks, and I congratulate each and every one of them as they pass, giving fist bumps and high fives to the guys who offer them up first.

McCabe is the last one out of the box—the captain who refuses to leave anyone behind. When his head snaps up and he sees me standing there, his pupils dilate until his bright eyes are practically black. The look of hunger on his face has butterflies swooshing through my belly.

"AJ." My name is a low growl leaving his lips as he nods his head at me. I'm sure he's trying to sound professional, but his gravelly voice scrapes along my skin until I'm certain I'm wearing my desire all over my face.

When he steps past me, Charlie Wilcott is right behind him. And his confused expression tells me he didn't miss the way I was looking at his star player.

"Congrats on the win, Coach." I fake a lightness I don't feel now that my heart is pounding, wondering what he might think about that look he just saw.

"Thanks." Charlie's words are gruffer than normal.

"I saw that Evangeline and her partner came in third at that competition in Europe last week." I fall into step next to him, trying to distract him by talking about one of his favorite topics: his daughter, who is a pairs figure skater gunning for an Olympic appearance.

"Sure did," he says, his face lighting up.

"That Olympic run is looking more and more likely."

"Yeah, she was disappointed that the other US pair competing ranked higher than them, though," he tells me. "She said she wasn't feeling quite right, and changed a double to a single in their routine, which lost them some points. She seems tired, and I worry that the constant travel and competition are taking a toll. I'm glad she'll be home for a bit this summer before next season's competitions start back up."

I know exactly what he means. "I think we can all use the break," I say. "But first, congrats, Coach. The Stanley Cup Finals . . . you don't get *there* every year."

"Sure don't," he says, lifting his chin. "Congrats to you, too. Wouldn't be in this position if it weren't for you."

"It's a true team effort." I hate how cheesy it sounds, but it's true. This team, and the year we've had, wouldn't have been possible if everyone wasn't giving their all.

I skip the locker room because I don't trust myself to see McCabe with no clothes on. Funny how I've never had a problem standing in a locker room full of mostly naked men, until now, when one of them is mine.

My heart skips a beat at that word. *Mine.* But he is, isn't he? Just like I'm his.

And I really like this for us.

———

"What do you mean, you used to work together?" Jules screeches, her eyes huge as she looks back and forth between McCabe and me, where he stands ten feet from us, talking to Drew and Colt.

I let out a small laugh, hoping it doesn't clue her in that this conversation is making me nervous.

"Yeah, I recruited him when I was a scout in St. Louis, before I became the assistant GM there."

"And then?" Audrey asks.

"And then he played there for two years before he got traded to Boston, and a couple years later, I took the GM position here."

Jules nods, like she's following, but she's narrowed her eyes at me. "I thought Colt said there was some sort of bad blood between you two? But it doesn't seem like there is."

"There was," I tell her, wishing I could confide in Jules and Audrey the way I confided in Lauren. But for now, the fewer people who know, the better—just until the season is over. "But we cleared up a little miscommunication about his trade, and things have been better since."

I *really* need to tell him the full truth about how that trade went down, but I'm already afraid of how he'll react when we play St. Louis next week and he sees Chet for the first time since beating the shit out of him.

It's going to be hard enough to keep our relationship a secret. Knowing that there's even more to the story would make it impossible—there's no way he wouldn't react if he knew how Chet actually forced me into the trade. And if things between them turned violent again, that would be the worst possible scenario. I will prevent that, at any cost.

I'll tell him the rest of the story as soon as the playoffs are over—hopefully after he's held the Stanley Cup above his head and taken a victory lap around the ice, for the second time in his career.

He'll understand why I waited.

"Hey," Drew says, sidling up next to Audrey and snaking his arm around her waist as he pulls her into his chest. "Our table's ready."

An hour later, our group has polished off three bottles of champagne. I'm still sipping my second glass, and next to me,

Ronan hasn't finished his second beer. It's an unspoken agreement that we're keeping our drinking moderate, because we don't want to waste tonight's precious alone time. In fact, the only ones drinking heavily are Luke Hartmann and the birthday girl, Marissa Walsh. She's pretty drunk, probably from the birthday shots she did with some of the guys when we first got here.

Beneath the table, Ronan squeezes my knee, and it's so unexpected that I inadvertently flinch. I glance over at him as he leans toward me, then tilt my head toward him so he can speak directly in my ear.

"So . . . St. Louis for the finals. This mean you're definitely going to that gala?"

"I guess it does."

"It would be a shame not to see you in that dress again," he says, dragging his fingers up the inside of my leg while memories of the way he looked at me when I walked out of the dressing room last time we were in Philly float through my mind. The hunger . . . there's always hunger in the way he looks at me. My eyes flick up to his, and sure enough, he wants to devour me.

"Stop looking at me like that."

"Can't help it," he says, nudging my shoulder with his. "And stop changing the subject."

"You can't come with me to the gala, Ronan. It would be a disaster."

"Why?" His fingers creep up my thigh until they're almost at the apex of my thighs. I swat his hand away. The last thing I need is Audrey, who's on the other side of me, to look down and see his hand.

"You know why. Let's just get through the finals and then—"

"What are you two whispering about over there?" Colt calls out, and Jules elbows him in the side, which doesn't even phase him. He just sits there, smirking at us, like he knows exactly what's going on. *Shit.*

"AJ's going to some big fundraising gala when we're in St. Louis next weekend," McCabe says casually before I can chime in. "Her ex is going to be there, so I was saying she should have some of us come along with her."

"Why?" Zach asks, concern in his voice. "You need protection or something?"

My laugh comes out like a snort as I wave him off. "No, I'm fine. McCabe is just overreacting."

"Actually," Jules says, head tilted as she looks at me, "I think it's a good idea. If your ex is going to be there, why *wouldn't* you want people there in your corner?"

"Because we're not going to be boxing?"

"You know what I mean," she says with a roll of her eyes. "For emotional support."

I look around the table, about to make a joke about not bringing hockey players to a black-tie event for emotional support. But all the guys are staring back at me, jaws tight, nodding their heads like the decision is already made.

They want to be there for me.

The realization hits me so hard that I tear up. They know I have their backs, and they want to have mine too.

"I mean, I do still have five seats at my table." I let the admission slip out, even though I hadn't intended to say anything.

"I'll take one," McCabe says next to me, and gives my knee another secretly supportive squeeze.

"I will too," Colt says.

"Me too," Drew adds.

"Me three. Or four?" Luke adds. "Haven't gotten to dust off my tux in at least a month."

"Having to dress up in a monkey suit for some fancy event is *not* the motivation here," Zach says with a sigh. "But I'll take the last seat."

"Who else is going?" Luke asks.

"Wilcott and his wife. And your parents."

He leans back and tilts his head so it rests against the back of the booth, letting out a big sigh. "I didn't know I was signing up to hang out with my parents," he groans. "Walsh, take my spot instead?"

"No can do," Walsh tells him. "Marissa's coming out with the kids for the first two games."

"I suuure am," she slurs, reaching her head up to plant a sloppy kiss on his cheek. He just laughs and shakes his head as he looks down at her fondly.

"Besides, you have the best parents," I remind Luke.

"You just think that because they're not *your* parents."

"I think that because they're awesome." I want to tell him a bit about my parents so maybe he'll appreciate his own, but I'm aware enough to realize that I have no idea what his childhood was like any more than he knows what mine was like.

"You only think they're awesome because you don't have to see your nearly seventy-year-old dad making out with your mom every chance he gets."

I laugh. "There are way worse problems than your

parents being married for almost forty years and still being very much in love."

"Well," McCabe says next to me with a chuckle, "this is going to be fun."

Fun is not the word I'd use to describe how I'm feeling about this event. However, now that I know they're all coming with me, I feel slightly less sick to my stomach about having to go.

———

"I'm never . . . wearing . . . a dress . . . again." The words leave my lips on ragged breaths between kisses where McCabe has me pushed up against the door of my hotel room.

The way he fingered me in the back of the cab on the way to the hotel, bringing me almost to orgasm, then pulling out right as we arrived at our destination, has me desperate for release.

This is a dangerous game we're playing, making out in the back of a cab and sneaking around in the hotel when we could easily be caught. Thankfully, I gave him my second room key before we got out of the car, and we headed up separately, both managing to make it here without anyone seeing us. Whether he can get out of here tomorrow morning without getting caught remains to be seen.

"I love you in a dress," he says, pulling back to look down at me. The pure need I see in his eyes has me clenching my thighs. "Easy access to your pussy is my favorite thing. The way you were dripping all over my hand"—he licks his lips—"I just want to taste you now."

He drops to his knees, sliding his hands along my thighs, up and under my dress, then pulling my thong down my legs so I can step out of it. Pushing my dress up to my hips, he loops one arm inside my thigh and brings my leg up so my calf is resting on his shoulder. Then he leans in and breathes deeply, the act making me whimper. "God, the fucking scent of you," he all but growls. "You smell like sex. Like you can't wait for me to make you come."

"I can't." I'm so turned on, I'm having trouble catching my breath. "I need you."

"I need you too," he says, those green eyes flicking up to meet mine. "Not just like this, Alessandra. I *need* you in *every* way. Sometimes it feels like I don't know what I would do without you in my life."

I stare down at him, on his knees before me, thinking that it's too soon to feel that way, that we don't know each other well enough yet. But even though I keep telling myself this, the truth is, I feel the same. I don't want to go back to my lonely existence, where I used work as an excuse to avoid relationships.

"This . . . with you . . . it just feels right. It feels like this was meant to be," I tell him.

He lifts my leg as he shrugs out of his suit coat, tossing it to the side before leaning in, running his tongue from the bottom of my slit, all the way through my center, and up to my clit, where he circles it before looking up at me again as I moan. "Maybe this *was* meant to be. We met at the wrong time, under the wrong circumstances. We should never have ended up here, together." He presses another kiss to my clit. "And yet we did. Because this is where we were always meant to be."

I thread my fingers through his dark hair, wishing this cast was coming off soon but knowing I still have weeks of wearing it. "Yes," I say as he brings his face back to me, licking and sucking until I'm panting his name.

"Tell me you're mine," he demands, as he slips two fingers inside me and curls them up to hit the place he knows will bring me to orgasm.

"I'm yours," I say effortlessly, my hips pressing forward to meet his fingers as I try to increase the pressure of his tongue on my clit.

He pulls back long enough to say, "Promise me." And then he's licking and sucking and bringing me right to the edge of release. My jaw hangs open, and I'm gasping for air, incapable of speaking, so he stops right as I'm about to come.

"Promise me," he grinds out, the words sounding like he's in pain. "Unless you don't want to."

"I promise," I assure him on a shaky exhale. And then waves of pleasure ripple through me as he brings me right over the precipice, and I cry out incoherent promises of forever as lightning runs through my veins and every part of me lights up like I'm on fire.

I collapse forward, catching myself with my good hand on his shoulder, but he's standing, picking me up and carrying me into the room in the next second. My mind dazed and my limbs weak, I melt against him, kissing his neck along the way. Putting me back on my feet at the end of the bed, he turns me around and unzips my dress, letting it drop, and then unhooks my bra, tossing it to the side so I'm standing naked before him.

His clothes are off just as quickly, and he fists himself, his cock huge and hard in his grip. I pull my lower lip between my teeth as I look down at it.

"I'm not going to fuck you tonight," he tells me.

"W-what?" It's a strangled gasp, and my core aches in response.

"That's not what this is between us," he says, bringing both his hands to my neck and running his thumbs along my jaw as he holds my gaze. "Every time I'm with you, it feels less and less like fucking, and more and more like . . . I don't know. I want to make love to you."

"Is there a difference?" I ask, attempting a flippant tone as I try to keep that last, thinning wall around my heart, even as I wonder why I bother. He's so ingrained into my soul at this point, I don't think I could live without him. I couldn't protect myself from getting hurt now if I tried, and I'm pretty sure there's no need to keep trying.

"You tell me. You just came apart on my tongue and told me this was forever."

I did?

"Ronan," I whisper as my chest tightens. I have so many emotions rushing through me as I bask in his adoration.

After my failed marriage, I never thought I'd say "forever" again. But, I'm ready to say it now. Things with him are different than anything I've ever experienced—the closeness, the intimacy, his protective instincts.

He's my person, the one who would do anything for me. I was ready to go public with our relationship days ago, just so he didn't feel like some secret I was hiding.

I'd take the fallout. I'd lose the award I've worked my whole career for. I'd do it for him, and I'd do it without any regrets. Because he's worth it.

"Yes?" He smirks down at me.

With my heart racing, I reach out, stroking him in my good hand. "I need you inside me. I need to feel how only you can make me feel. And I need you to promise me that you're in this for good, too."

"Oh, Sunshine . . ." Picking me up with both arms, he puts a knee on the bed and leans down to lay me out below him. "I've never not wanted you. I've just been waiting for you to want me, too."

"Wanting me," I tell him, before sucking in a sharp breath when his lips meet my nipple, "is not the same as wanting forever."

He hums a disapproving sound, and the vibrations send shockwaves through my body.

"With you, it is," he says, and something about the simplicity of his words has me melting. He plants an elbow next to my head as he slides into me, bringing his lips to meet mine. And as I wrap my legs around his hips and thread my fingers into his hair, nothing has ever felt so right. The way our bodies fit together perfectly, the way he takes care of me physically and emotionally, the way my body feels as he slams into me over and over leaving me panting with need. It's exactly what I need.

He is exactly what I need.

The fact that the sex is so good, that he has me coming again in a matter of minutes, has more admissions of my feelings tumbling out as the pleasure overtakes my senses. No matter how good it is, I could live without the sex. But I'm not sure I could live without *him*.

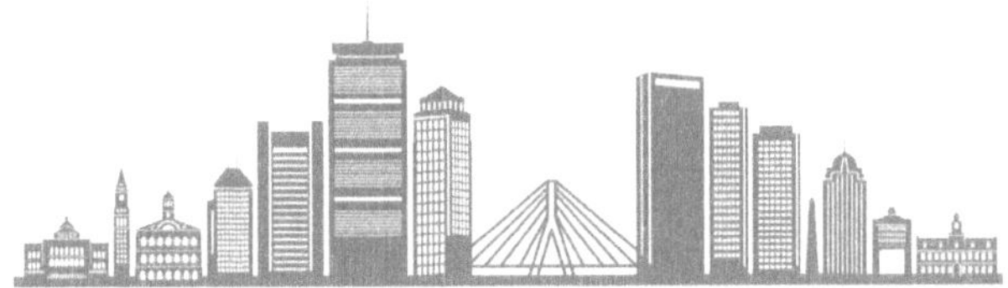

Chapter Thirty-Six

McCabe

My sister's flight home tonight got canceled,
so she's staying with me.

Oh, okay. So this is my warning that I
shouldn't sneak across the hall in nothing
but sexy lingerie tonight?

I want you to meet her. But yeah, preferably
with clothes on.

I thought our plan was to keep our
relationship a secret until after the playoffs?

We're keeping it a secret from the general
public. A small group of people close to us
already knows. Of course I was going to tell
Sloane.

SUNSHINE

Meeting her still feels like a really big step.

MCCABE

Too big?

SUNSHINE

No. It's just that you didn't ask me to meet
her earlier, so I wasn't expecting this and
now I'm just trying to wrap my head around
the idea.

MCCABE

The only reason I didn't ask you to meet her
earlier was that she was only here for the
day and I was having lunch with her, and I
knew you had that big meeting all day. Plus,
I wanted to tell her about us before she
met you.

SUNSHINE

* Deep breaths *

MCCABE

Stop being weird about this. Your brother
already knows we're together and now my
sister does too. Obviously we're going to
meet each other's families.

SUNSHINE

Yeah, but when you meet my parents this
weekend, we're still going to be pretending
we're not together.

MCCABE

That's getting harder and harder.

SUNSHINE

That's what she said . . .

MCCABE

SUNSHINE

What time do you want me to come over?

MCCABE

How about right now?

———

"Oh my god, you did not!" my sister's peals of laughter ring out after AJ tells her about the time she intentionally wore a vibrant pink suit to a dinner with all the GMs, because one of them had insinuated that women didn't belong in the upper echelons of hockey management.

"I did. I was the only person there not wearing black or navy blue. And you know what? If that asshole hadn't made the comment, I probably would have worn a black suit too, just to fit in. Instead, that night made me realize that maybe I wasn't meant to fit in. Maybe I was meant to stand out."

"You're my fucking hero," Sloane says with a big smile. "Like, seriously, someday I want to be a girl boss like you."

I'm not at all surprised that these two have hit it off. Sloane's in healthcare management, and as a single mom to two active girls, she's balancing work and life as best she can. She has big aspirations but hasn't had the luxury of putting in the time and effort it would take to advance in her career like I know she wants to. It's part of why us living in the same city had been so appealing—we'd have been able to help each other out.

"Just be careful you don't girl boss so hard that you forget to have a life. I went down that route, and don't necessarily recommend it." AJ's gaze slides to me, a small smile gracing her lips as she looks at Abby, who is currently cuddled into my chest, sucking on her pacifier. I'm sure her eyes are half-closed, because she feels like dead weight, exhausted after the video chat we had with Sloane's daughters before AJ came over.

"Now that my kids are both in school, I finally feel like I can be a bit more dedicated to my job. Like this trip for these meetings today wouldn't have been possible before, but because my neighbor has kids my kids' ages and she could just bring mine home from school with hers, I got to come to Boston."

Sloane had gotten her girls on the bus this morning before heading to the airport, made it to Boston before lunchtime so we could have a quick meal together, then had an afternoon full of meetings at a hospital in the same network as the one she works at. She was supposed to be home by bedtime, but bad storms in the Nashville area grounded some flights, and her plane never left the airport to head to Boston. Instead, she's scheduled on a flight home tomorrow in the late afternoon.

"Not being able to step up like this before," she continues, "held me back from advancing in my career. Not that I'd change the time I had with my kids when they were younger. But it does feel nice to be recognized for my skills at work, too."

AJ studies my little sister as she talks, and I think she senses her need for validation. "Can I give you some unsolicited advice?"

"Sure." Sloane looks at AJ with open admiration, but I'm a bit worried about what AJ is going to say. She can be blunt, and I don't want her to unintentionally dim my sister's newfound enthusiasm.

"Do the best job you can do at work, but only insofar as it doesn't take away from your family. I know I don't have children, so I don't know what it's like to balance kids and a career, but looking at it from this side . . . I'd trade my success for a family any day. The validation you get from work will only carry you so far in life. The love you get from your family"—AJ swallows, and I think she's talking hypothetically until she looks at me and I realize that she's not. She's talking about us—"it's so much more important."

Sloane smiles and says, "I want to be you when I grow up."

"Honey," AJ says, reaching over to take Sloane's hand and squeezing it. "You're going to be so much better. Because you're getting this whole work/life balance under control a decade before I did. You're going to crush this."

I clear my throat, because suddenly I'm a bit choked up, and that startles Abby and she lets out a whine.

"Here," AJ says, standing. "Let me put her to bed so you two can have some more time together. I'll be back in a bit." She takes Abby from my lap after I give her goodnight kisses, cuddles my baby into her chest, and carries her toward the hallway that leads to the bedrooms.

Once she's out of earshot, Sloane says, "Holy shit. She's amazing."

I nod, because there's no denying it. "She is."

"And to think that you used to hate her." Sloane has had years of hearing me bitch about AJ, so she was appropriately shocked at lunch when I told her how things had changed.

"I think it was just easier to hate her."

"Why's that?"

"Because look what happened when I stopped."

"What happened? You're both happy for the first time, maybe ever? Sounds just *terrible*." She laughs lightly with a shake of her head.

"When did you become such a smartass?"

"I was born this way."

"Is it going to bother you if she stays here tonight? She pretty much sleeps here every night now."

"Why would it bother me?" Sloane furrows her brow.

"I don't know. I'm just making sure."

"I love this for you. I love that you're happy. I love that you guys found each other and are so good together. And I love the way she is with Abby . . . how she talks to her and treats her like she's her own little person. I've dated guys who . . . I don't know. Who treated my kids like they were an inconvenience, I guess?"

"This is when it's good we don't live in the same place, because I'd probably want to kill a guy who treated you and the girls that way."

She opens her mouth to respond, but Abby lets out a shriek that has me standing. "Let me just go check on them. I'll be right back."

I rush down the hall and find Abby's door cracked. I'm about to push it open and walk in, when I hear AJ, her voice soft and calming, saying, "Yeah, if I had to burp like that, I'd probably scream about it too."

In the corner of the room, she's rocking Abby in the

glider, rubbing her back in a circular motion as she hums a song. I've never heard her sing. Didn't even know it was a talent she had. And yet, there's something so inevitable about this scene . . . her sitting in my daughter's room, rocking her and singing to her before putting her to bed. She really was meant to be a mom, and I want this for her more than anything.

I want her here in my house every single day.

I want her to be Abby's mom.

I want her to be my wife.

————

"Dude," Hartmann says as he steps up to me in Walsh's backyard late the next morning.

All around us, the families of our teammates are talking and laughing while children run wild at this team party, celebrating the Rebels making it to the finals. My eyes don't leave the other side of the large stone patio, where AJ's holding Abby's hands to steady her as she takes tentative steps. Next to her, Sloane chats her up.

"You didn't tell me your sister was so hot."

That gets my attention. "Alright, Lover Boy. Don't even think about going there. Besides, she's too old for you."

Granted, she's maybe four years older than him. But given his reputation, I can't picture him with someone with kids. He's not the type to settle down. I also try to ignore the fact that she's closer to his age than AJ is to mine.

"I don't know," he says, his eyes back on AJ and Sloane. "Older women are kind of hot."

He's not wrong.

"Do not fucking *look* at my sister," I threaten. "The last thing in the world she needs is a child like you chasing after her. She's already raising two kids of her own."

"She seriously has kids?"

I don't miss the way his eyes travel up and down her body when he asks this question.

"Yeah, and an asshole of an ex-husband, so just keep your distance. Besides, she lives in Nashville and is flying home tonight. Put her out of your mind."

"I don't know, I think she's *burned* in my mind now." His chuckle has me realizing that he's just trying to piss me off, so I punch him in the shoulder, muttering something about him being an immature prick. I watch AJ pick Abby up and hand her off to Sloane before she holds her phone up, shielding her eyes from the midday sun.

AJ turns and walks away, to the far side of the lawn, while Sloane walks toward me, carrying Abby. "You going to introduce me?" Hartmann asks.

"Get lost. For real."

He's laughing as he turns and walks away, but not before I see him wink at Sloane.

Abby reaches for me as soon as I'm close enough to take her, and then she snuggles her head into the crevice between my neck and shoulder, yawning. "Walking is hard work, huh, baby girl?" I say as I rub her back.

"I can't believe you were even thinking about leaving," Sloane says quietly as she stands next to me, her gaze sweeping across this scene. "You have this whole family you've created for yourself here."

"Well, this thing with AJ is still very new, and I was thinking of leaving *before* it started."

"I mean, even what you have with your teammates is great. The way you guys are there for each other . . . the way you give each other shit like actual brothers would. And then just add AJ on top of that, and the way she is with Abby, and how much you two clearly adore each other. Don't walk away from this," she insists.

"I'm not planning to," I tell her. "I've been meaning to talk to you about that, actually. I'm really hopeful that my new agent can work out a contract with the Rebels after Trevor almost screwed me over. But if for any reason he can't, I'm going to retire. There's just . . . there's no way I'd even think about leaving her."

"Normally, if anyone told me they were ready to give up their career and change their whole life for someone they'd been dating for less than a month, I'd have a lot of questions and probably be pushing back. But somehow, between you guys, I don't know . . . it makes sense. It feels like you're already in a long-term, committed relationship. And AJ was clearly born to be a mom. You guys going to have more kids?"

"It's complicated." Even though I don't think AJ would mind Sloane knowing about her hysterectomy, it's not my story to tell.

"Well, no matter what you guys choose, she'll still have Abby. That girl adores her."

Abby lifts her head when she hears her name, but she's too tired to hold it up and her cheek crashes back down onto my shoulder. It's definitely getting close to her nap time, and all that walking around with AJ seems to have tired her out.

"You know, spending this time with you guys yesterday and today makes me wonder if I should be thinking about moving up here with my girls, instead of you moving down to Nashville. We have friends and neighbors down there, but nothing else is really holding us to the place. It's not like Wayne ever sees the girls, now that he's moved to Florida."

I hate her ex-husband and how he's treated her, but that dirtbag moving to Florida and being out of their lives is the best possible end to that situation. Her moving up to Massachusetts would be even better.

"I'd like that," I tell her, smiling. "If there's anything I can do to help sway you in that direction, let me know."

"I need to think about it a bit more," Sloane says, right as AJ walks up to us. The look on her face is almost joyous.

"You're never going to believe who that was on the phone," she says to me.

"You going to make me guess?"

"No," she laughs. "It was Aidan Renaud."

"Oh yeah? Is that asshole finally coming back?"

"I thought he was your best friend?" Sloane says, head tilting as she looks up at me.

"He is. But he got injured last summer, and since he's been out this season, I've heard from him exactly two times."

"Well, I hope he's not on your shit list, because he just got cleared to play."

"In the finals?" I don't know if this is good news or not. He's a fucking talented winger and has been on my line for most of the time I've played in Boston, but we have a solid first line now and we've played together all season without him. I'm not sure what it would be like introducing him back into the rotation.

"No," she says. "His last surgery was only a few months

ago, but his doctor is confident he'll be back for pre-season training this fall."

"Good. I want him back for next season," I say, and when her eyes meet mine, there's worry in her gaze. Neither of us knows whether I'll be playing for the Rebels next season, and I haven't told her that I'll be here with her regardless of whether I'm still on the team.

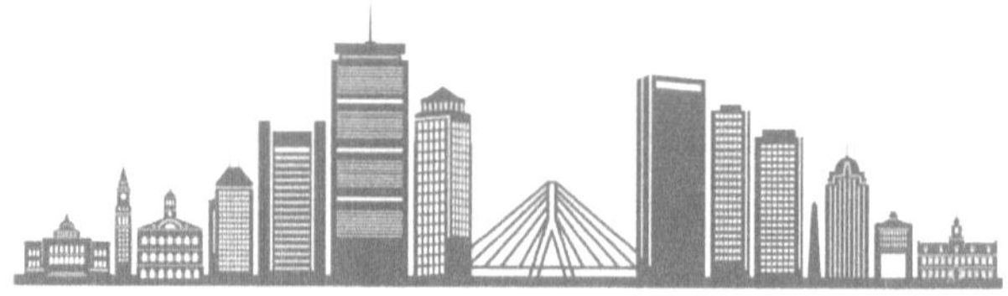

Chapter Thirty-Seven

McCabe

I'm not sure what I expected to feel when I saw Chet again last night during Game 1. As AJ and I have grown even closer in the last week since the semifinals, and settled into a routine that has her basically living at my place with Abby and me, I expected to feel the same rage I felt the last time I saw him. Especially now that I know that his berating AJ in the hallway that day wasn't a one-time occurrence, but rather a pattern of behavior.

But when I saw him standing behind the bench, sporting a clipboard and a receding hairline, I had no desire to pummel him again. In fact, I wanted to thank him.

He disappointed her in every way, leaving the door wide open for me to show her exactly how she should be treated. He never deserved her, and in the end, she's getting someone who does. Or who is working every day to deserve her.

Scoring the winning goal in Game 1 last night was also its own kind of reward, and I made sure to skate past St. Louis's bench and make eye contact with Chet after I did. My smirk and head nod had his face and balding head turning bright red.

But tonight, as I walk into this charity gala in downtown St. Louis with my teammates, I realize how difficult it's going to be not to let my feelings for AJ show.

I wouldn't care if my teammates figured it out. These guys are starting to feel less like people I work with and more like family. I'm pretty used to being a lone wolf, just like Renaud, which I suspect is why the two of us were always close. But this season without him has made me realize that hockey's actually more fun when you open yourself up a bit to your teammates and step up and act like the captain they expect you to be.

But don't open up so much that they realize you're dating your boss, I remind myself.

"Alright, so what's the plan?" Hartmann asks. "How are we keeping AJ away from her ex?"

"I think the best plan is just to make sure one of us is with her at all times. Hopefully then he won't even approach her," I say.

Colt eyes me, and it's like I can see the gears turning in his head as he catches the protective tone in my voice. "You know we're not only here for her, right?"

I shove my hands into my pockets as we walk across the ornate lobby with its walls of gilded mirrors, plush velvet couches and chairs, and chandeliers of crystal dripping from the ceiling. My high school prom was held here, and I'm pretty sure not a single thing has changed. "What are you talking about?"

"You clearly think she needs backup here, which means

you know more than we do. AJ doesn't share personal information about herself with *anyone* on the team. But she clearly has with you. So we're here for you, too. And for whatever's going on between the two of you."

I suck in a sharp breath as I glance beyond Colt at the rest of my friends. Only Hartmann looks surprised. "Huh," he says, as his head bobs with understanding. "I had often suspected some partiality, especially on McCabe's side."

"Did you just fucking quote *Pride and Prejudice*?" Zach laughs.

"Yeah, Evie makes me watch it at least once a year."

"Who the fuck is Evie?" Drew asks.

"Wilcott's daughter?" Hartmann says. "My best friend."

"Wait," Colt drags out the word with laughter in his voice. "You're best friends with Wilcott's daughter? How . . .?"

"We grew up together. Her mom works with my mom, training equestrians."

Frank Hartmann made his billions in business, but their family owns a lavish home on the North Shore that's also an equestrian center. He throws a holiday party there every year for the team, and it's like walking into a mansion from the Gilded Age—like you're on the set of the Great Gatsby or something. It's hard to imagine growing up with that kind of wealth, but Luke is somehow still well-adjusted and down to earth.

"Isn't Wilcott's daughter a figure skater or something?" Drew asks.

"Yeah. She's a pairs skater. Just took third in a big competition in Europe, but she's coming home soon. She's always home for a month or so in the summer, before the training and competitions gear back up. Hence, the annual viewing of Darcy and Lizzie."

Zach huffs out a laugh. "The BBC version, or the newer movie?"

"Always the BBC version. All eight hours of it," Hartmann groans. "Why? Are you a fan?"

"I mean, Ashleigh's made me watch both versions several times."

"Uh, so back to the point," Colt says, turning his head toward me. "This is . . . *a thing?*"

I can tell he's being careful not to use AJ's name here, as we approach the doors to the ballroom, and I appreciate his discretion. "It's a long story, and one I'll tell you when we're not here."

"Alright," he says with another nod. "Top secret. Right, guys?"

They all mumble their agreement as I give the people at the doors our table number, and when we sweep into the room and all eyes are on us. This is a room full of St. Louis's wealthiest residents, and I recognize a fair number of people who have connections to their hockey team.

"It didn't occur to me that Boston players might not be welcome here," I grumble as our group moves toward the bar.

"Fuck 'em," Drew says. "They're just pissed they lost you years ago *and* you scored the winning goal last night."

I see AJ across the room and stop short at the sight of her. Her back's to me, and she's wearing a sparkly pale pink dress with a low V in the back. I know it has a matching V in the front, and as sexy as I thought she looked when she tried it on at that fancy department store a couple of weeks ago, I didn't consider how I'd feel about other people seeing her look so gorgeous in it.

She does a lot to keep herself buttoned up and professional at work—suit pants and jackets, trousers and sweaters, and dresses that don't reveal anything except the lower half of her muscular legs.

But tonight, with her hair curled in loose waves and pinned to the side so it falls forward over one shoulder, her back is on display and so are the curves of her hips and ass. I know that dress has a long slit up one side of the front, so when she takes a step, her entire leg will show.

Suddenly, as I watch her move from one group of people to another, I note the way men look at her and I'm feeling incredibly territorial. I want to tattoo my name across her collarbones so that anyone looking at her knows she's *mine*.

"Put your fucking tongue back in your mouth," Colt growls at me, and it's only then that I take stock of myself. My tongue isn't literally hanging out, but I have stopped, frozen in place, to gawk at her. My eyes slide around the room to see if anyone else has noticed, and at a table in the front of the room, Chet is watching me closely. He follows my gaze to AJ and his lips curve up in . . . I don't even know what. It's not a smile, or a look of disgust. It's more like he's plotting something, and that thought has my stomach turning sour.

"Dude, you're down bad," Hartmann mutters with a laugh.

"It's mutual, though?" Drew confirms.

"Yeah, it's mutual."

"Let's go get a drink," Zach says. "Maybe try not to gawk

at her if you don't want everyone in this room to see what's now so obvious to us."

"I'm fucking trying, alright?" I grumble, turning toward the bar off at the side of the room.

I manage not to scan the room for AJ while we order our drinks, and once we have them, we head straight to our table. As we arrive there, AJ approaches with a couple that I've never seen before. But I immediately know these are her parents—she's got the same dark hair and eyes as her dad, though his is run through with gray now, giving him a distinguished look, and the same straight nose, full lips, and sharp jawline as her mother.

"Guys," AJ says, nodding toward us, "I'd like to introduce my parents, tonight's hosts for this event."

She goes through a relatively formal introduction that has me wondering if she was a debutante or something, and when she's done, her dad says, "I should have known my daughter would invite the opposing team tonight." It's said without pride or hostility, like he's trying to break the ice and make us laugh.

But I watch the way her shoulders stiffen, and I know she feels slighted, or maybe even attacked. "Just the kind of ballsy move you'd expect from the best GM in the league, huh?" I say.

Instead of seizing on the opportunity to compliment his daughter, Mr. Jones says, "Well, that remains to be seen, doesn't it?"

My free hand curls into a fist at my side.

"Nah," Colt says, stepping up next to me, like he's trying to make sure I keep my mouth shut. "We don't need to wait for the final round of voting to know she's the best. She proves it day in and day out with how she's turned our team —and our whole organization—around."

And then he's spouting off statistics showcasing what she's accomplished, and comparing her to other GMs in the league—even though now the final round of voting is down to only two people: AJ and her mentor, Joey Connelly.

Frank Hartmann and his wife walk up as Colt is wrapping up his pitch for AJ winning the GM of the Year award, and the way the Hartmanns greet the Joneses, I realize that they run in the same circles despite living in different regions of the country—which tells me even more about AJ's background.

And as the two couples chat, AJ turns toward us, walks through our half of the circle so we turn to follow her, and then stops to look back at Colt.

"You didn't have to do that. But . . ." She takes a deep breath, then relaxes and gives us a small, relieved smile. ". . . thank you."

———

I'm headed toward the empty bar on my way back from the bathroom, when Chet steps into my path. I should move around him and keep walking, but I'm so caught off guard by how he popped out of nowhere that I stop.

"Still following AJ around like a little bitch, I see," he says.

My jaw clenches, but I force myself to relax as I consider how I can manipulate his insecurities rather than react to his words. "Some people are born leaders; it makes it easy to support them. Not that *you'd* know anything about that."

His face starts to turn red like last night when I scored

the winning goal, and I realize how good the years have been to AJ, and how unkind they've been to him—not just in terms of their looks, but their successes as well.

"You think having her attention is something special? That the way she looks at you is some sort of prize?" he sneers.

I should be worried that he's seeing something between us, but I'm not. I want him to be jealous. I want him to feel her loss so much that he can't be happy. Because losing someone like Alessandra Jones is the kind of thing that could destroy a man. And I want to revel in his destruction.

I give him a smirk instead of a response.

"You'll see what it's like to live in her shadow," he says.

"I'm not in competition with her," I tell him. "I have *my* career, and I want her to achieve everything she sets her mind to in *her* career. I want her to be happy and fulfilled. The level of success she's achieved . . . man, the only people who'd be threatened by that are those who are weak, those who can't let other people succeed without trying to tear them down. So I guess what you have to ask yourself is: why did you have to make her feel small in order to feel good about yourself? Sounds like a personal failing to me."

The way he shifts his weight, his body rigid, resembles a bull stomping his foot as he gets ready to charge.

"I should have pressed charges when I had the chance," he sneers. "I thought forcing her to trade you instead would get you out of the picture."

Blood thrums through my veins, adrenaline rushing my system. Instead of chasing the rush I'd feel if I pounded him into the ground again, I force myself to breathe deeply and stay calm—despite his apparent admission to blackmailing or bribing her to trade me.

I know that, more than anything, Chet wants me to react. He's goading me, trying to get me to throw a punch like I did all those years ago. And as much as I want to take out my anger about AJ hiding this truth from me, I refuse to let this weak man provoke me.

"How'd that work out for you?" I ask instead. "Because she divorced your ass and ended up in Boston, so I'd say I ended up on top."

"Of course that little slut would follow you."

I shove my fists into my pockets, feigning nonchalance at his pettiness. Karma's going to be such a bitch to him in the end.

"There was absolutely nothing going on between AJ and me back then," I say. "But I'm sorry that you were so incapable of keeping her happy, of satisfying her, that you worried she'd be looking elsewhere."

"Quite the opposite. I had to look elsewhere because she couldn't give me what I wanted. You know she can't give you kids, right?"

The selfish bastard doesn't even try to hide his true colors.

"Of course she can. AJ was born to be a mom. Just because she can't carry a baby herself doesn't mean she can't have kids, and only a spineless asshole with serious inferiority issues would think otherwise."

"There you are, McCabe." I hear Zach's voice from behind me before he steps up next to me.

No one feels threatened by Zach; he has a Zen-like calmness about him that puts people at ease. But the one and only time I ever saw him lose his shit, fighting Ashleigh's ex-boyfriend, I learned how deadly he actually is. And the tone in his voice that's letting me know he has my back.

Chet doesn't have the good sense to back down, even with my teammate standing next to me. "Just because you're her newest fuckboy—"

Zach's hand shoots out, thumb and fingers splayed across Chet's collarbones and resting at the base of this asshole's neck. "I'm going to stop you right there. If you can't speak with the appropriate level of respect about our GM, we're going to have a serious problem. And I guarantee you, you don't want to have a problem with us."

Realizing that he's in a losing position, Chet takes a small step back, looks me in the eye, and says, "This isn't over."

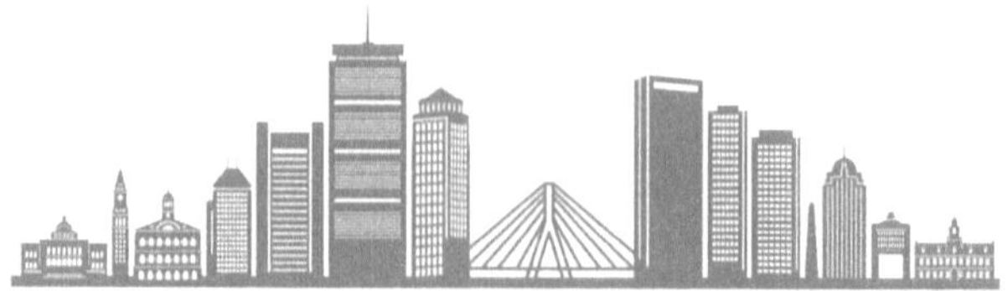

Chapter Thirty-Eight

AJ

I'm standing here talking to Chet's parents, because of course they're here and wanted to say hello. My third glass of champagne is going down easy, and I'm realizing that this night hasn't sucked as badly as I thought it would.

Conversation at our table over dinner was great because I was surrounded by people I know and trust. We laughed and talked throughout the meal, and it was so natural and easy, not like any dinner I've had with my own family.

And that's when I realized that these people *are* my family. My team, the Hartmanns, the Wilcotts, my girlfriends, McCabe and Abby . . . this is the family I've created for myself.

In fact, I've never had this much fun or felt this loved at a single one of my family's events, and I'm not going to let a conversation with my former in-laws derail my night. I owe them nothing.

I'm about to excuse myself, when I feel the warmth of McCabe's large hand on the small of my back. "I'm so sorry to interrupt," he says, "but I need to steal AJ away for a minute."

Chet's parents start to say goodbye, but McCabe turns and guides me away, as he dips his head so his mouth is right next to my ear. "We have a problem."

Thinking he's about to make a joke about how he can't wait any longer to get me naked, or something like that, I flirtatiously reply, "Oh yeah, what kind of a problem?"

"The kind where your ex-husband knows we're together and just said 'This isn't over.'"

"The fuck?" I groan out the question as my heart pounds so hard I can feel it in my throat.

"I'll explain, but we need to get out of here."

"It's going to be obvious if we leave together," I tell him.

"We can leave separately if you want, but the guys have already figured it out, and so has Chet."

"The guys? Meaning your teammates?"

"Yeah." His word is clipped, and it occurs to me that maybe we were stupid thinking we could hide this. Maybe inviting them here with me was a mistake, because how could anyone not notice the way we look at each other, how we always gravitate toward each other? Try as we might, it's impossible to hide our feelings, even with stakes this high—in this ballroom with my family, half of St. Louis's management team, and our own team owner, coach, and players.

How did I think this was a good idea? *Because your judgment is clouded.* It's always my father's voice I hear in these moments of doubt.

Maybe my judgment *is* clouded, but actually . . . I don't give a shit.

Perhaps for the first time in my life, I've realized that shoving down all my emotions and putting work above all else didn't actually keep me safe. The only thing it "protected" me from was the kind of relationships—professional, friendly, and romantic—that could bring me great joy.

"Let's go. We'll talk about this back at the hotel."

We don't say our goodbyes on the way out, and we don't discuss whats going on during the quick car ride back to the hotel. Instead, he texts his teammates a vague update and I reach out to Lauren, scheduling a call in fifteen minutes.

But the minute the door to my hotel room is shut, I rest my forehead against his chest, and he wraps his arms around my lower back.

"Alright," I say, relief washing through me as I find comfort in his arms. "Tell me what happened back there."

He walks me through his conversation with Chet, and then says, "Learning that there's more to the story about my trade from Chet, instead of from you, made me feel like I was set up."

I sigh, knowing that , he's right. "I didn't want to risk reopening that wound. I was afraid you'd go after Chet when you saw him, and we'd be right back to where we were eight years ago, with you facing assault charges."

"But instead, he came after me, so why don't you tell me about these assault charges that I know nothing about." His voice is level, and I can tell he's trying not to be angry at me for withholding information.

"That whole altercation in that hallway eight years ago was captured on the security cameras. And it clearly showed

Chet yelling at me, before you came out of nowhere and beat the shit out of him. He never even threw a punch, and didn't even have time to defend himself."

His chest rumbles with what feels and sounds like a growl, and I'm sure he's remembering everything that happened that day, just as I am. I've spent years trying to put that day behind me, but there's no way to deny that it was a tipping point—for my marriage, for my career, and for McCabe's career too.

I smooth my palms against his chest and tilt my head up to look at him. "He threatened to press charges. Assault and battery carries a minimum sentence of seven years in Missouri, and if the court had considered your hands as deadly weapons, which wouldn't have been much of a stretch given that fighting on the ice is part of your job, you could have spent half your life in jail if convicted."

"Alessandra," he whispers into my hair as he presses a kiss to my forehead.

"That's what I meant, when I said I didn't have a choice but to trade you. Not only would it have been impossible for you to play for Chet after that, but if I didn't trade you, he was going to try to send you to jail."

"Why didn't you just tell me?"

"Because that was part of the agreement. If I told you, he'd press charges."

"That's blackmail."

"In the legal world, I think they call that a plea bargain," I say with a sad shrug.

"Only if I had known and agreed to the offer."

"You would have."

I don't mean to sound dismissive, but what other choice

would he have had? The low rattle in his throat is his tacit agreement.

"I wish I could have told you, because then you'd have understood that I wasn't choosing Chet over you. If anything, I was choosing you. And then, I couldn't even tell you when I came to Boston, because the statute of limitations in Missouri is five years. If he'd found you knew, he still could have pressed charges. That video footage was so damning. There's no way you wouldn't have been convicted."

He runs his thumb along my jaw and tips my chin up as he says, "That means you could have told me three years ago. The statute of limitations would have expired . . ."

"Three years ago, you hated me. We had a decent working relationship where we kept our distance, and you weren't doing anything that could risk your career for me. It seemed safer to leave the past in the past."

"Were you afraid that telling me might have led us down this path sooner?" His hands move along my shoulders, down the sides of my breasts, and to my hips, where he grips me possessively.

"I don't know," I say honestly as I bring my hands up to cup his jaw in my palms, smoothing my fingers across the perpetual stubble that I find along his cheeks. "I thought I was protecting you, and I was probably also trying to protect myself. Honestly, I just tried to put it out of my mind."

"Because . . . ?"

"Because when you've been married to someone like Chet, when you've been fooled and made a fool of, it's hard to trust your own judgment. When it comes to work, I'm always sure what the right thing to do is. But in my personal life, I don't know . . . it just felt easier to only focus on work."

"You deserve so much more than what he gave you," he says. "You deserve *everything.*"

I press my eyes closed as I try not to let the tears fall. It feels so good to be with someone who always has my back and wants what's best for me.

"And that's what I feel like you're giving me. I just hope I can do the same in return."

"I'm not sure why you would even question that. You are everything I never knew I wanted. Your strength and determination, your tenderness with Abby, the fierce way you protect the people you care about . . . how can you even doubt that you could be that person for me?"

I gulp over the lump in my throat. I'm about to respond when my phone rings. "Shit," I mutter, moving to open the small bag that hangs from my shoulder because I recognize the ringtone for a video call. "It's Lauren, I have to get this."

"Alright, I'm going to call Jameson," he says, but his phone buzzes just as he pulls it from his pocket. "And right on cue, that's a text from him telling me to *fucking call him.*"

He heads into the bedroom, and I take a seat at the desk in the small living room. Once I've updated Lauren on the situation, she agrees that the best course of action is to get ahead of the story, and she suggests we pull Morgan into the conversation. Together, we craft a statement, and Morgan has a plan for some social media coverage to "make us the couple everyone's rooting for."

I'm hopeful she can soften people's view of us together.

"You should get Frank and Sarah's approval first," Lauren says, when I tell her that McCabe just read the statement I'd texted him and gave me a thumbs up. "As much as it sucks to say this, you're not releasing this statement as an individual. You're releasing it as a representative of this team."

I want to call bullshit on that, because this is my private life we're talking about, but she's right. If I weren't the Rebels' GM, I wouldn't need to put out a statement about being in a relationship with their team captain.

"I'll tell them I'm releasing a statement. What it says isn't up for debate. We've already worked through that, McCabe's good with it, and they'll need to trust our judgment here."

"It's up to you how you want to handle this," Lauren says, pulling her long red hair back into a bun. "But I also know you're a realist, and we don't know what the public's perception of this will be. It could really go either way."

"No matter what happens," Morgan says, "we're here for you. Just try to block out the noise for the next few days, because people will have opinions, whether they're entitled to them or not."

When we're off our call, I text Frank and Sarah with an update and a link to my statement.

FRANK

This is the right statement, given the situation. Go for it.

SARAH

Hold up.

Yes, the statement is good as is. But I think this needs to come from the Rebels, so it's clear that the organization is aware and supporting you in this.

I'd like to update PR and have them send the statement out to the media, immediately. Are you both okay with that?

FRANK

Sounds like a smart move.

This is all happening so fast; I want to pause for a minute to just breathe. I hate that I feel like I'm spiraling, like there's a crisis that I'm trying to manage before it's a catastrophe, all because Chet won't stay out of my life.

But I don't have the time to pause because we need our statement to go out before Chet can say anything, so it appears proactive, rather than reactive.

AJ

Go for it.

I hope I don't regret this, I think as I toss my phone and it clatters onto the desk.

"Everything okay?"

I jump at the sound of McCabe's voice behind me, and spin in the chair to find him sitting on the couch, legs spread, elbows on his knees. His tuxedo jacket is off, the bowtie is gone, and the top few buttons are undone. With his sleeves rolled up and his muscular forearms on display, he looks like dessert, and I'm suddenly starving.

Get your fucking hormones under control. This is a crisis, not the start of a sex scene.

"Yeah, it's out of my hands now."

"Meaning?"

"Meaning the Rebels are going to release the statement. Morgan said the best thing we can do is stay off social media for the next few days. Oh, and she wants to take some pictures of us when we're back in Boston—domestic stuff like us playing with Abby, to use on social media and release to the press."

He clears his throat. "That's fine, but we're not staging them. The way you are with Abby—the way you play with her, and feed her, and rock her to sleep—you treat her like she's your own kid. Morgan can capture *those* pictures, not something that looks forced. I don't want anyone claiming that your relationship with Abby is just for show."

"People will say it anyway, Ronan. You need to prepare yourself for that. There will be people who love this for us, and there will be haters. The haters will be way louder."

He tilts his head, looking at me like he's assessing me. Then he looks down at his hands, before looking back at me. "You're scared." It's not a question.

"I'd be a fool to act like this isn't going to be a big deal. I know I seem like I don't give a shit what people think, but deep down, I don't know . . . " I look out the window, but all I see is the darkness of the office buildings that surround us. "I like being successful. I like being good at what I do. I like the respect and admiration it's always granted me. And the thought of losing that—"

He stands so abruptly that I stop speaking, and in a few quick steps, he's in front of me, kneeling. "You're wound so tight about this, I'm afraid you'll snap."

"You would be too if your whole career was on the line."

"My whole career *is* on the line, AJ. And after I just accidentally revealed our relationship when Frank wanted us to wait, it's even more unlikely he'll keep me next year. You're not the only one who stands to lose something here. But *you* are the one thing I cannot stand to lose. So if this contract with Boston doesn't work out, I may retire early."

"What? No!" My whole body involuntarily pulls back from his embrace, but he doesn't let me go. What the hell is he talking about? He's one of the best forwards in the league. He *can't* retire early.

I stare up at him. "You can't do that."

"Yes, I can. Hockey has been my only love for most of my life. Then I stepped into my role as a dad, and now that I have you too, everything just feels . . . different. More complete. I'd miss playing, but I'm nearing the end of my career anyway. There's no way I'm packing Abby and myself up and moving somewhere else—not without you. There's no end to this situation that doesn't involve me staying in Boston."

"I don't want you to walk away from your career for me." It would add so much pressure to our relationship if one person sacrificed everything to be with the other.

"Really? Because I can't think of a single better reason to retire. I would do anything for you. And if you don't already know that, then I'll have to do a better job showing you. Which should be easier, to be honest, now that we're not going to have to hide this."

I know what he means, but nothing about going public is going to be easy—especially not during the finals, when we're competing for the Cup and I'm up for GM of the Year . . . or was, anyway.

"And I'm going to start by helping you relax a bit." He licks his lower lip and pulls it between his teeth as his eyes rake up and down my body so I have no doubt about his intentions. "But first, let's get you out of this gorgeous dress so I don't ruin it."

Standing, he holds out his hand, and when I take it, he

pulls me up and leads me back into my bedroom. There's a dressing area with a sink and a closet on the opposite side. He turns me so I'm facing the mirror above the sink.

"You remember the first time we had sex?"

Looking at him in the mirror, I nod. I remember every detail about every time we've been together—they're etched into my memory the same way he's etched himself onto my heart.

"Tonight, I want you to remember what I said that night. I want you to keep your eyes open and watch yourself come. I want you to see how beautiful you are when you fall apart on me, and I want you to remember that I'm the only one who's ever made you feel this way. The only one who ever *will* make you feel this way."

His promise and desperation come out in equal measure, and it pains me to realize he's less sure of my feelings for him than I am of his for me.

"Ronan," I say, my gaze still locked on him in the mirror as I bring my arm up and slide my palm along the back of his neck. "I meant what I said the other night. This is forever for me too."

He lets out a relieved sigh as his hands come around between us. The delicious drag of his fingers over my ass as he works the zipper down the back of the dress has me clenching my thighs together.

Will this ever get old? Will I ever be less attracted to him? God, I hope not. I hope that I still want to jump him every time I see him, even years from now. Even when our kids have run us ragged, and we fall into bed exhausted at night. He'll still be the person I reach for, no matter what.

"What?" he asks, pausing his movements as he stares at me in the mirror.

I press my lips between my teeth as my eyes fill with tears, and his arms wrap around my waist, pulling me back against him. "Holy shit, AJ, what's wrong?"

"Nothing," I say with a small laugh as I shake my head. "I just . . . I had this image of us, years from now. We had kids—a few of them—and we were crawling into bed, exhausted, at the end of the day. But still, we reached for each other, like we couldn't bear to be apart."

"I *can't* bear to be apart from you," he whispers against my hair, then kisses his way from my ear to my jaw and down my neck. "My life with you in it is so much more fulfilling, so much more rewarding, than I would have ever imagined. Hockey's been wonderful. But I'm not giving up our relationship to get in a few more years of playing anywhere without you."

"What about Sloane? I thought you wanted to move to be closer to her?"

"Well, now we're talking about the possibility of her moving up here, instead."

"You've already talked to her about this?" I don't know if I'm thrilled he's so sure, or upset that he's made these plans without talking to me first.

"I know what I want," he says, and his eyes focus on me in the mirror as he slips the straps of the dress over my shoulders and lets it fall to the ground. He looks down, and a low hiss of air coasts against my skin when he sees my lace thong and garter belt. All of it is nude, including the thigh-high stockings.

He squats to take my dress off the floor, and as I step out

of it, I go to kick my heels off. "Leave them," he practically growls as he wraps his hand around my calf. "You don't wear fuck-me shoes like that and take them off when I'm actually going to fuck you."

"Don't I?" I ask with a wink as I look down at him.

Standing, he turns to hang my dress in the closet before he's stripping his own clothes off slowly, making me ache with need as I wait for him to come back to me.

"God, you're fucking gorgeous," he says as he turns back to where I stand, my legs crossed at the ankles as I rest my ass back against the countertop.

His thumbs brush against my nipples as he steps up and plants one foot on either side of me. A low moan crawls up my throat as he rubs across my hardened peaks, and then he's turning me back to face the mirror as he says, "I love that you're always so needy for me. And tonight, I'm going to make you come until you can't stand on your own, until you fall into a deep sleep and forget about the last few hours."

"I don't want to forget," I say, staring back at him in the mirror. "Yes, the last few hours have been damage control, but we've also spent that time planning a future together. And that starts now."

I smile softly as I look up over my shoulder at him and he leans in to kiss me. It's tender at first—a promise of sorts— and then he's parting my lips and invading my mouth and taking total control of my body. His hands are everywhere, and as I reach behind me to grasp his hard length, he's pushing my thong to the side and rubbing circles around my clit until I'm moaning into his mouth. It doesn't take long. That first orgasm creeps up so quickly it takes me by surprise, and I'm using my thumb to circle the pre-cum around the head of his cock, gasping and chasing my release. But even though I'm right there, so close to tipping over the edge, I need him inside me . . . I feel empty without him.

I tell him as much, and he just smirks as he bends me forward and smacks my ass, hard. My gasp rings out and he presses his fingers harder against my clit.

"Come for me, and then I'll fill you," he promises. Waves of tingling electricity ripple through me as I clench my core together and my legs start to shake. But still, I don't go over that tipping point. I'm about to tell him I can't, when he takes my hand from his dick and moves it to the counter so I'm fully leaning forward. And then he's pressing himself against my ass crack, rubbing lightly against that opening as he circles my clit with one hand and cups my breast with the other, pinching my nipple between his fingers.

I'm panting and gasping as the waves of my orgasm roll through my body, and then he's biting my shoulder in between whispering filthy promises about how he plans to use me tonight. And while I'm still coming, he's sliding into me, his finger still working my clit, and demanding that I keep going. And I do. I've never had an orgasm like this, one wave right after the other, and I'm practically screaming his name as the intensity increases until my legs are trembling and the only thing holding me up are his powerful thighs pressing me forward into the countertop.

"Good girl," he purrs next to my ear as he continues fucking me, even after my orgasm ends. "I knew you could give me a second one. I think we need to go for a third."

"Oh my god," I pant. "There's no way."

"I didn't take you for a quitter, Sunshine."

He pulls out, spins me around so I'm sitting on the countertop, and then spreads his legs wider, bringing my legs up around his hips as he slips back into me. Then his mouth is on one of my nipples, sucking it against his tongue over and over while his fingers toy with my other nipple. It's like there's an invisible string connecting them to my core, and with each deep pull of my breast into his mouth, I can feel my muscles spasming around him.

"That's my girl. Look at you taking me . . . so fucking greedy."

Whimpering, I look down at where our bodies are joined, and the sight of him, huge and hard, pushing into me, the sound of our bodies meeting, the sight of my tits bouncing each time he bottoms out—all of it makes my core clench tighter.

"That's right," he says, his voice low and encouraging, "keep squeezing my cock like that, and I'll give you that third orgasm you didn't think you could have."

I gasp as he holds my hips in place, changing the angle so he pushes into me hard and fast. The smooth glide of his hard cock against the front of my inner walls has the edges of my vision clouding as I tip over the edge with a cry of his name.

"You're fucking perfect," he grits out between clenched teeth as his body jerks and shudders with his own release as he holds my body against his. Bending down so his lips are right at my ear, he continues to give me everything with one more declaration. "You deserve every good thing in life, and I plan to make sure you get what you deserve."

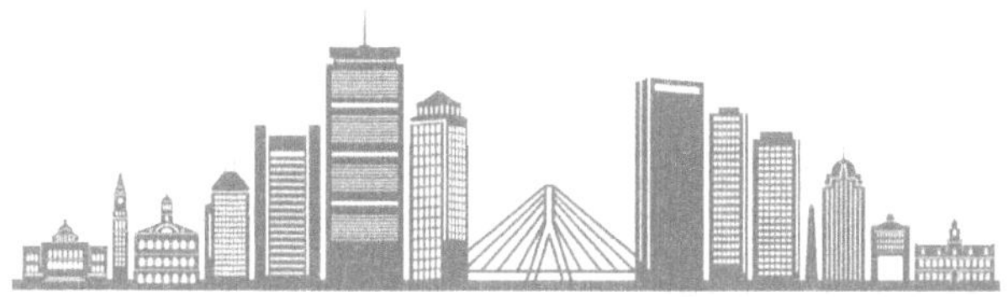

Chapter Thirty-Nine

McCabe

I watch from the back of the pressroom as AJ steps up to the podium, her eyes nervously flicking over to me before she focuses on the paper in front of her. The room is small, with the tables and podium at the front and only four rows of seats. Currently, the only sound in the room is the clicking of camera shutters, until she clears her throat and everyone falls silent.

Her hair is down and she's wearing the pink suit that must be the one she was telling Sloane about last weekend. The one that makes her feel feminine *and* powerful.

She looks fierce, ready to fight, and unfortunately, I think she'll need to. I really wish we were holding this press conference in Boston, not in St. Louis the morning before Game 2. I wish the whole Rebels organization was standing right outside the pressroom door, ready to show their support as soon as this was over. But that's not the situation we're in.

Me and my fucking mouth. I should have just acted like I didn't know what Chet was talking about, pretended that he was imagining whatever he saw between AJ and me. It would have been so much better for her if I had, and yet, she's remarkably calm about having to go public.

"Thanks for being here this morning," she says, holding her chin up and letting her gaze shift across the rows of reporters. "I want to start by saying that I'm proud of what we've accomplished in Boston in the six years that I've been the GM for the Rebels, and I'm confident in the team I've built and the direction we're heading. Because I believe in full transparency and have the utmost concern for professional ethics, I want to address the statement we released last night. As I said then, I've recently entered into a serious and committed relationship with Ronan McCabe."

She pauses, like she's expecting the press to jump in with questions like they normally do, but I think she's stunned them into silence by addressing this head on. No one even turns to look at me, which tells me they're still in shock.

"I want to assure you that nothing unethical has transpired. When our relationship extended beyond the professional boundaries of manager and player, I recused myself from all work having to do with his salary, his contract, and his playing for this team. However, I also recognize that a relationship between a GM and a player—even though I've been honest about it with our team's owner and with Human Resources—doesn't look good. For this reason," she pauses to swallow, but her voice is unwavering when she continues, "I'm withdrawing my nomination for GM of the Year award."

That announcement seems to spring the reporters into action—they're practically jumping out of their seats as everyone yells questions. Behind the podium, AJ sighs, then she starts pointing to different reporters and answering their questions.

Who is handling McCabe's contract? How long has this been going on? Did anyone else know? How does the team feel about it? The questions come at a fast and furious pace, and AJ answers each succinctly and professionally.

"Are you only making this announcement now because of the Brett Ivers scandal?" The question comes from a grizzled older reporter, one who's been around since long before I started playing.

"Let me be abundantly clear. Absolutely nothing unethical has happened here, and I stand by that. I'm making this announcement because I have nothing to hide, and hiding this relationship would call that fact into question. I've spent my career proving that a woman can succeed at this level in a male-dominated sport. And so, for most people who know me, or know of me, this relationship is going to come as a shock. But on a deeply personal level, I've sacrificed my own happiness and sometimes even my health, because I've been so committed to my job that it's always come first. And that is not sustainable. I deserve to be happy. I deserve to have a loving relationship. And if it makes people uncomfortable to see that I'm a woman who is prioritizing my happiness in a healthy, consensual relationship—then that's on them, not me. I'm proud of the work I've done here and the manner in which I've done it. And I won't feel guilty that the person I fell in love with also happens to work for the same organization I do."

I feel like the oxygen has been sucked from my lungs. *Did she just say she is in love with me?* Did she just tell that to the press, to the entire nation, before she's even said it to me? I must have made some sort of a sound in response, because suddenly all the reporters have turned and are yelling questions at me instead, asking about our relationship, my daughter, and how this has affected my game.

Fuck. This is AJ's moment, and I don't want to steal her thunder. At the same time, why should she be the only one bearing the brunt of this onslaught? I'm the one who got us into this mess. At every single phase of our relationship, I was the one who took the first step and then pulled her along with me. And now, I realize, I'm kind of mad that she beat me to saying the L-word.

"You all want a statement?" I raise my voice to be heard over them, and they quiet almost immediately. "Okay, here you go. Normally, I'm a pretty quiet guy. I put my head down and do my job, on the ice and in life. I prefer to listen rather than talk. I prefer to be in the background. And I prefer to let people speak for themselves. I've been told that this tendency can result in me coming across as grumpy or standoffish."

I smirk over at AJ, making it clear that she's said these things, and pause while the press laughs. I'm glad they find my self-depreciating remark amusing, as I was trying to lighten the mood a bit.

"So let me be crystal clear," I say, walking to the front of the room to stand next to AJ. I look down at her as I say, "I love this woman." And then I look out at the reporters when I say, "And I absolutely refuse to stand by if a single person calls into question anything that she's done in her professional or personal life. We are the team we are today because of Alessandra Jones. We would not be the winningest team in Boston hockey history if it weren't for the way she's rebuilt this organization, we wouldn't have the team camaraderie we do without her leading by example, and we sure as hell wouldn't have our eyes on our second Stanley Cup in six years if it weren't for her. No team is successful because of just one person, but I think you could ask anyone in the Rebels organization what AJ means to this team, and you'd get the same answer I just gave you. And *that* will be her legacy. Not some award, and not her relationship with me. What she's done here matters, and it will live on. And that's all I'll be saying about this." I turn to AJ, looking into her beautiful brown eyes for a moment. "You have anything else to say?"

"No," she says simply, like she can't trust her voice to say more. And the way her eyes are watering, I think she's more emotional than she'd want people to see.

"I think we're done here, then," I say, and taking her hand, I lead her out of the pressroom.

"Holy shit," she whispers when we step into the hallway, shutting the door behind us. "Did that really just happen?"

I don't stop my steps, leading her down the hall toward the exit. I want us out of this building. I want her far away from her old life in St. Louis—far from Chet and all the bad shit that happened here. I want to be alone with her, so I can remind her that I'll always be here for her. That no matter what happens, no matter how hard things get, I'll always stand by her side.

"You didn't have to do that," she says when we step out into the bright morning sun.

I don't know where we're headed, but I put my hand on her lower back and guide her down the sidewalk. "Maybe not, but I wanted to. Not because I didn't think you could handle that by yourself, but because I didn't want you to have to." I think a lot of AJ's life has been her figuring out how to handle things herself.

"Did we really just both say we loved each other to a room full of reporters?" she asks with a nervous laugh.

I wrap my hand around her hip, stopping her progress as I spin us toward the brick wall of a restaurant so we're out of the path of other pedestrians.

"We did, Sunshine." I smooth her long, dark hair behind her ear and cup my hand against the side of her neck. "Well, first, you did. And then I didn't want there to be any question about my own feelings. I'm just sorry I didn't say it to you first."

It feels like we both just adopted a *go big or go home* strategy, and I'm at peace with that. I want to love this woman out loud, and I've hated the way I've had to hide my feelings for her.

Her head tilts back as she looks up at me, full lips curling at the corners. "I never questioned how you felt."

I curl my fingers into her hips, and press a kiss to the top of her head before saying, "And I'll make sure you never do."

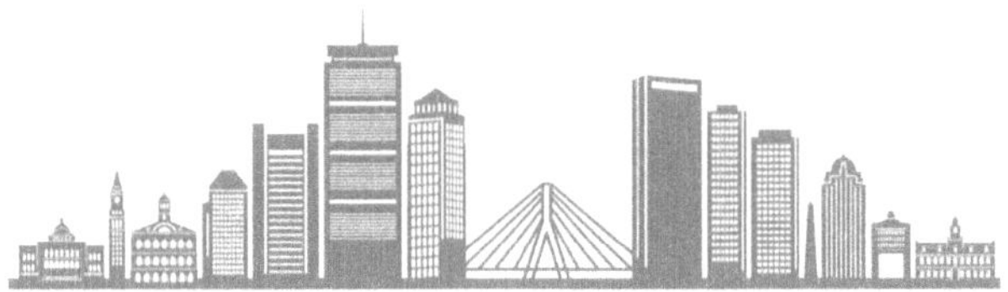

Chapter Forty

AJ

"I can't even tell you what a relief it is to know that you're going to be on board part time," I tell Morgan as I sit back in my office chair, watching her sign the consulting paperwork HR and our legal team drew up for her yesterday.

She laughs and relaxes in the chair opposite me, pushing her strawberry-blonde hair back over her shoulder. With her big eyes, fair skin, and freckles that sweep across the bridge of her nose and her cheeks, she doesn't look old enough to have earned an MBA and started her own company.

"I don't know why you think I'm some sort of social media miracle worker."

"Because you *are*," I say, picking up my phone and clicking on the most recent notification on Instagram. "Please don't sell yourself short. And I'm excited not only to have you on retainer personally, but to have you helping with the Rebels' social media also."

I glance down at my screen, noting how this morning's post already has thousands of likes. I don't even have that many followers, but Morgan had me post it as a collaboration with Ronan and because of his follower count it's completely blown up.

Of course it has. It's a series of six images of us at home together after returning from Game 2 yesterday.

I'm in a casual knit jumpsuit with a wide boat neck top that's slid down off one shoulder as I sit on the living room floor, building a block tower with Abby so she can knock it down, which is still her favorite activity.

He's sitting behind me in shorts and a t-shirt, his forearm casually wrapped around my waist, one leg stretched out the side with his knee bent and his elbow resting on it as he looks over my shoulder, smiling at Abby where she stands, arms up, ready to demolish the tower. In the next one, I'm laughing as the blocks come tumbling down, and he's looking down at me with complete adoration written across his face.

The whole series of images is so "us," that I felt good about posting them. They were exactly what Ronan wanted to showcase when I mentioned Morgan coming over to take photos—the three of us in our natural element, nothing about it staged except for the way I took extra time doing my hair and makeup because I wasn't looking for people to comment on how much older I am than him.

All the positive comments in the post almost make me forget that we lost Game 2 in St. Louis. But then my eyes land on the most recent comment, and I hiss out a breath. Even though I love the photos, and a lot of other people clearly do too, there are still trolls emerging in the comment section.

"Delete and block," Morgan reminds me, and I glance up to see her watching me closely. I'm sure she knows exactly the kind of shit I'm reading by the way I froze up just now, and the sigh I let out in response. "You don't owe anyone—especially not someone who doesn't even know you—the luxury of posting shit about you online."

"People are entitled to their opinions, unfortunately. Even when they're wrong." I set my phone between us on my desk, so I won't be tempted to keep checking the notifications.

"But they're not entitled to post them on *your* profile. Delete. And. Block." Her voice is decisive and commanding. "Do you want me to take over your social media for the next few days, just to keep an eye on it, reply to comments, delete the shitheads—that type of thing?"

"That's something you can do?"

"Yeah, it's part of what you're paying me for. I do the same thing for Jules and Audrey with their business account."

"That would be amazing. Honestly, it's validating to see all the likes and the positive comments, but I don't need to see the negative shit. It doesn't change anything. It doesn't make me question the relationship, or whether it was the right decision to go public."

There are two quick knocks on my door, and my assistant, Colleen, cracks it open enough to slide half her body through it. "Uhh, McCabe's here to see you." She eyes Morgan sitting across from me, and I get the sense that she hadn't wanted to interrupt us, but he forced her hand.

"Send him in," I tell her.

"I told you she wouldn't mind." His voice comes from the other side of the door as he pushes it open and strides right past her. "Morgan," he says, nodding at her as he comes around my desk and bends to plant a kiss on the top of my head.

Across the room, Colleen shuts the door.

"Have you seen this news?" he asks, holding his phone out to me. On the screen is a headline from Boston's sports news network.

NHL Commissioner Refuses Jones's Withdrawal from GM of the Year Award

My breath catches, and I have to clear my throat. "What the hell is this?"

"Apparently, you and Connelly are both still in the running for the award."

"I don't understand how that's even possible. I withdrew."

"Can you voluntarily withdraw?" Morgan asks, arching an eyebrow as she looks at us.

"If I don't think I deserve the award, why couldn't I?"

"*Do you* think you don't deserve it?" McCabe asks. "After everything you've done this season, do you really believe that us being together means you don't deserve that award?"

I glance down at my lap, then look up at him. "No."

"Well, apparently, the other GMs and the league officials agree with you," he says.

"Take this for the immense compliment it is," Morgan says. "And we probably need to respond on social media. I'll work on that today."

"We're not responding publicly until I understand how this happened," I tell her, shaking my head. I'm so caught off guard, I don't even know how to react.

"What do you mean?" McCabe asks as he comes around to the far side of my desk and takes the seat next to Morgan.

That's when my phone rings, and the name of the Commissioner of the NHL appears on my screen. All three of us sit there, staring at my phone buzzing where it lies face up on my desk. Morgan's eyes are huge, because although this job is the first she's had in the sports industry, her dad is a big hockey agent and even she knows who Timothy O'Leary is.

"You going to get that?" McCabe asks, amusement in his tone.

I grab for the phone, standing as I walk over to the wall of windows overlooking the rink. Practice is over, but there are kids' lessons going on right now, and I watch them as I answer.

"AJ!" Tim's greeting is friendly and full of excitement. "I suspect you've heard the news?"

"Yeah, and I'm pretty shocked. How exactly did this happen?"

"Well, none of us on the committee felt like you *didn't* deserve the nomination. So even though you thought you could withdraw yourself from contention, we don't accept your withdrawal."

"Does Joey Connelly have something to do with this?" What I'm really wondering is if Joey doesn't want to win this year by default, just because the other two nominees withdrew.

"All I'm going to say about that is that he's one of your staunchest supporters."

My chest aches with the realization that my mentor, the man who first hired me as a scout, then promoted me to being his assistant GM, before ultimately pushing me to move forward in my career, is proud of me.

"This really isn't just because he doesn't want to win by default?"

Tim's deep, low chuckle fills the line before he assures me. "I can't tell you anything that Joey told me in confidence. So I will just say, he doesn't question whether you deserve this. And you shouldn't either."

———

The stands are completely packed before Game 4, our second home game in the finals, and I know the fans are all hoping for a win tonight. Being down 2-1, after losing Game 3 at home two nights ago, puts our team in a less than ideal position. I'm hoping to check in on Wilcott's pre-game pep talk before the guys hit the ice.

But as I round the corner into the hallway leading to the locker rooms, I almost run into Chet. There's no one else around to hear him ranting as he holds his phone in front of his mouth.

"You need to fucking handle it. What do you expect me to do from Boston?"

"I'm not asking you to handle anything," the woman's voice is quiet, and the hurt is evident in her tone. I can't help but wonder why he thinks this is an appropriate conversation to have on speakerphone. "I just wanted a little support from my husband."

"We're about to start the fucking game, and you want a goddamn pep-talk because your sister canceled on girls' night again?"

"I forgot about the time change," she says, her voice even smaller and more defeated.

I really don't want to be here for this conversation. But I need to be in that locker room and he's standing in my way. I'm just glad that his back is to me and he hasn't seen me yet.

"Stop feeling sorry for yourself." He says it as though she disgusts him—the exact opposite of the pep talk it sounds like she was looking for. "I've done nothing but try to provide a good life for you, and it's never enough."

"You know that's not it. You've provided a great life for me and the kids. It's just—"

"I have to go." He cuts her off. "We're flying home tonight after the game, so I hope you're in a better mood when I get back in the morning."

I don't know why I'm angry on this woman's behalf. She knew he was married to me when she started sleeping with him, so I want to believe she got what she deserved. But does anyone really deserve an asshole who love bombs you, only to turn around and treat you like shit once he's locked you down? Didn't I fall for the same man? He can be awfully convincing when he's wooing you.

He steps up to the visiting team's locker room, and as he reaches out toward the door, I hope that he will enter without realizing that I overheard his phone call. But as luck would have it, he pauses, arm outstretched and hand flat against the door. And then he turns his head, looking down the hall at me.

"How long have you been standing there?" It's an accusation more than a question.

"Long enough to see that tigers don't change their

stripes." My mirthless laugh slips out, even though I don't mean it to.

"Still a superior bitch, I see." Dropping his arm, he turns toward me.

"I feel bad for your wife," I tell him. The only thing I truly regret in life are the years I wasted on him. "Maybe one day, she'll have the courage to divorce you too. Because there's nothing and no one who can make an unsuccessful narcissist like you happy."

A nervous energy courses through me as I go to move past him, intent on seeing my team. When he grabs my arm, I'm prepared and easily spin out of his grip, but I wish I hadn't engaged with him in the first place. I don't feel safe down here with him. Even though we're in a public place, there's no one else around until the teams leave the locker rooms about ten minutes from now.

"I'm not unsuccessful," he sputters, small pieces of spit flying from his lips.

I cross my arms over my chest, resting my cast on my good arm. "It's been over seven years since we divorced, and you *just* got back the job you lost then. You're unhappily married, look about ten years older than you are, and from what I hear," I say, thinking of the rumors that have been circulating over the last week, "your team hates you. So congrats, you're *super* successful."

"I would be if it weren't for you!"

"Yeah, I'm the problem. Sure." I nod at Chet as I see Joey Connelly turn into the hall behind him, probably coming to see his team like I've come to see mine. I focus my eyes back on Chet, because I don't want him to know Joey is there. I'd prefer to let his GM see his true colors.

"You fucking bitch," Chet seethes. "You think you walk on fucking water, but now that everyone knows you're just a little slut for your players, let's see what the rest of your career looks like. At least if you get that award, everyone will know that it's really for your 'service.'" He uses a crude hand gesture to indicate that the 'service' he's referring to is something sexual.

I watch Joey's eyebrows shoot up his forehead when he sees the gesture Chet just made off to his side, but nothing about this interaction phases me. This is exactly how he talked to me when we were married—like an entitled little prick any time things didn't go his way.

I'm not shocked that he hasn't changed. It makes me happier than ever that I got out of that marriage when I did, and even more thankful to have found a man who treats me right.

"The thing is, Chet, I never cared about that award in the first place. I only ever cared about leading this team without reproach. And regardless of what you think about my relationship with McCabe, that's exactly what I've done. Whether we win or lose the Cup, and even if I don't get that award, I'm proud of the work I've done in Boston. I'm even more proud of my team, and how they've played. And nothing you do or say is going to change that."

Chet's scoff is so loud I'd be surprised if they didn't hear it inside the locker room. "Yeah, sure! Better run along," he says, nodding toward the door to the Rebels locker room. "There are probably players in there that need blow jobs before the game."

From behind him, Joey asks, "Is that what you think I plan to do when I go into our locker room?"

Chet's jaw tightens because he knows he's just been caught acting incredibly unprofessional. Something that only one person—McCabe—has ever truly seen him doing before. "Connelly," Chet says, turning halfway so he stands between us. He's using that schmoozing voice he only uses with other guys, his upper-crust version of bro-talk, I guess. "Didn't know you were down here."

"Clearly." The muttered word is dry and unimpressed. He's not falling for Chet's attempts to downplay his behavior. "So? Is that why you think I'm down here? To give our players blow jobs?"

The fact that he utters this question without a hint of embarrassment, amusement, or anger leaves me wondering how he's feeling about what Chet just said.

"No." Chet laughs it off, and just the sound of his voice has my stomach turning. "Of course not. Unlike Alessandra here, you're not involved with your players like that."

"From what I've seen, AJ is in a committed relationship with a man who is nothing but respectful toward her. Unlike your behavior just now."

"She's fucking one of her players!" Chet sputters, incensed that Joey isn't taking his side here.

"What business of yours is that?" he asks, and I could not love his no-nonsense approach toward my ex-husband any more than I do. When Chet doesn't immediately respond, he says, "Especially since you went sticking your dick elsewhere when you were married to her."

It's only then that I realize that Joey, happily married for the past twenty years and having witnessed the dissolution of my and Chet's marriage, is *completely* on my side. He didn't show all his cards when we both worked in St. Louis, but now I understand that this is at least part of why he agreed to send Chet down to the AHL, and keep him there for nearly seven years.

"That's different," Chet insists.

"Why?" Joey asks, raising his eyebrows toward Chet like he's offering him an opportunity to defend himself, even while we both know he can't.

"Because she put her job before our marriage."

"Did she?" Joey asks. "Or did she just have a more important job than you, and you were jealous?

"My job was important too!"

God he sounds like a fucking toddler, and I can tell Joey's thinking something similar by the way he's clearly trying not to laugh.

"You were an assistant coach," Joey reminds him, "and completely replaceable. Even now, you're replaceable. In fact, your services are no longer needed."

"But," Chet stutters, "we have a game."

"And somehow I think the other coaches will manage without you."

"It's the playoffs. You can't head into this game short one coach." Chet's eyes flick to me, as if this situation is my fault. Over the years, I'd occasionally wondered if he ever learned how to take accountability for his actions instead of blaming everyone else. Apparently not.

"Watch me," Joey replies, crossing his arms over his broad chest.

"You can't do this," Chet says, eyes wide with rage and bewilderment. "I have a contract."

"Yes, and you're an at-will employee. Seems I no longer have the will to employ you."

"You're doing this because of *her*."

His glare has absolutely no effect on me. I just cross my arms and sigh. "Chet, grow the fuck up. Learn to accept responsibility for your actions, and just . . . stop being such a shitty person. Go crawl back home to your wife and hope she forgives you for losing your job by being an asshole. Again."

Once Chet's stormed off, Joey turns to me, clasping my biceps in each of his hands and giving me a supportive squeeze. "At the risk of sounding like a patronizing old man . . . I'm proud of you. The way you left, moved on, and did so much more with your life once you rid yourself of him, the way you've led this organization," he says, letting his gaze roam around the hallway of our home arena. "You deserve all the good things coming your way."

"About that," I say with a smile. "Pretty sure I withdrew from that award nomination . . ."

"Pretty sure you deserve it anyway," he says, giving me a wink before he turns and heads into his team's locker room.

I take a deep breath and exhale, letting the tension go as a deep sense of peace washes over me. Whatever happens in this game—in this series—I'm proud of this team. And I'm proud of myself, too.

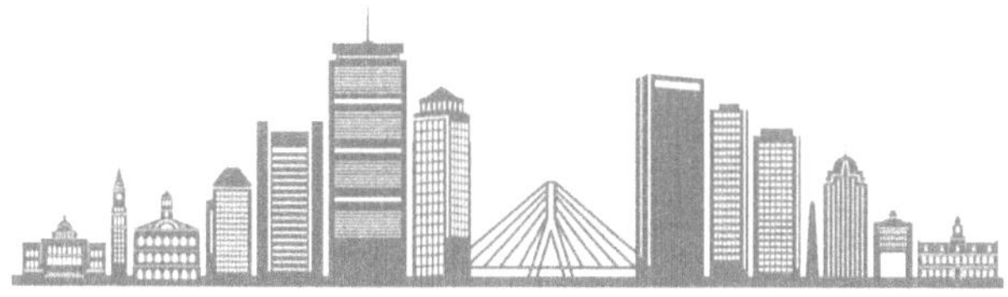

Chapter Forty-One

AJ

The crowd in the locker room before Game 7 is unlike any I've ever seen. Normally, Charlie likes to keep it just coaches, players, me, and occasionally Frank. But because the GM of the Year announcement will be made during tonight's pre-game programming, the large TV on the wall of the visitors' locker room is on, and every member of the Rebels organization who has traveled to St. Louis for the final game is standing here in this huge semi-circle that extends around the perimeter of the room.

In the middle of the room are two cameramen on their knees, with their cameras pointing at me. Behind me is the same reporter from the press conference a month ago—the one who asked our then-surly captain about fighting in the stands. It makes me realize that I never gave him the opportunity to make that right.

On my left , Ronan has had a tight grip on my hand since

they said they'd be back with the announcement after the commercial break. On my right, Lauren's arm is linked with mine.

I'm trying not to let the pressure of the series or the award get to me, but I feel like I'm strung so tight I'm about to burst.

"Relax," he whispers, low and dragged out in the same way he might say it if he were sliding into me, and my thighs clench in response.

"Not helping," I mutter, and his low rumble of laughter tells me he knows exactly what that word has done to me.

Dropping his voice even lower, he leans over and says into my ear. "Don't worry, I'll take very good care of you later tonight."

I don't have time to respond before the programming starts back up and a hushed silence falls over the room as we watch the compilation video highlighting each GM's journey and the reasons we were nominated for the award. Joey is first, and I'm as proud of my mentor now as I have been the other three times he's been nominated. When they get to me, I'm listening but not watching.

Instead, I'm looking around the room, keeping an eye on my players and coaching staff, and I'm beyond proud to see the way they are all nodding along with the list of strategic moves I made throughout this season to give us the best chance of getting to the exact place we are right now—about to play in the final game, hoping for the honor of bringing home the Cup.

My hand squeezes Ronan's so tightly I'm afraid I might actually be hurting him. It's not about the award; I just want to make the men and women in this room proud.

"And this year's General Manager of the Year . . . is Alessandra Jones of the Boston Rebels!"

In the second that follows, I close my eyes and press my lips between my teeth, willing myself not to cry. I know that the cameras are on me, and the last thing I want hockey fans to see is a woman at the pinnacle of her career crying about it on national TV.

But when Ronan sweeps me into his arms and spins me around, when the people who love and support me crowd around me with their congratulations, I can't stop the few tears that escape. Wiping them away, I accept all the hugs and congratulations until a camera is shoved into my face and the female reporter steps up next to me.

"Can you tell us what receiving this award means to you?" she asks me.

"It means she's amazing," Colt yells, and I can't help the small laugh that bubbles from my lips as I gently wipe any moisture from under my eyes.

"Honestly, it's just an honor to get to do what I do every day," I say. "And to be recognized for it in this way, by my colleagues and the league and the media—it's the honor of a lifetime. But now the work begins again. We have a game to play, and fans who are counting on us to bring home the second Cup this decade."

Cheers rise up around the room and I turn away from the cameras, signaling that the interview is over. There will be an awards night later this month where I'll have to give an actual speech, but right now, the focus needs to be on this game.

The press is ushered out of the room, and most of the Rebels staff leaves too, until it's just Charlie and the other coaches, the players, Frank, and me. Charlie doesn't give his normal pre-game pep talk. Instead, he takes a deep breath and says, "We've played six games against St. Louis. We've won half and they've won half. I don't need to go over their strengths or their weaknesses—you already know them. What I do want to tell you before you take the ice tonight is that *you* are the better team. You deserve this win. But it will only happen if every single one of you goes out there and gives it your all for the next sixty minutes of play. No distractions. No mistakes. Do. Your. Job."

With that, he claps his hand against his clipboard, quickly glances at his phone, and tells the men to line up. As they do, he whispers something to his assistant coach, Larry, and steps out the door. He never leaves the locker room before our players, and goosebumps prickle the back of my neck as I watch the door close behind him.

Larry makes a few more comments that I'm only half listening to, and then he holds the door open, fist bumping every player on their way out. Colt and Hartmann bring up the rear, and I follow behind them.

Charlie is halfway down the hall, his clipboard tucked between his elbow and his ribs as he holds the phone to his ear with one hand, and presses a finger against his other ear. I see the worry on his face when he looks up and his eyes meet mine.

"Okay. Keep me posted," he says into the phone. "I love you too."

"Everything okay?" I ask, coming to a stop in front of him as he pockets his phone, just as the line of players finish filing by.

"Eva just was sent to the hospital. Helene is flying to New York—"

"Wait!" Hartmann says, spinning back around to face us. "What's wrong with Evie?"

My eyebrows dip. I know the Wilcotts and Hartmanns are family friends, but the concern in his voice borders on panic.

"We don't know yet," Charlie tells him. "She was rushed to the ER during the layover on her flight back from Europe. I'm sure everything's going to be fine. Now get out there."

The worry in Charlie's tone doesn't imply that he's sure his daughter is okay. In response, Hartmann nods then slowly turns around, and I watch his shoulders tense as he walks to the back of the line of his teammates.

Making a mental note to check in with Charlie about Eva after the game, I head in the opposite direction to meet up with Nicholas and Abby. I find them at ice level, with most of the families waiting to see the players during warmups, and Abby's wearing the infant-sized McCabe jersey we got her for the occasion.

When Ronan sees us there, he skates over and taps the glass to get Abby's attention. She's got small, pink noise-canceling earmuffs on, but when she sees him there, she starts kicking her feet in excitement, and her face splits into a huge smile. She's got four teeth now, and a never-ending volume of drool, so I take the cloth hanging out of Nicholas's back pocket and wipe her chin. When she turns her head to look at me, her smile grows wider.

Glancing up, I see that Ronan is looking down at me from the other side of the glass, nothing but love in his eyes as he shifts his gaze between me and our baby.

Our. I don't know that I've ever used that word in relation to Abby, but it feels right. She and Ronan are mine . . . the family I never thought I'd have.

God, not having to hide this anymore is the best feeling in the world.

I can't wait until later tonight when I can show him the custom tank top I'm wearing under this suit coat tonight. As GM, I can't show up in his jersey to a game. But I can have Jules make me an incredibly sexy top with the number 9 sewn onto the back, and I can have her make me a matching thong. And most importantly, I can model them both for him in the privacy of our bedroom, before he strips them off me and takes care of me like only he can.

As if he can read my mind and already knows about my plans for later tonight, his pupils dilate while his eyes focus on my lips. The ever-present hunger is written across his face, like it is any time he sees me.

"Knock it off," Nicholas mutters from beside me as he watches us. "No one needs to see this."

I shake my head slightly as I snap back to reality. He's right, of course—not here, at work.

"Good luck," I tell Ronan. "You've got this."

He gives me a wink, blows Abby a kiss, and skates back to his teammates.

We're up 3-2 heading into the third period, and so far, it feels like things are going our way. We're in sync, playing a clean, strong game while St. Louis has made some sloppy mistakes. For the first half of the last period, as I watch our team play their hearts out, I'm feeling great about our chances. Rather than feeling dread whenever St. Louis takes a shot, I let the confidence wash over me. *We've got this.*

And then, it all goes to shit.

Colt goes for a fake shot, and when he realizes his mistake, he plants his skate and pushes off the blade to dive across the crease, sticking his glove out and miraculously catching the puck.

The Rebels fans breathe out a sigh of relief . . . until Colt doesn't get up off the ice. The refs skate over to him and then nod toward our bench, and that's when it's clear he's injured. He's pulling off his glove and blocker, and I glance up at the Jumbotron where the camera has zoomed in on him as he pulls off his mask, and his face is twisted in pain. A few seats down from me, Jules gasps.

"No," she whimpers, "no, no, no." On either side of her, Lauren and Audrey plant their hands on her thighs for support, and my heart sinks because I can imagine how she feels. Wanting to rush down the steps, jump the glass, and slide across the ice to him—because it's exactly how I'd feel if it were Ronan.

My eyes scan the players, and when I find him standing next to Drew at center ice, he's looking at me, too. Then Walsh nudges him with the end of his stick and he turns back to talk to his teammates. They don't hide their worried looks as Colt grasps his right knee. The trainers come out onto the ice to evaluate him, splint his leg, and help him skate off.

When Hartmann goes in, and I can tell something isn't right.

The rest of the game is like watching a train wreck, and

my body is plagued with wave after wave of nausea as I watch my team fall apart before my eyes.

Hartmann looks like a goalie we just pulled up from the beer league. Our defensemen aren't doing their job keeping the puck away out of our defensive zone, and shot after shot is fired on Hartmann. He stops the first two, barely, and then one slips between the pipes. Then another, and another.

Before I know it, we're in the last two minutes of the game, and trailing by two goals. Drew manages to score, bringing us back to life, and the team rallies, threatening St. Louis's net for the rest of the game . . . until one of their forwards gets a hold of it and takes off on a breakaway.

He moves right and fakes the shot, and as Hartmann butterflies down to block it, the player takes the puck behind the net and easily slips it into the goal on Hartmann's opposite side.

When the final buzzer sounds, St. Louis's players stream onto the ice in celebration, while we hang our heads in shock and dismay. Our fans stand still, stunned, all of us collectively wondering what the hell just happened.

I would expect nothing less from our players than the classy way they line up to shake hands with the other team, despite how the game fell apart so dramatically.

In the weeks to come, I know that we'll analyze the third period of this game over and over. Even as I immediately start focusing on how we can learn from this game, my heart breaks at the way our players, *my* players, file off the ice, heads hung low.

The victory lap around the rink with each player taking their turn holding the Cup . . . that should have been us. And maybe next year, it will be.

I take a deep breath, remembering how these men protected my honor, intelligence, and integrity, and cheered for me every step of the way this season. Now, it's my turn to support them by identifying the cracks that emerged, and fixing them so we can move on to the next season even stronger than we are now.

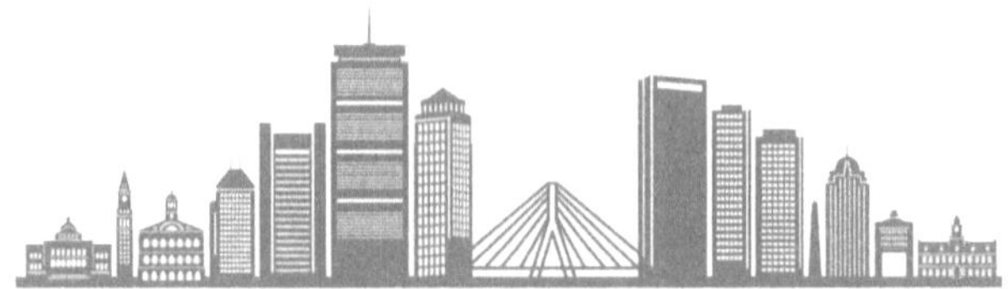

Epilogue

AJ & McCabe

McCABE

Three Weeks Later

"You need to stop fucking apologizing," I tell Hartmann, dropping my voice low so no one at this fancy awards ceremony will hear me. "Shit happens. Shit *games* happen. All you can do is learn from them and move on. You keep living in the past like this and it's going to fuck with your game."

His laugh is humorless. "Could my game possibly be any more fucked? And how exactly is this in the past, when every time I turn around another sports pundit is analyzing that third period, and debating how I could possibly have sucked so bad?"

"You did suck," I say, because there's nothing good that

will come of trying to cover up that truth. "But it was half a period, in one game. It doesn't mean you suck as a goalie—"

"Right, just Game 7 of the Stanley Cup Finals, no big deal."

"Listen, there's no two ways about it—it was a big deal. But you're still early in your career. You're still learning and growing as a player. Don't let it fuck with your head. Learn from it. Whatever had you so distracted, cut that shit right out of your life," I say, but the look on his face has me realizing that whatever it is, he's not cutting it out of his life. "Or learn how to keep that shit off the ice. *Everyone* has bad games. I had two of them in the playoffs, and both were because I was too focused on AJ and Abby. I had to learn how to compartmentalize when I was on the ice."

I don't know if whatever's distracting Luke is something important, or if his inexperience was why we lost Game 7.

Then, he looks over my shoulder, and his eyes light up. I turn to see what he's looking at, and entering this huge venue are Coach Wilcott, his wife Helene, and his daughter Evangeline—who I now know is Hartmann's best friend. But he's not looking at her like she's his best friend; he's looking at her the same way half the guys in this room are—like he wants to peel that dark green dress off her.

"Dude," I say, as I turn back toward him. "Wipe that look off your face. If Coach catches you looking at his daughter that way . . ."

His head snaps toward me. "I wasn't looking at her *any* way."

"Uh-huh." I take a sip of my drink, feeling like some puzzle pieces are clicking into place. Coach Wilcott leaving the locker room early before Game 7, AJ telling me post-game that his daughter was sick, Hartmann playing like shit. *He knew, and that's why he was distracted.* "You have feelings for this girl?"

"What? No. She's my best friend."

"You keep saying that, but Renaud's my best friend and I sure as shit don't look at him the way you're looking at her. Was she the reason you were so distracted in Game 7? The fact that she was sick?"

His guilty look is all the answer I need. "How'd you know she was sick?"

"How do you think?"

"I keep forgetting you're with AJ. That's still so . . . weird. How you hated her so much, until . . ."

"Until I didn't." I still haven't told my teammates what changed, because there's no way to talk about our history that doesn't involve telling them about how AJ's ex treated her, and that's not a path I'm going down. I'll figure it out, eventually. Right now, things still feel new and somewhat fragile, even though she basically lives with me. Even Tabitha has moved over to my condo, and I don't know what AJ was talking about—that's the most friendly, loving cat I've ever seen. With Abby and me, at least.

"You're staring at her again," I warn Hartmann as I follow his gaze to where AJ now stands talking to the Wilcotts. She's in a cream suit, the slim cut of her blazer barely showing the pearl-lined cream corset beneath. With her long wavy brown hair falling over her shoulders, she looks sexy and powerful. "Let's go."

"Where?"

"I'd like to meet your *best friend,* Lover Boy."

"Dude," Hartmann says, "do not call me that in front of her or I'll never live it down."

"She doesn't know your reputation?" I ask as we make our way toward the entrance of the huge auditorium.

"She does," he says, his words practically a groan. "But just because women flock to me doesn't mean I'm *doing* anything to earn that reputation."

I think back to earlier this spring, when it first came out that Colt and Jules were engaged, and he told me that just because I'd seen him *talking* to a lot of women didn't mean he was actually sleeping with them. I wonder if the same applies to Hartmann? "Huh."

As we step up to the Wilcotts, I slide my arm around AJ's waist and press a kiss to the crown of her head. Even with those three-inch nude heels she's wearing, I could still rest my chin on the top of her head.

"Still not quite used to this," Coach says with an awkward laugh.

"You'll get there," AJ and I say at the same time, and I chuckle as I pull her tighter against my side.

All I want to do, all the time, is to be close to her. Sometimes I worry that I'm being too clingy, always needing to have some part of my body connected to hers. When I told her I was afraid she was going to get sick of my constant need to touch her, she just laughed and said, "Never."

Hartmann introduces us to Eva, and as she extends her hand to shake ours, AJ tells her how much she loves her nail polish. I wouldn't have noticed if she hadn't said something, but it's a matte forest green that matches her dress. Her dark hair is slicked back into a high, fluffy ponytail that bounces as she talks, and her dark eyes with long eyelashes stand out against her pale skin. Standing next to golden boy Luke, with his light brown hair and blue eyes, they strike me as total opposites. While he's outgoing and talkative, she's measured and reserved. She's the dark to his light.

"I'm so sorry to hear you were sick a few weeks ago," AJ tells her as her parents move on to chat with someone else. "You feeling better now?"

"Yeah, I was just exhausted and dehydrated," Eva says. "The end of competition season really did me in." Her sideways glance at Hartmann has me wondering if there's a bit more to the story than that.

"She's doing fine now," Hartmann says as he brings his hand to her lower back. "But—"

The announcement asking everyone to please take their seats interrupts us.

"Where are you guys sitting?" AJ asks them.

"Our parents have a box over there," Eva says, nodding her head toward the side of the room, where theater-style box seats line the circular perimeter, facing the stage.

"Okay, we're on the floor," AJ says, "we'll see you later then." Taking my hand, she leads me toward the front of the auditorium.

"That was weird," I say.

"What was?"

"You don't think there's something going on with those two?"

"Pretty sure they're like siblings," she says. "Frank talks about her like she's his daughter. There's a picture of her and Luke in his office from when they were toddlers."

"Okay." Now isn't the time to dig into how he absolutely was not looking at her like she was his sister, much less his best friend. When I think about it, though, she was cool and detached. Nothing she did made me think she had feelings for him. But I am absolutely giving him shit about it later, because nothing will ruin their friendship faster than him pining after her.

We take our seats next to Colt and Jules. Colt is receiving the Goaltender of the Year award tonight, and I don't envy him having to make his way up the stairs to the stage on those crutches. Luckily, he doesn't need surgery, but he's going to be on crutches for another week and in that knee brace for a couple more weeks after that. He'll be out of the brace just in time for Jameson's wedding later this summer.

All things considered, he's damn lucky. In his mid-thirties, a knee injury could have ended his career, and I know he really wants to finish out the last year of his contract next season. After that, I wouldn't be surprised if he retires. He's already one of the longest-playing guys in the league.

As the lights dim and the program begins, I think about how I normally hate shit like this. Unlike other awards shows, everyone already knows who's won each award. There are no surprises; it's simply an opportunity to celebrate people's accomplishments.

Nine years ago, when I won the Rookie of the Year award, I hated every minute of the experience—getting dressed up, everyone congratulating me, having to go up on stage to accept the award, and having to give a speech. The only thing that made it tolerable was sharing that evening with Sloane and Grandma.

For a guy who spends a couple of days a week playing hockey in front of twenty-thousand fans, I really don't like being in the spotlight. But what I do really love is seeing AJ get the recognition she deserves. Which is why I love being here with her. And why, when her name is announced as the GM of the Year, I stand with her in celebration and pull her into a huge hug, whispering, "Good job, Sunshine," into her ear and watching the goosebumps rise across her neck.

I clap and cheer for her as she takes the stage, the red soles of the sexy heels I bought her catching my eye with each step. And when she stands at the podium, facing a sea of hockey's biggest supporters and holding her award, her eyes land on me before she looks out at the audience.

"For someone who's known they won this award for a few weeks now," she says, "I still find myself struggling to find the words to explain how much it means to me. It's impossible to stand here as the first female GM of the Year without saying that, while I might be the first, I won't be the last."

The thunderous applause is a shock in the best way possible. She'd been worried how people would respond when she brought up her gender, and the role of women in hockey, but I'd encouraged her to mention it, no matter the response.

"The road to this stage wasn't easy, and I'd be remiss if I didn't mention the women who helped me get here—whose friendship, assistance, and advice allowed me to grow and flourish both in this role, and as a person. This year, especially, I've come to realize the importance of friendships between women who want to see each other succeed in all aspects of life. The world is stronger when women work together instead of against one another, and I'm working hard to surround myself with these types of women, in my personal life and at work as well.

"I also owe a particular debt of gratitude to three men in

my life. First, Joey Connelly, the other nominee for this year's award, who was the most amazing mentor I could have hoped for. He took a chance on me when I was coaching D1 women's hockey, bringing me on as a scout and then promoting me to being the first female assistant GM in the league. And then, he encouraged me to spread my wings, to look for a GM position when he could have easily kept me exactly where I was, working for him.

"Second, Frank Hartmann, the owner of the Boston Rebels, who gave me the opportunity to lead this organization. He'll tell you I deserved the job, but when I started at the Rebels, there wasn't a single woman in upper management, and I know he took a leap of faith bringing me on, knowing I'd shake things up, and trusting me to do so. I wouldn't be standing here without him in my corner for the past six years.

"And finally, Ronan McCabe, who has steadfastly stood by me through some of the most trying times in my life." Her eyes are back on me, and I wonder what she sees reflected back on my face. I didn't know she was going to say anything about me tonight. I didn't expect it, and I'm not sure I deserve the adoring way she's looking at me right now. "I might still be standing on this stage even if it weren't for you, but I wouldn't be the person I am today. And for the first time in my life, I really like that person—the one who understands that vulnerability is a strength, not a weakness. I'll forever be grateful that we took a chance on each other, when it would have been easier to walk away. This award means so much more to me because you stood next to me when I won it."

I'm not sure why my eyes are all wet like this, but as I

shake my head at her, I can't stop smiling. The woman I love just accepted the most important award in her field, and I couldn't be happier for her, or for us.

If anyone had told me before this season started that it would end this way—me navigating fatherhood, AJ and me living together, a new agent and a contract for three more years with the Rebels making more than I've ever made, and being here with AJ as she accepts the GM of the Year award —I'd have been certain they were crazy.

And maybe that's what this life is . . . crazy, but beautiful. Maybe the beauty is in the unpredictability—in accepting changes you weren't ready for, and being open to possibilities you couldn't imagine. Because I never could have envisioned being this happy.

AJ

"God, you were so fucking amazing tonight." Ronan's breath is hot against my ear, his head dipped to whisper as I stand, leaning against the wall of the hotel elevator with my eyes closed. I'm exhausted in the best possible way, after what is quite possibly the most amazing night of my life.

Getting to stand on that stage tonight, to thank the people—especially Ronan—who helped me get where I am, and knowing that I'm paving the way for other women to do the same . . . it was everything.

"I hope you know I'm going to marry you someday," I mumble, not even able to open my eyes because I'm so tired.

"I was already planning on it, remember?" His low chuckle fills the space, and his chest shakes against my arm as he reminds me about how he said he was going to ask Frank for my hand when the time came.

"Oh, related to that," I say, cracking my eyes open. "Guess who texted me about an hour ago?"

He lifts an eyebrow. "Who?"

"My father."

To his credit, Ronan doesn't say any of the things he's probably thinking. Instead, he traces my jaw with his thumb and says, "Oh yeah?"

"Yeah. He congratulated me on the award and said he and my mom would like to see me again sometime soon."

"How do you feel about that?"

"Worried."

"Why?"

"Because either he's extending an olive branch, or it's a trap. And I'm not sure I want to explore either option."

"The beauty of being an adult is that you don't have to if you don't want to. But if you change your mind, I'm happy to be there with you . . . if that's what you want."

"I don't know what I want, and I'm too tired to think about it right now."

"There's no rush, Sunshine. You don't owe them anything."

The doors open on our floor and he sweeps me into his arms, carrying me down the hallway. I don't even protest, because while I'm in love with these gorgeous nude patent leather heels, my feet are killing me, and I'd rather be in his arms anyway.

"Maybe going out for drinks after the awards ceremony wasn't the best idea," he says, brushing his lips against my forehead before he sets me down at our door so he can find the keycard in his pocket.

"I'm not drunk, I'm just tired."

"I know. But I've been watching you all night in those sexy heels and that pearl corset you're wearing, and all I can picture is seeing you in nothing but those tonight."

I lean against the door frame as he taps the keycard on the lock. "That can probably be arranged."

"Not if you're too tired," he says, his tone making it clear that he's looking out for me, not that he's disappointed.

"I can rally," I tell him as I unbutton the single button on my blazer, then step through the door that he's holding open for me. I let the jacket slide off my shoulders and down my arms, dropping it in the hallway as I walk into our hotel room. It's not a full suite, but it's got an entire sitting area, with a couch and chairs next to the wall of windows overlooking the lights of Las Vegas.

"Alessandra, really." Coming up behind me, he places a hand on each bare shoulder to stop my progress mid-way across the room. "You've had a big night. Let's just go to sleep."

I look over my shoulder at him, taking in his close-cropped beard and that dark hair that's perpetually a little messy, and noticing the way his bright green eyes are focused on my lips. The dull ache low in my abdomen is growing hotter, spreading like a fire that wants to consume me. Flames lick through my body until I'm just a touch less tired and a lot more turned on.

It's amazing to me that just looking at this man can have this effect. Or is it the way his thumbs are running back and forth along the tense line of my shoulders, trying to soothe me? Or the way I can feel the heat rolling off his body and warming my mostly bare back?

My fingers meet at the waistband of my pants, and I'm thankful that the cast came off a few days ago as I quickly undo the single button and drag the zipper down before pushing them past my hips. With the wide legs of these suit pants, they pool at my feet, and I carefully step out of them, wearing nothing but my corset, nude thong, and the heels he loved so much he insisted on buying them for me.

I walk toward the window, sweeping my hair over my shoulder to give him the full view of my body. "You can go to sleep if you want, but I'm going to admire this view."

He huffs out a laugh as I approach the window, leaning one shoulder against the metal frame that runs from the floor to the ceiling, supporting the huge panels of glass. "Yeah, this view is really something."

I hear him undo his belt, then the drag of his zipper and the swishing of his clothing as he strips it off. And in the next few seconds, he's behind me, his hard, hot, muscular body cradling mine as one of his palms slides across my belly, pulling me against him.

"I hope these windows are mirrored on the outside," he says.

"Why?" I ask coyly, turning toward him as I drop to my knees, grasping his cock in my hand and bringing it to my mouth. "Afraid someone's going to see us like this?"

He groans as I swipe my tongue over the sensitive skin on the fat head of him while my fingers grip his shaft. "This view . . . you on your knees for me . . ." He loses his words when I take him to the back of my throat, sucking him between my tongue and the roof of my mouth as I swirl along him repeatedly. "These moments . . ." he grits out, ". . . are *ours*."

I slip my thong to the side and run my fingers through the slickness between my legs, using it as lubrication as I bring them to my clit, trying to soothe the throbbing ache there. He hits the back of my throat again, and it makes my eyes water as I look up at him.

"You are a fucking vision," he says, bringing his hand down to the base of my skull. "Look at you fingering yourself while I fuck your mouth. You want me inside you, Alessandra?"

"Umm hum," I murmur, and his entire body is wracked with a shiver from the vibration.

"Take your top off," he says. "I want to see you play with your tits, and then I'll fuck you like you want."

My inner walls clench in need, and I moan as he slides himself into my mouth at a faster pace.

"You like that, huh? You like thinking about your pussy being so full of me you can barely breathe?"

With my eyes on his, I nod as I bring my hands behind my back and undo the clasps along the seam, then toss it to the side. He doesn't even have to ask again; my hands cup the sides of my breasts, pushing them together as I pinch my nipples between my thumbs and forefingers. The sensation has me moaning again, and that's when he pulls out of my mouth, steps back, and sits on the couch facing the window.

"Lose the underwear, then get up here."

I never thought I'd like being bossed around, but as it turns out, I like it a whole lot in the bedroom. I'm eager to please him because he always leaves me satisfied.

I stand and, hooking my thumbs into the straps of my thong, I bend at the waist as I drag it down my legs, leaving it on the floor at my feet. Then I plant one knee on either side of his waist, and look down at the man of my dreams, lowering myself until he's filled me, until we're joined and moving together as one, until his hands and his mouth are everywhere and nothing exists except our pleasure and the love we share. I ride him until my legs are about to give out, and then he brings his thumb between us, slowly pressing into my clit with every rock of my body, bringing his lips to my nipple and teasing me, until he's tipping me over the edge.

When I come, it's not with his name on my lips, it's with the words "I love you so much."

And when he finds his release, he presses his forehead to mine, whispering, "I love you more."

I think I fall asleep before he even cleans me up and carries me to bed, because the next morning, that's where I wake up to the angry buzzing of my phone. I panic, worried that it might be Nicholas or Nicole telling us that something is wrong with Abby.

But when I pick my phone up from the nightstand, I see that I've missed several texts in a group chat with Charlie and Frank. I tap on the most recent message.

Filling my screen is a photo of a man's left hand, a gold wedding band circling his ring finger. The woman's hand, laying over the top, has one of the biggest diamond rings I've ever seen. I'm so focused on the size of that ring that I almost don't notice the matte green nail polish.

And then, another message pops up.

FRANK

We have a BIG problem.

Want more McCabe and AJ? Get their bonus epilogue here.

Curious about Zach Reid? He has his own novella, THE TRADE UP, which you can download here.

THE END

GOAL LINE

Boston Rebels, Book 4

Luke & Eva

This steamy best friends to lovers
(and so much more) story is coming soon!

Books by Julia Connors

FROZEN HEARTS SERIES

On the Edge

Out of Bounds

One Last Shot

One Little Favor

On the Line

BOSTON REBELS SERIES

Center Ice

Fake Shot

Cross-Checked

Goal Line

Acknowledgments

Normally when I finish a book, I have some combination of feelings that basically add up to me wondering if there's any way I can put myself through this process again.

Cross-Checked is the first book I've finished where I didn't feel like I needed to go into hibernation mode, didn't question whether I could sustain a writing career, and didn't feel like my family was falling apart as a result of me devoting so much time to writing.

What changed? *You.* You changed my life, and the trajectory of my career. Every single person who has picked up one of my books . . . you helped make this my full-time job. You allowed me to achieve the dream of going from working full time and writing pretty much all the time, to "just" writing full time. You allowed me to regain a sense of balance I'd lost, spend more time with my family, and really enjoy writing again. For that, I am forever grateful.

Being an author is so much more fun when you're not burning the candle at both ends! It's also a lot more fun when you have people in your corner, helping you and cheering you on. And for these specific individuals, I'm not sure how I'd have done this without you . . .

Victoria, Ashley, and Jenn – I have no doubt whatsoever

that our daily writing sprints are an enormous part of what made writing this book feel so effortless. *LET'S GO GIRLS!!!*

Rachel and Joelle – Thank you for being the gut check I needed when it came to McCabe and AJ's story—for letting me know what was working and what could be stronger, and for sometimes talking me off the ledge. Having you beta-read this book, and the comments you left me along the way, were invaluable. I'm so grateful for your time and your efforts to help me write the best book possible.

Melissa – Thank you for the valuable insight and feedback you've given me throughout the writing process, and for never letting me settle for less than my best work!

Brooke and Chelsea – Thank you for your attention to detail, and the way you stepped in at the last minute!

Kait and Autumn – Thank you for keeping me on track, for reading this book as I wrote it, and for being pillars of stability during the most challenging year of my life.

Elizabeth, Rachel, Melanie, and Alexandra – Thank you for not being mad that I kept my author life a secret for so long, for always being the first people to cheer me on, and for keeping our charcuterie and cocktail meetups a priority as our lives have gone in different directions.

Mr. Connors – Thank you for being a good listener, and for knowing enough to ask whether I'm looking for solutions or just need to be heard. This has been *a hell of a year.* One I hope we'll never have to go through again, but there's no one else I'd ever want to climb these mountains with.

And thank you to everyone else who has helped, supported, and guided me along the way – my author friends, my promo and ARC teams, and my family.

And the hugest thank you to my readers, because without you none of this would be possible!!!

Afterword

Thank you so much for reading! If you enjoyed the book, please consider leaving an honest review. Reader reviews mean so much to authors, and your time and feedback are appreciated.

Sign up for Julia's newsletter to stay up to date on the latest news and be the first to know about sales, audiobooks, and new releases!

juliaconnors.com/newsletter

About the Author

Julia Connors grew up on the warm and sunny West Coast, but her first decision as an adult was to trade her flip-flops for snow boots and move to Boston. She's been enjoying everything that New England has to offer for over two decades, and now that she's acclimated to the snowy winters and finally found all the places to get good sushi and tacos, she has zero regrets. You can usually find her in front of her computer, but when she stops writing she's most likely to be found outdoors, preferably with a pair of skis or snowshoes strapped to her feet in winter, or on a paddleboard in the summer.

goodreads.com/julia_connors

amazon.com/author/juliaconnors

instagram.com/juliaconnorsauthor

tiktok.com/@juliaconnorsauthor

facebook.com/juliaconnorsauthor

pinterest.com/juliaconnorsauthor

www.ingramcontent.com/pod-product-compliance
Lightning Source LLC
Chambersburg PA
CBHW061104310726
48974CB00002B/390